SHE WAS ALMOST HOME FREE . . .

. . . when a DEST operator strolled around the corner toward her.

In a millisecond she evaluated her options. The frightened little girl within screamed for her to turn and flee into the inviting maze of the warehouse, away from the bad man in black. But that was death; it would take Ninyu Kerai Indrahar's ninjas no longer to find her than it would take all the wine to spill from an upset bottle.

When the frightened child inside her screamed, Cassie's reflex was to snap into "kill" mode. But the agents suit would stop a slug from her pistol, even if there were time to draw it.

She would have to do this bare-handed.

DISCOVER THE ADVENTURES
OF BATTLETECH

CLOSE QUARTERS

by

Victor Milán

A ROC BOOK

ROC
Published by the Penguin Group
Penguin Books USA Inc., 375 Hudson Street,
New York, New York 10014, U.S.A.
Penguin Books Ltd, 27 Wrights Lane,
London W8 5TZ, England
Penguin Books Australia Ltd, Ringwood,
Victoria, Australia
Penguin Books Canada Ltd, 10 Alcorn Avenue,
Toronto, Canada M4V 3B2
Penguin Books (N.Z.) Ltd, 182–190 Wairau Road
Auckland 10, New Zealand

Penguin Books Ltd, Registered Offices:
Harmondsworth, Middlesex, England

First published by Roc, an imprint of Dutton Signet,
a division of Penguin Books USA Inc.

First Printing, September, 1994
10 9 8 7 6 5 4 3 2 1

Series Editor: Donna Ippolito
Cover: Boris Vallejo
Interior Illustrations: Earl Geir
Mechanical Drawings: Duane Loose

Copyright © FASA Corporation, 1994
All rights reserved

 REGISTERED TRADEMARK—MARCA REGISTRADA

BATTLETECH, FASA, and the distinctive BATTLETECH and FASA logos are trademarks
of the FASA Corporation, 1100 W. Cermak, Suite B305, Chicago, IL 60608.

Printed in the United States of America

To Sean, with thanks for the loan of the research material

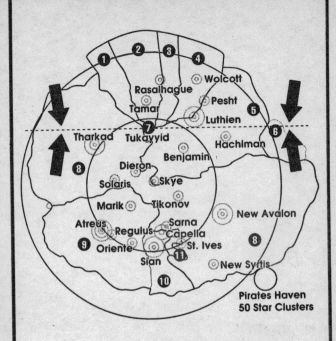

MAP OF THE SUCCESSOR STATES

CLAN TRUCE LINE

1 • Jade Falcon/Steel Viper, 2 • Wolf Clan, 3 • Ghost Bear,
4 • Smoke Jaguars - Nova Cats, 5 • Draconis Combine,
6 • Outworlds Alliance, 7 • Free Rasalhague Republic,
8 • Federated Commonwealth, 9 • Free Worlds League,
10 • Capellan Confederation, 11 • St. Ives Compact

Map Compiled by COMSTAR.
From information provided by the COMSTAR EXPLORER SERVICE
and the STAR LEAGUE ARCHIVES on Terra.

© 3056 COMSTAR CARTOGRAPHIC CORPS.

Prologue

It is the year 3056. The uneasy truce between the Clans and the Inner Sphere has run almost a third of its course. The vast Federated Commonwealth, which once seemed destined to reunify the Inner Sphere for the first time since the fall of the Star League, is feeding upon itself in the frenzy of civil war.

The Federated Commonwealth's orgy of self-destruction brings little comfort to Theodore Kurita, all-powerful Coordinator of the Draconis Combine. Such vulnerability in the Combine's greatest rival is the answer to the prayers of generations of Kurita rulers before him. But Theodore knows that the turmoil in the Federated Commonwealth creates not only opportunity, but the potential for disaster. The Clan menace has only been stalled, not stemmed. The Successor States must pull together—or face certain annihilation when the Truce expires.

On Hachiman, wealthiest world of the Combine, Theodore's cousin Chandrasekhar Kurita plays a secret game of his own—a game Theodore's spymaster Subhash Indrahar believes is treason. And a scandal involving a member of the Combine's ruling family might well put paid to any hope the Coordinator has of stopping the Clans when Kerensky's superhuman warriors resume their relentless march toward Terra.

But that's politics. The real story begins two decades earlier, on a backwater world of the Capellan Confederation. . . .

Part One

Nightmares

1

Cassie was three when the 'Mechs came to Larsha.

"Mommy, mommy, where's Daddy?"

A crack like lightning rattled the windows of the small house on the outskirts of Kalimantan, capital city of Larsha, on the distant fringe of the Capellan Confederation. Alexandra Yamaguchi Suthorn shuddered violently but tried to keep the terror from distorting her face and voice as she spoke to her young daughter.

"He's gone away now, Cassie. He'll be back"—a crash from outside; her blue eyes darted toward the window again—"as soon as he can."

Cassiopeia Suthorn writhed in her mother's grip. She was a small child with bare brown arms and legs and big gray eyes. All the neighbors—old Mrs. Wu next door, Dr. Bandaryan down the block, the Aungs across the way—never stopped commenting on how intelligent and cheerful she was. Cassie was always happy, always playful, and almost always getting into mischief of some sort. But she had such a pretty smile, such an innocent way about her, that no one could stay angry at her for long. Not even Mrs. Sanders, who lived on the other side of the Wus and was known for throwing rocks at older neighborhood children who tried to pick apples from the branches that hung down over her back wall.

Cassie wasn't a happy child now, fighting as much to keep a grip on her yellow teddy bear—worn and one-eyed veteran that he was—as to escape her mother's restraint. It was still dark when the sounds awakened her that morning—sounds from the next room—the intense whispers of her parents, who somehow imagined their excited hissing would not alert her keen child's senses. She had crept out of bed in one of her father's undershirts which she wore as a nightgown, peered around the doorway from the hall to see them standing in the middle of the living room, Mother in her robe, Father in his dusty-green military clothes with the darker green leggings and forearm braces and simple yellow tabs of his commander's rank on the collar.

Immediately Cassie too became excited. She loved when her father dressed up in his soldier clothes. He looked so handsome. And sometimes he took her along to parades, where she would see rank on rank of young men in their swept helmets and pretty uniforms and the big tanks that sometimes—if she were very good—a little girl might get to climb on. And sometimes she might even glimpse a BattleMech gleaming in the hot Larsha sun like a giant, fearsome metal man.

But the way her parents were acting told Cassie there would be no fun excursions today. They had the serious looks that grownups seemed to get when talking of things they didn't want children to hear.

"—just an alert," Commander Manoc Suthorn was saying. His handsome mouth tightened. "We're forbidden to evacuate, the orders say. They don't want to spread panic."

Cassie's mother clutched his arm. "Is there any chance the fighting will reach us here?"

"I don't know." Her father shook his head. "I wish we'd dug a shelter below the house."

"Don't blame me!" Alexandra Suthorn's voice shrilled and almost broke. "You can't blame me! We had other things to spend the money on, and never enough—"

"There was always enough for the party dresses, the whole round of you and all the other refugees trying to recapture the status we knew back in the Combine." Gently he detached her fingers from his arms. "Yes, yes, I know . . . the status I lost for us . . ."

He kissed her forehead. "It's too late for blame now," he said, "and if there is any, it's mine as much as yours. Take care of Cassie."

And then he turned and saw Cassie standing there, the child no longer making any attempt to hide, her bear dangling from one small fist. And he swept her up and crushed her in his strong arms and called her his little girl and told her to be good. Then he was out the door.

It was two hours later that the sirens began their banshee wail, rise and fall, rise and fall, rise and fall. And then a rushing roar across the sky, like a mighty windstorm passing, and Cassie's mother with a death grip on her daughter's arm to keep her from going out, tear tracks gleaming against the smoothness of her ivory skin.

Another crack. A red flash lit the street, followed by a *whoomp*. The smell of ozone and then the spreading Sandusk olive tree in the Suthorn's tiny front yard crashed past the window, branches burning. Alexandra let go her grip on her daughter, raked her flawless cheeks with her nails and screamed.

There were men moving up the block, men in the Aung yard across Resplendent Glory Lane. Men in the distinctive olive uniforms and helmets Cassie knew so well. "Daddy!" she shouted, wriggling with redoubled energy. "It's Daddy."

"No, dear, no," her mother said, somehow fighting down her panic. "Those are just soldiers dressed like Daddy. You can't tell—"

What cut off her words was a bolt of blue hitting the ground in front of the Aung house, the blue fire momentarily blanking Cassie's vision. Through great maroon clouds of afterimage she saw the big front window shimmer and simply melt away, felt a rush of heat on her face like the hot breath of air when she squatted too near while her mother slid her baking in and out of the oven.

In the Aung yard, men were on fire. Cassie uttered a shriek that seemed to tear the lining out of her throat. Dropping her bear, she broke from her mother's arms and ran out the front door.

The burning men had fallen to the ground. The whole front of the Aung house was in flames. Next to Cassie the fallen tree was ablaze with popping sounds.

From somewhere came a heavy pounding, like slow footsteps, but magnified a thousandfold. Out of the house ran Alexandra Suthorn, tail of her robe flying. She swooped Cassie up into her arms and carried her across the street at an angle away from the burning house, into the Fabricants' front yard. Then she was down on all fours, dragging Cassie along, burrowing like an animal into an azelia bush, hung now with wilted yellow-orange blossoms.

The hammerfall sounds drummed closer. Again Cassie escaped her mother, crawled out to stand upright on the Fabricants' lawn, staring back at her house.

An enormous figure suddenly loomed up behind the house. With a great splintering crack, it shouldered aside the evergreen oak that Cassie, to her mother's despair, loved to climb. The little girl stared up at the giant as it raised a giant metal hand, then smashed it down onto her house.

"Teddy," she said in a lost and tiny voice.

The giant BattleMech gazed down at her, its death's-head a gleaming metal parody of a human face. Slowly it raised its left arms, until Cassie was staring directly up the huge tube mounted on the end of it. Deep within the black tunnel, rings of blue light began to glow. Crouched behind Cassie, her mother began to whimper.

Whatever the giant machine was about to do didn't happen because the next moment a rocket slammed into the side of the 'Mech's head with a ringing sound like God's own sledgehammer. The metal monster rocked, turned. The blue lightning from its left arm hit the next street over, sending a rush of debris riding skyward on an orange fireball. But the giant was not felled. The 'Mech caught its balance, lowering its right arm to send an eye-hurting column of ruby light stabbing into the rubble of Cassie's house, followed by an immediate gush of fire. By then the monster was already striding away, wading through the Wu house and buckling the blacktop of Resplendent Glory Lane with its awful weight.

Cassie Suthorn stood and watched the gigantic beast that had destroyed her life as it lumbered off, heedless of the destruction it left behind. Tears streamed from her eyes; blood streamed from eardrums ruptured when the missile struck the BattleMech's head.

Little Cassie began to scream.

Somewhere deep inside, she never stopped.

2

Kalimantan, Larsha
Sian Commonality, Capellan Confederation
19 July 3047

Cassie was sixteen when the 'Mechs came back to Larsha.

"Hey!" Rat called from a corner of the darkened store. "*Royals' Pride* is on!"

The sudden murmur of voices from the holovid set perched on a shelf of the electronics shop was interrupted by a crash and tinkle of coins as Pachinko and Rusty finally pried open the register's cash drawer with the ludicrous sword-bayonets issued them along with their bolt-action rifles. In their enthusiasm they popped the drawer all the way out, so that it crashed onto the floor, scattering money across the scuffed tiles.

Recruit Cassie Suthorn sat in a corner formed by a glass display counter and a wall of shelves holding portable holo viewers and recorders. Her drab uniform was several sizes too large for her and hung on her skinny frame like a sack; the rifle propped in the corner next to her was almost as tall as she was. She was chewing on a mango she'd found in the back room, ignoring the antics of her compatriots as they scuttled around the store, scooping handfuls of green and orange Capellan currency off the floor.

"C'mon, Cassie," Tango called. "Free money! Grab your share." He held out a handful of bills. He was always trying to please her.

She snorted. "What for? Use it to wipe yourself and all you get are smudges on your fanny. Anyway, it's too scratchy." Cassie might not understand the concept of inflation—though House Liao assuredly did—but life on the streets had taught her enough about its effects. Just as it had taught her so much else she lacked the experience or education to understand in depth.

Tango shook his head at her inexplicable indifference to this newfound wealth, which, as far as he was concerned, had fallen from heaven into their laps. He stuffed it into the blouse of his threadbare, hand-me-down battledress and turned away.

Cassie's nostrils flared in amused contempt. It was no surprise to see the troopies of Glorious Redemption Detachment 325 thinking and acting like small-time crooks. That was, after all, exactly what they *were*.

The Capellans were poor people, government propaganda said, kept that way by the selfishness and invidiousness of their neighbors, specifically evil House Davion of the Federated Suns. Capellans could not afford to throw anything away. Not even their criminal scum.

The front window suddenly rattled to an explosion, and Cassie felt the muscles between her shoulder blades go tight. For a moment she was back in that long-ago day when her whole world died. . . .

Rusty looked out the window and bit her lower lip. "Wonder if the *gweilu*'ll come this way." Rusty herself was fair-skinned, with red hair and blue eyes that lacked the epicanthic fold, but she saw nothing incongruous in calling the raiders "round-eyed devils." She was Capellan, and they were Davions.

Ba Ma shook his head, his ears sticking out from under his helmet like jug handles. "No," he said in his standard, authoritative way. "They're hitting the 'Mech base east of town. They won't come into the city."

"Then what's that?" asked Snake, pointing her grubby finger out the front window. "A hopping ghost?"

What looked vaguely like a man made of pewter had risen above the skyline to the north and was sailing across the dirty overcast in an upright posture. A lance of red light pulsed from its head. Then it sank from sight again on jump jets that flared from its club feet.

"*Wolverine*," said Rusty. The stocky recruit was something of an aficionado of BattleMechs, as well as an accomplished smash-and-grab artist.

Cassie felt the back of her throat fill with stinging vomit. Thirteen years of nightmares rose up yammering to crowd her skull.

"Ours or theirs?" Tango wanted to know.

Rusty gave him a pitying look. "Confederation don't *make* no *Wolverine*s," she said, "and the Ever-Conquerin' Army sure didn't take it as battle honors—'cause we never win any battles."

Cassie threw aside the half-eaten fruit and clutched her rifle across her chest, knowing how futile the gesture was. Even a full-automatic rifle would have been small protection against one of those metal monsters, while all she had was one of the bolt-actions issued the members of the Glorious Redemption Detachment. Even if the guns weren't—as scuttlebutt would have it—more than a thousand years old, the design probably was. But they were cheap, and expendable ... like the jailbird troopies of the GRDs.

She forced herself to breathe as Guru Johann had taught her: slow, deep, controlled, mastering panic. The wavy-bladed *kris* he had presented Cassie on her twelfth birthday seemed to pulse with a heartbeat of its own in its hiding place beneath her battledress blouse. Indeed Guru had assured her the weapon *was* alive and that it remembered every moment of its history from the day of its forging in Terra's Malay Archipelago twelve centuries before.

Cassie loved her guru and honored his memory. But that didn't mean she believed everything he'd told her. Still, Blood-drinker's presence reassured her.

If nothing else, she could take her own life with it before the metal monsters took her.

"Hey, you clowns, quiet," Pachinko called. "I wanna hear this. Archon Alison is confronting her wayward daughter."

" 'Confronting her wayward daughter'?" Ba Ma repeated. "You been watching too much vid, man. You're starting to talk like somebody in a story."

"Who cares about that *gweilu* garbage anyway?" Snake sneered.

"I do," Pachinko said stubbornly. "I used to watch this show every day even when I was on the street."

Why a Davion-made dramatic series—especially one about mythical royalty of the alliance recently forged between Houses Steiner and Davion, now jointly known as the Federated Commonwealth—should be wildly popular on Larsha, a fringe world of the Capellan Confederation, was anybody's guess. An even greater mystery was why House

Liao's censors let it be imported via ComStar's interstellar communications network, let alone broadcast.

Not that Cassie gave a frak about it. She didn't have much curiosity about anything not intimately connected with survival. She'd heard an explanation, though: Old Hsu from the neighborhood where Cassie and her mother had moved after the 'Mechs came claimed the government let people watch the show because watching the antics of imaginary round-eye royalty kept their minds off the antics of the Confederation's own rulers, notably Chancellor Romano Liao, who some said was as mad as a bagful of ruby-eye scorpions. That was shortly before the Special Services Branch of the Maskirovka disappeared Old Hsu for running off his mouth.

He had it coming, Cassie reckoned—not that she had any love for the SSBs or any other brand of police. It was what he got for worrying about things that weren't important. It just set your mind in an uproar, distracted you from essentials.

"Suthorn," Lance Corporal Sugiman said. "Take a look outside. See if you can tell what's going on."

Cassie's blood turned to ice inside her. She didn't move. *The monsters are out there.*

Sugiman frowned. He was ranking member of the little squad because the lance sergeant in command—a Capellan regular busted to the unit on a disciplinary—had ducked out fifteen minutes before, ostensibly to "check things out" himself. No one was expecting to see him again, at least not until after the raiders were safely gone.

"Cassiopeia," he began, making two mistakes simultaneously: pleading and using Cassie's full first name, which she loathed.

She shot him an obscene hand gesture. "Bug off, Pretty Tony."

"But I'm in *charge*."

A crash from the back of the shop. Instantly Cassie was on her feet, rifle ready. She didn't have to take it off safety because she hadn't remembered to put the safety *on*.

When they were tumbled out of barracks at oh-dark-hundred this morning, that was how she had known they would be seeing real action that day: they'd been issued bullets. It was the first time any of the gutter-sweepings of the GRD had handled live ammunition, even including the several weeks of brutal hazing that had served as their basic training.

Heriyanto came backpedaling out of the stockroom, sweat running down his neck, his nose mashed flat under the muzzle break of a stubby Tseng machine pistol.

Four more figures crowded into the shop behind the Tseng-wielder, ballistic-cloth armor vests bulking out their uniform blouses and dark visors obscuring their faces: Maskirovka Guardsmen, the blunt end of the dreaded Liao secret police.

Cassie felt sweat running down her cheeks and the back of her neck, which still felt naked without the comforting weight of the braid she'd worn since childhood. Two nightmares in one day was a lot even for her to stand up to.

Another Guardsman stood behind the man with the gun, surveying the scene with gauntleted hands on hips. He was the shortest of the four, but not the least wide. On his collar were the green pips crossed by three transverse slashes of a force Leader.

"Well, well, well," he rasped in a voice rough-hewn by a Guardsman's diet of arrack, *bhang,* and harsh Larsha tobacco, "what have we here?"

"Look like shirkers to me, *tuan,*" said the one who had her piece pressed into Heriyanto's pale face. The backs of her bare, pudgy hands were covered with ginger fur, like an orangutan's, but curly. Cassie stared in fascination.

"What're you gawking at, guttersnipe?" a burly Guardsman demanded, backhanding Cassie across the face. She flew back into the shelves, dislodging her outsized tin hat and giving a nasty crack to the back of her skull. Vidchip boxes cascaded over her as sparks danced manic behind her eyes. The Guardsmen laughed.

"Where's your sergeant?" the Force Leader demanded.

"G-gone, *tuan,*" Pretty Tony said. *Tuan* meant lord in Malay; it was local slang for "boss." Most of Larsha's variegated populace had roots in ancient Indonesia. "He, uh, he went out to check the situation."

"Shut," the Force Leader said. Tony shut. "You—stand up."

Numbly Cassie complied, simultaneously knocking a Daewoo radio off the shelf and over her shoulder; it shattered at her feet. She stared fixedly at the Guardsman's sleeve where it displayed the sword-arm patch of House

Liao, the pips and triangle trim signifying SSB, to which the Guard belonged. Her face was hot, her vision blurred.

She'd been only nine the first time one of her mother's many lovers raped her. Afterward he laughed at her and said that if she told anyone he'd make her Mummy disappear. He could do it, too; she'd seen this same green patch on his sleeve as he pulled on his jacket and buttoned it over his huge, hairy gut. Then he'd placed his visored helmet over his head and stepped from the shack into the monsoon rain that drummed against the tin and tarpaper roof and walls like demonic monkey fists.

"Where's the proprietor, huh?" the Force Leader demanded. He was standing directly in front of Pretty Tony now, shouting up into the lance corporal's face. Tony was taller, but the Guardsman had a good twenty kilos on him. Plus he was a *Guardsman.* Street scum like Tony grew up dreading the Maskirovka Guard in their bones, even when they didn't have reasons as personal as Cassie's.

"He was gone when we got here. Honest. Our lance sergeant told us to come in here, and hold, and then he left—"

The Force Leader's gloved hand cracked across Tony's face. "Shut," he said again, then turned away from Tony to survey the squad huddled in the little shop on Marshal Chiang Avenue. "I know who you are," he said. "Don't think I don't. Glorious Redemption—what a joke."

The other four Guardsmen all gave nasty laughs. "The Army and the Planetary Governor may buy that they can redeem the likes of you scum. *I* don't. I been dealing with your kind all my life. *I* know what you did. I think you came in here to hide from the fighting, and rousted out the shopkeeper so you could rifle his store. Am I right? *Am I?*"

"No, honest—" Pretty Tony began. Without even looking, the Force Leader reached back and grabbed him by the lobe of his right ear. Thick-gloved fingers twisted. Tony dropped to his knees with a squeal.

"Look around," the Force Leader said. "It's quite a little mess you made, isn't it?"

He twisted again. Tony squeaked affirmation.

"Now, this morning the PG issued an edict forbidding the people to evacuate the city. You don't believe the merchant scumbag who owned this hole had enough in his sac to defy our glorious leaders, do you?"

Tony moaned. The Force Leader threw him to the ground

and stepped over him to the holovid set, where Pachinko stood trembling like a reed in a stiff breeze.

"What's this?" the Force Leader said, cocking his helmeted head to the side. "Davion trash? I don't believe it. You're all sworn to be loyal servants of the Chancellor, and you're watching this filth."

Pachinko stuck out his underlip. "But the government lets them show it. How can it be wrong?"

He was interrupted by a blow across the face that sent him to his knees. "Silence!" roared the Force Leader. He whipped a mirror-chromed snubnosed revolver from his belt and put a round right through the Archon Alison's angel face. The report was so loud Cassie wondered that the shop's front window didn't blow out.

"Treason's what I say it is, you muck-apes!" he roared over the ringing in GRD 325's ears. "Your even daring to *exist* is an offense!"

He looked around at them, the contempt shining through his opaque faceplate like the beam of a seven-centimeter laser. They looked back at him like animals awaiting ritual slaughter.

The squad outnumbered the secret policemen two to one, and at least half of them had rifles in hand. Yet not one of the troopies made a move to resist.

It was not just that three of the Guardsman were covering the room with their machine pistols, but that the people of the Capellan Confederation were used to obeying harsh demands. Larsha was a poor little garrison world, hard against the hostile Davion frontier and too close for its own good to the bandit worlds of the Periphery. Its government was repressive and corrupt even by Liao standards. Here, as throughout the Confederation, the most visible symbol of that repression was the faceless Maskirovka Guardsmen. To resist would be to overcome a lifetime of conditioning. That was a lot to ask, even of former street criminals.

Not long after Cassie's twelfth birthday, her mother's lover tried to use her again, as he had so often. This time, she threatened him with Blood-drinker. He laughed until she laid the back of his hand open and told him she'd kill him if he tried to touch her again.

He left, vowing to come back with his squadmates and make her disappear. Threats against her mother had less effect on her by that time.

When Cassie told her mother what she'd done—and why—Alexandra Suthorn slapped her across the face. "You little fool," she said, her still-lovely face contorted with anger and fear. "Can't you leave well enough alone? Don't you know when we're well off?"

Cassie left the house then, taking nothing but the clothes on her back and her kris. *She never went back.*

The Force Leader thumbed the catch on his revolver, turned the piece sideways so the cylinder swung out. He ejected the contents—one empty, five live cartridges—into his gloved palm. He stuck one round back into the cylinder and slammed the weapon shut.

"Let's play a little game, street scum," he said, rolling the cylinder down his left forearm. "A little Maskirovka roulette, eh?"

He held the pistol behind the kneeling Pachinko's right ear. Pachinko squeezed his eyes shut. Tears leaked out of them. His lips worked silently.

The gloved finger tightened on the trigger.

The hammer snapped.

The Force Leader's laugh was as jarring as the shot everyone had been expecting to hear. "Well," he said, "you are one very lucky young guttersnipe."

Sobbing, Pachinko tried to climb to his feet. The Force Leader spun the cylinder again, cocked the weapon and pressed it against the bridge of the boy's nose, forcing him back to his knees.

"Not so fast," he said. "I'm not done having fun yet. Let's see if you're *really* lucky, shall we?"

The next instant, walls and floor began to shake violently, knocking more electronic gadgets off the shelves. A ripple of flashes lit the front of the building opposite to a roar like jackhammer thunder.

Disregarding the Guardsmen and their weapons, the members of the Glorious Redemption Detachment ducked, instinctively seeking cover. The Force Leader waved his snubby in the dust-choked air. "What's going on?" he shouted over the whistling roar that rose around them like a typhoon wind.

"SRMs!" Ba Ma yelled. "And them's jump jets. 'Mech coming!"

For once he was right. A gigantic manlike figure, painted matte blue and gray, suddenly appeared in the air above the commercial buildings across the street and then landed in the avenue half a block away with a sound of shattering pavement.

Deep inside Cassie Suthorn, something burst like a bomb and burned like a nova.

$$=== 3 ===$$

Kalimantan, Larsha
Sian Commonality, Capellan Confederation
19 July 3047

Quick and fluid as a mongoose, Cassie stopped to snatch her antique rifle off the floor. She raised it to her waist and aimed it at the Force Leader. "All right," she hissed. "Out in the street—all of you!"

He looked at her a moment, then laughed, throwing back his head so she could see his open mouth under the bottom of his visor. His teeth were stained and pitted with dark caverns.

He was not the man who raped her. But he wasn't much different.

Knowing the Guardsman's armored vest would stop a small-arms round, Cassie dropped the long barrel of her rifle and shot the man through his unprotected thigh.

He screamed and fell, clutching his leg while Cassie worked the bolt and aimed the rifle at the apish woman, who froze in the act of trying to bring her Tseng to bear on the girl.

"Out," Cassie repeated. "Now." The Force Leader writhed on the floor, crying.

"But the 'Mech will see us," another Guardsman gasped.

Cassie smiled. "That's the idea."

"He'll kill us!"

"He might miss. I won't." She jerked her head toward the injured Force Leader. "Take that trash with you. *Go*."

Letting their Tsengs hang by the slings, the woman and the Guardsman who had spoken stooped, caught their leader under his shoulders, and hauled him into the street. Their two comrades followed.

A machine gun crackled as the door shut behind the Guardsmen. Cassie lowered her rifle and looked around at her comrades, who were all gaping as if she'd suddenly grown horns.

"Out the back," she said. "Hurry. We haven't bought much time."

She made pitchforking motions with her rifle for emphasis, prodding the squad through the door to the backroom and out into the alley. The last one out, Cassie, paused and turned to look out the window.

She saw a Guardsman scuttling across the street, hunched over like a crab, then a line of light stabbed down to touch him with a searing crack. He exploded in a gout of flash-heated pink steam and chunks of meat.

Cassie turned and ran after her mates.

"Why'd you have to *do* that, Cassie?" Pretty Tony whined. His voice seemed to buzz up through the urine-stench and dingy light that filled the deserted apartment's stairwell like a swarm of mosquitoes. He was wheezing a little. They all were, after the four-block run from the electronics shop. "We'll get reported sure. We're all for the high jump, 'cause you shot that water buffalo."

"Yeah," Tango said. "They musta read our names right off our blouses. They'll hunt us down once this is over, and then—"

"Shut up," Cassie said without looking back to see how many of her squadmates were following her to the roof. She didn't care. *She* was the one who had broken free; *she* was the one who had made the move. She was done with fear—or at least done with giving in to it. She was past caring about consequences.

The feeling of liberation was intoxicating.

The door that gave onto the roof was supposed to be locked, but somebody had jimmied it long before this and it had, of course, never been replaced. Cassie pushed the door open and started out.

What she saw next made her heart jump into her throat, abruptly teaching her a lesson about making assumptions. Standing there on *top* of another three-story building not five blocks away was a 'Mech. This one was much smaller than the *Wolverine,* more humanoid and with a single antenna protruding hornlike from its slanted, boxy forehead. Instead of having all its weapons built in, the 'Mech seemed to be carrying something like an outsized firearm in two-handed patrol position at about hip height.

Cassie froze. *"Stinger,"* Ba Ma said, ducking to peer under her armpit. "Twenty-tonner, light 'Mech. That's a medium laser it's carrying."

"Pretty solid building if it ain't caving in," Heriyanto said.

"See how he's standing on the ramparts? 'Mech jock's good," Ba Ma put in authoritatively.

"That's a bank," Rusty said, pouting because Ba Ma had beat her to identifying the 'Mech. "I wish he *would* cave it in."

"Why'd you bring us up here, Cassie?" Tango wanted to know. "That thing'll *see* us. We'd be safe in the street."

"What?" Rusty sneered. "Tango thinking about anything but loot?"

"His ass," Snake said.

"What are we doing up here?" Pretty Tony demanded.

With a bit of searching, Cassie found her voice. "You want to go scuttle around and wait to get stepped on," she growled, "go right ahead. I'm staying up here where I can *see.*"

"But that thing can see *us,*" Tango hissed. " 'Mechs have all kinds of sensors and crap."

Cassie felt her heart skip a beat, and just at that moment the *Stinger*'s head swiveled to look straight at them . . .

Then tracked right on past. The next moment the BattleMech crouched, leapt into the air, its jump jets taking it southwest toward the center of town.

Cassie felt a surge of something like triumph. The metal monster *hadn't* seen them. 'Mech's weren't all-seeing, after all.

Somewhere deep inside she dared to suspect the behemoths might not be invulnerable either.

"Come on," she said, and stepped out into such watery

light as managed to make it through the thick, low-hanging clouds. Duckwalking to keep below the parapet, she moved forward until she could peep over the edge.

The district was mostly commercial and light industrial, with few buildings rising more than three stories; the skyscrapers were clumped downtown, toward which the bulk of the invading 'Mechs seemed to be heading. It also seemed to be attracting defenders from the opposite direction. The monsters were all busy shooting at each other, which suited Cassie just fine.

"Looks like they want to hammer on the PG," Ba Ma said, hunkered down at Cassie's side. "Seat of Government is that way."

"Wonder if they'll hit the Big Pink Whorehouse too," Rusty said from the other side of her. That was what everybody called Planetary Governor Pang's elaborate residence in the hills to the west.

Just then, somebody gripped Cassie's upper arms, but even without looking or thinking, she broke the grip and twisted the offending hand back on itself. Guru Johann had been a practitioner of *pentjak silat,* but he'd also incorporated bits and pieces from other arts too, including aikido. Nobody touched Cassie without permission.

There was a thump as a body hit the graveled roof. Glancing over, she saw Lance Corporal Pretty Tony lying on his back.

He was pointing with his free hand. "That way, dammit! Look what you've got us into!"

It was their old friend the *Wolverine,* stalking the streets two blocks away. Cassie felt a wave of emotions—anger, hatred, resentment, fear—boiling inside her like water in a pot. But as she watched the top of the monster's head vanish behind a taller structure, she felt those emotions distilling into determination to *do something.*

Periodically they could see the flashes as the 'Mech blasted targets with its lasers, then pause as it came to an intersection. From out of nowhere a rocket came buzzing in to strike it in the chest. But the 'Mech showed no damage, only raised its right arm and answered with a rippling burst from the autocannon mounted there.

The weird little bulb of a turret mounted right in front of what Cassie took for the beast's head pulsed brilliant light. A crack, and power lines strung across the intersection parted company with a building and fell into the streets, drooling sparks.

"You don't like the lines," she breathed. "I've got you, you bastard."

She had released her grip on Pretty Tony, who was sitting up, massaging his wrist, looking at her strangely. "Cassie? What the hell are you talking about?"

She was looking around. The lines came into this building . . . right *there*. "Fire axe," she said.

"What?"

"Get me a fire axe. There was one in the case two flights down."

"Hey, I'm ranking man here—"

She turned her glare on him. Her eyes, normally a smoke-gray not much different from today's sky, were almost blue. "*Get it.*"

The lance corporal scrambled up and disappeared by the stairway. Cassie hunkered down to track the *Wolverine* in glimpses and laser-flash as it stalked the district, clearing out pockets of resistance. Just when she thought Pretty Tony had done the sensible thing and kept on running, he emerged from the darkened doorway with axe in hand.

She laid her rifle down and took it from him, then crawled along the parapet to the point where the power lines entered the building. She braced, took a two-handed grip on the axe and raised it over her head.

"Won't you get electrocuted, Cassie?" Heriyanto asked nervously.

"I don't know," she said, and swung.

Sparks exploded around the axehead as it smashed through insulation and cable. Huge blue sparks popped out at her like angry wasps. The wooden handle must have been a good-enough insulator, for the woven metal cable parted and dropped into the street. Grinning like a wolf, Cassie let the axe fall after it.

"Now what?" said Rusty, peering over the edge at the severed cable.

"Now we find a—a mop handle," Cassie told him. "And then we go hunting."

The 'Mech's footsteps, reverberating like thunder between the buildings flanking General Tso Street, were accompanied by the dull crackling of pavement giving up the ghost beneath the monster's fifty-five tons. As it neared the corner, Recruit Cassie Suthorn popped around and spanged a shot off the glacis of its chest armor.

The bullet could no more damage the behemoth than would an equal weight of spit, much less catch the attention of the warrior piloting the machine. Cassie's intention had been to put it right through the Mech's transpex faceplate, but she was a poor shot. The monster may not have noticed the puny bullet, but it did pay attention to the tiny, impertinent figure in baggy Liao battledress.

The little laser-bulb tracked, fired. The beam exploded concrete where the figure had stood just a moment before, but the figure was no longer there.

The monster hesitated, then rumbled forward. There were certain ... proprieties ... to thirty-first century warfare that must be observed. One of them was that a worthless little gnat of a groundpounder shouldn't dare to challenge the invincible might of a BattleMech—nor the invincible ego of a MechWarrior. It did not happen.

By now Cassie was running flat-out down the next street over, backtracking the direction the monster had been heading. Hearing the thunder of its footfalls nearing the corner behind her, her heart fluttered in her chest like the wings of a frightened dove. She felt *wonderful.*

For thirteen years the nightmares had haunted her. Now she was striking back against the steel demons who had robbed her of her Daddy and her house and her childhood. She might die—that laser finger might reach out and change her instantly to a steam-blasted, flaming, tumbling rubbish doll any time now. But live or die, she was no longer helpless. She was exhilarated.

She ducked into a doorway just as the 'Mech rounded the corner. It stood, casting around for its impudent foe.

Cassie knew that the killing beam of its laser moved at the speed of light, though she wasn't sure what that meant, except pretty damn fast. But the monster's response time wasn't so hot. From her perspective, it was dead slow.

She stepped into the street, shouldered her rifle, fired at the thing's head, chambered another round, fired it too. Then she lowered the piece and waved her hand in the air.

"Hey," she shouted, "Hey! Over here, you big slugface. Hey!" She could barely hear her own voice over the ringing of the shots in her unprotected ears. But just now she didn't need to hear to know she had the monster's attention. Moving in that man-underwater manner, it swiveled its torso, raising its right hand.

Like a rat, she darted back into the doorway, which was dim and stank of varnish and disinfectant. Apparently somebody in this crudhole still gave a damn, which would have been almost funny if she'd had time to think about it. Stairs disappeared into the murk to her right, but Cassie bolted straight back to the rear door, reaching it at the same instant the autocannon burst hit the front.

Glass shards and flame and explosive stink and raw shattering *noise* pursued her. She let the solid-metal rear door slam on them all, crossed the narrow, reeking alley in two steps, and blew in through another door. Down another cramped corridor that didn't smell *half* as good as the last one, out into the street where she'd left her squaddies in ambush. "Hey," she shouted as she ran across the street toward the apartment on whose roof she'd halfway baked her audacious plan of attack. "Hey, get ready!"

No answer. Her buddies had abandoned her, one and all.

No surprise. Nor bitterness. They didn't owe Cassie anything. Nor she them. Like her, they were just a bunch of street trash, losers by definition, who had managed to get the hard but damned near unguided arm of Liao law laid on them through bad luck or stupidity. Forget them. Whether the plan worked or not, they were just window dressing anyway. Their pitiful single-shot rifles couldn't hurt the monster any more than hers could.

She stopped before the apartment building, looked upon the street. She hoped the *Wolverine* pilot realized she'd kept running and would follow her around the corner.

But he surprised her, the 'Mech coming *through* the same buildings she had. First came an almighty crashing and banging, and suddenly there it was, looming up nine times the size of life in a giant cloud of dust and debris. The *Wolverine* was raising its autocannon-hand even as it appeared.

Cassie stood a moment, gaping in horrified dismay. Then survival reflexes honed sharp by years on the street took over. She dove away from the burst of cannon fire, rolled as fragments whistled over her, then regained her feet and darted over to the mop handle she'd left lying in the gutter.

The weight of the severed power line that had spot-welded itself to the steel-frame head was surprising when she hefted the handle. Since it wasn't spitting sparks at this moment, she had no way of telling whether it was live or not. Well, only one way to find out ...

The monster had turned to track her, still aiming the autocannon. The pilot must have learned that she was too shifty to nail with the laser, but figured that sooner or later the projectile spray would catch her. Or better yet—

With a vast creaking and groaning, the 'Mech raised its right foot, strode forward to crush the insolent little bug. Cassie hefted the mop-handle like a spear, taking care to keep the unshielded cable clear of her. Then she did the last thing in the world a MechWarrior would expect from a groundpounder caught in the open by a BattleMech: she charged.

Cassie ran into the shadow of the vast upraised foot. As it descended, she screamed and hurled the mop-handle upward and past it, straight at the great round joint of its knee.

With a cascade of sparks, the live power line flash-welded the metal giant's knee joint. Not much, but just enough to lock the joint.

In fighting a larger opponent—which in Cassie's case was just about anybody—she had been taught by Guru Johann to always go for the joints. A lesson that seemed to apply here.

The 'Mech pilot obviously had no idea what this impertinent insect might be up to until his machine tilted forward to put its weight onto a leg that utterly refused to extend to accept it.

The moment she released the mop handle, Cassie dashed away up the block, sprinting thirty yards before spinning to watch the *Wolverine* topple with majestic slowness into the apartment building. The structure collapsed right down the middle, chunks of cement block splashing like water from the awesome impact. Cassie just stood there flatfooted, gaping.

After a while the catastrophic rumbling and crunching noises subsided. There was silence in the street, except for the rustle and thud of occasional pockets of loose debris falling and random pings as metal cooled.

Cassie was completely stupefied by what she had accomplished. Never had she actually expected to bring the monster down. Instead of being jubilant at her victory, she felt totally at a loss.

"Not bad," she managed to croak at last.

No sooner had the words left her mouth when Cassie felt a shadow fall across her. She whirled, only to see another of the monsters standing right behind her. So enthralled had she been in watching the *Wolverine*'s fall that she hadn't noticed anything else.

A thunder of multi-ton feet, and then another giant 'Mech appeared at the far end of the street, beyond the fallen behemoth. Cassie realized that her victory's sheer unexpectedness had made her very stupid indeed if all it did was let her get surprised by a hundred tons or so of metal.

She sprinted toward a doorway. The monster's machine gun snarled behind her, pitting cement in front of her feet. She stopped.

There was no place to run. The 'Mechs were in danger of crossfiring each other if they used their heavy weapons. On the other hand, they could totally fill the street with machine-gun bullets bouncing like the steel balls of the game that had given Pachinko his name—and no more feel them than hail.

I'm gonna die, she thought. It was the logical sum of her childhood nightmares. Now the moment had come and she wasn't really afraid. Angry, yes. But mostly just drained, and eager to get it over with.

Thirteen years was a long time to run.

With a convulsive motion she drew her *kris,* though she wasn't sure what she was going to do with it. Maybe finish herself off and deny the monsters the satisfaction. At least die with Blood-drinker in hand.

"Come on," she yelled, waving the wavy blade at the nearer monster. "What are you waiting for, you big puke? Finish it!"

A sound made her turn. There was a man standing on the prone monster's hip. He was tall and brown, and his eyes and the hair hanging lank and wild around them were black. He wore the cooling vest and shorts of a MechWarrior and held a pistol in his hand.

The man jumped to the pavement and stalked toward her. Cassie dropped into a *pentjak* guard stance, *kris* held over her head, blade forward, as if it would do any more good against his bullets than against the metal giants.

"You little bitch," he said in heavily accented English, which was the lingua franca of the Inner Sphere. She understood it, as she did Chinese, pidgin Malay, and the Japanese her mother had insisted she learn and use at home. "I'm gonna teach you a lesson you won't forget."

From a loudspeaker mounted on the 'Mech behind boomed a series of what Cassie thought were words. She couldn't be sure; they sounded like a market woman chopping up a chicken on the block, with rising-falling tones added in. Not so many as in Liao Mandarin, but there. The dark man stopped, raised a fist, and shouted back in what sounded like the same tongue. Cassie saw that he was young. Maybe not much older than she.

As he started forward again, she took up the slack in her stance.

A whistling scream of a kind that had already become too familiar rose over a wet wind filled with the smell of smoke and burned propellant and lubricants and a tang of the roast-pork smell of burning human flesh. Her peripheral vision caught another 'Mech settling down out of the sky to her left, in front of the building the *Wolverine* had walked through to get at her. She paid it no mind. Another few steps and the angry 'Mech jock would be in blade range.

Machine-gun fire cracked from the newcomer as its metal feet crunched down. The bullets struck between Cassie and her advancing antagonist, stinging her legs with cement dust. His, too, from the way he jumped.

"Back off," a woman's voice said from the speakers of the new 'Mech, which was lighter than any of the others, but looked bigger than the *Stinger*. Like the *Stinger*, it carried an oversized weapon in its right hand. The weapon was pointed downward at the pavement, not at Cassie. "She's a POW, Wolf."

The dismounted jock turned to the new 'Mech. "I didn't know we were *takin'* prisoners this trip. If we are—this *puta*'s mine."

"No way, Bobby. You're a Caballero now, remember? We don't torture our prisoners."

"But she trashed Skin Walker!" he screamed in almost-frothing rage.

"More reason to keep her alive," the female 'Mech pilot said. "How often does a lone groundpounder down a 'Mech? Much less a skinny little militia conscript who can't weigh forty kilos soaking wet. She's got talent."

The 'Mech turned its round head to gaze down at Cassie. "What's your name, troop?"

"Suthorn," she replied. "Cassie Suthorn." She was supposed to give her rank and all that, she knew. But none of it seemed to matter just now.

From off toward the city center came the sound of heavy firing. "We're wasting time, Patsy," Wolf screamed. "Let me waste her before the Lousies are all over us like stink on a goat."

"Callate," snapped the woman. "Recruit Suthorn, I am Lieutenant Senior Grade Patricia Camacho of the Seventeenth Reconnaissance Regiment. Do you surrender yourself to me?"

Cassie rocked back on her heels. She could hear Bobby the Wolf growling to himself like his namesake. His hatred for her beat from his dark features like heat from a stove.

"It'll mean leaving your home and all your friends and family behind," the woman said, not unkindly. "But you don't have much choice, *hermanita,* 'cause we don't have much time."

Cassie gazed up at the 'Mech. Guru was dead. Her mother . . . the mother who had loved her and cared for her and sheltered her from harm had no more survived the pirate raid of thirteen years ago than had Manoc Suthorn. Cassie felt nothing for the walking, talking shell that remained. There was no one else.

With a flick of her wrist she sent her *kris* spinning upward. She heard servo whines as various 'Mech-mounted weapons zeroed in on her.

Blood-drinker spun down. She caught it by the tip and extended it hilt-first toward the 'Mech standing over her.

"I give up," she said. "Do what you want to me. I can't stop you."

Cassie's legs gave way then, and she collapsed like an abandoned rag doll. She was aware of the 'Mech stooping over her, reaching for her with a humanoid hand. And then she whirled downward into blackness.

Part Two

Survivors

4

Deep in swamp, a monster's footprint fills with water. Next to it a woman hunkers, nearly naked in the stunning, humid heat of this forgotten world on the edge of known space, assault rifle resting across lean, hard thighs. She reaches a hand down to feel the edge of the cut. The soil here is black and comparatively solid, or it would never have borne the seventy-five-ton weight of the behemoth who left the track. Ground seep has filled it.

The print is round and cloven-hoofed, so big around she could lie in it with arms and legs outspread and not come close to touching the edges. Weeds have sprouted through the compacted soil at the bottom of the print to thrust their heads above the brown water. The edges of the print are rounded. It is not recent. It tells her nothing she does not already know.

She raises her head and smiles. Among humankind her smile is reckoned beautiful. But hardly anyone would describe this expression that way. The print reminds her of what she has come for, makes it real and immediate.

She is hunting 'Mech.

Mercy is not her companion.

The footprint was left by a *Marauder*. Among the most dreaded of Inner Sphere BattleMechs, the *Marauder* is a foe even a Clan *Omni* has to respect, seventy-five tons of malice and thermonuclear flame. Cassie has long since learned the hard lesson that if there are gods out there somewhere in the blackness between stars, they don't listen to big, nasty girls who carry guns and knives for toys any more than they heed the cries of little girls with pigtails and teddy bears. But she still murmurs a fervent prayer that the *Marauder* will be hers.

A voice in her ear says, "Come again, Abtakha?"

Her lips say, "I'm moving in on the *basura* now," but no sound emerges from her mouth. She is subvocalizing for the tiny microphone patch taped to her throat.

"Be careful there, Abtakha," comes the voice of Captain Badlands Powell, the Scout Platoon CO, in her right ear. A ceramic dot speaker the size of a thumbtip is taped to the mastoid process right behind the ear, transmitting its vibrations directly into her skull. Someone could have his cheek pressed to Cassie's and still not hear a thing.

A momentary flick of tension at the corners of smoke-gray eyes. Nine years in the unit, and she is still an outsider. They call her Abtakha, the Clan word for a prisoner adopted into the unit that has captured her. Actually, it's a Clan loan-word, one of the things the Clans gave the Seventeenth Recon Regiment on Jeronimo, along with a world of hurt. Be that as it may, the term accurately describes the status of Lieutenant Junior Grade Cassie Suthorn.

"Right, Badlands," she says. Rising, she moves on toward a stand of palmack, the big, fleshy green leaves seeming to shoot straight up from the mud, their fringes looking as if they've been chewed on by the small, toothy creatures that inhabit the swamp. Her exposed skin is painted with a mottle of green and brown to break up her silhouette, her only clothing a strip of camouflage cloth around her small breasts and a thong bottom. A small, lightweight pack carrying her communicator and other essentials rides her back. Her feet are bare of her usual sneakers; the mud would only suck them right off or, at best, load them up into gobs of weight.

Cassie believes in traveling as light as possible. The baggy battledress most Inner Sphere groundpounders wear in swamp conditions does little to fend off the crawly sucking things that live there, though it did provide excellent cover for the local leech equivalents. As for the omnipresent thorns, they don't bother her. She flows between them like smoke.

It is a truism that the best scouts in the countryside are country-born. Cassie is the exception. She's city-trash born and bred—but she's adaptable.

The other members of Scout Platoon are true wilderness men and women from the harshest regions of the Trinity worlds of Marik space. What outsiders call the Southwestern worlds: Sierra, Cerillos, and Galisteo, the planets from which the bulk of the Regiment's members spring. Chiricahua and White Mountain Apache, Acoma and Zuñi from the deserts, *truchaseños* and hillbillies from the arid mountains. They had skills in their home environments that Cassie can, frankly, never match; it is as a *whole package* that she's unbeatable.

Compared to Cassie, the other scouts are actually at a disadvantage in this environment. Their homeworlds are dry and hot. Larsha, like this godforsaken Periphery outworld now named New Horizons, is hot and wet.

She slips into a bayou, stepping carefully to keep from tearing her foot on a snag or dropping into an unseen hole. She must swim partway, holding the bullpup-pattern M23 up out of the water with one hand. The assault rifle is supposed to be waterproof, but Cassie finds it hard to believe that it will survive being filled up with mud and silt and still be able to fire.

The water is opaque and greasy, but the facets of its everdancing surface take the ultraviolet-rich sunlight and blast it at her eyes like tiny laser cells.

On the far side Cassie slithers up the bank like an otter, making barely a sound as she parts company with the clinging water. She disappears into a bank of dense green undergrowth splotched white with flowers lobed like sea anemones, the branches barely stirring at her passage.

This planet had once been known as Crotch. It had been settled many centuries before by the usual assortment of misfits, outcasts, and outright bandits who came to the Periphery, finding life in the Inner Sphere dominated by the then-Terran Hegemony and the five Great Houses of Liao, Marik, Steiner, Kurita, and Davion too restrictive—or too hot—for comfort. The name Crotch might have suited the world's founders, but their descendants had apparently felt that tug of respectability that so often follows the waning of the roughnecked frontier spirit. Seeking an image upgrade, they had changed their planet's name.

The Caballeros, as the boys and girls of the Seventeenth Recon Regiment liked to call themselves, felt a lot of sympathy for misfits, outcasts, and bandits. Back in the good old days, the Trinity Worlds had themselves been a bandit kingdom, styling itself the Intendancy of New New Spain. Then the cantankerous three-world alliance had been conquered and absorbed by the Free Worlds League, a major coup that did much to win the fledgling League acceptance from the Southwesterners' long-suffering neighbors. The Caballeros didn't see anything wrong with calling this planet Crotch. Besides, it fit.

New Horizons was a reasonably remote world across the line from Qandahar Prefecture of the Draconis Combine's Pesht District. Its relative isolation, added to its wealth in water and metals, had enabled it to move from a pirate economy to a more or less trade-based economy. Accordingly, its unredeemed bandit king-style neighbors came raiding from time to time.

The Dracs, however, had gotten a bellyful of nascent pirate powers such as the Oberon Confederation coalescing on their borders, so when any of New Horizons' neighbors got too overweening, a passel of glory-hunting would-be samurai came booming forth from Qandahar to whack hell out of them. In return, the Planetary Syndicate that ruled New Horizons sent regular tribute to Qandahar Prefecture's military commander. Everyone's *wa* was on straight.

Then the Clans came swinging out of coreward space, crunching like an axe into the Combine in their cosmic smash-and-grab raid. Oberon and the other pirate states in the regions of space near New Horizons were smashed.

The lesser pirate realms on the fringes of the Clan advance *splashed.*

Captain Father Doctor Roberto "Call Me Bob" García, SJ, who was, among other things, the Seventeenth's leading history buff, was always happy to fill Cassie's ears with more than she wanted to know about precedents and parallels between current events and Terra's turbulent past. He liked to compare the effects of the Clan invasion of the Periphery to the great Movement of Peoples, pointing out how the eruption of a lone tribe of shaggy, smelly, pony-riding, sheep-eating, bow-shooting barbarians called the Hsiung-nu into Central Asia from the Gobi Desert had sent people flying as far as Scandinavia, Britain, Spain, and even North Africa, all of which Cassie understood to be worlds somewhere in the vicinity of Terra. She never really paid much mind to Father Bob when he was lecturing, any more than when he tried to psychologize her.

Cassie was not concerned with precedent; she was concerned with fact. The relevant datum was that one sizable glob of human detritus sent flying by the Clans had smacked *spang* into New Horizons. They brought with them the rapacious values of a true pirate culture, combined with the vicious and gratuitous cruelty of a defeated army—something Father Bob's history books never liked to talk about, but that Cassie herself had witnessed again and again in her nine years with the Regiment. These pirates worked hard to earn the name the Caballeros gave them: *basura.* It was Spanish for trash.

That was fine with Cassie. It made her job all the easier.

The New Horizons Defense Force had pretty well burned itself out fighting the original influx of pirate refugees. They had been overjoyed to let the Caballeros—themselves human flotsam from the Clan invasion—take on the job of digging the surviving pirate gangs out of the strongholds where they had gone to ground.

For its part, the Regiment had suffered severely fighting the Clans under the banner of the Federated Commonwealth. They were in sore need of rest and refit. This gig offered a nice chunk of change in return for a relatively low-intensity mission.

After going head-to-head with the Clans, it was a vacation.

This *basura* band had gone to ground in the Great Murchison Swamp on New Horizon's largest continent. They had 'Mechs, a dozen of them, all crouching down at the bottom of a big, stagnant lake off a bayou. Mostly they left them there, where murky water and substantial iron deposits beneath the lake bed made it tough to pinpoint their location with remote-sensing. The pirates issued forth mostly on foot, in literal pig-and-chicken stealing raids against the local Swampers. They didn't neglect the usual atrocities: torture, rape, and the burning of the Swampers' stilted shanties.

That let Cassie bring her special street-kid skills into play. Most of Scout Platoon were asocial loners, even more uncomfortable with outsiders than the average Southwesterner. Cassie, on the other hand, had come up a scammer and a hustler. The human environment was one through which she swam with ease and comfort.

She had been a busy girl these past two weeks, scouting the

basura camp and making preparations. The Swampers—an ethnic admixture of Cajun and Filipino *negrillo,* leavened with a bit of everybody else—had been *very* helpful.

Cassie crouches in a world of shades of green: dusty green, pale green, green so dark as to be almost black, green so pure and rich it makes the eyes ache. But she is there for the view, not the scenery.

From her cover in the dense, prickly undergrowth she looks out over a broad expanse of water. It stinks of stagnation and organic decay, the reek tinged by the scent of campfire smoke. On the far side of the dead lake a stand of silura trees bob shaggy heads above smooth, thirty-meter-tall trunks.

At the base of the silura grove the underbrush has been hacked back. Like multicolored fungus, a clump of settlement has grown up there: fading, once-colorful tents looted from the department stores of Medwick and Fiasco, New Horizons' largest cities; big white polymer boxes used for containerized cargo; shacks cobbled together from oddments of tarpaper and polymer; even huts of grass and native timber.

An outsider's eye might find it hard to tell the *basura* camp from the Swamper's rude dwellings. To Cassie there is no similarity. The Swamper shanties are rough in appearance, but they are highly efficient at keeping off the worst of the region's fierce weather, while not opposing too directly the strength of wind and water. They have an organic appearance; they fit the surroundings.

The *basura* shacks are the half-hearted improvisations of people so demoralized they can barely care about their own comfort. They stand out like a tumor on an MRI scan.

Moving without haste Cassie slips off her light pack. She lowers it to the spongy earth, unzips it. From it she takes a head-sized black box, sets it down beneath the sweep of a wall-eye bush, opens covers and presses buttons. Various pilot lights open like red rodent eyes.

"Diana, this is Abtakha," she subvocalizes.

"I read you, Abtakha," comes the voice of Lieutenant Senior Grade Diana Vásquez. The voice of the Caballeros' long-range artillery support. As sometimes happens in the Regiment, her call sign is the same as her name. "Go ahead."

Vásquez has the voice of a delightful little girl. The manner, too, despite her deadly job as pilot of one of the unit's *Catapult*s. She is shy and sweet, a slight, pretty woman with hands like brown doves, who likes to wear the extravagant local flowers in her hair. She is utterly different from the typical 'Mech jock, which is what makes it possible for Cassie to almost like her.

"Your beacon is in place and online," Cassie says.

"I have it on my screen now, Abtakha. Thank you."

Cassie grins. Diana, of all MechWarriors in existence, would think of thanking her for doing her job.

She stiffens, hearing the rustle of undergrowth, the thump of careless footsteps, a mutter of sullen voices. Then comes a shift of wind carrying the smell of cigarette smoke and unwashed bodies to her.

Damn, she thinks. The *basura* are habitually shiftless and lazy. Why this morning, of all mornings, do they have to send out a foot patrol? And why does it have to come *this way*?

She moves a few meters away from the live beacon. Most of the little surprises she has sown into the woods surrounding the *basura* camp are too well-concealed for chance discovery by a resentful, inattentive patrol. But if somebody trips over the homing beacon, hell will truly be out for noon.

She spots them, not thirty meters away and coming right at her: four of them, a woman and three men. Two actually have their assault rifles slung. Another carries his rifle by the foregrip, muzzle-down, like a good ol' boy coming back from a day's hunting.

Naturally, their left-flank man, the one walking straight as Cassie, is the only one who looks as if he has a clue as to what he's about. A bandy-legged, bearded little guy in a filthy tan tunic, shorts, and outsized jungle boots, with a DCMS jungle *képi* on his head and his assault rifle at patrol position. He might even be a Drac deserter.

The patrol slogs through a finger of marsh. Over the splashing, the woman's voice rises in a mosquito whine, complaining about the injustice of it all. Cassie grins. *Keep bitchin', sister.*

She sidesteps, becoming one with a flowering shrub, waits. The man in Drac cast-offs passes right by the bush, managing to make at least a trifle less noise than an *Atlas* with a bad hip bearing.

Making none, Cassie moves. Her left arm slides around his throat from behind, fingers clamping on the bearded chin and forcing his mouth shut. Her right pushes Blood-drinker through the side of his neck, a forehand stab. His body arches in agony. Keeping her grip, she pushes the wavy blade out the front of his neck in a god-awful gusher of blood.

In the holovids people die quickly and quietly from knife wounds. It isn't so. Cassie pulls him back down with her, rolls him over onto his face so that any sound that manages to get out his mouth—or the hiss of air escaping from his violated trachea—will be swallowed by the spongy earth.

His thrashings subside. Cassie poises atop him, listening, ready to spring up at the slightest hint that the man's comrades have overheard his death throes. They just keep grinding at each other, making more than enough noise to cover.

"Cassie?" Diana says. "You all right? I heard a noise."

She is scuttling on all fours back to the bush where she left her pack and assault rifle. "I'm fine, Diana. Tiburón? Abtakha."

Cassie cleans the *kris* blade with a flick of her wrist, then sheathes it. She pulls a hand unit the size and shape of a personal communicator from her pack.

"Tiburón here," someone answers. Deep and Spanish-inflected, it is the voice of a powerful man in late middle age. To Cassie's ear, it is also the voice of one both tired and sad. "Go ahead, Abtakha."

"You ready?"

The female *basura* has stopped twenty meters away. "Leo?" she says. "Leo, where'd you go?"

"Affirmative, Abtakha," replies "Tiburón," otherwise known as Colonel Carlos Comacho, commander of the Seventeenth.

The woman walks toward the shrub under which Leo's blood is pooling on already-saturated black dirt. "Where'd you get off to, Leo? You off takin' a leak somewhere?"

Cassie flips open the hard plastic cover on the unit in her hand. "Then let's take out the trash," she says. She presses a button and all hell breaks loose.

Numerous rockets suddenly hiss away from launchers concealed deep in the woods surrounding the *basura* encampment. Trailing streamers of white smoke, they arc across the clear blue sky and plunge into the dead lake,

where they make big bangs and raise geysers of ugly water.
It's all just pyrotechnics, mere skyrockets, but it *sounds* like
an incoming barrage of long-range missiles.

From the bushes near the scatter of hootches and dome
tents erupts the sound of machine-gun fire, the boom of grenades. These are more fireworks, firefight simulators emplaced by Cassie on one of those midnight belly-crawls
through the muck that have become her specialty on New
Horizons. Pirates explode from the dwellings like so many
quail. Some carry rifles, machine guns, rocket launchers.
Others are shrugging on MechWarrior cooling vests as they
dash for the lake.

Cassie rolls up to one knee, bringing her M23 to her
shoulder. Barefly four meters away, the woman stands gaping at her, rifle still slung. Tough luck. Cassie fires a single
shot as her front sight rises past the buckle of the woman's
cammie pants to bear on her bare midriff.

The *basura* falls kicking and screaming. Even over the
general commotion, the gunshot attracts her buddies' attention. They spin toward Cassie, fumbling to get their weapons
to firing position. She chops them down with quick, slashing
bursts.

Cassie is no longer a poor shot. She's learned much in her
time with the Regiment.

She moves again to the brush on the verge of the lake to
see that its surface has begun to boil. LRM simulators are
continuing to sputter into it sporadically, but that's not what
causes the disturbance: monsters are rising from the depths.

Cassie smiles as a *Locust* springs forth in a shower of
grimy spray. Lazy as they are, the pirates keep pilots in
some of their submerged 'Mechs 'round the clock—as the
NHDF found to their dismay on two disastrous raids before
they gratefully signed the problem off to the mercs. The little hopper is still a good half-klick away, clockwise around
the lake to Cassie's left. Not a problem yet.

"They're rising to the bait," she calls in. "Right on schedule. Get ready, Diana. Everybody else stand by."

She barely hears the acknowledgment. The surface has begun to churn for true. The big boys are rising, rising.

Adrenaline sings like a demon lover in her ears. That fear,
that age-old fear, is rising with the pirate 'Mechs. Cassie has
never conquered her little-girl's fear, her three-year-old fear,
but she has learned to *use* that fear. It is her companion in

arms, her goad and her guide; it is blasting into her now like a happy-drug into the veins of a Clan Elemental in a ruptured battlesuit.

A *Quickdraw* rises next, muck cascading from the sagittal crest fore-and-afting its round head, arms raised to pump dazzling laser pulses at phantom foes in the woods. Tree trunks explode in steam as the 'Mech rises high on its jump jets.

Cassie laughs out loud. "Diana, fire for effect."

"On the way, Cassie." Cool and confident in the cockpit of her hundred-ton 'Mech, Diana sometimes forgets to use call signs. It is appropriate that her style of warfare is to reach out and touch her foe from a distance that never lets her see him die. She could not withstand Cassie's style of war, where an enemy's lifeblood mingles with the dirt you and he have rolled in to form sticky, black, iron-smelling mud.

Diana's Arrow IV long-range missiles tear the sky as if it were a swatch of muslin. It is truly time to go; a short round will vaporize Cassie, leaving nothing but a memory. She doesn't care. She trusts Diana. And should a missile drop on her, it'll be over quick, ending Cassie's nightmares at last.

Her heart is singing now. Because that's her 'Mech rising now: the *Marauder* whose filled-in print she came upon. The long autocannon mounted on top of its hunched head-torso, muzzle covered with a red polymer cap, swivels back and forth like a finger looking for someone to accuse as the monster climbs from the lake floor.

"Yes," she whispers. *"Yes."*

No. It is not to be. An Arrow IV from Diana's first salvo lands directly on the MAD-3R's head, bursting it open like a potato in a microwave. Cassie utters a jaguar scream of fury and frustration as the *Marauder* sinks, gushing smoke and steam and then bubbling as the water closes back over its shattered carapace.

A rebel yell shrills in Cassie's ears as the Arrow thunder rises about her like a Larshan typhoon. *"¡Santiago y adelante!"* a man's voice yells. *Saint James and at them!* Coyote-yips and cries of "Ca-ba-*lleros*!" actually give the heavy warheads some competition. Somewhere Hachita chants his death-song as his *Hatchetman* wades down a bayou, axe hungering to split white-eye skulls. But at least he has the decency to do it offline.

Commo discipline is not among the Caballeros' strong suits—nor are most other kinds of discipline. Nonetheless, the war-cries quickly subside to let combat traffic through.

"First Battalion moving in," Tiburón says unnecessarily.

"Time to clear out, Abtakha," Badlands adds.

Cassie smiles. "Tiburón, make sure your people keep to the paths I marked," she says. There's not much soil in the Great Murchison firm enough to take the weight of even a small BattleMech. It's only because a shelf of bedrock lies under the lake bed that the outlaw 'Mechs can hide down there. That was one reason the government 'Mechs got themselves wasted wholesale when the NHDF tried to clean out the *basura*: the pirates had little beacons to mark usable trails. The Defense Force didn't. Their 'Mech jocks walked their machines into deep mud, then got mired while the *basura* slaughtered them.

Along with emplacing the various remote-controlled sound and light pyrotechnics, Cassie has spent the last two weeks scouting safe pathways and marking them with Caballero transmitters. She has also been playing some games of her own.

"Will comply, Abtakha," Don Carlos says. "Now pull back. Your job is done."

"I'm sorry, Tiburón," Cassie says, reaching behind her ear. "I'm having some trouble with my comm unit. Your signal's garbled."

"Git ye gone, rude girl," she hears Buffalo Soldier say. Like her, he is an outsider, a non-Southwesterner. Like Diana, he is nearly human for a 'Mech jock.

No foxtrot way, Rastaman, she thinks. She plucks the dot speaker from her skin and tucks it into the little pouch sewn into her top where her communicator rides. Now it's time for her.

Her duty to the Regiment is done. Now it's time for her. There are at least three pirate 'Mechs bubbling and burning in the lake. A *Wasp* is busy blowing up on the far shore, near the camp. The *Quickdraw* soars up on its jets again, and takes an LRM from the advancing Caballero company. Cassie must move quickly, or there will be nothing left for her.

That *Locust* has been crashing through the brush in her general direction. She frowns. It isn't as grand a target as the *Marauder,* no way. At the same time, it's far more dangerous to a groundpounder—fast and agile despite its lack of jump jets. And its cockpit is much nearer the weeds where an impertinent scout might think to conceal herself.

She stands, steps into the clear. "Hey, over here!" She raises her rifle and fires a burst at the 'Mech's head. The general uproar covers the sound of the shots, but the rattle of bullets off armor plate catches the pilot's attention. The *Locust* pivots, the underslung proboscis of its medium laser hunting around for whoever has been impertinent enough to attack it.

The laser spurts light. The flowering bush explodes in a gush of steam followed by smoke. Cassie is long gone, swimming with splashing strokes across a bayou. The 'Mech jock picks up her wake, blasts for her with its arm-mounted machine guns.

Hearing the whine of arm actuators, she has already gone deep. Small arms rounds lose most of their energy after two meters of water. A few spent rounds gurgle past her, trailing strands of bubbles through opaque water, but they lack the power to penetrate even her bare skin.

Moving mainly by memory and feel, her rifle trailing by its long sling, Cassie swims into another channel, crawls along the muddy bottom and up into the reeds of the bank. Through the waving tufts of long grass she sees the *Locust* standing above the bodies of the patrol she whacked. She raises her rifle, cracks a single shot into the left arm-mounted machine gun. Maybe she can break something, though that's a secondary concern.

The 'Mech turns. The laser turret can swivel, but the head/torso combo cannot. It must move its feet to change the pilot's field of vision.

Behind it an enormous splash. The *Quickdraw,* having managed to stay out of the way of Diana's incoming volleys of giant Arrow IV rockets by continuing to jump as high and as often as jets and heat sinks permit, has jumped into a direct-fire salvo of LRMs from the advancing 'Mech battalion. Strikes to the head and chest have not penetrated the heavy armor there, but they have tumbled the gyros, making the sixty-ton 'Mech topple off the columns of jump jet exhaust and lose lift. It has just plummeted headfirst into the swamp.

Ignoring the fall of his fellow MechWarrior, the *Locust* pilot gathers up his 'Mech on bird legs and springs. The machine cannot actually jump, but it uses its myomer muscles to hop across the little arm of brackish water onto the strand of relatively solid land behind which Cassie shelters.

The pilot is good enough to pull off the maneuver, but he almost loses it on landing, lurching and swaying as one foot sinks in deeper than anticipated. The problem with the dodgy little *Locust* in these surroundings is that its birdlike feet make it a relatively high ground-pressure machine. The lordly *Marauder,* by whose old print Cassie had paused on her way in, could move its seventy-five tons of bulk through the muck with far greater aplomb. Its great, lily-pad hooves loaded the surface with many fewer kilos per square centimeter.

Hoping to catch his antagonist by surprise, the *Locust* pilot begins to rake the weeds at its feet with his machine guns. Canting way forward, the 'Mechs sends up a geyser of steam and hot mud from its laser for good measure. But Cassie isn't there. Even as dirty rain from the laser-blast into the bayou spatters the 'Mech's viewscreen like dark bird droppings, that annoying *ping* of a rifle bullet bouncing off armor plate is drawing its attention.

Deeper and deeper into the Great Murchison Swamp the *Locust* pursues its foe. A *Locust* is one of the fastest of all 'Mechs, far faster than any mere human. But this one is severely hampered by the need to follow trails delineated by the pirates' beacons. A mired 'Mech is a dead 'Mech. Especially with an enemy force of unknown but obviously substantial size crunching into the area.

Behind the *Locust,* a fierce but one-sided battle is raging. Cassie's noisemaker barrage started the hidden 'Mechs nicely for Diana's long-range destruction. The survivors have left their watery hideout to find themselves caught in a fire-sack as the three Caballero companies of First Battalion close a pincers around their clearing and the stagnant lake.

Probably the *Locust* jock is thinking himself well away from that fiasco. If it occurs to him—or her—that his naked prey is sticking conveniently close to 'Mech-safe ground, he probably counts himself doubly lucky.

Yes, up ahead . . . there, from the far edge of a broad extent of marsh, the impertinent pedestrian is *waving* to the *Locust.* She salutes it with an unmistakable gesture of one finger, then turns and sprints for the concealment of a palmack grove at her back.

She has outsmarted herself. A beacon shines from the midst

of that marsh, bright and reassuring on the MechWarrior's tactical display. The *Locust* gathers itself, leaps again, landing with a titanic splash in the midst of the drowned field.

The impact must have just about driven the MechWarrior's spine out the top of his skull, but he is firing his laser and machine guns into the grove even as he hits. Thick boles fly apart in clouds of splinters. Huge leaves wilt in the heart and fray of the bullet-storm. In triumphant fury the *Locust* lays the stand of trees to absolute waste.

The outburst subsides. The *Locust* stands over the smoking wreckage of the little grove. The only sounds are the crackling of flames and the pinging of the heat sinks as they try to bleed off the waste heat from the Martell laser.

Suddenly the lone human breaks from the reeds almost at the 'Mech's feet, out of the submerged entrance of a swamp-otter burrow. Laser and machine guns blaze away, but she is already inside their effective arc. She is scooting between the *Locust*'s legs and off across the marsh, half-running, half-swimming.

She's caught now, though, out in the open and too far from cover. The *Locust* pilot raises his right foot and clutches-in the gyros for a quick right turn, only to find that the 'Mech's left foot has sunk more than two meters in the mud. The beacon's reassuring message of safety was a shining lie. At least, it became that once Cassie moved it to the middle of a bog.

The little *Locust*'s gyros torque it right off its feet. It spins around and falls into the mud, driving its laser into the muck like a spike. Its stubby right arm almost clips Cassie, who has characteristically cut things a little fine. The huge bow-wave of muddy water thrown up by the 'Mech's landing rolls over her like a *tsunami*.

She pops up immediately, though, mud-covered and grinning enormously. She pumps her right fist in the air and shouts, *"Yeah!"*

The *Locust* writhes like a snake with a broken back, but only succeeds in miring itself deeper. Cassie unslings her rifle, works the action, spinning an unspent cartridge away in a glittering arc, then shakes the piece to try to clear any mud that might have infiltrated during her swimming and burrowing antics. The presence of a den dug into the palmack stand by a two-meter swamp-otter was no more coincidental than

the misplacement of the *basura* beacon. Cassie has been
plotting this surprise for days.

With a hiss of air heated by bleed-off from the laser, the
main hatch opens. After first sprawling in the bog, the
helmetless MechWarrior picks himself up, stares wildly at
Cassie—standing with M23 ready in patrol position, not
thirty meters distant—then turns to run toward the smoldering ruins of the grove. He runs with the loose-jointed vigor
of the bone-scared, sinking halfway to the knee with every
step.

Cassie lets him go, grinning at his bulky vest-clad back.
The trophy is hers; he is irrelevant, and since he is wise
enough not to threaten her in any way, he gets to live. At
least until the Swampers catch up with him.

Her bare skin is warm, flushed, her whole body tingling
with the triumph of another kill. Her prey was not as mighty
as she hoped, but few groundpounders in the Inner Sphere
can boast of bringing down a BattleMech without the help of
power armor. She did not smash the beast, destroy it, as she
burned to do. But that is an advantage in a way. A *Shadow
Hawk,* Gabby Camacho's Red-tail, by the look of it, is already soaring her way, searching for the pirate 'Mech that
escaped a battle now almost ended. Don Carlos and his Regiment are in need of new 'Mechs to make good the awful
losses the Smoke Jaguars handed them.

Cassie wades to another palmack stand and sits down in
the shade to await the confirmation and salvaging of her kill.
She will miss the swamp, she thinks. This job has ended. After great debate Don Carlos has signed them on to a new gig
back in the Inner Sphere. Garrison duty—on a Kurita world,
of all things, distant from the Periphery and far enough below the truce line that Clan raids won't be a problem.

It will be a long time before she can again assuage her
burning need to smash 'Mechs and humble their pilots.

With a roar of Chilton 360 jets, the *Shadow Hawk* appears
above the high, bushy tops of a silura stand. It is indeed the
ride of Force Commander Gavilán Camacho, the Colonel's
son and commander of First Battalion. Cassie waves happily
as the 'Mech settles down toward the beacon she has emplaced on the *real* safe ground beside the bog.

She has taken prey. Whatever else comes, tonight she will
sleep without dreaming.

5

The room was dark. The plain white *shoji*—rice paper screens—that hid the ferrocrete walls reflected the dance of light from the shadow-show being enacted at the room's far end.

In its midst an old man sat watching, his long, hairless head slumped between sagging shoulders. His body, clad in a kimono of dark, lustrous silk, seemed to have melted into the motorized wheelchair that carried him. The colors of the puppets going through their motions on the holostage were reflected in eyes that were black and still sharp as an heirloom *katana*. He was eighty-eight years old and felt the weight of every minute like an ingot of lead.

The holodisplay showed a crowded, brightly lit auditorium. Metal beams exposed overhead testified to its impromptu nature. The place was obviously a warehouse of some sort, pressed into service. At its head was a podium.

At the podium stood a small, rumpled man, with thinning, disarranged hair and intense black eyes. He was framed by a giant full-body representation of the Kurita dragon, rampant, black against red. The man shook a pudgy fist at the audience and shouted.

"We demand the fall of the traitors who murdered Takashi, our noble Coordinator!" he roared in a voice of surprising strength. "*Kokuryu-kai*, the Black Dragon Society, demands *blood!*"

"*Blood!*" echoed back the crowd, which was exclusively male and mostly dressed in the garb prescribed for members of the Draconis Combine's Laborer class. A closer look revealed the occasional merchant or minor executive in finer cut and cloth.

"We demand the removal of the traitors who mislead our current Coordinator Theodore, blinding him to the golden opportunity represented by the disorganization of our enemies. Now is the time for the Dragon to strike, and strike without mercy! Our cry is *Hakko-ichi-u,* the Eight Corners of the World under One Roof!"

The crowd responded with wild enthusiasm, jumping up and waving fists in the air. *"Hakko-ichi-u! Hakko-ichi-u!"* they chanted.

"Our enemies the Steiners and the Davions are in disarray!" the speaker cried, almost immediately silencing the clamor—this was, after all a Kurita mob. "Our brothers of the Capellan Confederation are poised to strike! What cannot we and they accomplish together under the guidance of the Dragon?"

Whether the man intended to supply his own answer to that question, or whether it was simply rhetorical, would never be known. Just then came an odd explosive sound on the soundtrack, halfway between a spit and a pop, and then the speaker's face collapsed in red ruin.

For a moment silence ruled the makeshift auditorium. Then the crowd broke like an ancient vase shattering against flagstones. Some ran toward the podium to aid their fallen leader. Others—either better informed or simply with keener instincts for survival—bolted for the exits.

Either course was equally futile. The first ones to hit the doors to the outside were slammed into them by the rest of the crowd, then crushed against the door by their frightened comrades to the rear. The doors had been blocked from outside.

The camera operator now panned around to show men and women with their faces obscured by black faceplates and their bodies encased in black clothing from head to toe. They moved through the great chamber, back to front, killing as they advanced—first with stubby, suppressed assault rifles, and then, when the frantic Black Dragons closed with them, with the *katana* worn in scabbards across their backs.

The man who watched made a sound low in his wattled throat as he stabbed a switch set into the arm of the wheelchair. The holographic image froze, showing one of the black-clad operatives outlined against the Dragon banner, sword upraised.

The lights came up. "And this is happening here on Luthien," the old man murmured.

The much younger man on his right flared aristocratic nostrils. "Our colleagues—" he said, referring to Daniel Ramaka's dreaded Internal Security division of the Internal Security Force—"permit a hundred flowers to bloom, so they can lop the heads off."

"Indeed." The old man swiveled his wheelchair to face the man who sat on his left.

"The holocamera operator was one of our agents, of course," the second man said. He was younger than the man in the powered wheelchair, with flabby cheeks, a moist mustache, and a black beret perched on lank black hair. He wore a mustard sports jacket over an open-collared white shirt. A white scarf was tied around his throat. "He was briefed to record every detail of the raid."

"So I surmised," said Subhash Indrahar, Director of the Internal Security Force of the Draconis Combine. He paused for a moment, studying the untidy man in the beret with his fiercely glittering eyes.

"Do you still recommend that we release this recording to the media, Mr. Katsuyama?"

Katsuyama bobbed his round head enthusiastically. "Indeed, Subhash-*sama*. Suitably edited, of course. It's beautiful, just beautiful. At one and the same time it emphasizes the insidious nature of the *Kokuryu-kai* and the futility of their actions in the face of our pervasive and heroic ISF operatives—"

The man seemed inclined to go on in that vein, possibly forever, but Subhash cut him off by pivoting his chair to suddenly face the man seated at his right.

"Migaki?" he said.

The third man was younger than either of the others, tall and slim and dressed in the most up-to-the-nanosecond style of high life on the Combine capital of Luthien: a brightly patterned *happi*-coat worn open over a gray Sun Zhang MechWarrior Academy sweatshirt, black silk pajama-style pants, split-toed white *tabi* socks, and *geta* clogs. He wore his black hair in a topknot so long it hung over one shoulder. He uncrossed his long legs—covering a pause to frame his reply, Subhash did not fail to notice—and then shrugged with apparent casualness.

"Ernie-*sensei*'s the expert," said Takura Migaki, head of the Voice of the Dragon, the propaganda division of the ISF.

Subhash waited, but his subordinate chief had nothing further to say. Despite his good looks and carefully cultivated appearance of a carefree rake and dandy, Migaki was a man who never spoke a syllable by accident or default. His use of a nickname with the word for *master* or *teacher*, particularly delivered in his customary dry, near-contemptuous tone, was unorthodox, almost ungrammatical. So was employing an honorific when speaking of a junior. The effect was to emphasize both Katsuyama's mastery of the matter at hand and the eccentricity his dress suggested.

Subhash backed his wheelchair to a spot where he could view both men without needing to turn his head, though it taxed the waning muscles of his neck. In his day Subhash had been an athlete, a *kendoka* of great skill. It shamed him to have been brought to this helpless state.

Enrico Katsuyama was head of Benevolent Guidance, which handled media manipulation for Voice of the Dragon. He had been hand-picked for the position by Migaki, whose talent for propaganda was itself legendary; Migaki was the wizard who had dubbed Hanse Davion "the Black Knight," using the late Federated Suns' leader's own swashbuckling charisma to turn him into a larger-than-life villain in the eyes of the Combine's populace. Subhash Indrahar was not entirely comfortable with Migaki, though Migaki had never risen to the carefully dangled bait of hints that he might succeed Subhash in the Directorship, by means fair or foul. Migaki was just too smooth. But Subhash had no reason to doubt that Katsuyama was worthy of the position to which Migaki had promoted him. Migaki was too vain and careful to risk losing face by elevating an incompetent.

"We do not customarily publicize the activities of our operators," Subhash said.

"But why not start?" Katsuyama asked, bubbling over with enthusiasm. "These are trying times. The people need heroes. Why not the men and women of the ISF?"

Subhash looked at him. Even he found the notion of the public's regarding his well-feared secret police as heroes to be, well, novel.

"Besides," Katsuyama said, "this footage will certainly

put the quietus on rumors that the ISF itself is behind the Black Dragons."

Subhash exhaled a breath he didn't know he'd been holding. He cared little about the reputation of the ISF, as long as it was feared. But the ultranationalist *Kokuryu-kai* was already known to be taking advantage of rumors that it had allies highly placed in the Combine government. It would not do to let them draw spurious legitimacy from Internal Security.

There was an irony here, so great Subhash almost smiled—a surprisingly rare private event for a man still called "the Smiling One" at court. Takashi Kurita had not been assassinated, as the Black Dragon orator alleged. But not for lack of trying by Subhash and his ISF.

He nodded, the gesture all but imperceptible. Migaki, who had caught it, nodded in response and rose. Katsuyama, who hadn't, sat with hands clasped like a schoolboy, perched so far forward on his chair that he seemed in imminent danger of falling off onto his broad bottom.

"You may do as you deem best, Mr. Katsuyama," Subhash said.

Katsuyama bounced to his feet like a fat, floppy puppy. "Thank you, Director! I promise, you won't be disappointed."

Of course I won't, the Director thought as Migaki herded his subordinate from the room. Subhash Indrahar was a man who made few errors, and was absolutely ruthless in correcting them when he did. *I don't believe you have the courage to let me down.*

Subhash was alone. For a moment he sat, an old man with no company but his weariness. Then he blanked the holo image from the end of the room, erasing the Black Dragon Society from his mind at the same time. They were, for the moment, contained.

It was time to turn to a more pressing matter: the mission that had sent his adoptive son and successor-designate to the nearby world of Hachiman.

$$=== 6 ===$$

Masamori, Hachiman
Galedon District, Draconis Combine
27 August 3056

A festival atmosphere prevails here on the outskirts of Masamori, largest city of the Draconis Combine world of Hachiman. The ninety-plus BattleMechs of the Seventeenth Recon Regiment are arriving on-planet to take up employment with Hachiman Taro Electronics, Limited, the second-largest corporation on the planet. HTE is owned by Chandrasekhar Kurita, a distant member of the family that has ruled the Combine since its creation more than seven centuries ago.

"Behind me you can see the DropShip debarking 'Mechs of the First Battalion of Camacho's Caballeros, as the men and women of the Seventeenth style themselves. They will be marching into the city proper to take up security duties within the mighty HTE manufacturing complex, which lies on the west bank of the Yamato River in the city's Murasaki district. The notoriously fickle populace of the Masamori has turned the occasion into one of their rowdy *matsuri*, or street festivals."

The young man with the pencil-thin mustache half-turned to his left, allowing the holocamera to caress his beautifully chiseled profile as it zoomed in on a cantilever bridge spanning the Yamato River, which spread to a width of five hundred meters here as it flowed south into the metropolis. Crowds lined the approach, waving banners and bright, carp-shaped kites. Across the river, the late-afternoon light turned the skyscrapers of Masamori into towers of bronze.

"Behind me you see the Hohiro Kurita Memorial Railway Bridge. Like most highway bridges within the Draconis Combine, those leading into Masamori are designed to permit the passage of no vehicle heavier than nineteen tons, a feature intended to prevent enemy BattleMechs from using the bridges in the event of invasion. Only a railroad bridge will support the up to one hundred-ton weight of the mercenary machines.

"You can hear the crowd gasp as the leading BattleMech approaches the span. And well they might; perhaps not since the German *Stuka* of pre-spaceflight Terra has a war machine been so thoroughly identified with a mighty and implacable empire. For the 'Mech belonging to the Seventeenth's commander, Colonel Carlos Camacho, late of the Free Worlds League military, bears the unmistakable hunchshouldered, bullet-nosed shape of a *Mad Cat*—the very symbol of the fearful might of the Clan invaders.

"Striding behind the *Mad Cat* of his father comes the *Shadow Hawk* belonging to Force Commander Gavilán Camacho, his 'Mech painted front and back with the striking image of a hawk with outstretched wings and talons. Behind him the rest of First Battalion's machines take their place in line.

"But the *Mad Cat* with the shark's mouth painted on its snout is not the first vehicle in line. The honor of leading the procession into Masamori has fallen to a member of the Seventeenth's Scout Platoon."

The camera zoomed further, focusing on a solitary figure, seemingly insignificant as a bug before the terrifying bulk of Colonel Camacho's Great White. "Long and brilliant service to the Regiment has earned this distinction for Lieutenant Junior Grade Cassiopeia Suthorn. She leads this mighty procession of armor and firepower riding perhaps the humblest vehicles in all of the regiment: a thirty-speed Mikoyan Gurevich mountain bike."

Close up on Cassie, long braid hanging down her back, her assault rifle strapped across the bars of her bicycle, pedaling vigorously away. Then the camera zoomed out again to focus on the handsome young reporter in his immaculate bush jacket.

"Reporting from Hachiman, in Oshika Perfecture of the Galedon Military District, this is Archie Westin, FCNS."

"Good one, Archie," his camerawoman said, letting the holocam slide off her shoulder. Archie smiled almost shyly and bobbed his wavy-haired blond head.

"I beg your pardon, young man," came a gentle voice

from behind Westin's left shoulder. The newsman turned to see a man of middle height and years approaching from where he'd been standing by at discreet distance, waiting for the shoot to end. The wind plucked at the strands of dark brown hair combed over his bald spot. He had a mustache and dark eyes with lids so full they looked almost puffy; he also wore the white collar and dark sports coat over black tunic of a modern Catholic priest. Archie nodded politely to him.

"Might I have a few words with you, Mr. Westin?" he asked.

"Certainly, Father."

A shy smile. "I'm Father Roberto García, Society of Jesus," the priest said. "But you can call me Bob, if you like."

Archie grinned at that, bobbed his head. He was by nature both a polite and outgoing young man. It was a substantial asset in his lines of work—both of them.

"What can I do for you, then, Fa—Bob?"

"I couldn't help but overhear the reference to the *Stuka*. Are you by chance a historian?"

Archie laughed. "Nothing so grand. A history buff, rather."

The Jesuit's face lit up. "We have an interest in common then. Let's have a nice talk one of these days. What do you say?"

"By all means." Archie glanced to where camerawoman Mariska Savage was bent over stowing her holo gear. He grinned ever so slightly at the way her khaki shorts tightened over her buttocks. She was a touch stocky for his tastes, but strikingly well put together for all that; it was the way she was built, not excess. Professional principles and common sense kept him from trying to take their relationship beyond the already close friendship of those who'd shared danger. But he could look.

"I tell you what, Bob," Archie said, turning back to the older man. "Though I've met Colonel Camacho, and been briefed by Lieutenant Colonel Cabrera—and they've been the soul of courtesy, I must say—I don't really *know* anyone here yet, if you know what I mean. Since I'm assigned to cover the Seventeenth, I could really use a friend on the inside."

García nodded. "As it happens, I'm the closest thing to a public-relations officer the Caballeros have. It's one of several hats I wear—along with unit historian, psychologist, and *Crusader* pilot."

Westin's hazel eyes widened. "You're a MechWarrior?"

García nodded. "I have that honor."

"Rather unusual for a *padre* to be a combatant. Much less 'Mech-qualified."

"You're not familiar with the so-called Southwestern worlds, are you?" the priest said, to which Westin shook his head. "I'm going to have a lot to teach you then, my friend. To start with, we have only one noncombatant chaplain, Father Montoya. The rest of us—pastors and rabbis too—fight alongside the rest. It's the only way to win the respect of this bunch."

"Pastors, rabbis, *and* priests?" Archie asked.

"As I say, you've much to learn about us." The priest put his hand on the younger man's shoulder—which was something of a reach, Westin being the taller by a handspan—and turned him gently to face the procession of Caballero BattleMechs across the bridge and into Masamori.

"Now, tell me, as a student of history, does this scene remind you anything?"

Archie briefly chewed his underlip with immaculately straight white teeth, then shrugged. "Offhand, nothing I can think of."

"It reminds me," the priest said, "of the entry of the Catalan Grand Company in the year of Our Lord thirteen-oh-two into Constantinople."

Archie gave a slight shake of the head. "I'm afraid I'm not familiar with the incident, *padre*."

"The Ottoman Turks had recently begun to supplant the Seljuks. They were sweeping over the Byzantine Empire like a locust plague. To deal with them, the Byzantines hired in a company of Catalan *almugavars,* their matchless light infantry. They were the toughest mercenaries of the day, and their women were as redoubtable as the men—just as with our own Caballeros."

"Are you saying the Seventeenth are the toughest mercs of our day, *padre*?" Archie asked with upraised brow.

García shook his head. "Not while Wolf's Dragoons and the Kell Hounds still live, Mr. Westin, though any Caballero would die before yielding a centimeter, even to one of them."

"Call me Archie."

"Archie, then. No, it is rather the contrast in image that draws me. A painting from the nineteenth century exists that depicts the Company's arrival in the Byzantine capital. There sits the Emperor on his throne, with Santa Sophia behind his right shoulder and his glittering, painted retinue surrounding him in all its splendor.

"And before him march the Catalans: shaggy barbarians, to be frank, grubby and ferocious in their scale armor and metal caps, with their *azagayas* and shields slung over their backs. They look no different than their ancestors the Visigoths and wild Iberian tribesmen as they enter the greatest city then extant on Earth."

Archie laughed. "A striking image, to be sure. But not exactly one complimentary to your comrades, it seems."

"I am a Caballero born and bred, Archie. My family is one of the proudest of Sierra, my homeworld. But I know my people well."

Archie jutted his chin and nodded. It was a nice chin, square without being too overt. He was proud of it.

"How did the episode end, then?" he asked, watching the long shadows cast by the Caballero 'Mechs making their ponderous way across the shadow-bridge that lay upon the Yamato's slow water.

García sighed. "Not well. The Byzantines came to fear the Catalans' power and the ambitions of their leader, Roger de Flor. They invited Roger to a banquet in his honor, then set upon and murdered him and his retinue. At the same time they attacked the divided camps of the mercenaries, seeking to wipe them out."

"Did they succeed?"

"No, indeed. The Catalans not only defended themselves, but in their rage they laid waste to such of the Empire as lay outside the city walls, which they lacked the engines to breach. Then they sailed away to Greece and conquered the Morea from the Frankish knights who held it. And for centuries thereafter, a Greek who truly wanted to curse someone said to him, 'May the Catalan vengeance overtake you.'"

For a time the only sounds were the whistle of the wind, the distant shouts and hum of hovercraft engines as workgangs offloaded Caballero gear from the DropShip onto the grounds of the HTE-owned sports-training facility that would house the bulk of the Regiment, the low, slow thunder of the Caballero BattleMechs, walking deliberately out of step as they crossed the railroad bridge.

"Rather a grim omen, I should say," Archie remarked at length.

"If one believes in omens." The Jesuit clapped him on the shoulder again. "Come. I believe we and your charming young assistant might find something to drink, and then drive across into town in ample time to cover the arrival of our 'Mechs at the HTE Compound."

$$=== 7 ===$$

Masamori, Hachiman
Galedon District, Draconis Combine
27 August 3056

Here came Usagi and Unagi, your classic *ashigaru*, insepa-rable as twins, pelting through the mob with bare arms and legs and straight black hair flying.

"They're coming, Lainie," gasped Usagi, by a couple cen-timeters the taller. His name meant rabbit, which a glance at him showed to be appropriate. It was also *ingo*—underworld dialect—for petty thief. That was right too.

"It's the strangest thing," Unagi said, addressing the red-haired woman who was a good half-meter taller than either he or Usagi. She stood on the sidewalk surrounded by a small knot of hard-faced men, and around them another in-visible circle into which the putatively law-abiding citizens of Masamori did not care to intrude. Anyone giving the group only a casual glance would have surmised that this was a particularly tough street gang. He wouldn't have been far wrong.

Unagi stood and panted for a couple of breaths as the tall

woman looked down on him with folded arms. He was a
lithe little man whose movements, when he wasn't running
hell-bent, flowed like oil. His name meant "eel" and also the
fine, soft rope favored by second-story men. Which he'd
been before the Friendly Persuaders had nabbed him. He and
Usagi had shared a cell on Galedon V while doing their
"duty."

"They're being led by a woman," Unagi gasped, "and you
know what? She's riding a *bicycle*."

Away down Yoguchi Kurita Street you could see the loom
and sway of big BattleMechs on the move. The redhead
glanced over her shoulder at a man even taller than she was,
and as bulky as she was lithe. Some of this was fat, and
some was not. He had a shaven head, round, jovial-looking
cheeks, and wore the red-orange robes of an Order of the
Five Pillars monk.

The tall man stepped forward to where onlookers lined the
sidewalk's edge craning for a view. He made a sound like a
volcano preparing to belch. The onlookers turned around,
looked at him, and did a fast fade.

The red-haired woman took their place, her retinue flow-
ing into position around her. The citizens duly melted back
on either side like mercury from a fingertip.

The way was decked with elaborate, colored-paper
streamers, some held aloft by clumps of helium-filled bal-
loons, with flowers real and paper, with banners making the
foreigners welcome in *kanji, hiragana,* and *katakana* charac-
ters they undoubtedly could not read. Dancers in traditional
costume—Japanese, Chinese, Hindu—capered all but under
the metal feet of the 'Mechs. The *Masakko,* as the people of
Hachiman's capital were known, had done themselves
proud.

Of course, HTE's public relations elves had spread some
heavy jelly to guarantee a rousing welcome for the foreigners. But the street enthusiasm was perfectly sincere; Lainie
could feel it beating off the crowd like heat from a paper
lantern on a winter's night. The *Masakko* loved novelty, and
giant mercenary BattleMechs striding through the middle of
town were nothing if not novel. More than that, the people
loved the slightest pretext to pitch a *matsuri*—a festival, that
unique Masamori blend that was one part traditional celebration, one part street party, and one part riot.

"The Mustache Petes must be turning blue to see this

party going down for a lot of scrubby *gaijin*," said Shig Hofstra, a long, lean sort with sharp features and a shock of straw hair. He had been a suspected malcontent, pulling hard time in one of the Ministry of Peaceful Order and Honor's resort facilities in the Benjamin District—if they'd *known* he was a malcontent, they would have capped him—when the Clan invasion hit. Secretly, Theodore Kurita had opened a lot of prison doors to anyone who would volunteer for near-suicide missions. Though Shig had never been in a BattleMech in his life, neither did he want to rot in *teruho,* so he stepped right up there and signed on the line. After a ninety-day-wonder MechWarrior course, for which he showed a surprising natural aptitude, he found himself dropping into harm's way with *Heruzu Enjeruzu*—the Ninth Ghost Regiment. "Not to mention the fact that they're mercs."

Lainie chuckled. "Mustache Pete" could mean any traditionalist Kurita who was having trouble swallowing Coordinator Theodore's reforms. It specifically referred to that most conservative segment of Combine society, the *oyabun,* or bosses, of the yakuza crime syndicates. Like many of the non-yakuza members of the Regiment, Shig thought he really hated the "outside" yakuzas, those who were still civilian street gangsters.

Her smile folded itself and went away. He didn't *know* what it meant to hate the *oyabun.*

Lainie Shimazu did. She was yakuza herself.

The Rabbit and the Eel were right, she saw. Here came the procession leader, bare brown legs stroking at an easy pace despite the slow rise of Yoguchi Kurita. She was a small brown woman with long black hair hanging in a braid down her back. She looked like a generic Asian mix, might have been from the Combine herself. There was some *gaijin* blood thrown in too—her eyes met the tall woman's briefly, and they were gray with a hint of blue.

For an instant that eye contact held, and the small young woman and the tall one sized each other up. Then the rider was past, and the evil shape of a *Mad Cat* with a shark's gape painted on its snout was crunching by. The tall woman rubbed her chin.

"They don't look like much to me," said the handsome young man with the purple-dyed topknot as the mercenary 'Mechs came marching north on Yoguchi Kurita Street. He was a newbie with the Ghosts, some dipswitch second-son samurai kid from Miyada who had disgraced himself knocking up some Laborer girl. He was so hungry to prove himself that he was willing to roll all the way downhill into the midst of the hodgepodge of *gaijin,* yakuza, and *eta* who made up the Ninth Ghost Regiment. There was no accounting for taste.

Tai-sa Eleanor Shimazu had assumed the pose she always took when thinking about things in general: legs well apart, one palm on her temple clutching her mop of uncontrollable red hair. Dressed in khaki riding pants and a black vest over a white man's shirt, she would have been a striking figure even if, at 172 centimeters, she didn't tower over the predominantly diminutive population of Masamori.

She didn't pay any mind to the young lieutenant. Offhand, she couldn't even remember his name. He looked pretty flash in the cockpit of his 'Mech. But he hadn't earned his Golden Bullet yet, so the hell with him anyway.

Standing behind her left shoulder, Captain Buntaro Mayne chuckled. "You think the Smoke Jaguars gave that merc *oyabun* a *Mad Cat* as a gift?"

The new boot colored to his purple hairline. Mayne would have been as handsome as the newbie, but for the patch over his right eye. He was also a full two years younger. But Mayne had fought the Clans and lived to tell about it. To prove it, he wore a single round of live assault-rifle ammunition, vacuum-plated with a one-molecule thick coat of pure gold, on a thin chain around his neck.

"Look at that," the new man said, pointing, hanging gamely in there. "That *Locust* has trash all over it."

Following the heavyweights—the *Mad Cat,* an *Atlas,* a smaller but still substantial *Shadow Hawk*—came a little *Locust* bird-legging along. Many of the merc 'Mechs were painted in fanciful designs. The *Locust* was something else again. Glued all over it were myriad plastic toys and decorations—doll heads, models of 'Mechs, flowers, fruit—a fantastic encrustation. Garlands of plastic flowers were twined about its limbs and spiraled down the long barrel of its laser.

"I don't know," Unagi said. "I think it's—"

"—very mondo," said Usagi, who had a twin's habit of finishing his old cellmate's sentences.

"It's a shell trap," the samurai kid sneered, by his expression showing that he could still barely bring himself to talk to trash like the *ashigaru* twins. That was another stroke against him. Trash was what the Ghost Regiments were all about. "A round hits that crud, it'll stick and penetrate instead of glancing off."

"Nonsense," one-eyed Buntaro said. "The plastic's too soft. The decorations will simply shear away. It's kind of *kiza*"—the word meant kitsch—"but what the hey? I hear these boys fought the Clans too. They can do what they want."

"Like us," said a tall blond man.

The samurai shook his topknot. There was a fine line between tenacity and not knowing when to drop it. He was about to cross it. Maybe it was a further social disadvantage of being raised in the *buke*, the military caste: immersion in bushido, all that warrior's way *jarajara*.

"How much honor can they have if they let a *woman* lead them?" he said contemptuously. And then, realizing he'd really stepped in it, he added hastily, "Riding a bicycle, I mean."

Tai-sa Shimazu's eyes were an amazing auburn color, large and fine. When she was gripped by strong emotion— anger, commonly—they turned maroon as the eyes of some exotic beast. The eyes that glared down the purple-haired samurai reject were dark red.

"She has seen hell," Lainie Shimazu said. "As you have not, No-Name."

The newbie swelled. No-Name was about as offensive an insult as you could offer somebody of his class. He opened his mouth to challenge her—

And the air went out of him. The Colonel—*Tai-sa*—had clearly read his intent, and smiled. The penalty for challenging a superior officer in the Draconis Combine Mustered Soldiery wasn't death just for the offender, but for every member of his immediate family.

The young samurai knew, with a sudden insight flash, that he didn't have to worry about that. The yaks and Fraks and Hamlet People and other gutter sweepings who made up *Heruzu Enjeruzu* did not go running to the Assembly of the Grand Inquisitor every time someone farted out of turn. What *would* happen if he opened his yap was that the woman they called the Red Witch would take him up on any terms he cared to offer, 'Mech to 'Mech, blade to blade, or barehanded, and whatever was left of him would be buried without ceremony in a sandwich bag outside of town. A hell of a way for a samurai to go, *iie*?

The moment passed. The monk-robed giant put out a big soft hand, and without even deigning to look, pushed the young MechWarrior now irrevocably known as No-Name hard on the sternum. The newbie staggered back into a clump of civilians standing at a respectful distance. They squawked and scattered in terror, and the samurai fell on his skinny butt.

"Check across the way, *bancho*," Shig Hofstra said, pointing with his sharp chin between the legs of a passing *Wolverine* with the curious name of Skin Walker painted on it. "Candy-stripers mad-dogging us."

Lainie looked. A pair of Friendly Persuader police were eyeing the *Enjeruzu*, fingering their riot guns. She made sure they saw her as she laughed at them.

"Let 'em come," she said. "Let 'em bring all their friends. And we'll leave them alive so the Grand Inquisitor can pull them apart for daring to cross members of the glorious Mustered Soldiery."

The Ghosts all laughed at the cops then. When they'd been enlisted, Theodore Kurita's reps had pulled no punches: You're scum, said they, and born to die for the greater glory of the Dragon and House Kurita, amen. But if you sign on the line, you get to wait until the enemies of the Combine carry out your sentence. Still, there were advantages to being a Ghost and life member of the Order of the Golden Bullet. One that many of the boys and girls savored most was that the harness bulls of the Civilian Guidance Corps could not lay a gloved finger on them.

The cops saw. And glowered. And found somewhere else to go. The BattleMechs marched by like legendary giants made metal.

A middle-aged man built like a brick offered the fallen samurai a scarred blunt hand. No-Name stared at it a moment in distaste. The man was named Moon. He was *sabu*, subchief, to Lainie's *bancho*. He had been a member of *Toseikai*, the Voice of the East Gang, before coming to the Regiment. That meant he was of Korean heritage as well as a dirty *eta* yak.

"*Mujo*," the older man said. It was an ancient Buddhist term for the transience of life. In the unit it meant, roughly, *it don't mean nothin'*. It also meant *life is transient—so watch it*.

The samurai took the hand and let Moon pull him upright.

The Korean went to stand behind his commander in his customary position, where he could speak soft-voiced and only she could hear.

"A curious coincidence, is it not?" he murmured.

"Is what?" she asked.

"That Uncle Chandy should import a regiment of foreign mercenaries to protect his factories only days after our complement of 'Mechs has been brought up to full strength for the first time since Tukayyid."

"And?" Lainie Shimazu said.

"Hachiman is far from the treaty line," Moon said. "Do our masters contemplate that the Clan truce will be broken soon? Or perhaps that trouble will sprout from the soil of this world?"

"It could be what you called it," Lainie said. "Coincidence."

"It could," the compact man agreed, in a tone that said pigs might also fly—if they had wings.

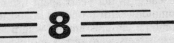

Masamori, Hachiman
Galedon District, Draconis Combine
27 August 3056

Cassie had never heard of the Catalan Company, and would have told Father Bob to put a sock in it had he tried to tell her about it. That was how she was: blunt to the point of rudeness, if not well beyond. But somehow no one much held it against her. Perhaps it was her smile.

Her wiry-strong legs pumped without effort. She leaned forward, letting arms braced on the straight bars take her weight for the moment, though the heels of her hands were starting to get weary. Her tailbone ached from the ride across the Hohiro Kurita bridge; those sleepers were bumpy. The ride into the Murasaki district was, by contrast, a piece of cake. Masamori was built in a wide valley above the bay from which the Yamato River emptied into the Shakudo Sea. That meant it was mostly flat.

Their prearranged parade route had parted company with the river not long after entering the city proper, exactly as she'd been briefed by Lieutenant Colonel Marisol Cabrera, Colonel Camacho's chief of staff. Cassie had led the procession first north, and then east into Murasaki. It took effort to resist the temptation to lead the column on a winding ramble through Hachiman's capital, spooking the straights and crunching up the pavement, but resist she had. Not for fear of the blood-curdling consequences with which *la Dama Muerte* Cabrera had threatened her if she pulled such a stunt. But out of respect for the tired old man in the *Mad Cat* trudging stolidly behind her.

The Murasaki district was mostly offices, with restaurants and small shops at street level. Though Cassie had no memories of life within the Combine, the area was a good deal more cheerful than she'd expected. Her impression had always been that life in the Draconis Combine was grim, and not just because of her years spent listening to official Federated Commonwealth propaganda and to the horror stories of the Combine émigrés among whom she'd been raised.

But these streets were broad and clean, the colors bright, and the *sararimen* and secretaries who made up most of the pedestrian throngs held at bay by Civilian Guidance Corps police, with their helmet-covered cowls and riot shotguns, were scrubbed and cheerful. The enthusiasm with which they greeted the mercenary procession was probably being carefully orchestrated by cadres within the crowd—that was the Combine way. In truth, the crowds seemed happy enough, probably because of sheer love of spectacle.

Many of the buildings were out and out skyscrapers. They tended to be built in the Yamato style, named after old Admiral Kurita's flagship from Terra's Second World War, a style that had been popular in the Combine in the late twenty-nine hundreds. The stylization was apparently based on some twenty-ninth-century architect's idea of what the Yamato's superstructure might have been: shapes vaguely like monstrously attenuated shark-fins, one terraced face slanting back toward a sheer vertical wall as if for streamlining, gleaming towers of glass and metal turned to bronze by the light of Hachiman's yellow-orange sun.

Cassie knew all this because she'd read a guidebook, which, along with a cursory pre-landing briefing by Rabbi Bar-Kochba, CO of Second Battalion and unit planetologist, was the Caballeros' only advance information about the terrain.

Her interest was not idle curiosity. Though Don Carlos may have been trying to honor her by letting her lead the parade, to Cassie, it was only doing her job: leading the Regiment into hostile terrain.

If these buildings go right up to the Compound, she thought, *snipers could sure have a heyday.* Some of the structures looked sturdy enough that light and maybe medium 'Mechs might even be able to get high up inside them. Which could be nasty if it ever came to a crunch.

Cassie had no idea who a crunch was likely to come *from*—yet. As a scout she was damned if she was going to take for granted that none would ever materialize simply because the unit was ump-many parsecs away from the nasty Periphery and even nastier Clans. A good scout always thought in terms of threats, no matter how much the brave MechWarriors pooh-poohed the possibility.

Cassie was used to keeping those boys and girls alive in spite of themselves.

The far side of the intersection ahead of her was blocked by a traffic barrier manned by cops in red-and white-striped greaves and armpieces. *If I wanted to bust that barrier, you bully-boys'd hop real pretty,* she thought, but then let it slide.

Backed up behind the candy-striped sawhorses were a bus and a throng of lorries and boxy little private vehicles that had apparently been caught en route when the Friendly Persuaders popped up to close off the street. The ordinary Kurita people were used to that kind of inconvenience. The vehicle occupants had all crowded forward to gape at the approach of the giant, manlike war machines, to clap their hands and chant with expressions of delighted amazement—

all carefully orchestrated by claques dispatched by Planetary Chairman Percival Fillington, the young Earl of Hachiman.

Oh, well, Cassie thought, not without sympathy, at least they're getting a show for their trouble. She hung a right, as indicated, onto *Tai-sho* Dalton Way.

The four-lane street slanted gently before her, stretching five hundred meters to gates that looked like real bronze and which were cut into forbidding ten-meter stone walls. The sun's falling light caught the designs raised on the metal gates and made the loops of razor tape topping the stone walls gleam like copper. Cassie bit down hard on the impulse to flatten herself over the handlebars and her strapped-down M23, slam-shift into high, and jam downhill as fast as legs conditioned by years of busting brush on a dozen hardscrabble worlds could take her.

But she resisted that impulse too. The Caballeros lined out behind her knew why she rode where she did, and like her, they generally did what Don Carlos wanted, even without his having to speak his desire, because Colonel Camacho *was* the Caballeros, their mind and soul. If they had a problem with the order of march, they could gripe about it, just as troopies always did.

But Southwesterners despised bicycles. No matter that bikes were an ideal low noise-heat-visual-signature scout vehicle, capable of going places not even the most agile Rat car could reach; their tiny MechWarrior minds didn't register considerations like that. To them bicycles symbolized the soft, urban, more-money-than-sense lifestyle affected by Trinity city-dwellers, people who looked down their noses at the rednecks and *bandidos* and wild bare-ass Indians who were the *true* Caballeros. If she put the pedal to the metal, the 'Mech jocks behind would regard it as a challenge of honor, something they could no more resist than a Clan mudhead could. Then *they'd* put the hammer down, racing their leviathans downhill, gyros whining to keep them from toppling forward, in a rush as undignified and out of control as first-graders heading for the play yard.

When those rambunctious little kids had an average weight of sixty metric tons, that was more than just undignified. It meant that even the specially reinforced pavement underfoot—presumably the reason for the officially designated route—would buckle under pounding monster impacts. And the racing MechWarriors would jostle each other exactly like rambunctious children, banging one another off building fronts at speed, which meant glass and stone and cement spraying into the street, and, not unlikely, a fair number of the spectators who had their faces pressed pale against lower-story windows.

That would not do. It could put a strain on relations with their new employer—which might not be that hard in any event, since he was a by-God Kurita, though distant from the all-important Line of Succession. Worse, it would make Don Carlos look bad in front of a passel of Dracs.

Cassie, behave. You've got to set a good example.

So she rode at a walking pace for the metal monsters, controlling speed with quick alternate flicks of front and rear brakes, coasting for the most part, though that was bad discipline indeed for a rough-country thrasher.

As she got close to Celestrial Splendor of the Dragon Boulevard, the broad avenue that ran parallel to the river along the compound's west wall, she began to gather a sense of just how big the place was. Those looming walls stretched out for a whole kilometer in either direction.

Now she could also make out the designs beaten into the metal of the gates. On the right was the Dragon-in-circle symbol of House Kurita and, by extension, the Draconis Combine. On the left was a samurai helmet with odd designs flaring like stylized antlers above, and below a *mempo* mask, features distorted by what might be martial fury or plain old mad laughter.

With a whine of servomotors and a creak of hinges, the gates swung inward before her.

Inside the walls, the HTE security forces were lined up to either side of the street in their powder-blue jumpsuits and helmets, assault rifles held in white-gloved hands at present-arms before their chests. Cassie rode between the silent ranks, still only beginning to grasp just how vast the complex was.

"A city inside a city," a voice murmured in the bone-conduction speaker behind her ear. Until now, she'd been ignoring the chatter off the 'Mech pilots' push. But this was the twangy Cowboy voice of Captain Kali MacDougall, Bronco Company's new boss, who happened to push about as many of Cassie Suthorn's buttons as was possible for a single individual. Her voice always went up Cassie's spine like nails on a pane of glass.

"Wonder if they got cathouses in there?" a male voice pondered. "Didn't see nothin' promising outside."

"Thinking with your small head again, Cowboy?" MacDougall asked. *Cowboy* was Lieutenant Junior Grade William James Payson's callsign as well as his ethnic affiliation. In the Caballeros you used the callsign your buddies gave you. The nicknames might not always be imaginative, but they usually *were* descriptive.

"Got my priorities straight, ma'am," the *Wasp* pilot replied with mock humility.

"And that's the onliest thing," came the voice of his buddy and mentor, Lieutenant Senior Grade Buck "Sawbuck" Evans, from his *Orion* named Buck's Bronc. "Least you got sense to think with the head has the *brains* in it."

"The one stickin' outta my collar."

"Not hardly."

"That *is* my small head," Cowboy announced triumphantly.

"Only in terms of utility," MacDougall said.

"I love it when you talk dirty, Lady K. Over."

"*Krasnyy Oktyabr,*" said Lieutenant JG Gorchakov.

"*Gesundheit,*" Evans and Payson said simultaneously.

"No, no," Gorchakov said peevishly. "It means 'Red October.' It was this big old tractor factory the Germans and the Soviets fought over during the battle of Stalingrad. First time a battle was ever fought in a giant industrial plant. It was big as a city, too, just like this place. One of my ancestors fought there."

"You puttin' on airs again, Tex?" Cowboy asked suspiciously. "Reckon I'm gonna have to pummel you some."

Older and wilier, Evans scored with, "Which *side* he fight on, peckerwood?"

That reduced Gorchakov to incoherent fury, as usual, sputtering about his illustrious forebear's heroism in the service of the Motherland in the long-dead Great Patriotic War. The Cowboys and 'girls tended to pick on Gorchakov, not because his family (one of the richest Cowboy households on Cerillos) still spoke Russian at home, but because they were descended from *Texans.* The bulk of Trinitarians, red, white, and brown, descended from residents of the ancient Terran states of Chihuahua, New Mexico, Arizona, and Sonora, all regarded Texans with the same fondness owls reserved for crows. Which was none.

In this case family tradition had let Tex down. Feliks Dzerzhinskiy was the tractor factory, not Red October. Good thing Father Bob wasn't there to set the record straight, or the honor of Texas and the Gorchakov clan might have undergone further battering.

"Come *on,* you guys," came Gavilán Camacho's voice. "Clamp it down."

"Yeah," Lady K added smoothly. "If your mouths are shut, there's a bigger chance your eyes'll be open. And there's plenty to see."

Gabby grunted. The Cowgirl's contribution had made him sound more like a leader and less like a whiny child, but he didn't like it.

Too smooth, Cassie thought in relation to MacDougall. She herself had never stopped looking. Lady K was right again, curse her cornflower-blue eyes. There *was* a lot to see.

Cassie knew little about modern manufacturing, and wasn't sure exactly what it was HTE made, other than consumer electronics. She was seeing ranks of long, low buildings that she guessed should be fabrication and assembly structures, but there, off to the left—north—were big, tall hangar-like structures that screamed '*Mech* in Cassie's mind.

What gets matched to the monsters in there? she wondered. Commo? Guidance systems? Control systems? She didn't know. HTE wasn't usually listed as a big military supplier for the Combine. Which just went to show how difficult it was for even the best of the Inner Sphere's intelligence agencies to infiltrate operatives into the Combine. But here, big as life, it looked like you could just climb up to the fourth floor of half a hundred buildings and see the damn sheds, she thought.

It gave her a chilly little feeling. She was, in a sense, coming home. But it was not a comforting thought.

Ahead loomed a building shaped like an ancient Japanese castle, with rising tiers and swept, pagoda-style roof-ends. Kurita-kitsch for true, in dark maroon marble veined with gold. Unlike the classic Japanese fortress, which was not intended for easy entrance, this structure had broad steps leading up to a huge doorway with a writhing dragon carved over it.

Standing at the top of those steps was a fat, bald man in a resplendent scarlet robe. Over that he wore a dark purple vest with dragons embroidered on both breasts and with shoulders that swept out like extravagant wings. Behind him the bronze doors were carved in the same pattern as the main gates.

The man looked like a decadent Buddha, and as she approached, Cassie could see that he was smiling immensely, as if he had just bet on a Taurian cook's apprentice against Kai Allard-Liao in the Solaris games, and the cook had *won*.

Next to him stood an immensely tall thin stork of a man, with long, grave features and receding gray hair. Dressed in conservative gray and mauve, this one looked like a typical Drac elder executive. Rapacious enough in his natural boardroom environment, and harmless outside it.

Or, so he would appear to most eyes. Cassie's gray-blue ones sized him differently. *Chief killer,* she thought, as she wheeled her MiG into position flanking the foot of the steps, as she had been briefed to do.

In spite of everything, she couldn't resist hot-dogging a little. Reaching her assigned spot, she locked up her front tire and threw her slight weight forward over the bars, lifting the thick, cleated rear tire right off the pavement. Balanced on the front wheel, she swung herself 180 degrees around and dropped back down with barely a thump of rubber on asphalt.

She glanced at the blue boy standing nearest, an armstretch away on her left. If his eyes had so much as flickered at her bravura display, she couldn't say. He might as well have been cast in concrete.

Some mighty strak sons of bitches, she thought. *On parade.*

Let's see if they shatter when the hammer comes down.

Just shy of the foot of the steps, the Colonel's Great White came to a halt. The *Mad Cat* knelt down like a trained elephant as a hundred powder-blue warriors presented arms, twirled them in salute, then clapped them to their shoulders. The hatch unsealed with a hiss, and Colonel Camacho proceeded to climb down to the ground.

At the foot of his monster, he stood there a moment, a dark-skinned, stocky man with receding black hair shot through with gray, an ash-flecked brush of mustache, and heavy bags beneath his soulful brown eyes. A *ranchero* to the bone, bandy-legged, with a potbelly hanging over his belt. But full of dignity, and giving the appearance of calm, quiet strength.

That appearance was a shell, Cassie knew. Touch him in the right way and it would all crumble and blow away as if his aura of strength were molded from a thin film of ash. He had been strong once, strong as the wind-carved mesas of his native Galisteo. But the strength had been scooped out of him.

He's our mind and soul, she thought. *Too bad the* tigres *cut our heart out on Jeronimo.*

Two 'Mechs came to a halt winged out on either side of Great White and just behind. One of them was Gabby's *Shadow Hawk.* The other, moving somewhat stiffly, was an *Atlas* borrowed for the occasion. It discharged the Colonel's chief aide-de-camp, Lieutenant Colonel Marisol Cabrera. *La Dama Muerte,* she was called: the Lady Death. Small, wiry, her features age-lined but still attractive, her hair auburn frosted with white. She was 'Mech-qualified but not current.

From it also climbed a tall, lean figure with an incipient paunch spoiling the lines of his flawless dress uniform, white with maroon trim, old-gold collar, and jackboots. This was Lieutenant Gordon Baird—"Gordo"—the Regiment's S2. His face was well-weathered, his hair silver, and he looked grand as hell.

They marched forward to take up formation on Don Carlos: Gabby at his right shoulder, the Lady Death at his left—the latter shooting Cassie a poisoned look behind the Colonel's back for that little show there at the end—Gordo Baird looming behind. As Don Carlos approached the steps, the others followed close behind.

At the foot of the broad steps Camacho stopped. "I am Colonel Carlos Camacho, commander of the Seventeenth Reconnaissance Battalion, *patrón* of the hacienda of Vado Ancho and Knight of Galisteo." He knelt. "My people and I are at your service."

The fat man in the robe beamed even more broadly, which Cassie would have sworn was impossible. "I am Chandrasekhar Kurita, Chief Executive Officer of Hachiman Taro Enterprises," he said in a soft and pleasant voice. "This is the *Mirza* Peter Abdulsattah, my chief of security."

The tall man beside him nodded his long thin head. His features were as ascetically drawn as his master's were round, his nose aquiline, his eyes dark and heavy-lidded.

"It is my great pleasure," the Kurita said, "to bid you welcome, Colonel."

He turned with a sweeping gesture of his scarlet-clad left arm. Somewhere a gong bonged. The great doors swung open.

Stately slow, Chandrasekhar Kurita entered his stronghold. His old retainer and his new ones followed him in.

Masamori, Hachiman
Galedon District, Draconis Combine
27 August 3056

It was a working-class bar two streets down *Tai-sho* Dalton Way and around the corner from the main gates of the HTE Compound. A handful of men and women in drab Laborer's garb looked up from their bottles of Borstal Boy beer as the door blew open as to a mighty wind.

Standing there was a tall, skinny *gaijin* in a leather jacket and baggy camouflage trousers, his thumbs hooked into a web gunbelt. On the heel of his right boot he wore a single silver spur. The outlandish figure's prominent Adam's apple traveled up and down with great deliberation as he tipped the toothpick he was chewing upward until it almost touched his long *gaijin* nose.

"Howdy," he said, and stepped inside the Permissible Repose Lounge.

He was followed at once by a mob of outside-folk, dressed with the studied roughneck casualness of the off-duty MechWarrior. The newcomers drifted to the bar and unoccupied tables and set the proprietor's three chubby daughters hopping to fill their drink orders. Being a *gaijin* mercenary was thirsty work, it seemed.

Tinkly music and shrill-sweet adolescent girl voices bubbled out of the musicbox in the corner. Images of the group, a current fave from Luthien called Purple Tailfeathers, danced upon the box's top with uncanny hologram precision: three adolescent girls, seeming to consist entirely of long legs, white teeth, big eyes, black bangs, and the eponymous purple feathers, alike as clones. It was what entertainment was coming to under the new relaxed regime. There were some who said the old dragon Takashi was turning over in his grave.

The sentiment seemed to be shared by the dark-haired gangly *gaijin* who'd violated the sanctity of the Permissible Repose. He went stilting over to the box and leaned his forearms right through the dancing doll-figures. He stood listening for a moment, his long *gaijin* upper lip curled in contempt. A moment more and he banged a fist down on the box.

Purple Tailfeathers missed a beat. A scan line flickered through their images. He struck again, harder, and the little-girl ensemble went wherever things like that go when they finally stop.

"Evenin'," the *gaijin* said. "Name's Cowboy. Y'all can call me *sir*. I'm declarin' this here boom box to be the o-ficial property of Radio Station KATN."

With the abrupt demise of Purple Tailfeathers, a few of the burlier Workers had started to their feet. Cowboy fixed them one at a time with the briefest of glances. "Y'all got a *problem* with that?"

The Workers one and all sat down. No, it seemed; there was no problem.

"Good," Cowboy said with a happy-goofy nod and grin. "Now, Zuma, whyn't you straighten out Mr. Barkeep over there on a thing or three. Like gettin' us some *real tunes* in here."

The intruders raised glasses and bottles and cheered. A few of them also threw back their heads in coyote-yips or trilling cries that ended with a nasalized "*ah*-ha!" A drink of water even longer than the one called Cowboy, with a single long braid extending down his back from otherwise close-cropped blond hair, rocked the walls of the Repose with a rousing rebel yell.

A little bandy-legged man with a neat black mustache and Mongol eyes, who had entered a few steps behind the herd in the company of a striking young woman with a long black braid, detached himself from his companion and walked over to where the bartender stood wringing his hands in his apron. The barkeep and proprietor was a tall, stoop-shouldered man with a long, saggy face and a tic that twitched the outside of his starboard epicanthic fold. Tonight it was fluttering like a shopman's awning in a stiff breeze. The Mongol-looking stranger touched him on the arm, then spoke with smiling earnestness.

After a few moments, the publican's eyelid almost ceased to flutter. He called for his stock boy, sent him scuttling out the back door into the alley. Then he straightened and looked around, and you could see him totaling the night's take by the gleam rising in his eye—despite the fact that most of the regulars had by now found cracks in the *tatami*-covered wood floor and sort of dissolved away through them.

Having finished his musicbox oration, Cowboy Payson hung an arm tipped by a bottle of Borstal Boy over the bush jacket-clad shoulders of Archie Westin. "So whaddaya think, Limey?" the MechWarrior asked.

A slight smile twitched the ends of Westin's mustache. "I think you lot certainly know how to make an entrance."

Cowboy laughed. "That's what it's all about, ain't it? Making your entrances count—and your exits, too."

He guided the reporter to the bar, against which Sawbuck Evans—the tall blond man with the tail—leaned with a bottle of Hotei Black Label whiskey clutched in his scarred fist. Beside him sat a third Cowboy, bearded to the others' clean-shaven but equally tall and lean. Tipped back over a mass of taffy-colored curls was a straw hat with a tattered red fire-bird feather stuck in the band.

"Right now, son," Payson said to Archie, who guessed the Caballero as maybe a year older than him, "I wanna introduce you to my brawlin' buddies Buck Evans and Rebel Perez."

He clapped the bearded man on the shoulder. "Don't let the name fool you, gringo. Old Reb here's a Jewboy through and through."

Archie felt his eyebrows crawl like blond caterpillars toward his hairline. "Jewboy?"

"Jewish Cowboys," Buck said. "Worst of a bad lot—mean as a Nova Cat who just found out he had a mother."

Reb touched the lip of his beer bottle to the brim of his hat. "Howdy," he said, in a voice like sand in a *BattleMaster*'s hip actuator.

"A pleasure," Archie said faintly.

"You're lucky old Cowboy dragged you away from Father Doctor Bob," Buck said. "He'll bend a body's ear till it breaks if you let him."

"By the way," Archie asked, "what do the letters 'KATN' stand for?"

"Kick Ass—" Cowboy began.

"—and Take Names," Rebel finished for him.

"Now," Cowboy said, "we're gonna buy you some drinks, and then we're gonna teach you how to talk to us Southwestern sons and daughters of bitches."

Holding a bottle of Hotei Black Label by the neck, Cassie left Zuma talking to the barkeep. Gentling the man like a frightened horse was more like it. She headed for the corner table, over by the currently quiescent musicbox.

As she was passing by, the Federated Commonwealth reporter with the blond hair and mustache came marching up to the bar where some of the *norteño* MechWarriors stood drinking and swapping lies, then said, right into the dark and handsome face of Macho Alvarado, *"Ódale, cabrón,"* in a horribly bright voice.

Macho turned ashy-pale. The next thing he had a knife in hand, slashing for the reporter's startled face.

The *next* thing was his skinny butt thumping on the rice-paper mats on the floor as Cassie, still holding her bottle, swept his legs from under him with a kick.

To those who later told the tale, Cassie reacted with her almost-mystical mongoose quickness. Since she never belied any of the legends about her, she never tried to set the record straight. The real reason she'd been able to respond so quickly when Macho pulled that knife, rattlesnake fast, was that she'd *already* been responding to what the stupid gringo had said. She'd known what Macho was going to do even before he did.

In an instant she was straddling the raging 'Mech jock with a forearm bar to the throat. "Macho, shut up and listen to me!" she shouted over his torrent of abuse in Spanish, English, and a couple of Indian tongues. "The *pendejo gringo* didn't know what he was saying. He was set up!"

Macho gathered himself. Cassie weighed maybe forty-five kilos even with her long hair full of water; he could outright *launch* her with one good buck. She read his body language, crossed the forearm bar with her other arm, got a good grip on the collar of his leather jacket, and blipped him out with a sleeper hold.

Then she climbed off him, picking up her bottle from where she'd set it upright on the floor as she went into the sweep. "Chango," she said to the nearest of the now-sleeping MechWarrior's buddies, "get him the foxtrot out of here. If he's still feeling peckish later, he can look me up. But if he messes with the gringo again he's gonna be eating Sierra Madre oysters for breakfast, and he *knows* where they're gonna come from."

Chango was a young stud as tough and full of himself as Macho was. But he just nodded and said, "Sure, Cassie," in a perfectly polite voice.

As Chango and friends scooped up Macho and dragged him out the door, Cassie turned to survey the Permissible Repose with eyes gone sky-blue. She caught sight of Cowboy Payson, Buck Evans, and Reb Perez sitting a ways down the bar, looking anywhere but at her, the very pictures of innocence.

They didn't so much as glance at her as she marched up and plunked her bottle on the bar. "Which one of you yokels pulled that little stunt on the Feddie?"

Payson was sitting on a stool between his cronies with elbows braced on the bar, hanging his bony face over a beer bottle. "Shoot, Cassie, I sure don't know what you're talking about—"

She kicked the stool out from under him. Payson's face banged the bar edge as he went down. Cassie's right hand caught him by his unruly brown hair.

As Evans stood to face her, Cassie's left hand came up, and all at once Blood-drinker was pricking the lanky blond Cowboy's Adam's apple.

Evans held his palms up. "Hey, no troubles, Abtakha."

"Damned straight. What got *into* you pinheads? If we kill off a gringo holoreporter, it'll make the Colonel look bad."

Despite her grip on his hair, Cowboy was trying to rise. Not too successfully, because his feet were tangled in the

stool legs. He was feeling his face. "HDLC, Cassie," he
whined, "what'd you have to go and do that for? You busted
my damn nose."

"No, I didn't." With a quick savage thrust, she rammed
his face into the bar again. There was a resounding *crack*.

"*Now* I did."

"*Owww!*" Cowboy wailed as he collapsed and covered his
face with his hands. Blood streamed between the fingers.

Cassie glared at Buck Evans, who shook his head and
stepped back. She tossed a glance toward Reb on Payson's
far side. He just sat there chuckling into his beer. The *kris*
went away.

"Come on," Cassie said to Archie. "Before I have to in-
capacitate any more of our manpower." She recovered her
bottle and walked away.

"That gal wants me!" Cowboy sang out after her back.
"This just goes to prove it. *Oww.*"

She turned and gave him a feral smile. "Keep dreaming,
Payson. Your own right hand would reject you, if it could
figure out a way to chew its way free of your arm."

The audience applauded as the bolt struck home. Cowboy's blood-streaked face became a stricken mask. "You
mean I'm . . . *coyote ugly*?" he said in tones of over-amped
tragedy.

"You got it, Red Rider."

Cowboy clutched himself over the heart with both bloody
hands, fell back onto a stool with his back against the bar.
"Shot through the heart!" he exclaimed. Cassie turned away.
Payson swiveled to drop both elbows on the bar, covered his
broken nose with his hands, and moaned.

Archie followed Cassie to a table, casting uncertain
glances back over the shoulder tabs of his bush jacket. "That
gentleman whose nose you broke keeps looking after you,
Lieutenant Suthorn."

"He's just watching my butt," Cassie said without looking
back. "Forget it. And don't call me 'Lieutenant.' Makes me
sound like a tin-man wannabe."

"Tin man?" he asked as she sat down with her back to the
corner.

"MechWarrior."

He took a place right around by her left side. "I hope you
won't think I'm too forward, sitting this close," he said.
"But I prefer to be able to see the room."

She shrugged and tossed off a shot of Hotei.

"I'm grateful for your assistance. But haven't you somewhat . . . overextended yourself? I mean, those men appear to have a rather rough-and-ready approach to life. And you *did* break one's nose and threaten the other with that unusual dirk of yours."

"Blood-drinker? Guru Johann gave her to me on my twelfth birthday." A shadow passed over Cassie's face, summer clouds sliding across the sun. "She's twelve hundred years old. He said not many *kris* have a female soul, but this one does."

She shook herself slightly, like a horse twitching a fly off its flank. "Don't worry about those bozos. It's forgotten already. They're good old boys; it's all a game to them—like setting you up to get carved on by Macho. They figured he wouldn't kill you, just cut you up some, add some character to that pretty profile of yours."

Archie glanced at her. He could not read the expression on that carved-mahogany face. It bothered him. He was used to being able to read women. Especially ones as attractive as his benefactress.

She sighed and leaned back in her chair. "Thing about the Caballeros is, they may go off on you and kill you if they think you've insulted them. Or they may just decide to pound on you for fun, with the understanding that you pound back and let's just see what you got, *hombre.* But it's like a sun shower. It all goes by quickly, and once it's past, it's gone. We don't hold grudges."

She poured another shot, stared into it. "Unless you work at it," she said. "Like what's between us and the *tigres,* the Smoke Jaguars. That's blood vengeance. An Elemental came through the wall in full battle armor right this instant, every man and woman in the room would be crawling all over the puke."

"And you?"

A grim half-smile. "Looking for something that burned hot and *clung.* Maybe see if I could whip up a Cerillos pancake—boiling sugar and lye, kitchen napalm. You can bake a mudhead like a Sierra foxtrot potato, if you catch him right."

Archie didn't quite manage to repress a delicate shudder. Quite uncomfortable, the matter-of-fact way this charming creature spoke of such unpleasantries. As if she talked from first-hand experience.

"Mudhead?" he asked.

"Pueblo term. *Indio, indigena*—Indian. Mudheads're supernatural clowns—a lot more sinister than the clowns you got back home, though. They're products of incest among the gods. Indians think the Clans reproduce by incest. Don't shine it on as prejudice, either; it's one way of looking at it."

He shook his head. "I don't, believe me. But you can also believe I am bewildered. By the terminology, by the, ah, the ethnic intricacies of your Regiment."

She laughed. "That's a good name for it. One bit of advice: never, *ever* use a Southwestern word unless you know stone four-by sure what it means. Like, whatinhell possessed you to say that to Macho?"

He chewed his underlip. "Lieutenant Payson"—he said it *leftenant*—"told me it was a comradely greeting that would help me get accepted."

She leaned forward and patted one of his hands. The contact sent a tingle up his arm like a breeze ruffling the short ginger arm-hairs. "Honey," she said, "they aren't *going* to accept you. I've served in this outfit nine years, I'm sworn blood-sister to half of everybody in it and have saved the personal butts of every last one of them a dozen times over. And I'm *still* a gringa. Will be till I die."

She settled back, and her lovely mouth took on a bitter twist. "Then I'll be one of them. Not before."

"They surely seem to accept you."

She shrugged. "I'm family. But still adopted. Abtakha, you know."

"You're not from one of the Southwestern worlds?"

"No."

He waited for her to elaborate. When she didn't, he said, "I confess I find myself at a loss, trying to understand the various groups and their relationships to each other."

"The groups? Cowboys, *norteños*, and Indians. Most of 'em are from the *caballero* class, landholders and retainers from the big ranches and haciendas, or from free-ranging tribes among the Indians. They look down on the city-dwellers, Urban Cowboys and *pochos* and Apples, almost as much as gringos."

"Now, I always thought gringo referred to, ah, a white man."

She shook her head. "Not with this bunch. Gringo is any outsider—even if his name is Gutiérrez and he hails from Mexico City on Terra."

"I see," Archie said without conviction. "And what about the people Lieutenant Payson called 'Jewboys.' "

"Jewish Cowboys, of course. Descended from Conservative Israeli refugees who didn't want to go along when many Jews went over to the Catholic Church in protest against certain actions by the state of Israel back on Terra. They didn't want anything to do with Orthodox Jews ever again, blamed 'em for messing up Israel, so they decided to get as far away from them as they could. Turned out to be the Trinity." She sipped her drink. "You don't have to be so hesitant with the word; they use it on themselves."

"It seems rather hard to discern what's safe to say and what isn't."

"You got that right. Keep it in mind and you'll pull through just fine."

"What about the Indians?"

"Far as I know, most of the Indians in the Trinity are actually Pueblos, but they keep to their settlements and don't go into space much. Ours're mainly Apaches and Navajos, which are almost the same thing but don't tell *them* that, and a few south Plains types thrown in—like Doc Ten Bears, our *curandera*. She's Kiowa/Comanche, off Cerillos."

"And all these types get along?"

"Depends on what you mean. Back home, they tend to fight a lot—feuds, raids, that kind of thing."

"As in people getting killed?"

"All the time. Now, understand, Cowboys are likely to be feuding Cowboys as anybody else, *norteños* versus *norteños*, that kind of thing. They make a lot of noise about hating each other, the different groups, but they're like as not to marry each other. And set 'em down at a table and get 'em drinking, there's not a gram of difference between them."

"And out here?"

She shrugged. "Everybody's butt goes on the firing line together. Stood down like this, some of 'em make faces at each other, other's don't care. It"—she made sinuous intertwining gestures with her hands—"shifts. Glows. Hard to describe."

He shook his head. "I don't think I'll ever understand."

"Don't sweat it," Cassie said. "Outsiders aren't meant to."

She looked up then and smiled. "Hey, Zuma. Got everything squared away?"

The Mongol-eyed man was walking over, holding a bottle of pale-yellow juice from some local fruit. Behind him came the proprietor, clutching a chip. He popped the cover on the musicbox, slipped the chip inside, turned to Zuma with a startling grin.

"Ready now!" he said, and walked back to the bar. The hammering strains of Chain Gang, a popular Davion band, came banging out of the box. A couple of Cowboys raised rebel yells, and several Indians got up to head-thrash.

Cassie laughed. "Don't know how you do it, Zuma."

Zuma pretended to clean his ear with a little finger. Though he smelled of soap even at this range, his hands were blackened with a mechanic's ground-in grime, the kind no amount of scrubbing could eradicate.

"You just gotta know how to *talk* to these dudes," he said. "Whew. The indios may love this stuff, but I can't hardly stand it. Sounds like what'd happen if you threw a drawerful of silverware and a coupla cats into a rock tumbler, y'know?"

Archie laughed. "That's as good a description of this particular band as I ever remember hearing."

Zuma gestured at the wall to Cassie's left. Set into it were several niches holding small paintings or statuettes before which candles burned. "I was admiring the *santos* here. Don't recognize any of them."

"Shrines to the *kami*," Cassie said. "Spirits."

"I thought the Combine officially frowned on worship of deities other than the Dragon," Archie said.

"Typical Davvy way of looking at it," Cassie said without heat, taking a pull from her bottle. "What's prescribed for the Workers is a type of Shinto. Basic animism—they worship everything from their ancestors to the spirits that lived here before they paved this part of the world over to Chinese gods to who knows what."

Archie was studying the images in their little nooks. "Well, then, what's that blue one there? If that's not Krishna, I'm John the Baptist."

Zuma laughed. "You'd look pretty funny with your head on a plate."

"It's Blue Boy, all right. Rabbi Maccabee—that's Force Commander Bar-Kochba—he says the population's mostly

East Indians mixed with Japanese. The ISF lets 'em slide Hindu gods in as *kami*. They're all supposed to be attributes of the Dragon, see."

At the mention of the letters *ISF,* the temperature of the bar seemed to dip a few degrees. House Kurita's Internal Security Force was probably the most feared secret police in the known universe. The Liao Maskirovka might be more sadistic, but the ISF was smarter. It was not very propitious to mention the name here in the very belly of the Dragon. Archie flicked his gaze around as if expecting to see *metsuke* lurking behind the musicbox. He had his own reasons for not wanting to be reminded of the ISF's existence.

With a start he noticed that Cassie was looking past them at the Repose's front door. Seeing her stiffen, he turned to follow her gaze, wondering if he should be diving for the *tatami*.

At first he had no idea what she was looking at through narrowed eyes. Then he realized she was tracking a tall blonde Cowgirl dressed in pale blue jeans and a blue silk blouse with tails knotted to bear her flat midriff. Shifting his mindset out of self-defense mode, he also noticed that the newcomer was well worth tracking.

The woman bought a bottle of the same stuff Zuma was drinking, paused to slap the shoulders of a couple of people at the bar, pass some easy talk around, then came sauntering over.

"Evening," she said, in a throaty alto. "Mind if I join y'all?"

Zuma smiled with evident pleasure. "Lady K. Good to see you."

She grinned and nodded to him, but she was looking at Cassie. "You can sit where you please, Captain," the scout said without warmth.

With a start Archie realized the newcomer was wearing a laser pistol in a tie-down holster on her right hip and had a big oval turquoise stuck in her navel. An altogether striking creature, he decided.

She turned a chair around and sat with her arms folded over the back. "Aren't you going to introduce me to your handsome friend, Cassie?"

"I don't know his name, Captain MacDougall."

The blonde turned to Archie and held out a hand. "I'm Kali MacDougall. I drive an *Atlas* for a living."

Archie took her hand. Her grip was firm. "Charmed," he said, and raised her hand to his lips. "I'm Archie Westin. Reporter for the Federated Commonwealth News Service."

She raised her eyebrows appreciatively. "A gentleman, I see."

"I try my best, Captain."

"Kali."

"She's the boss of Bronco Company," Zuma said. "Don't let the fact that she's blonde and an officer fool you, amigo." He tapped his temple with a forefinger. "She's sharp."

He drained his bottle, set it on the table. "Well, I better go see what the boys and girls managed to shake loose cakewalking their 'Mechs into town. Stay loose, Cassie. Nice to meet you, Mr. Westin."

Lady K reached out and touched Zuma on the arm. They smiled at each other, warmly, and Zuma went rolling out into the night.

The MechWarrior looked at Cassie, who seemed to have shrunk down inside the collar of her blouse. "I'm a little surprised to find you here, Cassie," she said in a friendly voice. "You're not usually the type to kick back with the other coyotes and howl."

Cassie raised her bottle and gestured around at the Permissible Repose. "This place is part of the terrain now. I'm a scout. I'm checking it out."

MacDougall made a face. "So that's why you aren't back at the Compound stalking the battlements. You're scouting the land here." She shook her head. "You need to learn to take time off, girl, take care of yourself."

"The Captain really doesn't have to waste her time worrying about me." Cassie stood. "I'd better get back."

She walked away, leaving her mostly full bottle on the table. Archie half-rose to follow her.

"Let her go, Mr. Westin," said Lady K. "She doesn't much like to be crowded."

Archie sat slowly back down. He looked at MacDougall. Some imp made him say, "Then why do you do it?"

A slow smile started at one side of her mouth and slowly spread across it, revealing brilliant white teeth. "I have my reasons," she said. "Now, why don't you rest your bones a spell and tell me why a big-time FedCom holojournalist is giving the time of day to a bunch of drag-tail mercs like us?"

* * *

Cassie walked back down *Tai-sho* Dalton Way with her hands thrust into the pockets of her baggy khaki trousers and her head sunk low. At sidewalk level the street was brightly lit; overhead the district's office towers soared upward, shadow masses occluding the stars. The streets were full of pedestrians, bicycle cabs with tinkling bells, honking cars. Unlike a lot of Drac worlds—and Larsha, where she'd been raised—the Hachiman police didn't bother trying to enforce a curfew except in times of civil unrest. And HTE, like the even bigger Tanadi Computer plant on the outskirts of town, ran staggered shifts, twenty-four hours a day. Which meant the Workers and Middle-Class *sararimen* were liable to be spending money around the clock.

A couple of cops standing at an intersection gave her a hard eye as she passed, playing with the safeties of their riot shotguns as they did so. Cassie ignored them. Even under Coordinator Theodore, *gaijin* were not a common sight on streets this deep inside the Combine; they had to make her for a merc. And if the Regiment's boss, big Buddha-belly Kurita himself, wasn't smart enough to keep the local police well-bribed ... She dismissed the thought. Kurita or not, if Chandrasekhar wasn't that sharp he'd never have been able to scrape up the ready to hire in a 'Mech regiment to hold his hand. Even one as semi-strapped as the Caballeros.

Why did she let the bimbo get to her, anyway? MacDougall had been with the unit since before Cassie was "recruited" on the DropShip lifting off from Larsha. She had taken over Bronco when the previous commander decided to retire after New Horizons. Cassie had never had much use for Lady K, to be sure, though she had to admit the Cowgirl was good at her trade. But it was only recently, ever since Captain Silva went home to Cerillos, that the blonde MechWarrior had begun to crowd the scout.

It might be getting time to back her off. Normally Cassie did not discriminate between men and women. Though women were sometimes treated like second-class citizens in the dominant cultures of the Trinity worlds, in practice that meant that any female who made it up to MechWarrior had to be at least as tough as her male counterparts, and generally meaner. Cassie had had her share of run-ins with women as well as men.

There was something about the taller MechWarrior that

discouraged Cassie from tangling with her, though. *What am I worried about? I can take her.*

But it wasn't that. It was something . . . else.

A knot of drunk *sararimen* with their ties off and their coats hanging open blocked the sidewalk in front of the stairs leading down to a basement strip club. They stared at Cassie with pie-eyed fascination, like so many sheep.

"*Bakayaro!*" she snarled at them. "Stupid idiots! Get out of my way!" The explosion of Japanese sent them scattering in all directions. Feeling slightly better, she continued on with head held high.

Well, okay, Miss High-and-Mighty 'Mech jockey, Cassie thought. *I will go stalk the battlements. I'll just load up my M23, and see what kind of perimeter security these* culebras *have put together.*

When she waved her way through a discreet little side door set next to the great bronze gates, Cassie was actually smiling.

10

Masamori, Hachiman
Galedon District, Draconis Combine
2 September 3056

Warm, humid air seemed to bounce off the pavement four stories below and back up into Cassie's face as she stood with one foot up on the rampart of the open-sided structure. The fumes from the ethanol mix burned by Drac ICE tended to produce formaldehyde, and it stung her eyes.

"Hey, Cassie," came the adenoidal whine of Private Absalom Sloat of Scout Platoon from behind Cassie's back. "Why we crawlin' around a parkin' garage, anyway? You ain't even got a car."

Ignoring him, she pushed her dark mad-dog shades farther up her forehead and scratched where sweat had begun to itch her skin. Fall might be coming to Masamori, but today it was muggy down here two klicks from the river.

"Just as I damned well thought," she said. "You can see the whole Sierra foxtrot *Compound* from up here."

A low dry chuckle rolled out of Scooter Barnes' big chest. "Give me a Zeus Big Twelve-Seven," he said, " 'n' I could sweep the place up pretty as a picture."

She skinned her lips open and blew air through closed teeth. "Yeah."

A half-dozen of Scout Platoon's complement had come along and were peering into the primarily boxy vehicles belonging to middle and lower-ranked Middle Class types. Platoon was a unit only by formality; the scouts generally operated lone-wolf or in pairs, rarely in larger groups. Unlike most Inner Sphere military organizations, the Caballeros encouraged their scouts to think small. After all, unless scouts were on ambush deployment, engaging an enemy usually signalled failure of their mission because it meant the enemy had been alerted to their presence. Bulk firepower was seldom much asset to the Seventeenth's scouts, whereas having a lot of people tripping over one another on patrol was a major liability.

Most military units weren't comfortable permitting their personnel to act as individuals, let alone encouraging them to do so, but people from the three dominant cultures of the Southwestern triad were individuals and damn anybody who tried to treat them differently; the secret to commanding them was to get them to cooperate and behave most of the time.

Scout Platoon was a repository for troops who were, even by Caballero standards, by and large cantankerous individualists. But troops like that tended to be self-reliant and self-contained, with both the skills and the mentality to let them spend days or weeks isolated in country hostile both in terms of enemy presence and, like as not, its own nature.

Badlands Powell, who took his callsign from the volcanic region of Cerillos which was his home, was more baby-sitter and director than actual commander of Scout Platoon. He knew and accepted the fact, and handled the job well. The natural leader for such a mob—to the extent that wasn't oxymoronic—was, of course, Cassie Suthorn.

He knew she'd agreed to accept promotion to officer after liftoff from Jeronimo only because Don Carlos had insisted. Cassie would do just about anything for him—especially with Patsy's death become a raw, gaping wound in his soul. She was the dominant personality in Scout Platoon; Badlands accepted that too. His wayward people might not be team players, but despite his own considerable gifts as a scout, *he* was.

Cassie's companions had come along mainly out of idle curiosity or just plain boredom. They obviously didn't expect much call for their services here in the heart of a metropolis, and were looking forward to getting back to the sport complex outside town where the other two battalions were bivouacked. There they could at least stretch their legs or get in some hiking and hunting. They didn't share Cassie's sense of urgency about scoping their surroundings, her obsessive drive to perform.

That was fine with her. No one she'd ever met could match her single-mindedness. Which had been to her benefit in encountering numerous enemies, and was a major reason she was still alive and they were not.

Cassie gave a quick glance around the floor to see if any of her buddies were slipping slim-jims into the windows of any of the parked and locked vehicles. Negative. She had promised to hurt anybody she caught boosting from the citizens on this little field trip. Even the biggest, baddest male chauvinist in the platoon—or the entire Regiment, for that matter—knew that Cassie was eminently capable across-the-spectrum of delivering on that threat. So they were behaving their little selves.

She turned to the dark little round-headed guy with big round glasses and an Aloha shirt who hovered by her elbow. "Yo, Preetam."

Preetam Masakawa, the HTE gnome assigned to be her guide on this little recce, bobbed his head and said, "Please?"

"We seriously gotta *do* something about this. You have any idea who owns this building?"

"Of course," he said proudly. "Uncle Chandy!"

"Uncle Chandy?"

"*Sri* Chandrasekhar Kurita. The big boss man."

That gave her a blink; *sri* was a common honorific back on Larsha, too.

A light dawned, slow as the primary squeezing its way out of Sodegarami, the *ukiyo* district east across the Yamato. "Who owns the buildings either side of this one?" she asked.

"Uncle Chandy. He owns everything fronting on the Compound."

Scooter Barnes whistled. The half-Kiowa Cowboy sniper was a bit more sophisticated than most of Cassie's mates in Scout Platoon, having spent some time coming up in cities.

"Piece of real estate like this'd go for a pretty penny," he said. "Single building'd cost as much as a BattleMech, sure."

Preetam laughed. "As a *battalion*," he said.

"Jesus," Billy Huckaby said.

That certainly explained a great deal. They had pretty much cruised where they chose on this reconnaissance run, with Preetam occasionally ducking aside for a few quick words with building security. Cassie had figured Uncle Chandy must have spread some jelly around with the neighboring landlords—or done some hard leaning; he *was* a Kurita. But all along the grease had been the fact that Chandy *was* the landlord.

"All right," Cassie said, turning away from the parapet to face Preetam, who was actually shorter than she was. "Now you take me to Uncle Chandy."

The little local was scandalized. "You no see Uncle Chandy! Why you want to see Uncle Chandy?"

"To ask for a raise."

No matter how highly she thought of herself, a drag-tail *abtakha* merc looie did not get to see Uncle Chandy just by asking, but Cassie operated on the principle of *you never know what you can get till you ask for it*, surprising plenty of people with what she'd gotten in the past.

And this time what she got was an interview with *Mirza* Peter Abdulsattah. It wasn't The Man himself, but it was impressive enough.

The *Mirza* raised his long narrow head to bring his gaze to bear on her while dismissing Preetam with a wave of spidery fingers. There was something in his manner, and Preetam's parting bow, that set little bells to ringing in Cassie's skull and her brain to wondering whether the guide was in reality the comic-relief goofball he seemed to be. Because Abdulsattah was a hard-core spymaster for true, and those appropriately spider-like fingers were meant to set marionettes dancing in the least expected of places—or else all Cassie's instincts lied.

If they lied, she died. This *Mirza* bore watching. So did little Preetam.

Abdulsattah rose up from behind his desk—and *up;* he must have been nearly two meters tall. He was gaunt as a skeleton, his olive skin drawn almost tight enough to burst over the fine ascetic bones of his face. He wore a skullcap and had a neat graying beard.

"You are the young woman who performed that caracole on her bicycle, out in front of the steps," he said, his voice startling deep.

"That's me," said Cassie, who was not one to be intimidated, by rank or height.

"Preetam said you had security matters to discuss with me."

"I'm surprised you agreed to see me," she said. "Women don't rate too highly in the Combine."

"Your Colonel speaks well of you," the *Mirza* said. "Please sit, if you've a mind to."

She did. Better, it got the HTE security boss to fold his length back into the leather-covered chair behind his modest hardwood desk.

"You speak with authority on Combine culture," he said. "Surely, your time within the Combine was too short for you to have learned much. I suppose the exile community on Larsha provided your education?"

"Peter-*sama,* with all respect, you don't suppose. You know."

The lids lowered over Abdulsattah's black eyes like impact-resistant shrouds. He gazed at Cassie a moment, his fingers dancing on the tabletop like a spider doing a jig.

She held his eyes steady with her own.

"You are a remarkable young woman," he said at length. "Your courage is proven by your record. But a word of caution, for your comrades as well as yourself: you are a long way from your homes."

"Is that a threat?" Cassie asked.

The *Mirza* shook his long, fine head. "Only a simple statement of fact, Lieutenant. I am not exactly a conventional Combine executive—"

Tell me something I don't know, Cassie thought. But she kept the thought quiet. She was a scout—cocky, not stupid.

"—and Chandrasekhar-*sama* is an even less conventional Kurita. But he is still a Kurita, and you and your people will encounter many here who are far less forbearing than either of us."

For a moment longer Cassie kept her eyes leveled at his. Then she nodded. "I bow to your wisdom, Peter-*sama*."

"Somehow I doubt that," he said, with the merest hint of a smile. "But as with so many things in life, you will either learn, or die."

Cassie put an arm over the back of the chair and settled into it. She felt no pressure from his words. *Learn or die* were the terms under which she'd lived since the age of three.

The *Mirza* rose and went to stand in front of what looked like a picture window opening onto a lush, sun-based oasis surrounded by dunes of gypsum sand so white they seemed to glow with their own light, as though heated in a furnace. It was an illusion, of course. Abdulsattah's office lay well within the Citadel, HTE's castle-like main administrative center. Had it possessed windows, they would have given out over the perpetually busy Compound.

Of course, windows would also offer a convenient way for foes to target the *Mirza.* Cassie wondered whether the precaution was merely prudence—life in the Draconis Combine tended to be a lot more turbulent than outsiders thought, particularly at the higher echelons of business and state—or whether there was a deeper game in play.

Abdulsattah gazed at the hologram for a moment, as if his hooded dark eyes could see beyond the horizon of that fantasy world, as if his vision were not limited by the scope of the lasers that had captured the image.

"What does *mirza* mean, Peter-*sama*?" she asked his back.

"It means 'prince' on my homeworld," he said, turning back to her.

"You are an Arkab?"

"Of a sort." He smiled. It seemed genuine enough. "Now tell me why it is a junior officer who requests a meeting regarding our security arrangements instead of your lieutenant colonel of intelligence?"

Because in Gordo's case, "military intelligence" truly is a contradiction in bloody terms, she thought. But again she didn't voice the thought. There were few rules in the Caballeros. Don Carlos allowed his troops to do pretty much as they wished, as long as they performed; those who didn't soon found themselves dumped with a cold-water ruthlessness that left them gasping. That was the way the unit had always been run, not a result of Colonel Camacho's withdrawal into himself in the wake of Patsy's death. It suited Cassie to the marrow.

But there *were* rules, mainly unwritten ones. And those Cassie honored—mostly. Foremost was the iron law of the Trinity: *when the hammer comes down, it's us against the Universe.* That law Cassie believed in passionately. Because it meant that when the hammer came down, she was no longer a gringa, she was a Caballero. They might call her Abtakha, but she belonged. It was a sense she had never known, except when she'd been with Guru Johann. She clung to it with a drowner's grip.

That law meant, among other things, that you did not criticize a fellow 'llero in front of outsiders. No matter how big a ragbag he happened to be.

"Lieutenant Colonel Baird's a busy man," she said in a carefully neutral voice. "And he concerns himself mainly with electronic intelligence-gathering."

The *Mirza*'s dark eyes bored into her like laser drills. She did not shy from the scrutiny; she knew that even the most penetrating probe could go only a certain distance into her skull, and no farther. But this truth was not buried that deep.

"Indeed," Abdulsattah said, resuming his chair. "What exactly did you wish to speak to the Chief about, Lieutenant?"

"I understand you—HTE—own the buildings that front on the Compound."

"It is so. The Chief felt they might prove a worthwhile investment." Was that a sparkle of merriment flickering well back in those anthracite eyes?

"Seems to me," Cassie said, "that there are some preparations that might be made inside those buildings. Some surprises for the bad guys, just in case somebody with hostile intentions were to happen along. Sensors, booby-traps—I'm sure I don't have to tell you."

The *Mirza* laughed—not the nervous-seeming titter Cassie associated with the few Arkabs she'd known, or most of the *Masakko* she had encountered, for that matter. It was a full-out laugh that seemed to come bubbling from the center of him.

"Indeed you do not, Lieutenant," he said, when the laughter subsided. He leaned forward and clasped his hands on the desk. "Perhaps this will surprise you, but neither Mr. Kurita nor my humble self have entirely overlooked the possibility that the property surrounding the Compound might prove useful for inconveniencing the ill-intentioned. The investment I spoke of was not entirely fiscal in nature."

Cassie shrugged. No, it wasn't a surprise. But she hadn't lasted this long by taking anything for granted.

"Still," the *Mirza* said, "hard as you may find this to believe, neither Chandrasekhar Kurita nor myself believe we know everything. I would like to hear what 'surprises' you have in mind, Lieutenant." Again that hint of amusement in almost impenetrable eyes. "I understand that surprising enemies is rather a professional specialty of yours."

11

Masamori, Hachiman
Galedon District, Draconis Combine
2 September 3056

"Leftenant Suthorn?"

Walking from her appointment with the *Mirza* with her hands in her pockets and her head down in thought, Cassie hadn't noticed the Federated Commonwealth newsie trotting after her. Great, she reproved herself. Get caught up in your own thoughts and lose track of your surroundings. It was under just such circumstances that she might have expected Guru Johann to come popping up out of nowhere to whack her upside the head for inattention.

The handsome young reporter was striding toward her with his hair gleaming gold in afternoon sunlight, his stocky black camerawoman trotting after.

"What can I do for you, Mr. Westin?" she asked.

He beamed, a real toothpaste-ad smile.

"Archie, please. I was wondering if you might be kind enough to show me around."

Cassie nodded at the camerawoman, a shy young woman with broad, pleasant features. "Scoping our dispositions, are you?"

He blinked, tittered nervously. "Nothing of the sort. Just doing my job."

She snorted. "Yeah. Well, I'm wandering over to see the astechs. No harm in you coming along."

They set off. The Compound was alive with purposeful bustle, the huge facility alone probably worth more than many a Periphery world. One of the effects of its size was that HTE workers were not forced to work in the desperately cramped conditions suffered by most Combine laborers. The actual assembly floors and production areas were more spacious than the norm; and on periodic rest-breaks HTE employees could actually go outside and stretch their legs.

The workers who strode by them in pastel HTE uniforms, the colors denoting subtleties of department and shift that Cassie had yet to untangle, held their heads up and moved in a way the Voice of the Dragon wanted outsiders to believe all Combine workers did, all aglow with *aisha seishin*, company warrior spirit. Normally that was just propaganda. Not here.

"Curious accent you got there, Archie," Cassie said casually, though she did consider the question mere abstract curiosity. Information about a person's background gave you clues to them, helped your threat assessment. And to Cassie, anyone who wasn't Regiment was a threat. Not that everybody in the Seventeenth wasn't; among the Drac exiles back on Larsha she had often heard the epigram; *tanin*—hostile strangers—begin with one's own siblings.

He laughed again, more relaxed this time. Mariska Savage hung back, discreetly out of the conversation, more as if she really didn't want to be included than as if she didn't think it was her place.

"Northfield was founded by people from the British Isles, you see," he said.

"So you're a Davion." Northfield was near New Avalon, capital of the former Federated Suns.

"I am a loyal, not to mention happy, citizen of the Federated Commonwealth."

She gave him a slantwise look out of those long, smoky eyes, the sort of look to make a man's heart skip a beat even though it was devoid of conventional coquetry. "Not too many of those these days."

An expression that might have been pain writhed across Westin's sculptured features like a sidewinder. "Perhaps not. Still, Westins have served House Davion loyally for generations, whether or not it was the fashionable thing to do. And now we serve House Steiner-Davion—in our own way."

They walked a while in silence. "If I may say so," Archie said, casting about for a flying subject change, "your own accent, while quite charming, is hardly orthodox. Those twangy American Western vowels, the somewhat staccato cadence of your Mexican comrades, mixed in with a sort of . . . well, *music*."

It was her turn to laugh—a sound Archie found quite enchanting, and indeed musical.

"I grew up in the Regiment," she said. "Not surprising that I talk like them. For the rest—" Cassie shrugged. "I lived on Larsha before."

"Before—?"

"Before I was captured," she said, her tone going flat.

"You're joking."

"No. I was in the militia. I was a street kid—we all were. Got trolled in on a random sweep, made for a couple robberies I didn't even commit."

"You . . . did commit robberies, then?"

She laughed. "Sure. I'd been on my own since I was twelve. Did a lot of things." A headshake. "Anyway, I got dumb, or unlucky, and I got caught. So they gave me an old bolt-gun and said I had to be a soldier. And then the Seventeenth hit town. Larsha's a border world, near both the Periphery and Davvy space—"

"I am familiar with it, yes."

"—and the Capellans had been launching border raids into the Federated Commonwealth, so the F-C sent a merc regiment in to teach them not to do that. I knocked down one of their 'Mechs—Bobby the Wolf's old *Wolverine*, before he got that *Griffin* he drives now."

Westin stared at her. She had to repress a giggle at the way his red-blond eyebrows arched, like caterpillars. "*You* defeated a BattleMech? A sixteen-year-old girl with a rifle?"

"A cut power line, actually. Spot-welded the knee."

"I say, they actually have above-ground power cables in the Confederation?"

"Did on Larsha. Anyway, Bobby was fit to be tied. He still hates me, not that he likes anybody else in the Sphere. And Patsy—the Colonel's daughter, she was a senior lieutenant and a *Phoenix Hawk* pilot then—she kept him from killing me. She's the one who asked if I wanted to surrender." Cassie shrugged. "They had me surrounded with three 'Mechs, so what could I do but say yes? It meant leaving Larsha, but it wasn't like I had anything keeping me on that hellhole."

She shivered then, keeping the gesture so small he didn't notice, or seem too. "Not since Guru Johann died."

"I see. And where is this Patsy Camacho now? I don't believe I've been introduced—"

"She died." The words cut across Westin's chatter like a cleaver chopping a rabbit's neck. "On Jeronimo. Fought five Smoke Jag Omnis. Smoked two, damaged the others, but they took her down."

"She destroyed two Clan OmniMechs in a *Phoenix Hawk*?"

"A *Vulture* and a *Puma*."

Westin shook his head in wonderment. "She must have been one extraordinary pilot."

"She was. The best PH pilot alive." Cassie drew a deep breath, let it out through flared nostrils. "She was our soul, Mr. Westin. And the only friend I ever had. Nothing's the same since she's gone."

"I can imagine," Archie murmured. He had a sense of intruding, and covered as best he could.

From ahead came the flicker-flash of an arc welder, blue-bright even in day, and the sound of a guitar. They rounded the corner of a building and there they were: the tall, hangar-like 'Mech assembly structures that had so intrigued Cassie earlier in the day.

Sitting on a flatbed trailer behind a tracked prime mover was the detached forearm assembly of an *Atlas*. The sight of it sent a shiver through Cassie.

A bare-chested man sat atop the 'Mech's forearm, strumming a guitar. His chest was covered clavicle-to-beltline with a peculiar tattoo. Standing by the trailer talking to him was a handsome woman in her thirties with lustrous auburn hair.

As they got closer, Archie could see that the tattoo depicted a woman in a cowled robe, surrounded by stylized radiance and standing upon a crescent moon.

"*Ódale,* Zuma," Cassie called.

The guitarist grinned beneath his mustache. "Hey, now, little sister. What's happening?" Belatedly Archie realized this was the man who had entered the bar with Cassie the night of their arrival.

The woman turned and smiled. "Hello, Cassie."

"Annie," Cassie said, more perfunctorily than she had greeted the man with the guitar. "Mr. Westin, I'd like to present Lieutenant Senior Grade Annie Sue Hurd and Master Sergeant Richard Gallegos. Lieutenant Hurd pilots a *Rifleman* for Bronco. Richard's our Senior Astech. Folks, this is Archie Westin from the Federated Commonwealth News Service."

"Hi," said the woman in the fringe. She was pretty in a watery way.

Gallegos—Zuma—nodded politely to Archie. "Understand you had a little run-in with my cousin. Hope nothing got shaken loose."

"Your cousin—oh, you mean Lieutenant Alvarado."

Zuma laughed. It was a big laugh for such a small man, but it seemed he had a lot of practice. "Macho? No. He's so stupid I wouldn't admit I was related to him even if I was, which thank the Virgin I'm not." He paused to cross himself. "I meant Billy. Lieutenant Payson."

"Cowboy," Cassie supplied.

Archie blinked. He seemed to be doing a lot of that. "Cowboy's your cousin? I thought—"

Zuma looked at the little scout. "He hasn't got it worked out about us yet, has he, girl?"

"Give him a chance, Zuma. It isn't like it's simple or anything."

"Please forgive me," Archie said. "I had garnered the impression that the lines between your ethnic groups were more sharply drawn than that."

"*Nothin's* sharply drawn with us," Zuma said. "Except the line between us and the rest of the universe."

"I see," Archie said.

"You're from the Federated Commonwealth?" asked Annie Hurd, rounding on him. He nodded. "Well, I just want you to know how deeply I feel for your royal family. I do so hope Victor and Katherine work out their differences soon. I just can't believe either of them had anything to do with their mother's awful murder."

Archie was opening and closing his mouth like a carp. Cassie laughed. "Avengin' Annie is a big fan of Misha Auburn," she said. Lieutenant Hurd nodded brightly.

"I . . . see." Misha Auburn, Countess of Tikonov, had been Archon Melissa Steiner's best friend and official historian for the court of the Lyran Commonwealth. Her astoundingly sycophantic histories of the Federated Commonwealth royals were the subjects of much amusement among the literary sophisticates of Davion space, among whom Archie counted himself with a touch of smugness. They were wildly popular with the general public, though, and not just within the Federated Commonwealth.

Like the Davion soap opera *Royals' Pride* of Cassie's youth, they had even become popular in the Capellan Confederation and the Combine, into which Theodore had recently permitted their legal importation—the warming of relations between the Draconis Combine and the Federated Commonwealth in the wake of the Clan invasion having been duly mirrored in Countess Auburn's works. Even people who did not much care for the F-C as a political entity were charmed by the antics of their ingenue nobility, it seemed.

"I adored *Melissa: The Triumph and the Tragedy*," Hurd bubbled. "Simply adored it. I'm still broken up over her death."

"I thought most members of your Regiment hailed from the Free Worlds League," Archie said delicately.

"Oh, yes. I'm from Galisteo myself. But the Regiment has served the Federated Commonwealth most of the time I've been a member. And I've been an admirer of your royal family since I was a little girl."

She shook her head, causing her auburn tresses to bounce around her shoulders in such an artless manner that Archie was instantly convinced she'd spent hours practicing the gesture. "I don't feel there's any reason for rivalry between the Commonwealth and the League, really I don't. After all, the Captain-General's son Joshua is a guest of Prince Archon Victor's at the New Avalon Institute of Science."

"Indeed," Archie said, a trifle hollowly. Among the cynics—and among those in the know—the ailing Joshua's status was considered to be more hostage than honored guest.

"Well, I have to get along or Bunny Bear will start to miss me," Hurd burbled with scarcely a pause for Archie's response. "Pleasure to meet you, Mr. Westin. If you ever want to chat about the royal family, look me up any time. Wonderful to talk to you, Cassie, Zuma." And she went bouncing off with a happy-schoolgirl walk.

Once Annie was safely around the corner of a building, both Cassie and Zuma broke into laughter. "Bunny Bear?" Archie asked.

"Her teddy bear," Cassie said. "Rides in the cockpit with her."

Archie blinked. "Senior Lieutenant Hurd seems a woman of pronounced tastes," he finally said.

"She's all right," Zuma said. "I mean, you take into account she's both an officer *and* a MechWarrior, she's really pretty, y'know, *normal*." Cassie gave him a look of pure skepticism, but she held her tongue.

"There seems to be a surprising amount of antipathy toward MechWarriors, for a 'Mech unit," Archie said.

Cassie shrugged. "I don't like 'Mechs, I don't like 'Mech jocks. I don't get paid to. I get paid to kill them."

Archie stared at her in surprise. If she was joking, the smooth, fine features and the long gray eyes didn't show it. Cassie Suthorn was a very hard number to read, Archie realized; but to the extent he could, she seemed to be speaking with utter conviction.

" 'Mech jocks are like kids," Zuma said, his cheerful voice bursting the brief tension like an invisible bubble. "You can't take 'em too seriously. Just spank 'em when they get too far out of line, and put up with them the rest of the time."

"Leftenant Gallegos—"

"Sergeant," Zuma corrected hastily. "Or Zuma. Or Richard, or just, *hey you*. The *patrón* keeps wanting to make me an officer, but I keep telling him I want to keep all my brain cells alive. Somebody's got to keep the tin men up and running in this outfit, you know?"

"That reminds me," Archie said, "if you don't mind my asking, where does the nickname 'Zuma' come from? I understand most of the callsigns I've heard in the Seventeeth, but that one has me stumped."

"It's short for Moctezuma," Cassie said.

"What else are you gonna call me?" Zuma said. "I'm the Head Aztech, after all."

A peculiarity of pronunciation of the common abbreviation *astech* clicked into place in Archie's mind. He laughed.

"You people seem to delight in wordplay," he said.

Zuma nodded. "Now you're startin' to get the hang of us, Mr. Westin. Caballeros play hard, and we play a lot, 'cause you never know when you're gonna get dead."

Mariska Savage had slipped discreetly off to the side and begun to record the exchange. She had a way of hanging in the background so one barely noticed her, not seeming to mind the role of ebullient Archie's shadow.

"Well, Sergeant—Zuma," Archie said, "will you plays us a song on your guitar? Our viewers in the Federated Commonwealth would be charmed, I'm sure." He glanced at his assistant, who bobbed her head and grinned encouragingly without removing her eyes from the eyepiece of the holocam.

"Sure, long as you don't insist I stay on key or nothin'." The Chief Aztech struck a chord, threw back his head, and declared, "Presentando el Capitán Carlos Camacho!"

He began to strum the guitar and sing in a good—if nasal and tobacco-roughened—tenor voice. It was a ballad sung in Spanish, and Archie couldn't understand a word beyond what he took for periodic references to Captain Carlos Camacho, the evident hero of the piece.

When it was done, he applauded heartily. "Bravo! That was quite stirring, though I confess I couldn't make most of it out."

"It tells the tale of how Carlos Camacho fought *los bravos del norte*."

"Was that when the Colonel was a younger man? Still in Marik service, perhaps?"

Zuma and Cassie laughed. "*That* Captain Camacho has been dead a thousand years," the Chief Aztech said, "if he ever really existed. *Los bravos del norte* were wild Indians of northern Mexico—Chihuahua, Sonora, where a lot of us hail from."

"They call us *bravos* and *bravas* sometimes, too," a clear Cowboy-accented female voice called from behind them. Ever so slightly Cassie ducked her head; if Archie had not been watching her as intently as his well-honed Northfield manners would permit, he'd never have caught it. "Us wild boys and girls from out in the desert and the chaparral."

Archie turned. "Captain MacDougall," he said. "A pleasure to see you."

"Likewise, Archie, Ms. Savage. Hi, Cassie."

"Hello," Cassie said, almost sullenly.

"I heard the tail end of your song as I came up, Zuma," Kali said. "I was trying to figure out which one it was—Carlos Camacho flying *Spitfires* against the Japanese, or fighting the Viet Cong, or taking on our hosts the Dracs in the First Succession War."

"There's a Carlos Camacho in every age," Zuma said, "and a ballad about each one."

"That's fascinating," Archie said. "What about your real-life Colonel Camacho? Will there ever be a song about him?"

Zuma shook his head. "I'd write him one—"

"Zuma's a pretty mean songwriter," Lady K said. "In fact, I'm not sure there's anything he can't do."

Zuma chuckled. "Sure got 'em fooled, don't I?" he said with a wink to Archie. "Anyway, he won't let me write one."

His expression set. "He won't let me write one for Patsy, either. Even though she's gone, and the way she went out should have won her a song."

The cheerful atmosphere cooled, as if the sun had gone beyond a cloud and let the incipient autumn bite to the air come to the fore. A few beats passed, and then Kali MacDougall said, "When do you think a bay'll open up, Zuma?"

"This afternoon, they said. You should see the 'Mech facility they got here, Kali." He shook his head. "They mate fire-control systems to them here. It's incredible what they got. And they said we can use them when one frees up."

"Great. I'll be glad to get Dark Lady back online—that's her forearm Zuma's sitting on. I don't think we can afford to let our guard down, no matter how far off the firing line we seem to be. Uncle Chandy's paying more like the Archon Prince than a Kurita, and we're getting near-Kell Hound rates." It was her turn to shake her head. "I don't think he's shelling out that much just to show off his pet *gaijin* regiment to his fellow CEOs. 'Least, I don't want to take that for granted."

Archie noticed that Cassie was watching the tall blonde officer closely as if reappraising her reluctantly. "I take it then, Zuma, that your role is more than administrative," he said. In most outfits, astechs were often grunt-level laborers, commonly hired in from the local pop.

"Yeah. In the Caballeros us Aztechs mostly handle the mechanical stuff. We leave the skull sweat, neurohelmets and all like that, to Astro Zombie and his crew."

"Astro Zombie?" Archie asked. "My word, I'm starting to sound like an echo, aren't I?"

"Cap'n Harris," MacDougall said. "Our Chief Technician."

"When you meet him," Cassie added, "you'll understand the name."

"*La Curandera*—that's Doc Ten Bears, our sawbones—she says he's the only psychosomatic hunchback in the Inner Sphere," Zuma said with evident pride.

"Cyberpuke," Cassie said, as if that explained it all.

"Indeed," said Archie, because it rather did.

Cassie had been edging almost imperceptibly away from MacDougall ever since the taller woman's arrival. "Zuma, they got a monkey pit in this joint?"

He nodded. "Down the line, past the end of the 'Mech hangars, they got a big old garage for their motor pool. If they didn't get a 'Mech bay open before long I was going to go hang out down there, see if I could pick up a few pointers. These here *culebras* seem to know a few things."

Cassie nodded. "Later," she said to the group at large, and strode away, braid flopping against the back of her blouse.

Archie gazed after her in consternation. "It seems that young woman is always running away from me," he said.

"It isn't you," Lady K told him. "It's me. Can I buy you guys a soda?"

The HTE garages were well-lit and sparkling clean, which anywhere else but the Draconis Combine would have sounded like a contradiction in terms. The techs were startled when Cassie addressed them in fluent Japanese. Despite her gender and her *gaijin* status, that gave her standing.

Much of Masamori's populace was Japanese, by affinity if not always extraction, yet far from all of them spoke the difficult tongue. Facility with the language of House Kurita was a mark of good class-standing in the Combine, and Cassie used Middle Class forms. The Workers treated her with automatic respect.

Hai, yes, they did have a grease pit that was currently unoccupied. *Hai,* she could use it. They didn't ask what for, but their eyes did.

Their eyes got even wider as she kicked off her athletic shoes, eeled down into the pit, and took up an obvious martial arts stance in the midst of grease that came almost to her ankles. She began to work through a sinuous *kata,* sometimes compensating for the slippery-treacherous footing, sometimes seeming to actually use it in her shadow-boxing. A crowd began to gather.

Cannier martial arts masters drilled their students in alleys and woods and rice paddies, not just on the neat *tatami*-covered floors of the *dojo.* One was seldom attacked in the middle of open, well-lit rooms, after all. *Pentjak-silat* took that a step farther; Cassie's Guru Johann had insisted she train on the worst footings imaginable: amid overturned furniture and broken bottles; in shin-deep mud; on a marble-strewn sidewalk; on pools of oil. *Most fighters crave good footing as an addict craves his drug,* Guru had told her. *Your enemy's prejudices and desires are among your most powerful weapons. Use them.*

Wish I could strip down for this, Cassie thought as she moved in the thick petrochemical muck to begin practice of *harimau,* the ground-hugging tiger forms of *pentjak-silat.* *But it'll make life tough for Don Carlos if I scare the straights too much.*

She bent from the waist until she was spread-eagled, arms and legs stretched wide, her flat stomach a centimeter above the waste oil and grease. The spectators oohed and ahhed at this, but for Cassie the outside world had gone away. Her heartbeat and respiration had slowed and leveled, and she was, for a brief time, again at peace.

Masamori, Hachiman
Galedon District, Draconis Combine
2 September 3056

"**N**ow what are you asking for, young lady?" Lieutenant Colonel Gordon Baird asked. Though born on a ranch on Galisteo, he'd been raised in Johnson City. His accent was that of an Urban Cowboy, not too different from any Free Worlds gringo, but his voice took on a nasty, waspy whine when he was trying to show that something was beneath his contempt.

Cassie got that a lot.

"Permission to do my job, Colonel," she said levelly.

"Your job." He looked around at the battalion and company commanders of the Seventeeth assembled now in the briefing room in the guts of the Citadel. "Your job, as I understand it, is to scout out unknown terrain and report back on what you find. Now, correct me if I'm wrong, but we are currently in the middle of a very large city, are we not? I don't see any scrub or swamp for you to reconnoiter."

"That's my job as *you* understand it," she said. Baird stiffened. *All right, so I behaved myself as long as I could.*

Don Carlos sat at the head of the table, chin sunk into his chest. He didn't appear to be listening, but Cassie believed he was. Maybe because she had to.

"My job is to monitor the Regiment's surroundings, wherever that might be. Just because we're in the middle of people and pavement and big, tall buildings instead of trees and flowers and chirping birds doesn't mean we're all of a sudden in a vacuum. Far from it."

"But what's the *point*?" asked Captain Angela Torres. She was Frontera Company's commander, callsign Vanity. "You want to know our situation? We're surrounded by *culebras*."

That was the word for "snakes," old unit slang for the Combine.

"Indian country," drawled Lee Morales, Deadeye Company's CO. Bobby the Wolf, who bossed Cochise, gave him the hot eye. Force Commander Peter White Nose Pony and "Stretch" Santillanes, the other two Indians present, just grinned.

"We're in the middle of millions of enemies, Cassie," Angela Torres said. "What more do we need to know?"

"There's more to life than how you look in the mirror, Captain Torres," Kali MacDougall said quietly.

Torres glared at her. "Excuse me?" she said.

"You're excused. We can't just assume every Drac's our enemy. Or have you forgotten that Combine troops shed their blood right alongside us at Jeronimo?"

Don Carlos crossed himself, but said nothing.

"We can't get complacent, either. At least, most of us can't." The tall blonde Cowgirl addressed this last to Baird, who stiffened. "Our employer is laying out a lot of change to have us here. If everything is just totally swell on this pleasant little planet, then *why*?"

"The Clans," Bobby Begay said moodily. "We can't trust those witches. Sooner or later they'll break the truce."

Kali looked from him to Cassie, caught her eye, and shrugged. From her many years in the Regiment, Cassie knew that a "Navajo wolf"—also known as a "Skin-walker" or shape-shifter—was a witch of the very worst kind of the *Diné*, which was why most of the other Navajos tended to shun Bobby the Wolf. One reason, anyway.

"Maybe that's so," Bar-Kochba said quietly, "but what'd make Uncle Chandy think we and the Dracs could hold 'em this time, any better than the last?"

Into the uncomfortable silence, Lady K said, "Perhaps Lieutenant Suthorn could tell us why she thinks it's so important for her to go underground."

All eyes turned toward Cassie, who stood at the foot of the table. "The last few days I've been investigating the buildings around the Compound with the *Mirza*'s people. They've been showing me the sensors and booby-traps they have in place, and I've been making some suggestions about what else they could do."

"I'll bet they're just thrilled," Angela Torres said.

Cassie clamped her mouth tight shut. "Go on, Cassiopeia," Don Carlos said, showing his first signs of life since the meeting began. He was the only person in the unit who dared call her by her whole name.

"I've been getting . . . feelings," Cassie said. "I can't be any more specific than that. Just something I pick up from the population—from the way people look at us, from the things they say when they think I don't understand: something big is about to go down, and it concerns HTE. Which means it concerns us."

The unit commanders traded looks. Baird sneered but said nothing. Caballeros of all flavors tended to trust their gut reactions. And they knew from long experience that Cassie's hunches were especially accurate.

"What've we got to lose?" Kali asked. "It's not as if we've got a lot of other jobs only Lieutenant Suthorn can do, after all."

"She's right," said Singer—White Nose Pony, Third Battalion's CO.

Bar-Kochba nodded. The Cowboy rabbi and the Navajo Singer—whose secondary occupation, which was also his callsign, was analogous to Bar Kochba's—were close friends. As experienced MechWarriors and leaders, their voices carried weight in council beyond even what their rank entitled them to. Because the two men thought along similar lines, they not infrequently found themselves forming a bloc against the younger and far more impulsive commander of First Battalion.

Cassie eyed Force Commander Camacho intently. Sometimes he seemed to go out of his way to ingratiate himself with her, sometimes to spite her. Gabby was hunkered down in his chair, a sullen expression marring his dark handsome features. Either he agreed with the older battalion commanders, or he was determined not to be shut out and lose face in front of his father, because he nodded abruptly and—uncharacteristically—held his tongue.

"What about the work Cassie's been doing?" asked Don Coyote, Adelante's CO. He was another lean and handsome *ranchero,* with a trim mustache, sideburns to the point of his jaw, and a devil's grin. Despite his last name, which was O'Rourke, and the color of his skin, which was black, he came from a Cerillos *norteño* family of great age and honor.

No wonder we give poor Archie fits, Cassie thought—incongruously, and to her own surprise, because in council she seldom thought about anything but her mission. She was still more surprised to discover that she thought of the FCNS reporter with more pleasure that contempt or even caution, though his real occupation was almost painfully obvious to her.

I'll have to steer clear of him, she told herself decisively.

"What?" sneered Bobby the Wolf, "touring the neighborhoods? Are we all going to take second jobs as janitors when things get too boring cooped up in the Compound?"

Singer's eyes narrowed in his weathered, leather-colored face. It was a tiny gesture that perhaps only Cassie caught; she never let any detail escape her and knew the Force Commander's expressions well.

"I like knowing about ground we might have to fight over," said O'Rourke, who thought that Bobby, Macho, Chango, and the other rougher-edged *norteños* were idiots. "Especially when it has the potential to contain, you know, surprises. For us or them—whoever *they* might turn out to be."

Don Coyote was a *Locust* pilot who specialized in recon work himself, frequently operating in close concert with Cassie. As far as she was concerned, even twenty tons of metal was a lot, and, no matter what kind of fancy sensors you had wrapped up with you in that armored cocoon, it basically isolated you from your surroundings. Within his limitations, though, he was good.

"Badlands can continue scouting the surroundings," Kali MacDougall pointed out. "If he needs or wants a 'Mech jock's perspective, I can go along. I don't have that much to do, either."

"First Battalion's rotating out to the Sportsplex tomorrow," Gabby Camacho pointed out in that bored voice he often affected when he was being contrary. In this instance, Cassie guessed he was fault-finding because Kali was a woman. Despite the fact that a sizable number of the Caballero MechWarriors were females, many of the men had trouble with that fact.

And Gabby's got reasons of his owns, she thought. Not that she was prepared to cut him any slack for that.

Kali shrugged. "So? Dark Lady's still likely to be down for a few days until Zuma gets the arm actuator fixed." As Senior Aztech, Zuma was entitled to attend the council, as was the equally absent Astro Zombie. Neither tech made any secret that he preferred working in the shop to sitting in on debates. "And it's not like it's that big a trip. I hop a train, and twenty minutes later I'm at the Sportsplex."

At least for a preliminary rotation, Colonel Camacho intended that each battalion remain on duty in the Compound for no more than a week. He knew full well how garrison duty sapped morale, something the Seventeenth could not afford.

His solution to the problem, as well as his doctrine in general, was incessant BattleMech drill. The intrinsically undisciplined Caballeros had one advantage over many regular soldiers they faced: most Caballeros—*norteño,* Cowboy, or Indian—had learned 'Mech piloting by handling AgroMechs almost from the day they learned to walk. Their gunnery skills weren't the greatest, their coordination was less than perfect, but as sheer 'Mech pilots they were right up with the Inner Sphere's best. Don Carlos was fanatical about keeping them sharp.

Tomorrow Adelante, Bronco, and Cochise Companies would depart by train and barge up the Yamato. Maccabee's Second Battalion—Deadeye, Eskiminzin, and Frontera—would take their places. First would drill with Third at the Sportsplex until it was Third's turn in the barrel.

"I've got training as a civil engineer," MacDougall said. "I know a little something about materials and structural strengths that might help the work along. And Father Bob can drill the boys and girls while I'm away."

The assembled commanders looked to Don Carlos. The Colonel's head had drooped again, his eyelids hanging low as if he were about to fall asleep.

He wasn't. Cassie knew what he was seeing on the insides of his eyelids.

How long can we go on, she wondered, *with him little more than a figurehead?* She feared this gig was bad for the Seventeenth, right now—the inaction, the loss of purpose that came with it. Yet the money Uncle Chandy was paying offered the prospect of a comeback from the terrible losses the Smoke Jaguars had inflicted on the Caballeros. The material losses, at least.

The other ones cut deeper. And they would be far more difficult to make good.

It had been the Colonel's best judgment that they accept this assignment among their ancient enemies, and his judgment remained sound. He still gave the Regiment everything he could. It was just that what he was *able* to devote to the Seventeenth kept diminishing.

Cassie tightened her mouth and gazed at the tabletop without focusing. Her world was in danger, and there was nothing she could do. She could only concentrate on those things that had kept her alive and functioning since childhood: her art and her work.

The Colonel raised his head and looked at her. The bags under his eyes seemed filled with lead.

"Do as you choose, Lieutenant," he said. "You're our scout. Keep us safe."

"Lieutenant? Talk to you a moment?"

Walking down the white anechoic corridor away from the briefing room, Cassie felt her jaw and the muscles between her shoulder blades go tense at the sound of that Cowboy-accented voice. She stopped.

"Sure, Captain," she said without turning.

Lady K came alongside her, stilting easily along on those damned long legs of hers. She looked down at the smaller woman with a guarded smile, then glanced around to make sure no one was within easy earshot.

"You seem to have some problems with me, Lieutenant," she said quietly. "In the past, that was fine—not everybody has to love me. But now that Suavecito's gone back to the League and I've got Bronco, we need to work together. I don't want any interference on the line between us if there's anything I can do about it."

Kali paused. "Let me buy you a drink and we can talk," she said, giving Cassie that dazzling smile that had surely melted many a 'Kicker heart throughout the Trinity.

Cassie ducked her head low and seethed. *Don't do this to me*, she thought furiously. *You're a MechWarrior and a blonde bimbo. Let it stay that way.*

Lady K's smile faded to a look of concern. "Please?"

Cassie sighed. "Yes, ma'am."

"Kali. Or Lady K."

Cassie just nodded. She didn't trust herself to speak.

Part Three

Dangerous Ground

Masamori, Hachiman
Galedon District, Draconis Combine
2 September 3056

The shiners Cowboy had caught when Cassie busted his nose were starting to clear up. He was in his usual spot by the bar, with the other usual suspects Buck and Reb, when Cassie and Lady K came into the Permissible Repose. The *former* Permissible Repose; the 'lleros had just about got Mr. Krishnamurti, the proprietor, talked into renaming the place The Sagebrush. They were even taking up a collection to buy him a new sign.

Cowboy rose and hoisted a glass to the two women as they walked toward the table by the musicbox in the corner of the mostly empty bar. "Evenin', ladies," he called out. "You two lovelies feelin' a trifle lonely tonight, here on this foreign world amongst all these Snakes?"

"Lonely, yes," Lady K said, "not desperate. Sit your skinny butt down, Cowboy."

His buddies laughed. After a moment he grinned and resumed his seat.

Kali paused by the table. Startled, Cassie realized her companion was letting her slide into the corner chair, from which she could keep an eye on the whole establishment. Grateful in spite of herself, she did so, while Lady K signaled to whichever of Mr. Krishnamurti's daughters was on duty tonight. The girl took their order, bowed, and scuttled away, making sure to steer a berth as wide as possible of the Cowboys at the bar.

A soft ranchero ballad played from the box, which had a sticker pasted on it for the mythical Radio KATN, printed up on some long-ago world. "I thought Cowboy was making some headway with one of Krishnamurti's girls," Kali observed. "Reckon this isn't the one."

Cassie looked at her. "I really shouldn't take too much time, Captain—" she began.

MacDougall sighed and shook her head. "Cassie, what have I done to get crosswise of you?"

"The Captain's behavior toward me has always been entirely correct," Cassie said in robot tones.

Lady K snorted. "That's a load of organic fertilizer if ever I heard one. All right, let's see ... maybe I can tell you what you don't like about me. I'm too tall, too blonde, and you reckon that maybe when the good Lord asked me what I wanted to help me along in this vale of tears, I said, Lord, give me a double helping of boobs, hold the brains. Am I dropping close to the target, Lieutenant Suthorn?"

Cassie stared at the other woman with enormous owl eyes while the chubby Krishnamurti daughter set a fruit juice down for Kali and a Borstal Boy beer for Cassie, bowed again, then scurried away again to elude Cowboy's amorous attentions.

Like a windowpane fracturing, Cassie broke into giggles. Lady K joined her. The giggles turned into gusty laughter as the male 'Mech jocks turned from the bar to stare.

Regaining control of herself, Cassie wiped tears from the corners of her eyes. She realized she had, well, overreacted again. Yet Lady K didn't seem to mind the display of somewhat inappropriate behavior. And she felt an undeniable sense of release that she could not explain.

"Yes, Captain," she said, "the target is destroyed."

Lady K sat back in her chair and took a hit of her juice. "The fact that I'm an *Atlas* pilot bothers you too, doesn't it? It was an *Atlas* blasted your house and killed your Daddy when you were a little girl, right?"

Cassie felt as if shutters had closed over her face again. Yes, it was, she knew now. An *Atlas* with nonstandard weaponry—not unusual among 'Mechs of the Inner Sphere, to say nothing of pirate raiders from the Periphery. When a warrior lost a major weapons system, sometimes he just had to jury-rig in whatever replacement was available. The system wasn't as smoothly efficient as the Clans' modular Omnis, but with enough ingenuity—or brute-force determination—it often worked. And a genius like Zuma on the job could often rival what the Clans could do.

"Cassie, Cassie, look, I'm sorry if I touched a nerve. I know why you feel the way you do about 'Mechs and MechWarriors, really I do. But, honey, I wasn't *there*. Shoot, I was maybe seven myself. Sure, I was learning to drive a busted-down old AgroMech around my daddy's spread back then, like any good little Cowgirl. But, believe me, nobody would've trusted me with an *Atlas* in those days."

Despite herself, Cassie found herself smiling again. It was turning out to be difficult to keep disliking the Captain. Maybe that was why she'd worked at it so hard all those years.

"Look, Cass," Kali said, "I can see why my looks put you off. A lot of people think I've got a little valve up here"—a hand fluffed blonde hair beside her left ear"—with a stencil next to it that reads, 'INFLATE TO ONE STANDARD LOCAL ATMOSPHERE.' And what the hey? I don't see any call to go 'round without bathing and with my hair hanging all matted in my eyes just so folks won't think I'm too blonde. I'm proud of the way I look. It's just that I don't let it define me. And if people think it does—"

The smile she showed then was not altogether pleasant. "—why, now, that can be downright useful sometimes, can't it?"

Cassie nodded slowly. Grudgingly. Her beer tasted flat.

"Besides, Cass, you don't come up any too short in the looks department yourself. Not by half, as that cute Limey newscaster would say, just to mention someone who follows you around as if his eyes were tethered to the seat of your trousers."

Cassie smiled, and to her astonishment felt her cheeks grow warm. "Me? I thought he—you—" She dropped her eyes, unable to look at MacDougall any longer.

"Some men like their women tall, blonde, and brassy. Others go for the dark, lithe, exotic types—you, for example. It's a big universe. And speaking just for myself, I'd be tempted to kill for that snub nose of yours and those almond-shaped gray eyes. Not to mention a metabolism that lets you eat like a Ranger bull in springtime and never gain a kilo."

Rangers were the main product of the Trinity worlds, gene-tailored crossbreeds of American bison, Spanish fighting bulls, Longhorns, and the Zebu, a.k.a. the Brahma bull. Father Doctor Bob said they almost perfectly reproduced the ancient aurochs, a strain of wild cattle so ferocious it hunted men. True or not, they were huge, monstrously strong, and unbelievably surly. There was a reason Southwestern ranch kids learned to pilot AgroMechs at a very early age. Rangers did not respect anything less—and a full-grown bull could take one down hard if the driver wasn't careful.

Cassie felt confusion bubble inside her, like silt obscuring the bottom of a clear mountain stream. She was aware of her attractiveness to men—had been much too aware of the fact, since childhood. She had put it to use often enough, as a street Arab and scam artist, and subsequently as a scout. Always the come-on, never coming across; she would never be a whore, no matter what. The memory of her mother was too strong for that. But Cassie could pull off the illusion.

It seemed that the only man she'd ever known who'd evinced no interest in her as a sexual being was Guru Johann. No, she knew what it was that had drawn him: the hunger inside her, that thing near madness that drove her from waking until dream-troubled sleep. It made her the perfect student, the ultimate receptacle for his lethal art, which he had poured into her like seed. Her hunger was to be his immortality, and so it had come to pass.

But Cassie had never thought of her physical attractiveness in such a benign way before. As if it might be something to enjoy for its own sake.

She felt a stab of hatred for the tall blonde captain then, so furious and white-hot it took her all aback. *I know myself, damn you!* she thought. *I know who I am and where I stand. And here you are, confusing things—*

She cut herself off before she could think the rest of the thought: *you scare me.* That was something she could never admit, that any individual made her afraid, especially not this pushy, pasty-faced *bolilla* bitch.

MacDougall had leaned subtly away. "I don't mean to rattle you, Cassie Suthorn," she said softly, as if gentling a frightened horse. "I like you, I admire you, I respect you. I know what you mean to the Regiment. I'm proud to call myself your comrade."

She reached out and laid a hand on Cassie's. "And if you'll let me, I'd be proud to call myself your friend."

Cassie raised her head. Kali MacDougall was looking at her, clear blue eyes level, mouth smiling. A smile of real warmth, not a pasted-on glossy grin. Cassie Suthorn, who could read most people's feelings as if they were written in LEDs across their faces, and who could hardly have said what she was feeling herself from one moment to the next, studied MacDougall's features as carefully as she had ever scrutinized anything in her life. She saw only friendship.

"I'd like that too, Captain," Cassie said before she could stop herself. Inside her a voice yammered, *I can't have friends! Friends always leave! Patsy was my friend, and she—*

"Kali," MacDougall said. She was looking past Cassie now, to spare the other woman the direct pressure of her gaze without actually looking away.

Cassie drew in a deep breath, from the diaphragm, the way Guru had taught her. Control your breath, and you can control the fear, he always said. She could not make it go away, but she could prevent it from mastering her.

She tried to pass discomfort off with levity. "I guess I made some assumptions about you, Kali," she said. "I thought you were more, like, well—Lieutenant Hurd."

Kali laughed. "I know what you mean. Annie Sue seems kind of naive at times, but she's a good enough kid." She sipped her juice. "Hmm, I call her kid and she's older than I am. Guess that's the way she is. But she handles that old *Rifleman* pretty fair, and Lord knows that isn't easy."

At sixty tons, the *Rifleman* was considered a heavy BattleMech. Most modern 'Mech pilots also considered it a deathtrap. It had a decent punch to it, particularly at intermediate ranges, and its two big Imperator autocannons provided highly desirable long-range, low-heat firepower. But it had the worst vices of both heavy and medium 'Mechs: a medium's armor mated to a heavy's speed. That made it a support weapon, like an old-style self-propelled gun; it couldn't survive in a furball. Caballero that she was, Avengin' Annie had gotten the most out of her Little Sure Shot in more than a score of battles.

"Yeah," Cassie said. "She's steady enough on the firing line. But, I mean, she carries that teddy bear in the cockpit with her."

"Bunny Bear," Lady K said, and shrugged. "I have a teddy bear too. Name's Albert. 'Course, I don't carry him around in Dark Lady with me, but, you know, whatever gets you through the night."

Cassie made a face, but nodded. *Whatever gets you through*

the night was something of an unofficial credo of the free-swinging, high-living Seventeenth. To the 'lleros, how a person lived was her own damn business, as long as she was there when it hit the pot—as the damnably clever Captain MacDougall had just reminded Cassie. There was something else in the way Kali was looking at her, not threatening, but unnerving in a way Cassie couldn't pin down.

She didn't get much chance to try, because just then the door to the street opened in a puff of smells of wet asphalt and exhaust fumes. The Repose was on a side street, off the approved hover-route, and though it was at basement-level, the short steps led straight down from the street without a dogleg or baffles to keep the customers from being blown into the jukebox whenever a blower cruised by. Outside it was raining.

A figure slipped inside, stepped quickly left to clear the doorway. He was a startling apparition, a young man with a wolf's face and a black eye patch, a shock of black hair, a leather jacket fallen artlessly open to reveal elaborate tattoos twining the right shoulder visible beneath his tank-top. He looked around the bar, tipped the toothpick he was chewing up to his upper lip and smiled.

"Uh-oh," said Cassie. Under her own jacket she made sure Blood-drinker was loose in her sheath.

"What do we have here?" Kali murmured, sliding down and around in her chair just enough for her peripheral vision to pick up the door without being obvious about it. "A man who's proud of his tats, looks like."

"Those are *irezumi*," Cassie said. "He's yakuza."

Lady K pursed his lips. "Trouble?"

Wearing a worried look, Mr. Krishnamurti started to bustle out from behind the bar. Unfolding himself from his habitual barstool, Cowboy sent the proprietor trotting back on his heels against the bottles on their shelves with a friendly backhand push to the sternum.

"Lemme handle this, Hawkeye." The boys had started calling the bar owner "Hawkeye" for no very obvious reason.

"Could be," Cassie said in answer to Kali's question.

Thumbs tucked into his belt, Cowboy rolled toward the newcomer with an exaggerated bowleg stance, despite the fact that he hadn't been on an actual horse in years.

"Howdy," he said. "Reckon you know by now you wandered into the wrong place. This here's an *exclusive* kinda establishment—"

The newcomer looked up at the lanky Cowboy, who was a head taller than he was, and smiled wider. Then he jammed a stiffened forefinger into Cowboy's solar plexus.

"Not any longer," he said in crisp, Drac-accented English as Cowboy doubled over. The newcomer glanced at Cowboy's two companions, who had jumped to their feet at the bar.

About that time Cowboy nailed the yak with a loopy right that originated down around his pointy-toe lizard-skin boots. The one-eyed man flew back against a poster of Purple Tailfeathers and kind of slouched there, sorting it all out.

"Whoo," Lady K said, getting to her feet. Cassie noticed that she was suddenly wearing gloves—ladylike buckskin gloves. Until a few minutes ago, Cassie would've chalked it up as an affectation worthy of Avengin' Annie. With her new perspective, it occurred to her that even light gloves enabled a body to hit somebody full-out in the head with a much reduced risk of breaking something. For the puncher, that is.

A few more yakuza came darting in, jackets slick with rain. One looked over at the still-dazed, one-eyed man. The other cracked his knuckles and began to advance purposefully on Cowboy, who, having delivered himself of a righteous payback shot, had returned to the important business of bending over and groaning.

Cassie made a face but did not rise. She wasn't much for recreational combat. Her go-arounds with Macho and Cowboy that first night in the bar had not been sport, but rather communication. She wouldn't back her buddies in a casual dustup, a fact that they all knew and accepted—but if things turned deadly, she'd be right in the midst of them, striking like a cobra.

"Stop." The word wasn't loud but it cracked, as if it carried the supersonic harmonics of a gunshot. The yaks froze. So did Reb and Buck, who were just making their way over from the bar.

Another figure now stood in the doorway, silhouetted black against a drizzle illuminated by the streetlight at the corner, so that it seemed to be a haze of drifting light-motes.

A moment, and then the figure stepped inside. It was a woman in tight leather pants and a bulky leather jacket, a woman standing taller even than Lady K's 170 centimeters. She had golden skin, freckles scattered across a snubbed nose, red-brown eyes with pronounced epicanthic folds, and a wild profusion of startling red hair, the kind of mop that can't be tamed, and shouldn't be.

The three male yaks snarled but fell back, convincing Cassie that this whole little scene was a put-up job of some sort. The yakuza—the Combine's well-organized underworld—had a strong sense of hierarchy, and the tall redhead was obviously in command.

Maybe literally, Cassie decided, because all four of the intruders wore patches showing a skull sporting wings. Obvious unit insignia. And she, of course, knew exactly which unit.

"Cowboy," said Kali MacDougall, who had stepped forward to face the newcomers. "Payback's a mother. Now let it ride."

"Aw, *Kali*," Cowboy said, straightening as if nothing had happened. The right leg of his cammie pants dropped back down to the instep of his boot. He hadn't quite got it hiked up enough while doubled over in apparent agony to get his hide-out dirk into play. At least he hadn't gone for the *left* boot, where the ten-millimeter double-derringer rode.

Cassie stood up and came forward. "Captain MacDougall," she said, "let me introduce *Tai-sa* Eleanor Shimazu, commander of the Ninth Ghost Regiment. Colonel Shimazu, this is Captain Kali MacDougall, commander of B Company, First Battalion of the Seventeenth."

"I'm honored," Shimazu said, and extended her hand for Lady K to shake. Then she turned to Cassie with one flaming eyebrow raised.

"And who are you, that you know who I am?"

Cassie grinned. "This is Lieutenant Junior Grade Cassie Suthorn," Lady K said dryly. "She's our best scout, and darned near as good as she thinks she is."

The Ghost colonel nodded. "A unit needs a good scout," she said, and then broke into a sudden grin. It was a good grin, but it passed quickly, like a leaf blowing down the street in the autumn Hachiman wind.

The one-eyed Ghost was standing without the help of either of his friends or the wall now. He rubbed his jaw and looked appraisingly at Cowboy.

"Good right," he said.

Cowboy snorted a laugh. "You sport a pretty mean finger, hoss." He stuck out his hand. "I'm Cowboy."

After only momentary hesitation the one-eyed man shook it. "Buntaro Mayne," he said, his voice giving no sign of the fact that Cowboy was trying to mash his hand to paste.

After a moment Cowboy's eyes got wide. Sweat started at the line of his dark hair. Another moment and the yakuza relented, letting the other man have his hand back.

"Buy you a drink?" Cowboy said, trying not to shake his mangled fingers.

"Sure thing," Mayne accepted with a grin.

Tai-sa Shimazu accepted a seat at the corner table with Cassie and Lady K. "Pardon my ignorance," MacDougall said, "but isn't *tai-sa* a few grades light to command the Ninth? I thought the Drac ... onians put only generals in charge of regiments."

Shimazu showed her half a smile. "Such is the common practice," she said. "But the regulars of the DCMS would be scandalized beyond measure were a yakuza to be granted general's rank. Much less a woman."

The on-duty Krishnamurti daughter came trundling up to take the newcomer's order. The colonel ordered Old Stick and Sack—Hotei Black Label—neat. Kali signaled to put it on her tab. Shimazu's eyes narrowed briefly, but the smooth skin of her face remained unwrinkled, and she said nothing. She was calculating the extent of the obligation the mercenary officer was laying upon her, and finding it acceptable, Cassie knew. She'd learned the same assessment reflex herself among the expatriate Dracs on Larsha.

Shimazu leaned forward. Closer in, her eyes glowed strangely in the muted yellow gleam of the lights. The strength of her personality seemed to glow from her like heat from overworked 'Mech's sinks; she was like a force of nature.

Cassie slid a little to the side in her chair, hooked one arm over the back. At the same time she saw Lady K lean slightly forward, place her forearm on the table. It was Cassie's way to bend to the forces of nature, Kali's to stand up to them—and neither woman's way to give in.

From the colonel's slight pause Cassie guessed she hadn't missed the unspoken dynamics of posture either. No surprise. In the Combine the unspoken—*haragei*, "belly talk"—could be as important as what was said aloud.

"I observe that there are an unusual number of women in your unit," Shimazu said, "with a fair percentage in positions of command. Is that often the way in the Free Worlds League, then?"

She was showing two could play Cassie's game of knowing. Just about every detail of any DCMS unit's composition and deployment was considered a military secret, but as a courtesy, the mercenaries had been provided the names of the commanders of the Combine unit on-planet, the Ghosts. Given the flamboyance of the Ninth's commander, it was inevitable that she became a recognizable presence. Uncle Chandy's security people, whom Cassie had invited to drinks in on-site commissaries, had plenty to say about her, most of it gossip.

Of course, all the Colonel had to do for information on the Seventeenth was ask. Chandrasekhar Kurita had been compelled to provide the planetary government a complete TO&E on his merc unit before they could get permission to drop out of orbit. What Shimazu was mainly demonstrating was that she too had done her homework.

Kali laughed softly. "Not hardly." Having made her point about personal space, she leaned back and relaxed again. "Fact is, our little corner of the League, what most people call the Southwestern worlds, is about as male-chauvinist as anyplace you can find, Colonel. So what's a lady with a taste for adventure—or at least, no taste for being an obedient little baby-factory and homemaker—what's she gonna do? Join the army and take it from there, basically."

Shimazu nodded. "I understand you fought the Clans on Jeronimo." Which proved she'd gotten intelligence digests from the ISF, too; Uncle Chandy hadn't been required to put *that* on any forms.

A faraway look came into Kali MacDougall's eyes, and she sighed. "Yeah, we did at that. Left near half our people there, too—rotting, 'cause we never leave the living behind. Fought alongside the Combine troops."

Shimazu nodded. "I know. I lost friends there, too. And against the Ghost Bears, when we fought them on Alshain."

The drinks came. Shimazu tossed hers back without showing a reaction, then leaned forward. "What do you think about how to fight them?" she asked. "Everybody knows we're going to be up against them again, too soon. Our Coordinator remembers that, even if the other Great House leaders have become distracted by their petty dynastic squabbles. Just as if the Clans had never come—the fools."

"Hon, you got that right," Lady K said. "What we learned when we went up against the Clans was that we had to remember two main things: how the Clans fight and how they think *we* fight. . . ."

Buntaro Mayne leaned his back to the bar with a whiskey bottle clutched in one hand. His two yak brothers sat at a table near the door, watching. They weren't expecting trouble, least of all from the Friendly Persuaders. But you didn't last long under *Tai-sa* Shimazu if you started taking things for granted. Since for most members of *Heruzu Enjeruzu* the alternative to service was slam, it paid to be attentive.

"How do you like being under the command of women?" he asked, taking a long pull.

"Well, it ain't what Daddy raised me for," Cowboy said. He sat facing the bar, propped on his elbows. "But honesty compels me to point out, Buntaro old pal, that Cap'n Mac ain't rightly my commander. She's Bronco's CO. I'm with Adelante."

He took a hit from his own bottle. "You?"

Mayne shrugged. "It took some getting used to," he admitted. "But the Colonel . . . is clearly most fit to command."

Cowboy nodded. "Well, I got to say that *el patrón*—that's Don Carlos, our Colonel—ain't one to just raffle off company commands. Pure and simple, Lady K's got what it takes."

"In more ways than one," Reb said through a haze of cigarette smoke.

"Don't underestimate the skinny little one, either," said Buck Evans, who was standing between Cowboy and Reb. "She busted old Cowboy's beak for him last week, just for runnin' a friendly little scam on a newbie."

Mayne looked at Cassie, who was sitting listening intently to the conversation passing between MacDougall and the Ghost commander. "What do you think they find to talk about with such interest?" he asked.

Cowboy shrugged. "Oh, the usual," he said. "Clothes, hair, all like that." He hefted his bottle. "Say, this thing's running low. Hawkeye, hustle your butt on over here and top off my tank before I die of thirst."

═══ 14 ═══

Masamori, Hachiman
Galedon District, Draconis Combine
3 September 3056

"**A**h, Eleanor-*san*," the man behind the big black desk said through a lipless reptile smile, "so good to see you."

Lainie Shimazu was glad of all her extensive practice at remaining expressionless as she approached the great man. "*Oyabun,*" she said. "The pleasure and honor it gives me to see you are without measure."

Which, as far as it goes, she thought, *is the absolute truth.*

The yakuza leader was a small man with an almost earless head perched on a skinny neck emerging from his black, Western-style suit coat. He looked quite like a turtle.

Behind him a clear wall—transpex, the projectile-proof synthetic used in BattleMech viewscreens—gave a breathtaking panoramic view of Hachiman's capital in all its chaotic glory. The orange morning sunlight filled the room almost tangibly, like a smell, softening the intentionally spartan decor and creating an illusion, not of cleanliness—the janitorial staff kept the offices spotless, of course—but of purity.

Kazuo Sumiyama's office occupied the 100th-floor penthouse of the Sumiyama Building, headquarters of Sumiyama-*kai*, the Sumiyama Society: the largest yakuza organization on Hachiman. It was all quite open; the Society's name and logo were displayed on the front doors of the building, in three-story letters on each face of the structure, and as *mon*, crests, on the right-breast pockets of the midnight blue blazers worn by the two goons who stood flanking the *oyabun* and slightly behind him.

Gaijin were always astounded by the overtness of the yakuza presence in the Combine. The yakuza conducted their aboveground operations with the full knowledge and tacit consent of the police, and by extension, the ISF. One major reason for that was simply tradition; it had always been thus, in the Combine and in pre-spaceflight Japan before. And in the Draconis Combine, tradition had nearly the force of law.

There were other reasons for police forbearance, too, of course. Lainie knew them well. And the new Coordinator's long-standing alliance with the yakuza clans was only one among them.

"Please sit down." Sumiyama gestured to a chair waiting before his desk. The desk itself was carved from a single piece of native Hachiman ebony, and gleamed like obsidian. With its high metallic content, the wood was dense and difficult to work. It was also supposed to be very effective at stopping small-arms rounds, and to take a while for a man-portable laser to burn through.

The chair of curved chromed-steel tubing and black synthetic leather was not comfortable, nor was it meant to be. Lainie dropped into it in as much of a sprawl as respect for the *oyabun*—"father figure"—would permit.

At that, she was crowding the envelope, no new experience for her. The bulkier of Sumiyama's bodyguards growled low in his throat. A gigantic man, much of him was fat and just as much was not. His face was the color of tanned boot leather, with a bit of purplish tinge. His cheeks bulged outward around an oft-mashed nose and thrusting jaw almost as if swollen by some disease. Above them, his eyes were sinister slits.

A *sumitori* forced to retire from competition by certain allegations of impropriety, the man went by the name of Emma. It was not the female given name, but rather the name of the Buddhist King of Hell and judge of the dead. It was also *ingo*—yakuza street slang—for pliers, for King Emma often used such instruments to pull the teeth of the unrighteous, to help put their minds straight. They were also used by this Emma for the very same purpose; that and a fancied resemblance to the literally bull-headed deity gave the former *sumo* wrestler his name.

Lainie ignored him. The other bodyguard, a round-eye named Sutton who was almost as tall as Emma and of a more conventionally athletic build, caught her eye and winked. Lainie ignored that, too.

I'm long past having to yield myself to the likes of you, lit-

tle man, she thought. And that was just one more obligation she owed the Coordinator.

No sooner had she sat than the *oyabun* rose and went to stand looking out the window-wall. "Ah, Masamori," he breathed, "precious jewel of the Combine. Yet how much you have changed since this young woman first came to you as a *kyakubun.*" The word meant "guest member." As in, of a yakuza gang.

He turned back to face her. "Not all the changes have been for the better. Don't you agree, Lainie-*chan*?"

The skin seemed to stretch itself almost to the bursting point over Lainie's high cheekbones. Adrenaline sang in her ears. *I will not let him see me react.* The suffix meant *treasure,* a phrase similar to saying, "my dear." Its use in this context implied possession.

"The reforms of the Coordinator, and his father before him, have been a blessing to us all," she said in a neutral voice. "But the changes brought by the Clans have not been favorable, surely."

It was Sumiyama's turn to swallow his reaction. For all that Theodore Kurita had legitimized the yakuza as never before by making them partners in the fight against the Clans, the reforms begun by Takashi and continued by his son did not sit well with the underworld.

Lainie's politics began and ended with loyalty to Theodore Kurita, though her *understanding* of politics was rather broader. She knew full well that criminals tended by nature to be intensely conservative. If anything, the yakuza were even more so. The status quo suited them wonderfully, and had for over a millennium, since long before any of them had left Terra.

Theodore Kurita had pressured his father to loosen the strictures on Combine society, and had himself continued the process. Of all the powers that be, the yakuza were the only ones likely to oppose such measures. The army adored Theodore, the former Gunji no Kanrei, or Deputy for Military Affairs. The Order of Five Pillars was serenely confident in its ability to hold the souls of the Combine's populace, at least in the face of temporal change. The dreaded ISF, headed by that master of expediency, the Smiling One, knew just how damned difficult it was to maintain the harsh controls on Combine life. And both organizations were run by personal allies of Theodore's.

Yakuza influence, iceberg-like in its proportion of seen to unseen, was enormous. By embracing the underworld in a qualified way, Theodore had opened to the Draconis Combine Mustered Soldiery an enormous pool of badly needed funds and manpower from the Unproductive class, to which all yakuza technically belonged. To most, that was sufficient explanation for the act. But Lainie knew that perhaps equally significant had been Theodore's desire to make it difficult for the yakuza bosses to interfere with his political agenda.

That didn't mean they all had to like it. Kazuo-*sama* certainly didn't. Which was why Lainie liked to rub his nose discreetly in it whenever possible.

It was her subtle way of reminding him that he no longer owned her. Because she *wasn't a kyakubun* anymore, wasn't the same terrified teenage runaway who had fled across a quarter of the Combine to escape the men who'd murdered her father. Back then she'd been forced to throw herself upon Sumiyama's mercy, and he had not hesitated to avail himself of the opportunity.

Theodore-sama *freed me from you,* Lainie thought. *And that's why I'll follow him till I die.*

"You have met with some of these new *gaijin* mercenaries Chandrasekhar Kurita has imported," the *oyabun* said. "What do you think of them?"

This was Sumiyama's way of reminding her he had spies in her outfit, which was no surprise. "They are seasoned troops," she said. "The ones I met seemed competent enough. Still, they're foreigners."

He nodded, pleased by what he took for her dismissal of the Seventeenth's abilities. "It is a scandal that he should import such trash," he said. "As if you and the Regulars were not enough to defend against any possible threat! Truly, it is a slap in your face, my child."

"Perhaps Uncle Chandy—"

"Do not refer to him that way! He is a Kurita."

Lainie bowed her head. "Yes, *oyabun*." Her eyes had gone the color of blood. "Perhaps Chandrasekhar-*san* intends them as playthings. Ornaments to his ego."

Sumiyama nodded. He liked that thought. "Chandrasekhar is a Kurita," he said, turning away again, "but he is a fruit that has fallen a very great distance from the tree. He was exiled from court in his youth for being a wastrel—yes, and a fool." He regarded her with hands clasped behind his back, giving her time to appreciate that *he* could speak of Chandrasekhar Kurita in any tone he wished.

"A fool," he said again. "And he has continued to play the fool on Hachiman."

He's such a fool that he built HTE from nothing until it threatens to rival your pals at Tanadi, Lainie thought, but she said nothing.

"You are undoubtedly aware that his security forces have taken to chasing our people from the vicinity of his Compound," Sumiyama went on. "Suddenly we are deprived of licensing and protection fees across a vast area of the city!"

Lainie had to drop her eyes then. The image of her new acquaintance Captain MacDougall in her 100-ton *Atlas* confronting Sumiyama's soldiers out extorting protection money from the small shopkeepers was almost too much. A sight she'd most definitely pay to see. She liked the mercenary officer, recognizing that the other woman was in her own way nearly as formidable as Lainie herself. Then again, the tall blonde didn't seem half so dangerous as her quieter, smaller friend. A coiled ball of malice, that one.

"But worse than that," the *oyabun* continued, caught up in his righteous indignation, "he has cut the hours of his workers. Again!"

This time Lainie had to bite her lip to keep from laughing. "Now he has them working ten hours a day. Ten! As if twelve was not a sufficiently scandalous indulgence! The other six hours of the proper workday he *gives* to them."

He shook his head as if trying to clear it of water before hauling it back inside his shell. "Oh, he says that his employees are still at work during those additional hours. 'The Dragon's time,' he calls it. He claims it is to be used by his workers to improve themselves or to bolster their bonds with their broods of squalling brats or otherwise work to strengthen the Dragon. Nonsense, I call it, and nonsense it is! I know these Laborers. A pack of lazy louts, all of them. The whip is all they understand. They will fritter the time away, mark my words. Fritter!"

He rounded on her furiously. "A man such as that eats away at the very foundations of our society. No matter how noble a family name he bears!"

Because they were speaking Japanese—which allowed Sumiyama to maintain the self-delusion that he was an important businessman, and not a thug who was virtually *eta*, a casteless pariah—Lainie was able to pass that off with a brief mutter that sounded like agreement. *Aimai*, that built-in ambiguity of the Combine overculture's tongue, had its definite advantages.

He took a deep breath, faced the window, placed his hands on it. Several kilometers away a barge chugged up the Yamato with the giant manlike form of a mercenary Battle-Mech strapped supine to its deck. Lainie wondered if it might be Lady K's *Atlas*. The pollution-haze made it impossible to tell. Hachiman was a clean world by Combine standards, but Masamori was not a very clean city.

"But there is a fresh wind blowing, Lainie-*chan*," Sumiyama said. "A wind that will blow the weakness and corruption from the streets of our city as the autumn wind off the Yamato dispels the smog. I can tell you no more now, my child—only that you and your men will have your part to play."

He smiled smugly at her. "I have every faith that you will continue to serve me as loyally as in the past."

Lainie rose and bowed to him. "I live only to fulfill my duty, *oyabun*."

And if you believe I owe any of that duty to you, you shriveled degenerate, she thought, *perhaps you will one day get what's coming to you.*

"There, there, little bird," said the man in the sports jacket with the extravagantly padded shoulders. "Why do you weep?"

The girl sat on a crate with a squawking blue-furred native heath-hen inside. Her dress-robe, cobalt blue with dark blue figuring, clinging to a slim but definitely unobjectionable figure, was typical of what a country girl might buy to wear to the big city for the first time. What a bumpkin might think fashionable without being too risqué.

The man knelt down next to her. He almost put a hand on her knee, but somehow managed to resist the impulse. He was large and blond and ungainly, and younger than he tried to come across.

Around them the street-market crowd flowed like a river. Graceful women balanced baskets of fruit and fowl-crates on their heads. Men cried wares from containers slung to carrying-poles braced across their shoulders. It was a side of

Masamori that might strike a stranger as incongruous, this village-market activity in the shadow of hundred-story bronze towers. But it was as vital a part of the city as the underground maglev trains and the glittering nightclubs.

It was also an area the Friendly Persuaders didn't like to enter. Even in pairs.

"Come on, now, missy," the blond young man said. "Why're you crying like that?"

The girl stopped and looked at him. Her mascara had run down her cheeks. The effect would have been comical had she not been quite so lovely, with her sculpted-mahogany features and slanted smoke-gray eyes.

"I . . . I'm from offworld," she said, her words so full of glottal stops from swallowed sobs that she might have been speaking some exotic language. "From Kawabe, in Matsuida Prefecture. I used up all my money to come and stay with my aunt because she was sick. And then I got here and find she's dead, and now someone has stolen my bag, and my papers are gone, and *annhh*—"

Sobs overcame her. She buried her face against his biceps. He clumsily patted her back, becoming aware of the smooth, sweat-damp skin left bare above the neckline of her robe and the way the garment molded itself to her body, which was trembling against his. Somehow he did not mind that her makeup was staining his coat, with its jags of color against a white background.

"There, there," he said. "Surely it's not so bad as all that."

"But I have no money and no place to stay and I can't even *work* if I don't have papers!" She had raised her head to suck in a ragged breath, then let it all out again in a tumbling exhalation of words. She inhaled once more, like a swimmer beached after nearly drowning. "I don't know what I'll do!"

A thought began to form in the mind of the man in the sports jacket. He tipped his snap-brim hat back from his forehead with his thumb. "Well," he said, drawing the word out long, "you don't always need papers to work."

She raised her head and looked at him. Another sob ran through her body like a temblor. "But the police—"

He chuckled. "The police don't know everything. Lots of things the police don't even want to know."

She stared at him, practically gaping. She really was a total potato, and what could you expect from a backwater hole like Kawabe? But the girl was truly stunning, in spite of that.

Suddenly she jumped up, tried to bolt. He caught her by the arm. "You're an agent of the ISF," she said, struggling. "You're trying to trap me. I know!"

He threw back his head and laughed, being careful not to slacken his grip. "Little bird, you watch too much holovid. I'm not with the Dragon's Breath—not even a Friendly Persuader. Though I do have connections. Here, sit down. People are staring."

People weren't—it didn't do to look at anything too directly in the twisty byways of Masamori—but the girl allowed herself to be drawn back down to sit on the crate. Its occupant shook its wings and muttered to itself, miffed that its cries of outrage weren't heeded.

"My name's Peter," he said. "What's yours?"

"M-Mitsuko."

"There, Mitsuko." He chucked her under the chin. "Like I said, not every place is so picky about papers. You just have to know the right people."

She sniffed. Her nose was snubbed. Her eyes were very large, rimmed by smeared dark makeup. "But I don't know anybody!"

"That's not true." He rose, held out a hand to lift her to her feet. "You know me."

$$=== 15 ===$$

Masamori, Hachiman
Galedon District, Draconis Combine
4 September 3056

The girl with the dress slit up to here and the lustrous black hair piled atop her head slipped through the mob at the Kit-Kat Klub like an eel through water. She dropped her tray on the bar, turned around, and gave the young blond man a smile as dazzling as his sports coat. "Peter-*san*," she said, "I have something for you."

His dull blue eyes lit briefly, before it dawned on him that she would hardly give him *that* here, in the middle of a crowded bar. "Oh," he said.

Spotting a mark is an arcane art. Cassie could not articulate exactly how she did it, though she'd tried once or twice for the benefit of the occasional confidante she'd picked up and kept as a pet back on Larsha. Nowadays she wouldn't try. It was too personal a revelation.

The two main considerations were straightforward, though. The mark had to a) have something the scammer wanted; and b) show signs that the scammer could get it away from him. It was spotting those signs that had made scamming an art and a challenge to Cassie as a child. Playing on them had always been the easy part.

Nowadays she only scammed when and as her job required it, but that didn't stop her from feeling a certain thrill of the hunt. Even when the object of the scam was to obtain a menial job as a waitress in a scummy dive.

The key was, it was a *yak* dive.

The task was not as easy as it might seem. Combine culture was very much a village culture, no less in a megalopolis like Masamori than on a hayseed world like Kawabe.

Mizo-shobai, the water trade, tended not to look too closely at the antecedents of those who practiced it. But you still had to know somebody. You couldn't just blow in off the street and expect a job—not from a greengrocer, not from a striptease club.

And especially not from a bar frequented by low- to mid-level yakuza soldiers. The yaks had a modus vivendi with the Civilian Guidance Corps—and, on a much more tacit level, with the ISF, based on the fact that the yakuza were loudly ultra-nationalistic, big boosters of the Dragon, and Subhash Indrahar didn't care diddly about street crime. Still, the bulk of yakuza operations were against the law, and the Friendly Persuaders had a façade of absolute control to keep up. So spies happened sometimes.

A bar was a sacred kind of place in the Combine. It was an accepted refuge where loyal servants of the Dragon, from the lowliest Worker to *sararimen* in their rumpled suits, could gather to relax after working their long hours. Those who didn't join their comrades for an after-shift snort were looked upon with suspicion, and sometimes even spied upon by the ISF for being insufficiently Harmonious.

Yak soldiers had shorter hours—if they wanted to work sixteen-hour shifts, they wouldn't be criminals and Unproductives—but they still loved the easy camaraderie of the watering-hole as avidly as the shop-floor warriors and grunt laborers with sunburned necks. And they wanted to be able to gossip and talk shop, just like everybody else kicking back in a bar. So they were particular who they hired, in their own way.

If there was one thing Cassie was good at, it was convincing people she wasn't a police spy. And she had good credentials: Peter Malloy was a rising young soldier—not rising fast, mind you, but steady, and palpably one of the boys. If he vouched for his little pal Mitsuko the Potato from Kawabe, she couldn't be a plant.

But big-hearted as Peter liked to think he was, his vouching was a favor. And favors came at a price.

Before Petey-pal could manifest too much disappointment, she pressed something into his hand, then stood on tiptoe for a quick peck on the cheek. "Thank you," she whispered into his ear.

Malloy stared down at the object she'd given him. It was

a combination pen and laser pointer, made of real silver and showing fine workmanship. It was just the sort of status symbol a soldier about to make the jump to junior management might like to flash.

The little waitress had picked up her tray and almost blended back into the crowd when the awful truth dawned on him: she had discharged her debt. That meant she would feel no obligation to bed with him.

Peter Malloy was in the strong-arm end of operations, and did not handle disappointment well. He tucked the pen into the inside pocket of his jacket—it was worth hanging onto, after all—then extended his arm and laid his hand heavily on the girl's shoulder.

She spun easily, without dropping her tray. "Hey," Malloy shouted. "You think you're gonna get off just like that? You *owe* me, bitch!"

"Eddie-*sama!*" she squealed, in a voice that cut through the babble and tinny music like a *katana*. "Eddie-*sama*, look!"

A giant figure loomed up behind Pete Malloy. His sports coat was in as garish bad taste as the soldier's, but the shoulders were almost twice as wide, and the difference wasn't in the extravagant padding. His face was the color of native ebony, and his rust-red hair was drawn up in a samurai topknot, a fashion currently reserved in Masamori for those who had attained at least *chunin*—subleader—status within Sumiyama-*kai*. Eddie Katsumori was not a very big fish in the Organization, but he was top barracuda in the pond of the Kit-Kat Klub.

"What?" Eddie asked in a voice like an *Atlas'* footsteps. He was a man of few words. They tended to put off hitting people longer than he liked.

With deft fingers the waitress twitched open Pete Malloy's sports jacket. "That silver pen you lost, Eddie-*sama*," she said. "See? This *chimpira* swiped it!"

It came into Pete Malloy's mind that he was well and truly sautéed. He opened his mouth.

Eddie saved him the disgrace of uttering a denial that would not be believed by smashing his face with a quick right that sent Malloy flying into the crowd. The crowd, anticipating just this turn of events, opened before him as if by magic, so as not to interfere with his flight time. His head slammed against the musicbox, making the Purple Tailfeathers squawk indignantly and jitter briefly, as if fire ants had gotten into their tights. Next to the box a tutelary statue of elephant-headed Ganesha, god of thieves, teetered and almost toppled from its niche. A hand missing its little finger caught the idol and eased it back in place.

Two of Eddie's *hatamoto* were flanking the hapless Malloy by the time he subsided into a heap on the *tatami* that covered the floor. One relieved him of the stolen pen. Then they caught him under the armpits, dragged him to the back entrance, and pitched him into the alley.

Eddie had already lost interest in the proceedings. He grunted and flipped a coin to the waitress and turned back to the bar. The crowd, meanwhile, had returned to the serious business of drinking.

Cassie caught the coin with casual aplomb, slipped it into a pocket, then resumed her rounds almost without missing a beat. She hadn't even watched her former benefactor's brief, inglorious flight.

She felt no remorse for his fate. She had tried to square things with him, but only because the whole point of the exercise was to hang around this locale for a while, rather than the fast fade that usually followed a successful touch. It was easier to pay off and avoid trouble.

She'd suspected Petey might not care for the coin he got paid in. But Cassie always covered her bets. If Malloy hadn't gotten greedy, big Eddie never would've had a clue as to the whereabouts of his favorite pen.

The issue was likely settled. The Sumiyama lieutenant thought she'd done him a favor, and had tipped her to get out from under the *on*, the obligation. If Petey showed his face in here again, he'd get it smashed again and worse.

Of course it might occur to him to lay for the presumptuous potato and settle accounts with her outside the confines of the Kit-Kat. But that would be the worst mistake of his life. Also the last one.

"Here, girl! Bring some more beer!" Cassie plastered a smile across her features and scurried to obey. Her mind was once again a Void, but her eyes and ears were open.

With a lifetime of practice at showing only those emotions she chose to, Cassie found it easy not to smile when she felt the jostle on the narrow noonday street.

She wore her long black hair coiled in a braid at the back of her head and a DCMS aerospace jock's jacket against the autumn chill blowing down the Yamato from the mountains. The jacket displayed no unit patches, and everyone knew the Combine wasn't wasting any of its aerospace assets, already stretched membrane-thin, on a low-threat world like Hachiman. To any onlooker the jacket would have suggested that Cassie was probably flight crew off a Drac merchant spacer, pushing the envelope of Combine sumptuary laws. Even before the current permissiveness, that would have been nothing out of the ordinary on Hachiman. The *Masakko* were loyal sons and daughters of the Dragon, but they figured their devotion entitled them to expect him to look the other way if they didn't hew to the letter of every last petty regulation his servants saw fit to impose. The people of Masamori reckoned that they and the Dragon were like *that*.

Observation of the rules tended to be especially lax here in Sodegarami, Masamori's lively *ukiyo*, across the river from the HTE complex.

Cassie was just cruising, like a spacer scoping the lowlife district in advance of a nocturnal excursion or one unwilling to wait for the sun to roll below the horizon. Anything that could be had in Masamori's Floating World—which was *anything*—could be had in daylight as easily as dark. But the semi-licit pliers of Sodegarami's version of the water trade were creatures of the night. In daytime like this, they were just going through the motions.

So she walked along with her hands in her pockets, craning around at the strip clubs, geisha parlors—which, around here, *was* a euphemism for "whorehouse"—and the pachinko halls as if undecided where she was going to blow the thick roll that bulked out the right rear pocket of her whipcord trousers.

Sodegarami's main drag, Camellia Way, was closed to vehicular traffic. When the rightmost of the two young men, seemingly lost in emphatic conversation, who loomed up from the pedestrian-stream in front of Cassie accidentally bumped into her, she knew that somebody had decided to make up her mind for her.

The dip was good, the touch feather-light. Even Cassie might not have noticed if her peripheral vision hadn't been tuned way out just as Guru had taught her, so that she made out almost no detail but was sensitive to motion in an incredibly wide arc.

Even before he could get her wallet out, she had the pickpocket's hand bent backward toward his forearm. "You make a single sound," she said into the ear of the young man whose arm she had trapped, "and you'll never make a touch with this hand again."

He gritted his teeth and nodded. A shock of black hair hung over his frightened black eyes. As if strolling with a friend, she steered him deliberately but purposefully into an alley so tight she could have spanned it with her outstretched hands.

She held him in the come-along, waiting. A few steady heartbeats, and his two accomplices appeared. One twirled a balisong knife with ebony handles. The other was uncoiling a thin chain from around his waist.

Cassie's left hand came up. It held a snubnosed, five-shot, 10-millimeter revolver, hammerless and matte-black. Civilian ownership of firearms was proscribed in the Combine, which of course didn't inconvenience those willing to bend the law. The local *Masakko* toughs, like criminals throughout the Combine, didn't actually use guns much, but that was out of personal preference. They preferred mayhem of a more intimate variety, the kind where you got to feel blood on your knuckles. But Masamori's punks and gangs knew enough about heat to recognize an altogether serious concealment piece, and draw the proper conclusions.

These two dropped their weapons and raised their hands without needing to be asked.

Cassie smiled. "Smart boys."

"You won't get away with this," groaned the one in the wrist lock.

"Save it." She spun him face-first into the wall—enough to give him a few lumps, but not draw blood. Also enough to stun him so he didn't immediately bolt. Then she put the piece away.

"You want what's in here?" she asked, fishing out the fat wallet. "Well, you can have it—some of it. And all you have to do is talk to me."

Yoshitsune Spaceport on the coffer-dammed floodplains east of town was an *ukiyo* of a different stripe. Even in the tightly regimented Combine, spaceports were filled with activity that could not always be overseen and shadows that could not always be penetrated by light. A vague sense of extraterritoriality always seemed to surround spaceports, as if they belonged to the Combine at large rather than to the world where they happened to reside.

Of course, most Combine worlds were much more orderly and obedient than Hachiman to begin with.

The recent opening of the Combine to greater intercourse with its neighbors had the effect of loosening the limits within Yoshi-Town—a miniature satellite city rising out of the reeds—even further. HTE, especially, had been doing an increasingly brisk business with the wealthy Federated Commonwealth, building a reputation for probity it wouldn't even have occurred to earlier generations of Kurita magnates to envy. Davion and Steiner spacers, accustomed to standards of personal freedom that seemed extravagant even in comparison to Hachiman's, had left their own marks.

Finally, though the yaks controlled the spaceport's dockworkers, they did not exercise that stranglehold on street crime that kept it to such a low level throughout the Combine—an apparently enviable state of affairs that outside commentators universally and mistakenly attributed to the iron grip of the Friendly Persuaders and the ISF. That meant the mean streets between the warehouses and the spacer honky-tonks were mean indeed.

But if there were secrets to be had on Hachiman, they would almost certainly filter through Yoshitsune.

Night was kind to Yoshi-Town, as to an aging whore. It hid some of the cobbled-together shantytown look of the place, and the bright, ever-dancing lights even gave it a certain semblance of exotic charm. At least to the upper-mid and lower-upper class *Masakko* who came slumming here, looking for adventure; the very claptrap ephemerality of the pleasure palaces tickled their sense of the *mujo*. But to the denizens of Yoshi-town and the spacers who had seen Yoshi-town under a hundred names on a hundred worlds, it was the same old dreary same-old.

The blacktop streets glittered with oil and recent rain. A shuttle lifting off from Number Nine pad sent a wave of glare rolling *tsunami* down the display windows of the rinky-dink curio shops and flesh bars, touching the faces of everyone on the street with the light of Hell with the hinges off. The three hookers talking to the diminutive spacer woman ignored it.

It was a shame about the spacer with the Davvy French accent, the hookers thought. She obviously had a fine figure, though she did her best to hide it with that heavy jacket and baggy trousers, and her features were quite lovely. But she must have felt disfigured by the port-wine birthmark that covered the right side of her face. When the street lit with exhaust flare, she ducked that side of her face into her collar by reflex.

She paid standard hourly rates just to sit and talk in a café. That made her almost transcendentally kinky. But none of the hookers was exactly averse to easy money.

Besides, she was easy to talk to. A working girl needed a sympathetic ear, now and again.

"Been some tough customers coming off the regular packet from Luthien lately," Lulu was saying, fiddling with her platinum wig. The breeze was blowing out to sea, and with the blast from the shuttle takeoff boosting it along, it kept trying to snatch the hairpiece off and send it skittering down the street like a frightened animal. "Men and women both. Hard faces and tight lips."

"Who gives a damn?" said Bonnie, short and tough, with neon-orange hair she claimed she'd been born with.

"That means they keep their wallets closed, too," Kimiko explained around her mouthful of chewing gum. "They don't exist for Bon unless they fork over."

"Who's got the time to mess with 'em?" Bonnie demanded.

"They don't say anything?" the Davvy spacer asked.

"Not to nobody I talk to," Lulu said. Kimiko nodded, chewing. After a moment Bonnie shook her head too. The spacer woman *did* fork over, after all.

"They just flash their papers and breeze through Customs," Kimiko said.

"What about their baggage?"

"Travel light, I hear," said Lulu. "Bag or two. Just clean clothes for the jump from Luthien."

"How about baggage shipped in the hold?"

The streetwalkers looked at each other. If any of them thought the *gaijin* woman's questions were strange, they didn't show it.

And if the Friendly Persuaders ever came asking—no,

they'd never seen a woman like that. They'd remember that birthmark, sure.

"I can ask Shiro," Kimiko said. "He's one of my regulars, offloads the packets. Drives the little carts, you know?"

"Watch it," Lulu warned. "He's Sumiyama all the way."

Kimiko made a dice-shaking gesture with her right hand to signify exactly what she thought of the local yak organization. Then she looked past the Davvy spacer's shoulder and her almond eyes got wide.

"Well, girls," called the man dressed in a robe and skull cap and walking up the street toward them. If one didn't look close and didn't know Combine dress customs real well, he might have been mistaken for a minor official of some sort. A large pair of shadows followed him. "So, so, so. You got nothin' better to do than hang out on the corner of Walk and Wait and break wind with this bimbo?"

"She pays, Rikki," Lulu said in a nasal whine.

Rikki stopped. Then his right hand lashed out and cracked the woman across the face. The heavy gold rings on his fingers left welts visible even through stucco-thick mock-geisha makeup.

"You get paid for making the futon bounce, baby," the pimp sneered, "not for running your face. Maybe Leon and Teruo oughtta rearrange that face a little, to help you remember." He nodded to the shadows, who stepped forward meaningfully.

Lulu whimpered. Then to her surprise the little spacer stepped forward.

"My money's good," she said. "What the hell do you care what it buys?"

"Excuse me?" Rikki had a long, narrow face and a little chin beard. It was a face well-suited to sneering. "I'm taking care of business now. You can butt out."

"As a matter of fact, I paid to talk," the spacer said stubbornly. "I'm not leaving until I get my C-bills' worth."

The hookers exchanged glances. Bonnie shrugged. *Oh, well. There goes the easy money . . .*

Rikki smiled. It was not a pleasant expression. "Well, well, well. What do we got here?"

"I dunno, boss. What do we got here?" asked Leon. His job description seemed to include *straight man*. Teruo just glowered and cracked the knuckles in his fingerless-glove clad hands.

"We got an interfering *gaijin* bitch here, looks like to me. One who's fixing to miss her liftoff. Found floating face-down in the canal, so sorry—"

He seemed about to expand on the subject, but words failed him abruptly. It might have had something to do with the three centimeters of wavy steel that were jutting out the back of his neck, just to the left of his spine.

Cassie twisted Blood-drinker, slashing outward in a spray of arterial blood that spattered Leon's startled face and ruined his suit. Rikki collapsed, writhing.

She stood holding her *kris* aimed midway between the two goons. "Who wants some?" she asked, not omitting to keep up her cute little Davvy space-cadet accent.

The thugs had started to reach inside their loud *zaki* sports coats. The look in the spacer woman's eyes made them pull their hands slowly out again.

"Looks like you did a hell of a job guarding your boss' body," Cassie said. "You boys better hunt up a new line of work."

Leon and Teruo looked at each other with frightened animal eyes. *"Now,"* Cassie added.

The pair turned and walked briskly off, presumably to seek new careers. Lulu spat on her former pimp, who had quit wiggling around. Kimiko turned and vomited.

"You're such a wimp, Kimmi," Bonnie said.

Kimiko stared at Rikki's form, face-down in a big dark puddle. "Who's gonna take care of us now?" she wailed.

"Me."

The three turned to stare at the diminutive woman in spacer garb. "You're just a little thing," Bonnie said. "Why would anybody take you seriously?"

Cassie shook the blood from her *kris* with a flick of the wrist and turned Rikki over with her boot toe. The lights of Yoshi-Town danced on his dead eyeballs.

"They could ask him, for a start," she said with a smile.

$$=== 16 ===$$

Masamori, Hachiman
Galedon District, Draconis Combine
5 September 3056

"Jesus boy howdy," Kali MacDougall said. "What would Colonel Cabrera say if she knew you were running a stable of pros?"

She giggled, looking and acting about fourteen. A well-developed fourteen, a certain jealous part of Cassie couldn't help noticing. Then, despite herself, Cassie giggled too. Lady K had that effect on her.

Have to watch yourself, her inner censor cautioned. She sobered at once.

An hour into the midnight shift at HTE's Masamori Compound, the commissary wasn't particularly busy. A couple of shirt-sleeved middle-management types sat in the corner, discussing production targets over cups of tea. Cassie and Captain MacDougall were the only mercs in the place, Kali wore jeans and a shirt tied up above her midriff; she'd caught a late workout at the well-equipped HTE gym, and had her bag beside her chair. Cassie still had on her jacket and baggy pants, though she'd scrubbed the waterproof birthmark makeup off with a special solvent.

"Hey, I'm paying money into the I & D pool," Cassie said, referring to the fund the Regiment maintained to cover injuries and disabilities to members and their dependents. "She ought to love me—I'm saving the Seventeenth cash." It was well known that Marisol Cabrera, who was, among other things, the unit comptroller, hated spending money as passionately as she loved Don Carlos.

Kali grinned and nodded. "You think these ladies know something?"

Cassie shrugged. "Maybe the hardcases from Luthien signify, maybe they don't. Right now what I'm concentrating on is getting my network in place."

"I don't envy you your job, hon. You don't even know what you're looking for."

'That's what makes it a challenge." Cassie leaned forward. "I just know it's out there." She touched herself over her flat belly. "In here I know."

In a quieter voice she said, "I trust my gut. Ignoring it's what landed me in the Larsha militia—"

"Facing down BattleMechs with a bolt-gun," Kali said. "We all trust your instincts, hon. Well, except for Gordo and Cabrera and that psycho Bobby Wolf."

"Don't forget Captain Torres."

"I'd like to. Anyway, you were telling me what you're doing out there on the mean streets of Masamori. I thought you got that waitress job to troll for info."

Cassie held up her hand. "What I'm looking for might pass through the club," she said, "but I'm not counting on it. I'm mostly there to get up to speed on the local street life."

"You're the perfect scout, as always, Cassie," Kali said, sipping her inevitable fruit juice. "Looking to get dialed-into your environment as quickly as possible."

Cassie watched her new friend closely for a moment. She saw no signs of falsity or deprecation—and she knew how to look for them. Strange as it was, the tall and flamboyant 'Mech pilot seemed to like Cassie for her own sake.

That made her dangerous.

"My idea," Cassie made herself say, "isn't so much to lay hands on the information directly. No matter where I go or what I do, that'd be a matter of sheer luck."

"And you never rely on luck."

"Not rely on it, no." She took a taste of her own soft drink. "But *somebody* has what I'm looking for, whatever that turns out to be. And as I get my contacts out there"— she made a spreading gesture with open hands—"the chance that somebody knows a man, who knows a man, who knows what I need to know, goes right on up."

Kali laughed and shook her head. "I love to watch an artist at work. It's no wonder you're the best."

"Thanks," Cassie said, guarded again.

Kali looked at her with those sky-blue eyes. "How's reception? You getting anything?"

"Bits and pieces," Cassie said. "The yakuza boss, Sumiyama, has it in big for Uncle Chandy. The *kobun* talk about it a lot over their beer in the Kit-Kat."

"Could that be what's bugging you? Man like that might be able to cause a mess of trouble. Even for someone named Kurita."

Cassie gave her head a quick shake. "That's not it. And there's word on the street that the Planetary Chairman is looking to squeeze HTE down to size."

"Childe Percy," Lady K said. "Percival Uyehara Fillington, Duke of Hachiman. Still wet behind the ears, by the look of him on holo." She looked at Cassie over her glass as she drank, her eyes alive with mischief. "He's pretty easy on the eyes, though, and I understand he's the planet's most eligible bachelor. Shoot, Cass, maybe you oughta think about settling down—"

The look in Cassie's eyes made Kali stop. "And then again, maybe not," she finished smoothly.

Cassie made herself emit a sound resembling a chuckle. Sort of. "What about you?" she asked.

"That skinny little eel?" Kali shook her head. "Not enough vitamins. I don't want a man with all the edges planed off him, no way."

"Also, it seems like Marquis Hosoya, CEO of Tanadi Computers, is getting nervous about the growth of Uncle Chandy's operation," Cassie continued. "The Fillingtons have been in Tanadi's hip pocket for generations. The Earl's official line has always been that if it's bad for Tanadi, it's bad for Hachiman."

"So is that the problem?"

Again Cassie shook her head. 'If Chandy couldn't deal with bugs like that—Percy, Hosoya, even the yaks—he'd never have scraped together the money to hire us in. No matter what his last name is."

Kali nodded slowly. "Makes sense to me. Even if Chandy made most of his roll off corruption and extortion, in high old Combine style, he's got to have something on the ball." She snorted a laugh through her nostrils, and managed to make it almost refined. "He can't be quite as harmless a fat fool as he looks. 'Cause nobody is, mainly."

"Or his hatchet man, Abdulsattah. He gives me the creeps."

"You? Whoa, *mamacita,* hang on. He must be a stone hardcase to get to a tough little number like you."

Cassie nodded.

"What is it then? Any clue?"

"No. But it's real. I'm not imagining this, no matter what Gordo and Cabrera say. The yaks sense it too; they're all jumpy as cats with a pit-bull convention coming to town. It's on the street. Everybody sees storm clouds building over the Compound, but nobody knows anything."

"Hmm," Kali said, her mouth crumpling into an expression that suggested she didn't much like the taste of what Cassie had to say. "You think maybe old Uncle Chandy had somethin' on his mind besides buying a new toy when he signed up the old man?"

Cassie just looked at her friend.

Kali sighed. "Ah, well. Should've known this gig was too cushy to be for real. You'll give us warning when the storm's fixin' to break. I know you will."

They sat a moment in silence. The managerial types in shirt sleeves had been working themselves into a noisy argument. Finally one square-faced man with a crewcut stood up, windmilling his arms and shouting Japanese, then stalked out.

"I thought these Combine types were all supposed to be subdued and polite," said Lady K. "'Cept when they're riotin', of course."

"We—they like to think of themselves that way," Cassie said.

"They put on an act for the *gaijin*?"

A smile. "And themselves. Self-deception is kind of the national sport in the Combine."

"Like it's not everywhere else?"

The tall blonde captain settled in with one arm slung over the back of her chair and gazed at Cassie. "So you had to waste the pimp?"

Cassie felt her jaw muscles tighten. "You think I had much choice? I figured it was drop him right then, or fight his bully boys. Or should I have just let them wax me?"

Kali patted her hand. "Easy, sister. You did what you had to, and frankly, it sounds as if Rikki-boy needed killin' anyway. But—" She shrugged. "But maybe it shouldn't get too easy, you know?"

"You've killed people," Cassie said tautly.

She expected to get back the usual 'Mech-jock line about fighting the man but killing the machine—how injury or loss of life was an unpleasant by-product, just collateral damage. But Kali nodded and said, "I have. And reckon I'm going to again. All I'm sayin' is, I don't know as it should ever be easy."

"What I'm doing, I do for the Regiment."

"Yep. And you do real well by us, and everybody with three functioning brain cells or better appreciates it. Shoot, even Cowboy does, and I'm none too sure he's got three still firin'. But maybe you might think about what you're doing for yourself once in a while."

Cassie shook her head. "I don't know what you mean."

Lady K's smile was sad. "No. Reckon you don't."

She stood, stretched, picked up her gym bag. "Well, we rotate out to the Sportsplex in the morning, give Second their turn in the barrel. Gotta get some sleep. Walk me back?"

Cassie nodded. She still felt wired and wary from what she took as MacDougall's inquisition. But Kali seemed willing to let it slide.

As they headed out, Archie the FCNS reporter strolled in with Father Doctor Bob, his friend and self-appointed liaison officer. Westin caught sight of the two women, his face brightening visibly behind his pencil-thin mustache.

"Ladies," he said. "How delightful—"

"Later, Archie," Kali said with a weary wave. "We're hitting the rack." Then she and Cassie hustled out even before his face finished falling.

"Thanks for getting us out of there," Cassie said as they walked down the short corridor to outside.

Kali shook her head. "I don't know why you work so hard at dodging Archie. He's a nice boy, not to mention terminally cute."

Cassie's response was more shudder than headshake. "He bothers me."

"Might not hurt you to loosen up and live a little, hon. Been a while since you had a gentleman friend, isn't it?"

"I'm not hurting," Cassie said briskly.

"Maybe not," Kali said. "But I sure don't mind looking at young Archie. Only he doesn't seem to know I exist."

Cassie made a noncommittal sound in her throat as they stepped out into the crisp autumn night. From across the broad Yamato came a crackle. Cassie paused, listened to the cadence, nodded.

"Firecracker strings," she said, walking toward the barracks. "Having another street festival in Sodegarami, not a riot. Yet."

"How can you tell the difference?" Kali asked.

"When you hear those automatic shotguns the candy-stripers carry," Cassie said, "that's when you figure it's a riot."

Kali grinned. "These Dracs sure know how to party," she said.

Cassie's room came first. She unlocked the door, started inside.

"Hold on a sec," Kali said, bending down to rummage in her bag. "I got something for you."

Cassie stood there, wondering. Kali turned and stuffed something soft and fuzzy and pink into her arms.

"Surprise," the Captain said.

Cassie looked down to see that she was holding a toy animal shaped like a plump polar bear with a big, friendly smile. Cassie jumped, made as if to throw it away.

"Whoa, there, girl," Kali said. "Settle down. She won't bite you."

Cassie held the thing out. "What *is* this?"

Kali bent over and pretended to examine it. "It's a teddy bear," she said. "Less somebody sneaked a bomb into my bag when I wasn't looking."

"Take it back," Cassie said firmly.

Kali shook her head. "Sorry. Can't. Against the rules. She's your teddy bear now. Deal with her."

Cassie opened her mouth, shut it. She felt as if her limbs and body had become hollow tubing and that cold condensation was seeping down inside her.

"You don't have to thank me," Kali said. "Just keep the bear." She leaned forward, gave Cassie a sisterly kiss on the cheek, and shooed her into her room.

The needle tip of Blood-drinker hovered a millimeter from the stuffed bear's button right eye. Cassie sat on the end of her bed, holding the thing in her lap. The hand that held her *kris* quivered with an emotion she couldn't begin to name.

She wanted to plunge her dagger into the thing, rip it

apart and strew its innards around the room. Instead she pitched it away with a convulsive heave.

"All right," she said. "All right. I'll keep it. Kali will be mad at me if I tear it up."

She went over and picked the bear up from where it had fallen next to the little dresser, hearing a voice in her head say, *What do you care what she thinks?*

"I don't know," Cassie said, sitting down again. She tapped the dagger against her thigh. The bear continued to beam fatuously at her.

Maybe if I just poke it some . . .

A knock at the door. She jumped, instantly twitching the stuffed toy behind her rump. The thought that somebody might peek in and catch her holding the thing horrified her—irrationally, since the door was locked, and not even Bobby the Wolf was crazy enough to bust down Cassie's door in the middle of the night.

"Who is it?" she called, surprised and appalled by the quaver in her voice.

"If you call her Snuggles," came Kali MacDougall's voice through the door, "I bet she'd answer. 'Night."

"Ooh!" The squeal of outrage burst out of Cassie as if she'd been punched in the gut. She wheeled and threw the toy bear against the wall, but it merely bounced back to land on the pillow, where it lay smiling with uninterrupted love and acceptance.

Cassie threw herself facedown on the bed and, entirely to her surprise, dissolved in hot and helpless tears.

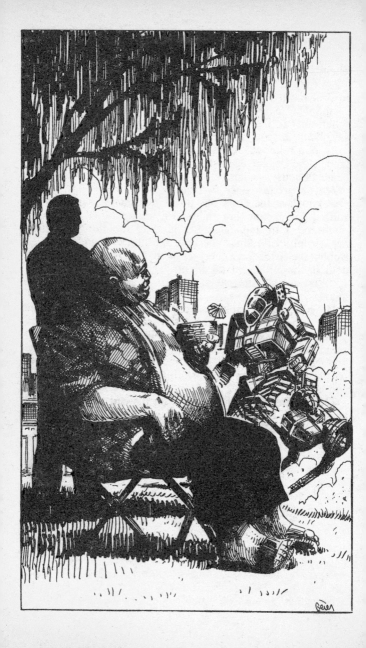

Masamori, Hachiman
Galedon District, Draconis Combine
6 September 3056

From the north a company of 'Mechs advanced along the Yamato as if bent on invading Masamori. Backs to the city skyline, a second company stood waiting to receive them. Diagonal blue stripes had been painted on their arms and legs.

"A lovely day for an exercise," said Uncle Chandy, who filled to overflowing a folding chair set beneath a pavilion erected in the shade of cottonwoods by the river. He was sipping an exotic rum drink served in half of a head-sized Vindhaya nut from the southern continent of Deolali. A tiny orange parasol peeped up from the frothy mix.

The sky was hurting-bright blue and cloudless, the sun hot enough to sting unprotected skin. The river smell rose thick and cool around them, and every now and again a breeze from the lordly, distance-blued Trimurti Mountains in the east took the edge off the morning heat, reminding the clumps of spectators strung along the riverbank that, no matter how warm and bright the day, fall was definitely bearing down on the Shakudo coast.

Seated on the Kurita's right, Colonel Carlos Camacho nodded gravely but did not speak. "You're absolutely right about that, Excellency," Gordon Baird said, leaning over the Colonel's shoulder. He was always ready to get a word in with the highly placed. "It's a lovely day."

The magnate ignored him. "I am not unappreciative of a pretext for an excursion out-of-doors on such a day, Colonel," he said. "Yet I am curious as to why you were so insistent that I come to watch what I gather is an entirely routine drill."

Camacho looked at him. "I wish the *señor* to see just what it is he's paying for," he said.

The young samurai with the purple topknot poked at his white polymer plate with a disposable fork and eyed the contents with suspicion. "What is this?" he asked, indicating a thick, finger-length cylinder wrapped in a corn husk and covered with brownish sauce.

"Dead rats and ground sewage," Gandaka said, unwrapping his tamale and taking a lusty bite. "Good, too."

The samurai shuddered fastidiously.

"What do you care?" asked Moon. "It smells edible enough. You'd have eaten worse if you'd been with us when we fought the Clans."

"Of if you'd been born in the same place we were," Gandaka said. He was a long, lanky type with a prominent Adam's apple and sideburns down to his jaw. His name literally meant "tall wild goose," and figuratively referred to what he proudly considered his most prominent physical trait.

The youth colored clear to his hairline, which had been shaved up to the crown in traditional fashion. These *eta* scum dared take him to task for his own exalted birth. And there wasn't one damned thing he could do about it.

"What about him?" he asked to cover his own discomfiture, pointing at Buntaro Mayne with the butt of his fork. The one-eyed MechWarrior stood away from the serving tables with his hands in his pockets, watching Cochise Company advance to the attack. Out front of him children and dogs ran about, chasing and playing, oblivious of the impending clash of titans.

"I'm waiting for the goat to be done," he said, jerking his head toward where several burly Aztechs, stripped to the waist, were turning a goat carcass on a spit above a pit full of coals.

Eleanor Shimazu was a woman of marked appetites. She was sated for the moment, though, her subordinates having insisted that she eat first. Perhaps it was because she never claimed such prerogatives that her outlaw boys and girls always pressed them on her.

Now she stood watching a few of her female MechWarriors shyly talking to mercenary women with babies in arms.

Several of them were MechWarrior themselves; the Seventeenth Recon struck the *Tai-sa* as a combination extended family, circus, and gypsy caravan.

That made the way her people and these outside-folk were beginning to take to one another seem entirely natural. *Heruzu Enjeruzu* were a lot like that, too.

"Which side are you rooting for?" Shig Hofstra asked No-Name the samurai. Meat and shredded cheese and lettuce cascaded down his chin from a taco as he tried to calculate the proper angle of attack to fit it into his mouth.

"White," the young samurai said primly. "Most of the people around us have white pennants."

Everybody glared at him. "What a ween," Gandaka sneered, picking up the stub of his tamale with his fingers and cramming it in his mouth.

"I'm rooting for Blue," Buntaro Mayne announced, nodding toward the defenders, who were beginning to deploy a light lance forward along the river, perilously close to the picnickers, who variously cheered or jeered and threw disposable cups, depending on affiliation. Inland a short lance of three medium 'Mechs advanced, on the right flank of the mixed heavy/assault lance waiting in reserve. "That's Adelante Company. Cowboy's in Adelante, and I'm the only one who gets to kick his butt."

"That's not what I heard," the large, shaven-headed man in the O5P robes rumbled. His callsign was Yamabushi, from the somewhat suspect suborder of warrior-monks to which he belonged. "I heard that little bitty scout girl with the bicycle busted his nose for him. More than *you* did."

"Where is she anyway?" Gandaka asked, wiping his fingers on his jacket and looking around.

"She's not your type, Gandaka," Lainie drawled.

"Why?" Gandaka demanded. "What's she like then? Girls?"

"Humans."

The Ghosts roared with laughter. The Caballeros nearby looked at them and grinned, none quite close enough to share in the joke. Gandaka bobbed his head and laughed with the best of them.

Lainie sipped Borstal Boy from a throwaway cup. Sunshine and satiety were working on her. Her mind was elsewhere, drifting backward on currents of nostalgia.

She *hated* nostalgia.

Lainie Shimazu had spent much of her childhood and youth as center of attention in sporting events, which was how the 'llero onlookers seemed to be taking this whole thing. Devoted to riding, an all-Combine class equestrienne, she possessed a facility for athletics in general and had competed successfully in various sports.

For most of her childhood she did not understand that what her father did for a living had anything unorthodox about it. He was filthy rich, to be sure, and surrounded himself and his family with husky young men with guns. But if you were rich in the Combine, that was simply what you did.

When she was about twelve, Lainie found out that her father was not just a remote yet indulgent old man who happened to be loaded, but the top *oyabun* on Kagoshima. She was a yakuza princess for true. Before that time she'd been inclined to be a bit of a tomboy, but was basically a good and dutiful daughter. The sense of betrayal the discovery evoked in her had given vent to a hitherto latent rebellious impulse.

Her rebellion had manifested itself mainly in getting herself expelled from several private academies, which Milos Shimazu found doubly irritating. Not only did he lose face, but he forfeited the bribe money he'd had to fork over to get the schools to accept her in the first place. Lainie was what was called an underachiever, which was to say her classes bored her; but that wasn't the real problem. The real problem was that she was a yakuza, and even though the yakuza had enjoyed a certain quasilegitimacy within the Combine even before Theodore made them his allies, they weren't considered fit for polite company.

Lainie was beginning to blossom from gangly and homely adolescence into striking young womanhood—and to consider options that would *really* have driven her father wild— when her world up and exploded. A coterie of five of Kagoshima's secondary *oyabun* decided their lifestyles would be improved if old Milos went the way of most of the planet's indigenous life-forms larger than a sparrow. Somebody—a trusted lieutenant would have been traditional, but Lainie never knew for sure—had let a squad of assassins into the family estate one pleasant autumn afternoon not much different from this one, and that had been it for Milos.

Another squad had arrived at the school currently in-process of giving Lainie the boot, intending to tie up that particular loose end. Only the intervention of a trusted retainer who hadn't gone over saved her life. He got her onto a freighter bound for Hachiman, where a cousin, Kazuo Sumiyama, was an up-and-coming yakuza boss. The servant was mortally wounded in the process.

Lainie had arrived in Masamori penniless and emotionally shattered. Aside from claims of blood, which the yakuza took every bit as seriously as *katagi*—straight—society, she had little to offer. She had her riding and athletic abilities, none of which was marketable in any significant way. She also had the usual skills instilled in Combine females born to families of pretension, skills designed to make them good little homemakers and ornaments. Those weren't in enormous demand in the underworld, either. Her only choice was to throw herself on her distant cousin's mercy as a *kyakubun*, guest member, and hope for the best.

Which did not materialize. It turned out that Kazuo Sumiyama did have a use for his fugitive relation, blossoming into womanhood as she was. So the quondam princess learned about yakuza concepts of duty and obligation the hard way.

Kazuo-*sama* had done Lainie one service other than tender refuge with a high price tag: he'd allowed her to study whatever she wanted, be it economics, history, administration, or the operation of his Sumiyama-*kai,* which he was building into the dominant organization of Masamori, and thus of all Hachiman. It was not that he was enlightened. He simply didn't care what his "protégé" did as long as her services were available when he wanted them.

For the first time in her life, Eleanor had been truly motivated to learn. She proved a very quick study. Not that her newfound knowledge did her any good; she had her niche as far as the *oyabun* was concerned, and she needn't expect to rise out of it.

Then, in the late forties, she'd learned that the Gunji no Kanrei was looking for bright, ambitious, and able recruits, regardless of antecedents, to fill the ranks of his Ghost Regiments. Sumiyama had actually given her permission to join.

He knew it never hurt to have contacts in the military, which were not so easy to come by because the Combine's High Command utterly despised the yakuza, mostly because of their hyperactive patriotic posturing. Besides, he'd begun to grow bored with her, truth to tell.

Eleanor Shimazu had never felt much attachment to the Draconis Combine, its ways and ideals. She had received the usual indoctrination, and paid as little attention to it as everything else her mentors had tried to drum into her as a child. She still felt little of that patriotic fervor the *oyabun* liked to make so much noise about.

But her devotion to *Kanrei* Theodore Kurita, later to become Coordinator, was absolute. Notwithstanding the fact that it was by his orders that Lainie had arrived back here in the hated presence of her cousin.

"What?" Lainie demanded, realizing that Buntaro Mayne was saying something in his usual laconic, wise-ass way.

"I said, you better get your bets down, *bancho,* because they're about to rock and roll," the one-eyed MechWarrior said.

Lainie grunted. "A hundred on Blue," she said absently. She became aware of tension in her forearms, glanced down at her hands.

They were balled into fists, so tight the bones threatened to burst through whitened skin. Pain darted up her arms as she forced her fingers to unclench. Her fingertips had left half-moon craters in her palms. Fortunately, her nails were short, the way she'd worn them ever since fleeing the school on Kagoshima and in spite of Sumiyama's frequent comments that it was the duty of any consort of his to appear suitably feminine. She had consented to wear false nails during that phase when he'd had her on display, but she'd never have grown out her own.

In fact, her hands, long-fingered and once considered exceptionally fine, were now coarsened and callused from rigorous toughening exercises. That too was a kind of rebellion.

On both sides of the vast stubble-fields where the exercise was taking place stood BattleMechs with black and white stripes painted on arms and torsos. These were referees, drawn from Bronco Company, which was not participating in today's competition. Not far from Lainie and the score or so of Ghosts accompanying her stood the *Atlas* that she understood belonged to her new friend Captain MacDougall.

The crowd whistled and cheered as a volley of rockets arced out from the advancing 'Mech to explode against Adelante armor. The rounds were low-powered and filled with paint; yellow splashes appeared on limbs and breastplates. Adelante replied with snarls of paint-filled autocannon bursts and powered-down pink laser lances. Low-power blue-green practice lasers played the role of particle projection cannon.

Buntaro Mayne sauntered up to Lainie, his plate filled with goat meat swimming in red chile. "Pretty poor shots, *bancho*," he said with his mouth full.

About then a volley of SRM-simulators struck the treeline some seven meters up and a hundred meters south of the Ghosts, spattering picnickers with the orange paint Adelante was firing. The spectators scattered, to the gleeful applause of compatriots fortunate enough to be out of range.

"Living lives of total safety doesn't seem to be much of a priority for these folks," Mayne remarked.

Lainie shrugged. "*Mujo,*" she said.

A light Cochise lance was racing along the cottonwoods to meet the Adelante lights. A referee *Rifleman* emitted a shrill simulated whistle through its loudspeakers and pointed the long-barreled weapons that served as its right arm at a charging White *Wasp*. Apparently protesting, the *Wasp* began to jump up and down and wave its arm in the air. The *Rifleman*'s right autocannon blasted, and huge black splashes blossomed on the *Wasp*'s front glacis, which was already liberally covered in orange. The little 'Mech folded its medium laser and its hand actuator over its chest and promptly toppled over backward.

Lainie laughed out loud. "I guess that means he's out of it."

A heartbeat later an Adelante *Wasp* with its torso painted in black and yellow stripes came jumping over Dark Lady's head and tackled an unwary *Valkyrie* with a butterfly painted on its chest.

"That's Cowboy!" Buntaro whooped, spilling his *cabrito* in the process. "Go, you skinny sonofabitch!"

"My word," Chandrasekhar Kurita said as White and Blue 'Mechs collided in a crash that went on and on like thunder. "They certainly are . . . exuberant."

A blue *BattleMaster,* Macho Alvarado's Macho Man, kicked out one leg on a White *Locust,* which sent the 'Mech crashing down to the ground. Dark Lady charged up, waving her arms and whistling. Macho tried to crack her in the head with the Fusigon Longtooth extended-range PPC in his 'Mech's right arm. Lady K blocked, then stuck her *Atlas'* right leg behind Macho Man's right ankle, put her right palm against his chest, and dumped the *BattleMaster* to the ground with a creditable leg-throw and a thump that made Uncle Chandy's teeth knock together with an audible clack.

Seated to Camacho's right, Lieutenant Colonel Cabrera winced.

Chandy shook his large head, which glistened with sweat. "Amazing. But don't your machines suffer damage, Colonel? I should think they would be expensive to repair."

Cabrera's face pinched again at the mention of expense. Don Carlos nodded. "The damage is primarily to armor and is fairly simple to repair." He spoke with something like animation. "Sometimes joint actuators are damaged, but our technicians work wonders."

"Indeed, they must."

"As for expense—" The Colonel shrugged, carefully avoiding his top aide's eyes. "I find the cost worth it. We are not such marksmen as the Nagelring or New Avalon turn out. Nor do we have the technology to match the Clans. But there are no finer natural 'Mech pilots than Caballeros. It is worth much to us to keep our skills honed. Everything."

"It certainly pays off, Colonel," Chandy said enthusiastically. "Truly your people are skillful MechWarriors, to maneuver their machines in such a fashion."

"You haven't seen anything here, Excellency," enthused moonfaced Father Montoya, the unit's sole noncombatant chaplain. "Now Patsy, *she* could pilot a BattleMech. I don't think there was a finer PH pilot in the Sphere. Not Allard-Liao, not anybody."

"Patsy?" Uncle Chandy echoed politely. "Who might this Patsy be?"

The momentary sheen had gone from Don Carlos' large dark eyes, leaving them empty and matte, like the eyes of a beaten dog. Marisol Cabrera glared furiously at Montoya, the look in her dark eyes revealing why she was nicknamed *la Dama Muerte,* Lady Death.

"Only my daughter," Don Carlos mumbled, half-apologetic. "She died. On Jeronimo—"

"So that's Himself," Archie Westin said, shading his eyes to peer at Chandrasekhar Kurita in the pavilion fifty meters north. He, Mariska, and their customary guide Father García were recording the game for the folks back home in the Federated Commonwealth. "That's what a Kurita looks like in the flesh."

"A minor Kurita," Father Doctor Bob said. "Fairly far removed from the line of succession. I gather the late Coordinator Takashi thought him something of a fool."

"That seems to be the consensus," Archie said, nodding. "He was thick with Theodore, though, back when the old man was riding roughshod over the boy. Took his side at court. Teddy still favors him today in rather a pitying way. That's where he got the nickname 'Uncle Chandy,' you know, playing uncle to Theodore when the boy was out of favor, even though they're really cousins. Truth to tell, Chandy's only a year or three older."

"You seem to know a great deal about our employer."

"Do I?" A boyish grin. "I suppose I do. I'm rather fascinated by the Combine's ruling family, truth to tell."

Father Bob smiled. "Most people find your own royal family more compelling."

"You're missing some great action here, Arch," Mariska Savage said, crouching to get a different angle.

Archie laughed. "I suppose I find them less exotic. Rather like members of my own family." His face clouded. "Though the current state of affairs between the Archon Prince and his sister is thoroughly distressing."

"I should imagine," murmured the Jesuit.

"Arch," Savage said.

"Yes, yes, in a moment." He was looking at Chandy again. "I wonder if he can really be quite such a harmless fool?"

About then his camerawoman hit him in a flying tackle that sent the newsman sprawling. She also hooked Father Bob by the cassock in passing and they all flew into a heap.

A heartbeat later Buck Evans' *Orion,* propelled by a kick from Marshal Waits' *Marauder* came crashing into the trees where the trio had been standing.

Then a White *Phoenix Hawk* came swarming after, land-

ing astride the *Orion*'s belly and pummeling the 'Mech with
its fists. A whistle, and Dark Lady bodily yanked the *Phoenix Hawk* back onto the field by one shoulder.

"Oh, my," Father Bob said breathlessly.

"Astounding, the way your Captain MacDougall gets
around in that great, unwieldy *Atlas*," Archie said, standing
up and helping the shaken Jesuit to his feet.

Savage, who carried her camera on a sling, remained
seated, blithely filming away.

"Rather a close-run thing," Westin said. He leaned over to
kiss Savage on the head. "Mariska, you're a love. Thanks
for saving us."

Savage grinned, but kept her eye fastened to the eyepiece,
as the two other zebra-painted 'Mechs hustled forward to
untangle Buck Evans and his *Orion* and from the splintered
cottonwoods.

"The officials are all from your Bronco Company, are
they not?" Archie asked. García nodded. "If you don't mind,
why aren't you among them? You're a highly respected man
in the Regiment."

Father Bob chuckled. "That's the key word, my friend:
man. The good Lady K's two assistants are likewise female.
We Caballeros have a chivalrous streak; we hesitate to offer
violence to a woman, even though our lady 'Mech pilots
give quite as well as they get. Were I out there"—a
shrug—"in the heat of passion, even a good Catholic might
forget I was a man of the cloth."

Archie shook his head. "You're a fascinating people, Padre."

"Yes, aren't we?" García agreed enthusiastically. "I love
my work."

"Speaking of women—Caballeras?—I wonder where that
little scout of yours is."

"Ah, the lovely Cassiopeia—" Father Doctor Bob began,
a faraway look in his eyes.

"On the job somewhere, Archie," Savage said, still filming from the ground. "She's a fanatic. Also, her only interest
in 'Mechs is blowing them up."

Archie blinked. "I knew that," he said.

The exercise came down—"degenerated" was actually the
word that sprang to Lainie's mind—to a face-to-face melee
that the Caballeros clustered around the Ghosts gleefully re-

ferred to as a *lucha libre*. There was much reference to a Captain Santo, commander of Infante Company, but he was in Third Battalion, whose members didn't get to play today. Lainie gathered a confused impression that Santo went by no other name, never appeared without wearing a silver mask, and descended from a family of nobles whose scions were inevitably masked wrestling champions. By this time she was thoroughly bemused, sunburned, and cradling some young Caballera MechWarrior's two-year-old daughter on her hip.

Bobby the Wolf went into a rage, and was disqualified when he tried to wrench the head off Cowboy's *Wasp*. That seemed to signal the end of the engagement, since all that remained standing were three Adelante 'Mechs: Raven O'Connor's *Raven*, Perez' *Awesome*, and Pipiribau's *Locust*, whose plastic-toy decorations had been removed before the rumble started.

Hooting, Buntaro Mayne began to dance around and slap the hands of Usagi and Unagi, who had backed Blue along with him. Everybody else but the *tai-sa* had gone White. Not out of consensus with the surrounding spectators, except for the stiff-necked young samurai, but because Mayne's new buddy Cowboy was on the Blue team.

"So what did we observe today, people?" The Colonel's voice cut through the celebration as Lainie handed the infant off to Captain Vásquez, the angel-faced *Catapult* pilot, who seemed to have charge of the younger kids.

"Some pretty hot 'Mech piloting," Mayne crowed. "Brothers, did you see the way Cowboy decked that damned *Banshee*?"

"*Banshee*'s a piece of junk anyway," grumbled Shig Hofstra.

"Yeah, I'd like to see *you* do that—"

"So would I," Lainie Shimazu said. But softly.

"What are you talking about?" the young samurai demanded, handsome face flushed. "These mercenaries are a disgrace! Wild, heedless, totally undisciplined—"

"Totally proficient pilots," Shimazu said.

The boy threw up his hands. "They acted without thought! They're mad! Utterly abandoned! Like—like animals!"

He used the worst word in Japanese, *chikusho*. Moon, who hadn't bet at all, dropped a square scarred hand on the samurai's shoulder.

"Son," the Korean said, "you'd best quit while you're ahead. That's warrior spirit you're describing. If you can show half that much when the PPC beams start to crackle around your ears for real, boy, you can die with your name restored."

═══════ **18** ═══════

Masamori, Hachiman
Galedon District, Draconis Combine
6 September 3056

Bent over, Cassie picked her way softly and silently over the tops of stacked polymer crates. Above her, lights hung from the ceiling trusses spilled soft illumination to the warehouse floor. She was careful where her shadow went.

To her surprise, it was her Kit-Kat gig that rang the cherries after all. A couple of grunt-level *kobun* soldiers muttering together in a corner about the big mysterious meet the boss was having the next night. One was grousing in his Old Stick and Sack that he was missing a big date with a dancer from Torashii Gyaru, currently the hottest strip club in Sodegarami. The other was commiserating.

They thought they were maintaining perfect security. There was nobody around but the little waitress with the smoke-gray eyes and perfect little butt.

So here was Cassie, snooping and pooping through a warehouse on the estuary just south of the *ukiyo*—perhaps significantly, in easy line of sight of the forbidding walls of HTE Compound. She was dressed all in black, and her face was blackened with non-gloss cammie plant. She was armed with Blood-drinker, a pistol, assorted burglar tools, and a palm-sized camcorder—straight video; she didn't want to be sending laser beams around at random in a place that might be lousy with detectors.

An intersection. A pair of burly goons in dazzle-pattern sports coats with padded shoulders—*zaki*, regulation gangster kitsch—stood with heads together. They carried submachine guns and in their ears were little buttons connected to their breast pockets by wires. There were more modern commo rigs available, even in the Combine; no doubt the yaks were fond of these.

She spidered back a few meters from the watchdogs, who occasionally remembered to look around, but—like most amateurs—never *up*. She gathered herself, leapt across the two-meter space between stacks, light and silent as a shadow. Then she was stealing forward, unsuspected.

The center of the big warehouse had been cleared of crates in a space about ten meters square, the boxes heaped hurriedly on top of the orderly stacks surrounding it. Two groups faced each other across the stained cement floor. Creeping forward, Cassie found a conveniently situated crack between crates and hunkered down to peer between.

One trio centered on a man of medium height and light build, with a turtle head jutting from the collar of his dark and well-cut suit coat and a slash of mouth. Cassie's first guess was that this was Kazuo Sumiyama. Also her second and third; she had heard the boys talk about him. Besides, she'd also seen his picture in the *Mirza*'s files.

Standing behind his either shoulder were obvious meat puppets, one bulky, one trim. They had the buttons in their ears too, but no obvious pieces, confirming them as bodyguards and not grunt sentries. Cassie dismissed them with a glance. They obviously thought they were long-range, low-heat, but their awareness was low; they'd never see her, and so could never threaten her.

The other three were as unlike the yaks as noon and midnight. The central figure was a tall man with a shock of red hair and a fist of a face thrust forward beneath it. His features had that seamed sort of ugliness you have to be born with and then steadily work on, with help from weather, fists, blades, and various other inputs. He wore nondescript Middle-Class clothes. Cassie had no idea who he was, but she knew him. From his presence and his poise, the way he stood with his weight forward on the balls of his feet like a boxer, he was Death.

His bookends were a different tale as well. Unlike Sumiyama's bodyguards they were compact, neither one as tall as the redhead, a man and a woman, faceless in head-to-toe black and opaque transpex faceplates. Each carried a compact Shimatsu-42 assault rifle. Each had a sword strapped across the back.

These were Death, too. Cassie had never seen those get-ups before in the flesh—only in intelligence digests and maybe a hundred action holodramas. That was Draconis Elite Strike Team drag, there. The suits were ballistic-armor cloth, sealed against chemical and biological agents. They carried a wide array of sensors, including infrared, and like BattleMechs had a view strip at the top of the inside of the faceplate, which condensed a three-sixty field of vision. Members of the Dragon's special forces were hard to sneak up on.

But DEST members didn't need the suits to make that claim. They were masters of martial arts, stealth, and every weapon system known to man. They were trained to the raw edge of psychosis, and ready to die *right now* if the Dragon demanded. Or should he feel even a passing whim.

Unless they were fakes—no. Cassie could *feel* the red-headed man from here, burning from the floor like a star of menace. If he willed it, he could down both of Sumiyama's men in the time it took them to blink, without his own guards have to so much as shift their weight. Such a man wouldn't even *bother* with guards who weren't fully qualified to wear DEST commando gear.

Cassie was reassessing her plans as she aimed her little 'corder through the crack between crates. Such a man would not bother with guards at all—visible ones, anyway—unless he wished to make an impression. He was wearing these two like a display handkerchief, but they were almost certain not to be the only ones on hand. The others were, presumably, doing what DEST operatives were supposed to do: not being seen.

And looking for her. Oh, they didn't know she was here—not yet, or they'd be crawling in her ears already. But they would be sweeping the warehouse with motion sensors and IR scanners and particle-sampling people-sniffers. Nor would they forget to look *up*. In fact, they were fairly sure to think of patroling the tops of the crate-stacks ...

Peering through the sight, she tracked the little 'corder

left, from Sumiyama's group to the redheaded man, then back, just to make sure she had identifiable pictures of both. The little unit had a highly directional sound pickup on it. She couldn't monitor it; she wasn't going to run around enemy territory with a plug in *her* ear interfering with her hearing if she could help it. Cassie wasn't much of a lip reader, and Kazuo Sumiyama didn't have much in the way of lips, anyway, but she was morally certain she caught his mouth framing the syllables "Chandrasekhar Kurita."

Then she was gone. Back toward the side door whose lock she had picked, not the way she had come, but close. She was quiet, but mainly she was fast. No art at her disposal could hide her long from the faceless men and women in black.

Twice she glimpsed black suits. Once down below her, ghosting along with assault rifle ready, once twenty meters away, spidering over the stacked crates. Both times she ducked away from the line of sight as quickly as she could.

The DEST faceplates provided a full circle of vision, but the images weren't very clear. Cassie had seen mockups of such miniature displays; it took a fair amount of training to make visual sense of what they showed you. They were wonderful for preventing anyone from slipping up and shanking you from the rear, but they were rather less motion-sensitive than the unaugmented peripheral vision of a trained, alert person.

And while the DEST operatives were as close to superhuman as might be fond outside a Clan Wolf or Jade Falcon sibko, even Kerensky's tube-born bastards had human limitations. These commandos were far more alert and observant than normal folk—definitely including Sumiyama's club-footed patrols. But they weren't really expecting anyone to be spying on this little confab. So they didn't stretch their awareness that tiny extra fraction that might have alerted them to the flitting passage of the eyes of the Seventeenth Recon.

Cassie reached a point from which she could overlook the door through which she had entered. It was still closed, and there was no one nearby. She let out a relieved breath, and slipped noiselessly down to the cement. *I'm out of here . . .*

Not yet, apparently, for a DEST operative chose just that moment to stroll around the corner toward her.

In a millisecond Cassie evaluated her options. The frightened little girl within her screamed to turn and flee into the inviting maze of the warehouse, away from the bad man in black. But that was death. Once alerted, it would take the rest of the DEST team no longer to find her than it would take all the wine to spill from an upset bottle, and there was nothing even the finest scout in the Inner Sphere could do about the fact.

But when the frightened child inside screamed, Cassie's reflex was to snap into kill mode. She was sprinting toward the black-clad agent even before she was aware of what she was doing.

The black suit would stop a slug from her pistol even if she'd had time to draw it. Ballistic cloth was notably less effective against bladed weapons than bullets, however, and she might be able to jam Blood-drinker through to flesh. But she didn't have a lot of time to poke around looking for weak points. She would have to do this bare-handed.

Two meters from the DEST man, Cassie left the floor in a flying leopard leap over the Shimatsu's rising barrel. This was *madi*-style *pentjak silat*, most difficult and demanding of arts. Only a perfect acrobat with drawn carbon for nerves could make the technique work.

Cassie was that. And motivated too.

Her leap was enough to actually clear the man's left shoulder. As she passed over, she seized his head in both hands. Slight as her body weight was, her momentum was more than enough to whip the head far back on the neck.

She twisted her body as it arced toward the floor, put a knee into the small of the man's back, and *heaved*.

The man's neck broke with a sound like a pistol shot.

Cassie landed on her feet, skidded, fetched against the ramparts of crates. She reached up and grabbed a protruding edge, pulling with all the might adrenaline lent her fine-tuned muscles. Crates tumbled with a crash, falling across the motionless figure in black.

She was out the door before the last crate came to rest. The night was her friend, folding her into its arms.

The midnight streets of the Floating World were thronged with pleasure seekers, a river of souls between neon-lit banks. The passing *Masakko* and the odd offworlder turned to stare unabashed at the four women who stood on the sidewalk peering at an unusually discreet neon sign beside a flight of steps headed down. Especially the tall blonde in the tight-fitting trousers.

"What's 'Torashii Gyaru' mean?" demanded Janine Esposito. Her callsign was Mariposa. Her 'Mech, Iron Butterfly, was the *Valkyrie* Cowboy's *Wasp* had attacked after Macho got called for unnecessary roughness. By now, though, the bruises and disappointment of the afternoon's exercise were equally forgotten. Tomorrow after Mass she would be marrying Lonny Ortega, a *Stalker* pilot from Infante Company. She was determined to celebrate her final night of freedom to the max.

"Trashy Girls," Lady K supplied.

"How'd you know that?"

"Abtakha's been giving me pointers in Japanese."

"She's spooky. Where is she, anyway?"

"Working," said Raven O'Connor. She was a wiry, acerbic blonde married to John Amos "French Fry" Ames, who like her, was an Adelante MechWarrior. He took his nickname from what he used to stick up his nose at parties, back in his wild bachelor days when he ran with the usual suspects: Buck, Reb, and the archetypal Cowboy, Cowboy. His *Phoenix Hawk* had been "killed" by Navajo Wolf that afternoon, and he had gotten pretty banged up himself in the process. He was in no position to begrudge his lady her night on the town.

"Doing those weird exercises of hers," said Mercedes "Misty" Saavedra, a giggly, round little MechWarrior from Bronco who was Janine's best friend and maid of honor-to-be.

"Dancing in there, for all I know," Kali said.

"Ooh, look," Misty said, peering at a sign on the dark door at the end of the half-flight of stairs. "It's ladies night. They've got male dancers too!"

"Let's go in!" Janine declared. "It's my party, and I'm ready to howl."

"Lonnie's probably in there himself, with Macho and the boys," Misty said. "Don't you know it's bad luck for you to see him the night before your wedding?"

"Oh, who cares? C'mon, let's go."

"Y'all go ahead, girls," Lady K said. "I'll amble on."

"What's the matter?" Janine demanded. "Chicken?" She'd already gotten a bit of a load on.

Smiling, Kali shook her head. "No. Just not in the mood

to have some total stranger dangling his participle in my virgin Mai Tai."

Raven laughed. "You oughta come in with us, Cap'n," she
said. "They'd probably recruit you. They love leggy blondes
in these parts; you could pick up some easy C-bills."

"Sierra Foxtrot, baby doll, what're you trying to do to
me?" MacDougall laughed. "If Cabrera ever found out I was
shucking my skivvies in a Floating World dive, she'd skin
me out for a lampshade for true."

"Aw, you're not afraid of *la Dama Muerte*," Misty exclaimed.

"You betcha I am. Anybody sane's afraid of that witch."

"HDLC," Janine sneered. "She's barely even a MechWarrior."

"Satan don't ride at all," Lady K said. "You reckon his
breath won't melt your refrigerated 'Mech-jock panties to
your butt?"

"I'd like to go in."

Everybody shut up and stared at Diana Vásquez. The *Catapult* pilot was so quiet people often tended to forget she
was there.

"I've never been in a place like this before," she said
shyly. "I'd like to see what goes on."

Diana was so retiring as to be often overlooked, but a case
could have been made that she was the most beautiful
woman in the Regiment. Like Kali, she had an engineering
degree, but her manner had an incredibly childlike, innocent
purity. As the joke in the Regiment ran, she had a two-year
old son, so she *probably* wasn't a virgin—but no one was
making bets.

"Will you join me, Captain?"

Kali sighed. "Sure, Di."

"You gonna drink with us for real?" Janine suddenly demanded.

"Say what, Mariposa?" Kali answered evenly.

"You gonna have a real drink, or are you just gonna keep
sucking down that fruit juice?"

"Janine," Raven said in a warning voice.

"Sokay, Rave," Lady K said. "You do what you like,
Janine. I got no problem with that. But I walk my own
path."

"Think you're too good to drink with me, *bolilla*?"

"Shut the foxtrot up, Janine," Raven said, pushing in between them. Janine started to cock a fist.

Then Diana was standing next to her, smiling sweetly. She laid a hand on Janine's drawn-back arm, and suddenly the tension just flowed out of the scene.

The artillerywoman looked a question at Lady K. "Don't worry about my anonymity, Di," Kali said. "I don't mind people knowing I'm drying out. I just don't go *advertisin'*."

Janine's truculent manner dropped right in the gutter at her feet. *"Hijo la,"* she moaned. "I'm sorry, Cap'n."

Lady K gave her a dazzling grin. "Never happened, Butterfly. Let's go ahead on in."

Part Four

Razor Games

≡ 19 ≡

Mirza Peter Abdulsattah appeared entirely awake, entirely collected, and entirely unsurprised at having been—presumably—roused from sleep in the belly of the night. He arranged his brown and black striped robes around his gaunt body and settled in behind his desk.

"Yes?" he said.

Cassie waited a few heartbeats, still braced. Dignitaries in the Combine were not notorious for their forbearance toward underlings. Neither was brass anywhere else, in Cassie's experience. But the expected blustering about what would happen if she had disturbed him without *damned* good reason never materialized.

She nodded briskly to herself. *Need to focus.* The night's events had shaken her in a way she did not truly understand.

"There was a meeting in Sodegarami tonight, in a warehouse down on the waterfront," she said. Still dressed in her anonymous spacer's outfit, Cassie pulled the palmcorder from an inner pocket of the jacket, popped out the disk, slid it across the desk toward him. "Guy I'm pretty sure was Kazuo Sumiyama played host. I was an uninvited guest. The guest of honor was somebody I didn't make, but I figure he has to be big."

Abdulsattah cocked an eyebrow at her. "And how big is 'big,' Lieutenant?"

"If his guards weren't DEST, then some holo-production company's missing a bunch of costumes."

Abdulsattah picked up the disk in forceps fingers. "Holo producers do not *make* movies about DEST in the Draconis

Combine," he said. He fed the disk into a slot on the desk, manipulated a keypad inset in the wood.

The lights dimmed further. Images sprang up where the desert scene had been. Abdulsattah nodded. "Sumiyama, indeed. And the other—"

The scene panned back to the redheaded man. Cassie, who knew what was on the disk, was watching the *Mirza*. Even in the darkness she could see that he paled.

On the sound-track, the slash-mouthed man's words were clearly audible: "—sekhar Kurita shall get what he has had com—"

Abdulsattah ran the brief sequence through three times, then froze the redheaded man upon the wall and turned up the lights.

"Tell me everything that happened," he said. "Everything you did, everything you saw. Even everything you *guessed*." He did not raise his voice, but the tension in it was unmistakable.

Cassie obeyed. After a momentary hesitation, she described the killing of the DEST operative and her improvised attempt to make it look like an accident.

"You killed a DEST agent *bare-handed*?" the *Mirza* asked incredulously.

"I had surprise," she said. "Also motivation."

Abdulsattah shook his long narrow head and muttered something Cassie could not understand. He popped out the datadisk, picked it up, and rose.

"Follow me," he said, leading her through a door in the rear of his office. There was a little chamber there, paneled in dark lustrous wood, with a framed scroll covered with an intricate interlocked design in black ink. A door in the paneling slid aside, and Abdulsattah led Cassie into a small elevator.

The car descended into the depths of the Citadel. The *Mirza* stood as if in his own world, humming tunelessly to himself, tapping the toes of his right foot on the sole of his sandal. Cassie tried not to look at him, but inside she was fascinated. The humming, the toe-tapping, were all but imperceptible—yet for a man who wasted so little motion, they amounted almost to a nervous tic.

At a level Cassie suspected was well below ground the car stopped. The door slid open, revealing a chamber about ten meters square. The walls were most obscured by lush hang-

ings and expensively elegant screens. In the center of the
floor was a conversation pit almost filled with silk cushions.
Amid them sprawled Chandrasekhar Kurita, a vast baby doll
in a scarlet robe.

Though Cassie had seen Abdulsattah do nothing to signal
their approach, Uncle Chandy seemed unsurprised to see
them. If he had been interrupted or awakened, he gave no
more sign than had his security chief.

"Lord Kurita," Abdulsattah said, "this young woman
brings us most unsettling news."

Uncle Chandy nodded his shaven head. "Thank you, Peter. I shall hear her story." He gestured toward the cushions
with a broad hand. "Come, child. Sit. Make yourself at
home."

Cassie hesitated, eyeing her employer narrowly. *My job
description sure as hell doesn't include rolling around with
a wad of greasy blubber,* she thought. Still, she doubted a
Kurita would take kindly to being refused. There was no
point in causing a war over what was on the face of it a
courtesy; plenty of time to fight when and if Uncle Chandy
demanded something unacceptable. She sat, keeping studi-
ously out of the fat man's reach.

Abdulsattah crossed to a small antique table, slipped the
datadisk into the mouth of what seemed to be a small, fat
dragon carved from blue Proserpina jade. Then he bowed
and withdrew into the elevator, which swallowed him without a sound.

Chandrasekhar Kurita sat studying Cassie for a moment.
His eyes were small and black as buttons, almost lost in
shiny rolls of fat. They were also hard and bright as obsidian.

"Speak, child," Uncle Chandy murmured. "Tell me your
tale."

He listened raptly, without interruption. It seemed to Cassie that his eyes widened fractionally at the mention of the
redheaded man.

"You are a young woman of formidable attributes," the
Kurita said when she had finished, "not least of which is
luck."

He clapped his hands, and said to the air, "Display the
recording now."

What had appeared to be a Bokhara carpet from ancient
Terra turned into a viewscreen displaying the warehouse

scene. Uncle Chandy nodded when the red-haired man came into view.

"Freeze it," he said, and this was done. "The first man, as you surmise, is my old friend Kazuo Sumiyama. Do you know who this other is, young lady?"

"No. Only that he must be important."

"Important, indeed. And more than important. He is deadly."

I figured that too, Cassie thought, but bit her tongue. Chandrasekhar Kurita almost managed to intimidate her, which made it all the harder to restrain her wiseass impulses. Fortunately, the preservation instinct was running strong in her, awakened by the warehouse encounter.

"His name is Ninyu Kerai Indrahar," Chandy said. "He is the adoptive son and heir-designate of Subhash Indrahar, the Smiling One."

Cassie caught her breath. She was far from easily impressed. But the realization that she'd been within spitting range of the second most feared secret policeman in the Inner Sphere caused her limbs to quiver and a roaring sound to momentarily fill her head.

She came back from her momentary distraction to hear Uncle Chandy saying, "—your impressions of what you observed, Lieutenant Suthorn."

She looked at him. He smiled, almost shyly. "You are surprised that I know your name? I wish I could claim to know the name of everyone in your Regiment, indeed I do. Just as I wish I could recognize each of my employees by sight. Alas, such is beyond my modest capabilities. The *Mirza* has briefed me about you. And, indeed, your own Colonel spoke of you to my agents, during our contract negotiations. Your talents as a scout were a significant selling point."

"You expected something like this." The words tumbled out before she could think about the ramifications of saying them.

He smiled benignly. "I expected *something.* One acquires certain instincts—spending years at Court, spending years in business, being born a Kurita."

So much for our easy ride. She could not bring herself to feel cheated; Uncle Chandy had never promised that he was hiring the Caballeros purely for show and without any risk of danger. For an outfit as little-known as it was, the Seventeenth charged steeply for its services. It was a lot to expect any man to pay out that much on a whim, even someone as allegedly rich and foolish as Chandrasekhar Kurita.

And while the *rich* part was beyond dispute, it was coming to Cassie that she had yet to see anything of the fool about Uncle Chandy.

She felt a tingling, a spreading sensation that was part fear and part welcoming a challenge. This game might prove to be as exacting as 'Mech-hunting—and perhaps even more dangerous.

"Sumiyama doesn't like you, Lord Kurita," she said, scanning his face for a flicker of the impulse to slay the bearer of bad tidings. The vast wheat-colored expanse of skin remained placid as a wind-sheltered pond. "For him to be holding a secret meet with the Smiling One's heir . . ."

She paused. "That looks like the ISF may be mounting an operation against you." The conclusion shook her like the concussion of a long-range missile.

Kurita raised one thin eyebrow. "Not simply interested in keeping an eye on my humble self?"

Cassie shook her head. "No." Absorbed as she was, she omitted an honorific. Uncle Chandy did not remind her. "Maybe I've gotten too many of my ideas about how the ISF works from the holo and Steiner and Davion propaganda, but it seems to me that the Dragon's Breath would have all the spies it needs without having to put the touch on the local yakuzas. I—I think they must be looking for a local base, and support, for a covert operation."

As she spoke, it was occurring to Cassie that here was a very unorthodox Kurita indeed. Uncle Chandy was not just consenting to listen to, but actually *soliciting* the opinion of an underling—and a woman at that. *Maybe that's why everybody thinks he's such a fool, because he pays attention to people who're supposed to be inferior.*

She suspected that tolerance endured only so long as the supposed inferior—or anyone else, for that matter—had something worthwhile to say.

He was nodding, still showing no sign of surprise or concern. "Why do you suppose the ISF does not move against me directly, then?"

Cassie may have lacked tact, but her survival instincts were more than active enough to take up the slack in time of need. This jolly fat man was a Kurita, after all. She bowed her head.

"Might your humble servant inquires as to why your Radiance deigns to listen to her opinions?"

Uncle Chandy threw back his head and laughed. Like the *Mirza*, his was not the high-pitched titter common among the *Masakko*, but a gusty roar. "Isn't it a little late to play the servile underling, Lieutenant?"

"Did not a wise man once say, 'Better late than never,' Lord?"

More laughter. "Undoubtedly. I've said it myself, not infrequently. But come, child, your *gaijin* impertinence is part of your charm. Even though you were born a daughter of the Dragon."

Her blood temperature dropped a few degrees. He really *had* taken an interest in her. She hoped that wouldn't have unfortunate ramifications.

"Besides," he went on, "you were the person on the scene. And the very fact that you were able to turn the tables on the cagey Ninyu and live to tell about it reveals how good you are. Or that you're very lucky—probably both. That is a fortuitous combination indeed, and renders what you have to say of interest to my corpulent self."

It occurred to Cassie that her employer was something of an old windbag—and also something of a self-parodist, another trait she wouldn't have expected in a Kurita. Despite the fact that she had grown up with little love for the Combine or its ruling family, or authority figures of any stripe, she was tempted to like the fat old fraud.

"Now kindly answer my question, daughter," Uncle Chandy said, an ever so slight note of command coming into his voice. She had to admire his technique. He had subtly established himself as an indulgent, appreciative master—but a master withal.

"I don't know much of substance about the Internal Security Force," she said, "but it seems to me that they don't have more than suspicion to work on. If they had the goods, they'd just up and arrest you, no matter who you were. As it is"—she shrugged—"simple suspicion should be enough to get you disappeared or killed, just as if you were a laborer or *sarariman*. But because you're Kurita, they feel they have to be sneaky about it."

She looked at him, then, her gray eyes large and questioning. He returned the gaze for a moment. His substantial brows drew together like thunderheads gathering above the Western Sea Range, and then he chuckled.

"You have an amusing way of asking an impertinent question by not saying anything at all," he said. "I am sufficiently amused to answer. No, I am not engaged in any activity prejudicial to the interests of the Draconis Combine, House Kurita, or my beloved cousin Theodore."

She bowed her head to the carpet. "Forgive me, Lord. But I had to know. My Regiment—"

"Is your family. And the matter has bearing upon its survival. I understand. But you already seem to have grasped the key element, that innocence makes no difference to the Dragon's Breath unless it can be conclusively demonstrated. Until that time, suspicion is a natural supposition of guilt. Even the guilt of one such as myself."

He gestured. A panel slid open, and a young woman with deep red hair piled atop her head and dressed in a diaphanous robe came in carrying a tray. She set it down between Cassie and Uncle Chandy, poured pale wine from a carven black lacquer bottle into beaten-bronze cups. She smiled at Cassie and glided out.

"So the vultures gather," Uncle Chandy murmured. "One thing you would likely not know, child, is that the warehouse where the meeting took place is owned by a subsidiary of Tanadi Computers."

She looked at him. This was, indeed, new information, but she couldn't say she was surprised.

"They're jealous of your success?"

He nodded. "And the esteemed Kazuo-*sama* of Sumiyama-*kai* hates me because I use my own cargo handlers instead of the ones provided by his alleged union, and do not permit him to shake down my people or the occupants of the properties I own for protection money."

He chuckled. "Actually, I think he finds it harder to forgive me for shortening my workers' hours, and otherwise behaving in a non-traditional way. Great preservers of the Dragon's holy tradition, our Combine criminals. And the Earl of Hachiman, who doubtless is involved, has probably perceived at last the true extent of the financial network I have constructed, and feels his power compromised—not to mention the powerful urge to cut himself in on a share of the proceeds."

"But the ISF," Cassie blurted. "If you're innocent, Lord, why are they—?"

"Suspicious of me? Dear child, it is the Smiling One's nature to be suspicious, as it is the nature of the tiger eels of the Great Bodhisattva Reef to bite and hold tenaciously. I am of the Blood, after all. Though I am distant from the line of succession, I would not be the first Kurita to regard that as a small barrier to ambition."

He shook his head, causing his jowls to wobble like gelatin glaciers. "The Combine has lived too long for the Pillar of Steel alone, and neglected the Pillar of Jade. House Steiner and House Davion are stronger than we, yet the Steiners are merchants first and foremost, and the Davions, while warriors of note, have never neglected trade. We are strong but poor.

"I have built what I have through my own wits and effort; I have never traded upon my name. That is perhaps the main factor exciting old Subhash's suspicion, his beginning to discover just how much I *have* built, using proxies and dummy corporations to hide my personal involvement."

He looked at her, the anthracite eyes shining with such earnestness that Cassie was instantly on her guard. "The Combine's weakness has always been that we viewed trade as an adjunct to war, all too often practicing it in a way nearly indistinguishable from conflict. Our reputation for double-dealing and outright piracy is appalling. What is the result? Our people suffer, our realm scrabbles for resources, while smugglers from the Federated Commonwealth carry on the bulk of interstellar commerce within the Combine—and reap most of the rewards.

"My goal is to change that. Not through force of arms—the Dragon knows we have tried, and it is like trying to push back the tide with our hands. Instead, my aim is to strengthen our economy by providing goods people are actually willing to pay for, at a reasonable price; and by always dealing honorably with my trading partners."

Cassie eyed him narrowly. This all sounded subversive to her.

"Not everyone in the Combine is in accord with such aims. I don't doubt that our Coordinator would be, but he was raised to concern himself first and foremost with war, and he is preoccupied with the threat of the Clans. Indeed, it seems he alone in all the Inner Sphere concerns himself with the great menace we all face, the Sword of Damocles that hangs over our heads by a hair fraying with the passage of each year. Meanwhile all the other princes scuttle and scrap for dynastic advantage that will become as meaningless as last year's cherry blossoms in a mere eleven years unless we find some means of countering Clan might.

"But others—Marquis Hosoya, the yakuza, perhaps even the Planetary Chairman—feel threatened by what I am attempting. They prefer the old days, when treachery, corruption, and outright force were the media of exchange. The concept of giving value for value undermines their whole existence. They will stop at nothing to stop me."

"Do you believe the Smiling One is in league with them, Lord?"

"He is *cooperating* with them through his alter ego Ninyu, that much we know—thanks to your own courage and skill, my dear." His eyes twinkled as he sipped his wine. Cassie had not yet decided whether he was trying to seduce her or not. That in itself was unusual; Kuritas did not *seduce*, historically. They took.

Of course, Cassie had never been relieved of Blood-drinker, either. She assumed that meant Uncle Chandy had snipers hidden somewhere behind those exquisite tapestries. In any event, she would not be easy to rape, alive.

"But I fear my own innocuousness has come, in a way, to work against me. In all my years I have done nothing that would indicate the slightest interest in the Coordinatorship. I have upheld Theodore, publicly and privately, even in the face of poor dead Takashi's displeasure—as did Subhash himself. Now the Smiling One learns of the power base I have built, on a foundation of money, not blood. And that arouses his suspicion. Why should I be so self-effacing, build such a shadow empire, if I did not intend to seize ultimate power? Such is the way the mind of Subhash works. But sometimes he is a man too devious for his own good."

"For that matter, why hasn't the Smiling One seized power, Lord?"

"Because his ambition does not extend beyond serving the Dragon. He is a monk, with a monk's devotion and self-denial, even as I am myself—I see you trying to hide a smile. I deny myself few pleasure of the flesh, child. But I deny myself ultimate ambition, and that for a Kurita is the greatest sacrifice of all. I indulge in those pleasures that it is traditional for a Kurita to spurn, but resist the craving for power to which so many of my kindred are enslaved. Like Subhash, my only desire is to serve."

He sighed volcanically. "But, alas, the Smiling One cannot believe that of any but himself. And perhaps his adopted son, who has graced our planet with his presence."

Chandrasekhar fingered his topmost chin and his gaze went to some faraway place. Cassie settled back onto her haunches to wait. Patience did not come naturally to her, but she had practiced until she could fake it.

Circumstances, however, were not making it easy for her to cool her heels. She felt a surging need to jump up and run out to warn Don Carlos and the rest of her comrades of the danger they faced. Had she not dedicated herself to the Regiment's safety with the fanaticism of an acolyte of the Order of Five Pillars? This was the greatest threat to the Caballeros since they had escaped the Smoke Jaguars.

Just as she was about to start fidgeting, Uncle Chandy came back and blinked at her with amphibian eyes. "You are as resourceful as your Colonel claimed," he said. "And, as adept as are the *Mirza* and his operatives, I fear that the ISF has long since compiled fat dossiers on all of them. They will not have had time to learn much about you, however. You must continue to investigate this matter. From now on you will work for me directly."

Cassie bowed her head to the floor again. "Your pardon, Lord, but I must keep my Colonel informed of everything I learn."

His face clouded up impressively this time. Indulgent Uncle Chandy though he was, no Kurita expected to be contradicted. Especially by a female junior officer of *gaijin* mercenaries.

The passion subsided. His face smoothed again to pudding blandness.

"You risk much, daughter," he said, a trifle huskily. "Perhaps you should meditate upon the distinction between bravery and folly."

"As your Excellency said, my Regiment is my family," she told him, raising up to look him in the eye. "Surely Chandrasekhar Kurita can appreciate risking all for family."

Again he laughed, his great belly shaking. "I like you—may the Smiling One dip me in acid if I don't. We shall accomplish much together, Lieutenant, if I'm not compelled to kill you."

Or I you, Cassie thought, bowing again as the big man gestured permission to withdraw. Despite his parting shot, she felt unaccustomed warmth in the pit of her belly as she stepped into the elevator, which slid open at her approach.

She trusted the old man. Within sharp limitations, to be sure—but still, she trusted him.

Trust wasn't something that came easy for her. Since Guru Johann died, she had trusted few people—the Colonel, Patsy Camacho, and now, grudgingly, that smooth blonde bitch of an *Atlas* pilot.

Take care, a voice inside her warned. *Trust makes you vulnerable.*

Cassie shuddered as the elevator bore her upward. She had spent a lifetime struggling to armor herself against all imaginable weaknesses. Yet she was unwilling to give up her trust, in Don Carlos, or Lady K, or Uncle Chandy.

Am I losing my edge? she wondered.

The ComStar acolyte who handed Ninyu Kerai the message sheaf bowed as deferentially as the *Dictum Honorium* might prescribe. Nonetheless, she seemed distracted, and almost rushed away.

Ninyu Kerai Indrahar could not have been described exactly as an *understanding* man, but he knew what the acolyte's problem was: technological advances were breaking up ComStar's monopoly on faster-than-light interstellar communications, while the dissident Word of Blake sect—with Free Worlds League ruler Thomas Marik as their main supporter—was threatening to destroy them as heretics. So far the schismatics relied mainly on sporadic terrorism, but like ComStar itself, they had a powerful modern army. An army that might soon be backed by Free Worlds 'Mechs—if not the forces of Marik's son-in-law to be, Sun-Tzu Liao.

Presumably the acolyte's concern was more abstract than immediate; the Combine had a longstanding concordance with ComStar. Both Marik and Liao were being extremely conciliatory of House Kurita at the moment, hoping to forge an alliance against the troubled Federated Commonwealth. And Captain-General Marik had recently received the heads of some seven Word of Blake terrorists, packed in canisters of dry ice, men who had been impertinent enough to try to conduct operations within the Combine. At least in the heart of Kurita space, ComStar was secure.

Ninyu smiled thinly. It might have occurred to the acolyte not to trust in Combine goodwill too implicitly. And that was wise.

Never forget who we are, his adoptive father was fond of telling him, *nor what we are. Leave honor to the samurai, in their perpetual adolescence. Our only honor is what best serves the Dragon.*

Ninyu was about to ascertain whether he might best serve the Dragon by committing *seppuku.* He opened the folded slip with steady fingers.

The message was written in a private code known only to him and Subhash Indrahar. It read, *Do not be concerned, adoptive son. Even if an intruder penetrated your meeting with Sumiyama, it is of small consequence.*

In the meantime, I am sending an asset which I believe will prove useful.

There was no salutation or farewell. Ninyu nodded as he crumpled the thin yellow paper. He approved of his adoptive father's lack of sentiment. The old man was weak in body, but he still breathed with the spirit of the Dragon.

That Ninyu was not deemed to have failed significantly—and so could go on living—he took note of without elation or relief. Had he not long since learned to live as one already dead, the Smiling One would never have chosen him as son and heir.

As he stepped into the muggy night to burn the message slip, he wondered briefly just what useful item Subhash Indrahar might be sending him. Except for the matter of the unexplained death of agent Collins in the warehouse, he thought he had the situation well in hand.

Blood-drinker in hand, Cassie moved as if underwater through the movements of a fighting form. Her quarters were dark, the curtains drawn against the light of the blue moon, Benkei. It was good discipline to practice without sight, and it helped to focus her mind.

But the fear inside her would not be stilled. Even her art could not completely calm her, and the Void of meditation escaped her as it had not in years.

At last she gave up and crawled into bed. Tears overwhelmed her, hot and sudden.

You're overextended, she tried to tell herself. *This is a re-action to physical and mental exhaustion, no more.* But she knew that was a lie.

For years Cassie had been awakening in terror from night-mares in which giant metal men pursued her, destroying ev-erything she loved or ever had. In reaction, she had turned herself into a killing machine as deadly as any Clan OmniMech. Every BattleMech she destroyed won her respite from the terrifying dreams.

Deep down, she still feared 'Mechs. But she had long since learned to live with that fear—to use it, to mold herself into a consummate weapon, to wield her body and mind and skills as deftly as a *kenjutsu* master wielding a blade. For all the awesome might of the giant battle machines, they had their weaknesses—and Cassie knew them all, and lived within them, as a rat lives within fortress walls.

But the red-haired man—he was a killer, and he com-manded black legions whose training and technology could negate most of her hard-won skills of stealth. She survived against BattleMechs because they were huge and unwieldy, their pilots insulated from the outside world by tons of armor—and their own MechWarrior arrogance. She defeated them because they could not see her unless she chose to let them.

But she could not hide from the black-suited agents of DEST; they were as small and alert and agile as she. The red-haired man could use her own weapons against her, a re-alization that terrified her to the core of her soul.

Fear for her had a new face. A new name. *Ninyu Kerai Indrahar.*

Only then did she realize she was clutching the stuffed bear Kali MacDougall had given her, its pink fur wet from her tears. She made as if to hurl the soft hateful thing across the room, but the fear overcame her again, and she huddled in on herself, clutching the toy and weeping, until at last fa-tigue drew her downward into sleep.

Masamori, Hachiman
Galedon District, Draconis Combine
21 September 3056

The scarfaced spacer smiled through a haze of cigar smoke at the diminutive woman in the aerospace jock's jacket as if he didn't mind the port-wine birthmark covering half her face at all.

"Yeah, I'm sure," he said. She could not place his accent. His clothes gave no hint to his origin, which wasn't unusual in his line of work. "Them was Clanners we brung down to the surface."

Cassie stared at him. She resisted the impulse to look wildly around the spaceport dive to make sure no one was paying too close attention. She had greased the management well to permit her to install a few telltales of her own to detect bugs. And as the one-eyed woman who ran the place said, Cassie was doing *her* a favor because it meant being able to guarantee complete privacy to her patrons.

Of course, in the water trade, loyalty tended to stay bought only until a higher bidder came along. On the other hand, Cassie wasn't too worried; word of the fate of Rikki the pimp had gotten around. People would not trifle with her lightly.

But *lightly* did not begin to describe how the red-headed man could lean on a body, either. Cassie realized she was becoming paranoid, but she wasn't going to take anything for granted, either.

"Are you sure?" she asked. "What were they, warriors? Elementals?"

He laughed. "Sure I'm sure. Don't know what caste they was from, nor Clan neither, and they wasn't wearing any kinda badges to identify 'em. Only thing I *am* sure of is that none of 'em was Elementals—no nine-foot mounds of muscle, them. But they were Clanners, right enough, from the cut of their clothes, and that *look* they have." He shuddered. "Once you see 'em, you don't never forget. Had hold of me and my crew for a while on Twycross, 'til Kai Allard-Liao sprang us. Got a bellyful of 'em then, and more."

Cassie had spent the last two weeks working the streets and clubs and tending her own intelligence network like a lithe gray-eyed spider. She had even gone back to work her regular shifts at the Kit-Kat, overcoming a terrified conviction that somehow the Sumiyama yaks knew she had been in the godown and were only waiting their chance to grab her and torture her.

They didn't. They didn't know a damn thing, only that some boxes had fallen from a stack and busted the neck of one of Ninyu Kerai's arrogant, black-clad bully-boys. They got a pretty good laugh from that over their Borstal Boys.

Beyond that, beyond the fact that the second-in-command for the whole ISF was on-planet and like *this* with *Dai-Ichi* Sumiyama, the soldiers down in the Kit-Kat knew nothing. Neither did anyone else with whom the far-flung tentacles of her network came in contact.

Though frustrating, that didn't surprise her. Ninyu surely wasn't about to discuss his plans with the yaks. He'd tell them what he wanted when the time came, and if they were smart they'd see he got it with a minimum of fuss.

Cassie did pick up rumors that the red-haired man was staying at Stormhaven, the Fillington estate north along the coast from Masamori, but she hadn't yet penetrated high Hachiman society to any great extent. The *geisha* houses and gambling establishments that catered to the elite were a little tougher to crack than the Kit-Kat Klub and Torashii Gyaru, where, as a matter of fact, Cassie *was* dancing every once in a while, to see what she could pick up on. But she was not prepared to call attention to herself by pushing too hard anywhere.

Ironically, when a nice juicy fly did blunder into her web, it had nothing at all to do with what she was looking for. Or maybe everything.

"Where'd you pick them up?" Cassie dug into her pocket for her wallet, using the opportunity to skim the room with her eyes. No one seemed to be paying them any attention.

Not that that was any real surprise. Minding other people's business was a fine way of fetching up dead in Yoshi-Town.

"Out on the Priff," he said, using spacer's slang for the Periphery, "just across the line from Gravenhage. Too close to Jag territory for comfort, even though the Wolves and the Bears are givin' 'em most of all they can handle these days. 'Course, that close to Clan space, the Snake patrols got better things to do than look for us."

"You ran suspected Clanners into the Combine," she said in wonder.

"Told you we did." He chuckled. "Hey, you don't think we had a license from the Dracs to run out beyond the Fringe, do you? Might as well get hanged for a sheep as a lamb, whatever that means."

He took a drag on his smoke and shrugged. "Besides, we weren't sure they was Clan to start with. Only that they wanted a ride to Hachiman, and were willing to pay."

"C-bills?" No spacer Cassie had ever met would even consider risking Kurita anti-smuggler patrols and their summary notions of justice for payment in the unstable H-bills issued by the Inner Sphere's Great Houses. Of course, the C-bills issued by ComStar, once the foundation of Inner Sphere exchange, were also beginning to fray at the edges these days, thanks to pressure from the Word of Blake zanies.

"Gold."

Cassie made an appreciative face, nodded.

She had never intended to get quite so involved in the less-licit water trade as Rikki the late pimp's impulsive nature had led her to become. But here it was paying off big time. It was amazing the things a lonely spacer—or just about anyone, to tell the whole truth—was capable of telling a total stranger, just because they happened to be sharing a table. Or a pillow.

"Like I said," the spacer was saying, "they didn't identify themselves as Kerenskys or nothin' when we DropShipped 'em aboard the *Daisy Belle.* It was just—they didn't act quite right, you know, like they wasn't comfortable around people, or at least raggedy-ass Inner Sphere types like us. They was polite enough and all, just—remote. *Different.*"

"Where'd you take them?"

This time his colorless eyes made a circuit of the crowded bar, and he rubbed the stubble on his thin cheeks thoughtfully with a palm. It made a rasping noise until Cassie lifted her own hand off the table to reveal a roll of C-bills.

His eyes lit. The Blakies hadn't yet messed ComStar currency up *that* much.

"Took 'em out in the middle of the Aventurine Sea, clear t'other side of the world," he said.

"How'd you keep from being spotted?"

He tipped his head and gave her an odd, birdlike look. She realized she had taken a false step. Below the edge of the table, her hand edged toward the bent hilt of her *kris*.

"You know how spotty Hachiman traffic control is," he said, "don't you?"

"I made planetfall as cargo, myself."

The suspicious crow's-feet smoothed out from around the spacer's mouth and eyes. He nodded. "Well, take it from somebody who knows, their coverage is more hole than net. Piece of cake to do a touch'n'go. Reckon the yak like it that way."

"Could be," Cassie said. "What about the Clanners?"

He stubbed his cigarette in a bronze ashtray and immediately lit another. "Dropped 'em at a map reference in a Zodiac boat. Blowin' a gale, waves toppin' ten meters, and they never flinched, just went puttin' off in that Z-bird as if they had never a care in the whole damn world."

"Any land in range?"

"Not a chance."

"Did you spot their pickup ship?"

The spacer snorted. "Didn't even look. Didn't care. Tell you some truth, I was glad to see the last of 'em. And if they went straight to the bottom of the ocean, so much the better. Not even ISF interrogators can get much out of dead Clanners."

He stood up. "Reckon I done as much talking as my health can stand," he said. He lifted his right hand, encased in a fingerless glove, and riffled through the stack of C-bills Cassie had slipped him.

"Easy money, I guess," he said. "Sure you don't wanna help me spend it?"

Cassie looked up at him and nodded slowly. He shrugged and was gone.

She sat there, vision unfocused, allowing her senses to gather impressions from the tavern and the throng around her: smell of tobacco and various smokable drugs, sweat, a tang of fear; muttered conversations, spikes of anger, hissed shushings, the tinny Moroccan-roll music currently popular among Inner Sphere spacers; looks of anger and greed and lust and plain despair. Slow, smoke-laden currents of air and the pressure of many presences.

Guru had taught her to sense the presence of danger simply by allowing her senses free rein and not allowing her conscious mind to interfere; to let her instinct sift the input for nuggets of menace. Of course, it didn't always work. Guru Johann stepped on a glass cobra and died before his spasming brown body hit the ground in front of his shanty on the outskirts of Larsha. Cassie had been so distraught by the death of the one living human in the universe that she cared about that she'd let herself get trolled in by a random street-sweeping police patrol two days later.

But she'd been through so much since then. Both her senses and her subconscious processing of what they brought her had been sharpened on a score of worlds and in a thousand potentially lethal situations. There was no danger here.

No *immediate* danger, she amended mentally. Outside, it was as if the night had become a vast sea of menace; she could feel its pressure, as she always imagined she'd be able to feel the crushing pressure of the ocean in a submersible a thousand meters down.

She had no idea what significance the presence of Clanners on Hachiman might have, for her, for her employer, for her surrogate family. But she knew in her DNA that it was significant. As significant as the presence of the red-haired man—and as potentially deadly.

Some of the unattached men in the bar were beginning to slip her sidelong fondling looks. To have to injure or kill somebody would call attention to her. The *last* thing she wanted was for anyone to remember that the woman with the florid birthmark had been talking intently to the lanky spacer who at one time had had his face opened up from his right eyebrow to the tip of his long chin. She had chosen the port-wine mark because it grabbed attention, was all anyone would recall of her appearance. But she was under no illusion that ISF psych-techs lacked ways to pry a more complete picture from a witness' subconscious.

Though her instincts were shrilling for her to get *out of here,* she made herself sit and pretend to smoke a cigarette,

to set an interval between her informant's departure and her
own. Then she rose and slid casually out through the rowdy
crush of drinkers.

Outside the night was bright with the holographic blan-
dishments of Yoshi-town. Cassie gave the street a quick surveillance. A knot of stevedores made their drunken way
toward her, singing a bawdy song in the Rasalhague tongue:
have to navigate around them. None of her stable of hookers
was in view—she'd picked the meeting-place to be well
clear of their turf—and if somebody was lurking in shadow
to watch her, they were damned good.

She put her hands in her pockets. The right closed reas-
suringly around the black rubber grips of her snub-nosed
10-mm hideout. She began to walk down the street as if she
were heading somewhere in particular, but nowhere very urgent.

Uncle Chandy was lolling among his cushions eating
spiced fruit when the *Mirza* escorted Cassie from his private
elevator into the CEO's chambers. The Chief was not alone.
A pair of his play-pretties lounged with him, clad in skimpy
harem garb and with their hair piled on their heads. They
watched Cassie like cats whose domain has been invaded by
an unknown feline; their eyes tracked her like gunsights, and
she could almost see the tails twitch.

Have no fear, she thought. *I wouldn't be where you are for
anything in the world.* Even if *la Dama Muerte* thought she
was a total slut—and that *without* knowing that Cassie was
dancing naked at Torashii Gyaru.

"Ladies," Chandy said, "if you'll excuse me . . .?"

They rose, gave Cassie a last if-looks-could-kill-all-that'd-
be-left-of-*you*-is-smoldering-boots glare, and hip-swung out
of the chamber.

Chandy patted the cushions beside him. "Come, sit with
me, daughter. Enjoy some fruit."

Cautiously Cassie sat, but not quite as near his bulk as he
had indicated. He picked up a pale green grape. "These are
Terran grapes, marinated in a blend of native herbs. Really
quite exquisite."

"Thank you, Lord." Cassie was still too much of a street
child to turn down free food. She accepted a serving on a
golden plate and began to eat. Despite the fear that sim-
mered inside her, she munched with appetite.

Chandy nodded approvingly. "You are too thin, daughter; a little more flesh on those fine bones will buffer you against illness, mark my words." He lay back among the pillows. "Now, what have you brought for me?"

Between mouthfuls of sweet-spiced fruit, she told him what the spacer had said. He pursed his great mouth and sat very still.

"So. Someone on Hachiman treats with our great enemy." He fingered his chins. "Perhaps the Smiling One suspects their presence; that may be why he has despatched his pet blood-beast here."

Cassie froze with a slice of unknown purple fruit halfway to her mouth. If the redheaded man thought Uncle Chandy was treating with the *Clans* . . .

"*Mirza.*"

"I serve."

"Put all your resources on this matter. At once."

"But the matter of Ninyu Kerai Indrahar—"

"Will wait." A smile. "In the fullness of time, he no doubt will come to us. In the meantime, learn what you can about this Clan business. Lieutenant Suthorn will of course continue her inquiries, which have already proven so fruitful. But we have assets not even our resourceful *abtakha* can match."

A chill sizzle ran down Cassie's spine; the use of the Clan loan-word seemed ominous, though it had been her callsign since 3051.

The *Mirza* hesitated. "Chief Executive—?"

"Speak."

"It seems to me that only one entity on Hachiman would have the resources to smuggle Clan members onto the planet."

"Tanadi." Uncle Chandy rolled this around in his mouth, then set his great head back and laughed. "That would be choice. The Marquis assists Ninyu Kerai in destroying me for a crime the Marquis himself is committing! Delicious irony indeed."

He raised a pudgy hand as if delivering his blessing. "Go. We do not *know* it is Tanadi. Nor can we act until we have more information."

Abdulsattah bowed and withdrew. "Must you rush away, Lieutenant?"

She paused, caught off balance. *What's wrong with me?*

This is happening far too much these days. Yet there was no denying that Uncle Chandy was an extraordinary man—an unorthodox Kurita, indeed, but a Kurita.

"I—" She held her hands up. "I feel the need to *do* something, Lord."

"As a scout of your experience," he said, "I should think you understood the uses of patience."

She bowed her head. "I think I'm out of my depth here, Lord."

"No." She snapped her head up. "I do not believe you are, child. But that is something you must determine for yourself." He shifted his weight. "Are you sure you won't stay with me a while? I quite enjoy your company."

She tensed. "You can let that wild-animal look out of your eyes, Lieutenant," Chandy said, grinning abruptly in a way that made him almost boyish. "As you can see, I am quite adequately supplied with bedwarmers. While it's true that you are, in your quiet, underfed way, as lovely as the loveliest of them, I have no interest in seducing you. Nor coercing you, for that matter."

"Then what does your Excellency wish?"

"That you would sit with me and tell me marvelous tales of the deeds you've done and the sights you have seen. Why the look of surprise? Do you think I'm some kind of supernatural being, with no need for entertainment? Even the *kami* love a good story."

She sighed, sat. Tension flowed out of her. She had no choice, and in a way that was tremendously liberating.

Like the loss of control she got from alcohol or drugs, it was not a release she cared to permit herself too often.

"That's better," said Uncle Chandy. "Now, Lieutenant, before you tell me of your exploits, there is one thing I must ask you: do you indeed plan to inform your compatriots of what you have learned this night?"

She drew a breath deep, let it go. "No, Lord."

He nodded, smiled. "Your wisdom increases, little one. Now, how is it that you came to be scout for these mad men and women from the Trinity?"

21

Masamori, Hachiman
Galedon Diistrict, Draconis Combine
22 September 3056

Cassie was walking across the black dirt of the HTE Sportsplex outside Masamori, flattened to the consistency of cement by the passage of 'Mech feet, when her peripheral vision caught something flying at her face from the right.

It was too late even to draw Blood-drinker. All she could do was wheel into a twisted *pentjak* stance, hands open and raised to defend.

A red plastic ball covered in blue and yellow polka dots flew into her hands.

"Hi, Cassie!" a little square brown girl in a pink smock and jet black pigtails called. "Nice catch!"

She grinned. "Thanks, Nopalita. How's it going, gang?"

The dozen or so children from the day-care group crowded around, bouncing up and down and hugging Cassie. Little ones loved Cassie. She wasn't afraid to play with them.

"Gotta run now," she said shortly, disengaging herself from the pack. She waved to Diana, another of their favorites, who spent most of her free time working the Regiment's day-care center—and headed off for the rec hall.

Even before she got there Cassie could hear the shouts and cheers over the musicbox caterwauling that ancient favorite, *El Camino Real de Guanajuato*. It sounded as if something more spirited was going on than the usual debates of the merits of singing-*vaquero* star Tino Espinosa over Johnny Tchang, the martial-arts holo god who'd defected to the Federated Commonwealth from the Capellan Confederation in '49, just before the Clan invasion erupted.

She stepped inside to find the Ping-Pong table stacked

against a wall and a space cleared where two men, stripped to the waist, faced each other with knives. The holo set was playing in the corner, a kickboxing match from Luthien that was being ignored as comprehensively as the musicbox. Archie Westin, boy reporter, was hopping around the fight's perimeter like a nervous terrier.

"Ah, Leftenant Suthorn!" he said, spying her. He bounced to her side. "You've got to do something!"

"Why me?" Cassie said, watching the combatants circle each other. One was Macho, weaving a slim-bladed knife out in front of him. The other was a Kiowa from Captain Santo's Infante Company who went by the name Metalhead. He was a great big man, with a round dark face, hawk nose, and something of a gut, who was currently holding out a huge-ass Bowie, blade up. "Father Doctor Bob and Lady K both have rank on me."

The Jesuit was standing to one side with hands stuck in his pockets and a slightly glum expression. Kali MacDougall stood at the edge of the combat ground with her back to the wall, holding a pool cue in her hands.

"They're no bloody help," Westin said, distressed. "Captain MacDougall is actually *officiating.*"

Cassie nodded at Mariska Savage, who was ducking and weaving like a boxer, working the angles with her holocorder. "At least your faithful camerawoman is getting it all down on disk. Be a good show for the folks back home; you haven't had much exciting to show them since the mock battle."

"Good afternoon, Cassie," Father García said, materializing on her other side.

"*Buenas,* Father. *¿Qué pasó?*"

"I'm afraid our young friend from the Commonwealth is distressed by the barbaric side of our character."

Cassie made a face and shrugged. "They're letting off steam. Could be worse; might be settling their differences with Shimatsu forty-twos."

"Your Colonel permits this?" Archie asked, his brows horrified arches.

"He encourages it, discreetly," Father García said. "MechWarriors—especially those from the Trinity—have a way of insisting that honor be satisfied. And the damage they can do to each other with knives, or even machine pistols, is nothing to what would happen if they squared off in BattleMechs."

"Oh," the reporter said, with the air of one over whom a light is belatedly dawning.

"Even the Kell Hounds and Wolf's Dragoons have their duels," the Jesuit pointed out. "We try to keep things somewhat less intense."

A wolf-howl from the crowd. Archie and the others turned to see Metalhead lift his hand from a long, red-dripping slash traversing his paunch, and Macho grinning all over his dark face. Archie turned green beneath his freckles.

"It seems adequately intense to me," he said.

"Risky's getting right into it," Cassie said, using the nickname the unit had hung on the FCNS camerawoman. "Better watch it, or she'll throw you over to cover the underground free-fight circuit in Capellan space."

Archie arched an eyebrow at her. "You're joking, surely." Nonetheless he cast a worried glance at his photographer.

About that time Metalhead slashed toward Macho's face with a speed that belied his mass. Macho leaned way back, whipping up his smaller blade to parry. The Kiowa lashed out and swept the *norteño's* lead leg right out from under him, then swarmed into him, straddling him and pinning his knife-hand to the bare wood floor.

"Life is worth nothing in Guanajuato," the mournful musicbox sang.

With a howl of triumph Metalhead reversed his grip on the Bowie and reversed it to plunge into Macho's chest. Before that could happen, Lady K's pool cue came whistling around and whacked the inside of his wrist with a savage crack. The knife spun from his fingers.

"That's enough, boys," Kali said cheerfully. Dressed in sky-blue jeans and a barely blue shirt tied just above the midriff, she looked like a country girl off for a ride in the hills on a warm spring night. "Honor's satisfied. Time to shake hands and call the deal done."

"Who says?" Metalhead snarled, and lashed at her. Kali didn't dodge the roundhouse swipe; instead the butt of the poolcue smashed into the Kiowa's lantern jaw and threw him flat on his back. Before he could get up, Bronco Company's commander was standing over him with the tip of the cue at his throat, socketed in the notch of his collarbone.

"I says," she said. "You accepted me as ref, you accepted

any decision I made in advance. You got that, or do you want to spend the last couple minutes of your largely wasted life tryin' to learn how to breathe through the other end of your alimentary canal?"

Metalhead held his big hands up. To Archie's astonishment he laughed. "No problem, Yellowhair. Heat of the moment, y'know?"

She nodded, reaching down with one hand to help him up. Cassie saw Archie wince as the warrior took it and rose to his feet.

"Now what's the matter?" Cassie demanded.

"I—" He moistened his lower lip with his tongue. "I felt certain that individual would try something desperate when the Captain offered her hand."

"Why?"

"I suppose—I suppose because that's what happens in the holodramas all the time."

Father Doctor Bob laughed and laid a hand on the reporter's shoulder. "We Caballeros take our honor seriously."

"Besides," Cassie said as Metalhead was led off to have his cut dressed, "this is play to them."

Archie shook his head. "I admit it; I'm perplexed."

"By what?" Lady K asked, walking over. She had returned the cue to the rack. "By our occasionally bizarre play behavior? Hey there, Cass."

She and Cassie traded hugs. "Let's sit down and take a load off," she said. The four of them settled down at a table, one as far as Lady K could get from the musicbox.

"You ladies both used the word *play,*" Archie said seriously. "It does strike me appropriate, considering the names you give yourselves and your machines, the fanciful costumes some of you affect, the decorations plastered all over one of your 'Mechs. I know too that MechWarriors traditionally use callsigns, but with so much that you do, there does seem to be an aspect of, well, *unreality.*"

"I believe the word you're looking for is *make-believe,*" Father García said.

Lady K nodded and took a swig from a half-liter bottle of juice one of her Bronco jocks had brought her. "It's like this, Arch," she said. "All around the known galaxy, to this very day, kids grow up playin' cowboys and Indians. Right?"

Archie looked at her sideways for a moment, as if suspecting a trap. "Yes," he agreed cautiously. "I played it myself, growing up."

"Well, see, hon, we *are* Cowboys and Indians. So we figure that gives us license just to go on being kids forever."

The reporter blinked at her, uncertain how to respond. Finally he grinned gamely.

"You know, Captain, that explanation almost makes sense."

"Speaking as a trained sociologist," Father Doctor Bob said, "it's as good an explanation as you're going to get."

"So all this make-believe—you're simply playing a role?"

"We're all born to die, Archie," Lady K said. "The Trinity's a violent kind of place, at least out in the desert and chaparral and mountains where the real Caballeros roam, *norteño*, Cowboy, and Indian alike. We all know from early on that no one gets out of here alive." She shrugged. "So, long as you're taking a one-way trip across the stage, might as well make the show as good as y'can, *¿qué no?*"

While Archie struggled visibly trying to digest all that, Mariska Savage came up, excited as a new Lab puppy. "Wasn't that something, Archie? I got it all down. Hi, Lieutenant."

"What's happening, Risky?"

The camerawoman beamed. She claimed she'd never had a nickname before, but no one knew whether she was joking or not. Even though the Caballeros' subversive campaign to pry her out of her shell was slowly working, they still couldn't read her.

"No underground fight circuit for you, Ms. Savage," Archie said sternly.

"What?"

"The Capellan free fights are out, young lady. They're no place for a well-brought up person such as yourself."

"Archie, what are you talking about? Did you bump your head on something?"

Cassie caught Lady K's eye. "Talk to you a minute outside, Captain?"

Kali nodded. Archie turned to look stricken as the two women rose. "Lieutenant Suthorn! Must you rush away so soon? I'd really like to interview you about your mysterious comings and goings since your Regiment arrived—"

Lady K gave him a sweet smile and patted his cheek. "If she told every holonews reporter in the Federated Commonwealth about them, they wouldn't be mysterious anymore, would they? Don't fret, hon. We'll be back directly."

"Cassie—" Archie sputtered, but she was already gone.

The Jesuit laid a fatherly hand on his forearm. "Listen to the Captain, son, and don't get your insides in an uproar, as our Cowboy brethren would so picturesquely put it." He looked after the two, and he seemed rueful too. "Might as well try to catch the wind in your hands as try to hold on to that one."

Outside the sun was a gigantic molten-bronze ball about to drop into the unseen Shakudo Sea. A *Hunchback* strolled along the western perimeter, in silhouette looking as if its head was lowered in contemplation. Diana Vásquez had shepherded her charges back inside.

"What's on your mind, Cass?" Kali asked. She stepped to the side of the doorway, started to lean her shoulders back against a wall that looked to be made of wood planking, hesitated, and then went ahead and leaned. Their ever-helpful liaison Preetam Masakawa had proudly informed them at the dorms and auxiliary structures at the Sportsplex were made from panels of a synthetic processed out of sterilized human waste at an HTE-owned sewage treatment facility. Further evidence of Hachiman Taro's unusual interest in environmental preservation, not to mention Uncle Chandy's resourcefulness.

Lady K, like all the Seventeenth's ranking officers, had grown accustomed to complaints about the smell. Preetam insisted there *was* no smell. Kali had just about decided it *was* all in everybody's mind, but every now and then she caught a whiff of, well, *something*.

"That going on a lot?" Cassie asked.

Kali frowned, and suddenly she was a company commander confronted by an impertinent question from a lieutenant JG. Cassie braced herself for the blast. *See?* the taunting voice within her jeered. *You opened yourself to her, and she's going to treat you like dirt. Solitary means safe.*

Instead, the stiffness went out of the Captain, and she nodded. "More and more. Usual garrison-duty fever. Only so many holo games a body can play, only so many times you can watch Tino Espinosa singing his handsome little heart out as the bad guys close in for the kill."

"Is it just that?"

Lady K started to bristle again, then sighed. "Good thing we're a family," she said, "and *you're* such a long-range, low-heat scout. You'd drive the brass crazy in most outfits."

"You think *you* wouldn't?"

Kali laughed.

Long-winged nightgaunts flitted around them, uttering mournful croaks as they feasted on the twilight swarms of late-season sedge midges. In a few weeks first frost would come, and the insects would disappear.

"It's more than just the usual boredom," Kali admitted. "We've had a lot more dust-ups, and the casualties are getting worse. Ever since you brought us the cheerful news about the ISF taking a close personal interest in our favorite uncle, the boys 'n' girls have got to feeling as if we're sitting smack in the middle of the V-ring, waitin' for ol' Ninyu to drop the hammer on us."

Cassie kept staring at her. The ends of Lady K's mouth cut slowly back into her cheeks in an expression that wasn't a smile.

"You could cut me some slack, here, Lieutenant."

"You forced your way into my life, and made me take that damned bear. Forget about slack."

Kali laughed humorlessly. "All right. Yeah, Don Carlos has been sunk even deeper than usual into a funk lately. All this inactivity gives him plenty of time to brood about Patsy. People are starting to wonder if he's lost it."

"*El patrón*'s still got more on the ball than any self-obsessed 'Mech jock in the Regiment!" Cassie said heatedly.

"HDLC, hon, don't hang the messenger. I'm just passing the word on what's been happening on the home front while you've been out snoopin' and poopin' and trading in fallen women."

"Sorry," Cassie said. "It's just that Don Carlos has done so much for us. He's the only thing that's brought us this far."

"Yeah," said Kali, "and you can go ahead and skewer me with that wavy-blade toadsticker of yours for saying so, but he's not gonna bring us much farther if he doesn't pull together and get a grip."

Cassie turned away. Unexpected tears stung her eyes. To her Don Carlos was not a commanding officer, not an authority figure. He was the sole element of stability in a universe of uncertainty and destructive change.

"Hey!" a voice yelled from inside the rec hall.

They poked their heads back in through the door. It was Cowboy. He and Macho's other sidemen had gathered by the bar, consoling their fallen champion. The lanky Cowboy was pointing at the holovid display.

"Check it out," Cowboy said. "Our boss made the nightly news!"

The Masamori Broadcasting Company evening news was on. MBC was supposed to be private—it was a Tanadi subsidiary—but of course, all media in the Combine danced to the tune the Dragon called. The young woman reporter, who had undoubtedly been selected for her wholesome, earnest-yet-cheerful appearance, was saying, "According to reports from elsewhere in the Inner Sphere, Masamori's own Hachiman Taro Enterprises is on the verge of announcing a breakthrough in faster-than-light communications technology."

"This advance would complete the breakup of the monopoly on interstellar communications long enjoyed by ComStar's hyperpulse generator network already begun by Federated Commonwealth research into recently recovered technology," the earnest yet cheerful six-square meter face said from the wall of Uncle Chandy's pleasure dome.

Chandresekhar Kurita sighed, a sound like a two-moon tidal bore rushing down the Yamato. "So that's their angle of attack," he said.

Standing by his master, the *Mirza* Peter Abdulsattah nodded solemnly. "The Word of Blake has not accepted that the loss of the hyperpulse monopoly is inevitable," he said. "Their fanatics will be swarming here like flies to a honey pot to put an end to our heresy."

"With a little covert help from Ninyu Kerai Indrahar, no doubt." Kurita steepled his fingers before his pursed pudgy lips. "Have you any of those clever and illicit tales of your Mullah Nasruddin to cover this set of circumstances, old friend?"

"None suggests itself, my lord."

Chandrasekhar Kurita nodded. "We must step up our precautions. Order the mercenaries to recall some of their troops from the Sportsplex."

Abdulsattah paused. "If the Chief Executive permits—"

"Out with it! Why should I take the risks entailed in employing a member of a forbidden sect, if not to avail myself of his full range of abilities? I depend upon your candor, my Sufi friend."

"In military circles—if not always in the DCMS—it is considered the best command form never to command."

Kurita stared at him. His black eyes were matte, impermeable. After a moment a smile extended itself across the vastness of his face.

"You suggest I voice my concern, and allow my ferocious *gaijin* to take the initiative by boosting their forces within the Compound?"

Abdulsattah bowed. "You have suggested it yourself, Chandrasekhar-*sama*."

Uncle Chandy laughed uproariously. "You are a clever charlatan, Peter."

"I am, as you say, a Sufi, Lord."

22

Masamori, Hachiman
Galedon District, Draconis Combine
23 September 3056

The red-haired man stood on the terrace of Stormhaven, the Fillington ancestral estate set high against breathtaking rock cliffs towering a hundred meters over the self-devouring surf of the Shakudo Sea. Whoever had built the place had sited it excellently for defense.

Presumably his host had nothing to do with that.

The wind ruffled Ninyu's hair like fingers heavy with the scent and slightly tacky feel of salt water, tinged delicately with the smell of autumn-flowering blooms in the Earl's gardens. The sun was setting, the western sky banded in slate and indigo and fire. Field crickets trilled uncertainly, warming up for their nocturnal concert.

It was not in Ninyu's nature to appreciate such things. That was something his adoptive father was trying to teach him. *You are not a bushi, a warrior, you are ninja. Yet you must learn from the samurai, for all their posturing and self-deceit. And one thing you must learn is that a warrior without appreciation for beauty is like a blade without an edge.*

The image of the Smiling One promulgated within the Draconis Combine was of a benevolent aesthete, of discriminating tastes and affable manner, a man who might pat schoolchildren on the head when they visited his own extensive gardens to present him poems they had written in praise of the Coordinator. Outside the Combine it was generally assumed that Indrahar would be happiest boiling those happy schoolchildren in a pot. Even Liao's dreaded Maskirovka viewed him thus, and admired him all the more for it.

Ninyu Kerai knew the truth. His adoptive father would boil those schoolchildren in an eyeblink if his duty to the Dragon demanded it. But he would take no pleasure in it. *Giri overcomes ninjo;* duty overrides human sentiment. That was the law of the Dragon.

Yet Subhash constantly badgered his heir not to neglect those human feelings, *ninjo.* Ninyu did not fully grasp that. But his father bade him, and he obeyed; so he was learning to appreciate sunset and salt-spray and the perfume of Hachiman lilacs.

But not so much that he didn't note instantly the scuff of a shoe against the paving stones. Something clicked, paused, clicked again, like someone trying to emulate the cricket's stridulation with a pair of dinner forks. He grimaced, and felt the muscles between his shoulder blades tighten. Just as he began to grasp that serenity toward which his adoptive father guided him, here came the hateful Katsuyama to spoil it.

He turned and there he was, dressed in his ludicrous beret and smock. In his hand was something that suggested a chronometer, though there were tiny dots and numbers arranged around the perimeter of it, and slim pointers, and no space for a digital readout.

Ninyu Kerai bit back his anger at the interruption. *In the past, your anger has served you as a magnificent weapon, adoptive son,* Subhash had told him. *Yet it can turn in the hand and cut one like a Muramasa blade; it is a servant which can easily become one's master. The time has come to learn to put it aside.*

Ninyu was trying. But he'd hated Enrico Katsuyama on sight.

"What do you have there, Associate Director?" he barked.

Katsuyama held the device up in his face, clicked the knob on top of it. Ninyu resisted the impulse to seize it and hurl it over the cliff into the sea. He observed that the thinnest pointer was sweeping around the circle, and the middle one more slowly.

"It's a stopwatch," the lumpy man said.

"Ridiculous. How would one ever read such a thing?"

Katsuyama turned it, peered at it as if he'd just found it under a leaf in the garden. "These hands sweep around and point out the time."

Ninyu scowled. "You joke."

"No, no, truthfully, Assistant Director. This is a very special stopwatch. It's almost a thousand years old. It was used in the credits and framing sequences on the ancient Terran flatvision show *60 Minutes*."

"Indeed," Ninyu grunted. He actually had no idea what was appropriate to say, but he was damned if he'd let this toad set him at a loss.

Katsuyama bobbed his head enthusiastically. Moisture glistened at the corners of his mustache, Ninyu noticed with disgust, as if he had been chewing them.

"It's the newest addition to my collection," Katsuyama said. "I have Joseph Goebbels' microphone, a half-meter tall statue of Mickey Mouse, Indiana Jones' fedora, and the sweater worn by Franklin Roosevelt in his fireside chats, though I suspect it's merely a replica. All from the twentieth century."

"Why this obsession with that particular era?" asked Ninyu, who had no idea what Katsuyama was on about.

"Why, that period saw the dawn of the era of mass communications!"

Ninyu's eyes narrowed. "So?"

"So it also saw the dawn of media *manipulation*. Joseph Goebbels first discovered the principle of the Big Lie, on which all public-opinion molding is based. My relics are artifacts of Herr Goebbels and other greats of the art, who specialized in shaping popular opinion, whether through manipulative entertainment, cleverly biased news reports, falsified polling, or direct rabble-rousing."

"Are you sure that thing is real?" Ninyu asked. "It doesn't *look* a thousand years old."

Katsuyama blinked at him. "Why wouldn't it be?"

"Gentlemen."

Both turned to see the Right Honorable Percival Fillington, Earl of Hachiman, walking toward them from the great house. He was a slender young man in his early thirties, with pale, handsome features and curly hair on the light side of brown. He carried himself well enough, but inwardly Ninyu sneered. The man's fitness was that of the gym, of trainers and saunas and masseurs. He practiced *kendo*, as was almost mandatory for the Combine's upper classes. He had even seen brief action as a BattleMech pilot. But he was no warrior; he was soft at the core.

Which is why we conduct our real business with the yakuza, though policy requires me to treat with you.

"Have you heard? MBC has just picked up a story from elsewhere in the Inner Sphere that Chandrasekhar Kurita has discovered some kind of hyperpulse communications technology!"

Ninyu did not glance at Katsuyama, but he felt the little man's grin like warmth from a 'Mech's heat sink. The Planetary Chairman blinked from one of them to another. His eyes were large, brown, long-lashed, and slightly protuberant.

"You both know of this," he said, in a tone as close to accusing as a Planetary Chairman dared get with the number two man in the ISF and the deputy chief of the propaganda branch.

"The story originated with Associate Director Katsuyama," Ninyu acknowledged grudgingly.

The Earl's mouth became a startled "O." "But that will bring Word of Blake fanatics swarming to Hachiman!" he exclaimed. "They'll do anything to keep the hyperpulse monopoly intact, even under ComStar control."

"So it will, Mr. Chairman," Katsuyama said smugly.

"But, Ninyu-*san*, I thought the ISF was conducting a campaign against the Word of Blake."

I have to tell the fool something, don't I? He might prove inconvenient if his ego is not massaged. Tact was another quality Ninyu's adoptive father was trying to instill in him. The Smiling One was nothing if not exacting.

"We have firmly repressed all efforts by the Word of Blake to carry out attacks against ComStar facilities within the Combine, my Lord." He smiled, an expression not at all suited to his scarred lips. "If they agree to leave ComStar alone, Internal Security is willing to allow them some leeway in handling other matters."

"Oh," the Earl said. A *kabuki* actor's concept of a conspiratorial expression stole across his face. Ninyu had to bite down a laugh. "So you're going to let them put fat old Chandrasekhar in his place for you, eh?"

Among other things, Ninyu thought. His representatives were on the alert for feelers from the Word of Blake at any time. The Blakes knew better than to try to work the Combine without clearing it with the ISF, now.

As he indicated to Fillington, Internal Security was going to grant the Word of Blake permission to deal with this new heresy—as long as they accepted guidelines, which he and Subhash were certain they would. He and his adoptive father were also sure that, in the Word of Blake's eagerness to smash HTE and its presumptuous Chief Executive, they would compromise many of such assets as they had managed to infiltrate into the Combine without the ISF's knowledge.

The Smiling One was a master of games within games.

Fillington looked from Ninyu to Katsuyama. "Well, I'll just leave your gentlemen to fine-tune your plans. Dinner awaits after you've had enough of our fine evening sea air." Being around Ninyu seemed to make him nervous.

As the Planetary Chairman made his way quickly back inside the house, Ninyu stood there, willing Katsuyama to follow. The lure of a full table wasn't something the little man was much good at resisting.

But Katsuyama insisted on hovering at his elbow, gray in the twilight, like a lumpy ghost. "You have done well, Associate Director," Ninyu said.

Katsuyama bobbed his head gratefully. "Thank you, **Lord** Ninyu. Thank you so much." He made no move to leave.

Ninyu turned to him and raised an eyebrow. "Well?"

Katsuyama's tongue crept across his lips like a rat across temple steps. "I know you are skeptical of the value of me-

dia manipulation, Lord. I was hoping this demonstration
would open up to you the glories of the art."

"It appears to be working adequately in this case. My
adoptive father displayed his usual wisdom in sending you
to me."

"I trust you'll soon see his wisdom in bidding me stay
with you to see this through." The media man took off his
glasses, began to polish them with the tail of his smock.
"Have you never heard the phrase, 'Let them eat cake,' Lord
Indrahar?"

It was incorrect for Katsuyama to refer to Ninyu in that
way. He would have to reprove him for it—eventually.

In the meantime he nodded, warily and slow. "I've heard
it."

Katsuyama's face lit like a star-shell. "And do you know
who said it, Lord?"

"Some queen or other, in the days before spaceflight." A
moment's thought; Ninyu's adoptive father had urged the
study of history upon him. Life had been so much simpler
when he'd been merely an ISF agent. "They cut her head off
for it, I believe."

"That's the one. Only she *never said it.* It was invented by
the royal family's political opponents. On the basis of that
bold lie the king and queen were beheaded, an ancient mon-
archy deposed, the social order of all of Europe ultimately
overturned." Katsuyama shook his head. His eyes glistened
with moist devotional fervor, as if he were being privileged
to view the Coordinator on his birthday. "Do you not see the
transcendent power and beauty of propaganda, Lord? That
very same lie is used to good effect by social activists to this
very day, put in the mouths of those who oppose their reforms, to discredit them."

"We usually have to put such activists to death, don't
we?" Ninyu asked.

"Well, yes." Still the toad refused to be squelched. "Yet
the *principle* remains valid. Very valid indeed. As we've just
now demonstrated again."

"We have?"

"Do you have any evidence that Chandrasekhar Kurita has
the slightest interest in faster-than-light communications,
Lord."

"No."

Katsuyama showed him his uneven assortment of large,

yellowed teeth. Fortunately, it had gotten too dark to discern much detail. "Then what is this news report but a Big Lie? And you'll see, it will serve us as well again."

"Let's hope it doesn't have to." Ninyu looked out at the sea. A hint of purple iridescence seemed to lie upon the restless water, bled from the sungleam that edged the bottoms of the banks of black clouds. He turned to see that one of Hachiman's lesser moons had begun to peek over the great Trimurti Mountains, far inland. A few stars shone tentatively overhead.

"I'm going in," he said brusquely.

Katsuyama adjusted his beret to a jaunty angle. "I do believe I'll join you."

"The conditions out here are absurd, *papá*," Gavilán Camacho's handsome face was saying from the communicator on Don Carlos' desk. "We haven't been able to hire adequate support staff. The plumbing keeps seizing up. The food is terrible. The—"

The Colonel tuned his son out. *Mother Mary forgive me,* he thought, *for I have made the boy what he is. But I cannot bear to listen to his whining any longer.*

The MechWarriors of First Battalion were actually a good group, but like soldiers throughout time they loved to gripe. Instead of dealing with it, or simply disregarding the bulk of it as sheer white noise, the younger Camacho's solution was to pass it along to his father.

Gabby was a good boy, within his limitations. But even his proud father Don Carlos could see that his maturity left something to be desired.

Gavilán's appointment as battalion commander had caused a certain friction in the ranks. The other battalions were commanded by a rabbi and a Singer. The Protestant chaplains, Reverends Odegaard and Poteet, and the Catholic padres alike sometimes wondered aloud why no good Christian cleric had been given a battalion.

It wasn't an easy question to answer—at least, not to the faces of the men who asked it. Poteet was a blustering fool. Odegaard was not command material. Neither was Father Elfego Goldstein, whose family had been pious Catholics ever since the era when many politically alienated Jews had converted to the Church of Rome. Don Carlos' own confessor, Father Montoya, wasn't even a combatant. As for Father

Doctor Roberto García—he'd never take such a job, fortunately. He was not exactly a leader, either. And the Colonel could hear Father Montoya now: *But we wished you to appoint a* Catholic *as Battalion Commander, my son. Instead you give us a Jesuit.*

Ah, well. Gabby was a fine MechWarrior, everybody acknowledged that. He had even graduated from House Steiner's elite Nagelring military academy, as his sister had gone through Davion's New Avalon Military Academy. He had proven himself in combat.

Even so, he was no more than a shadow of his sister as a MechWarrior, Don Carlos told himself. *You could never forgive either of them for that, could you? And so Patsy killed herself, and Gavilán spends his life in endless pursuit of a ghost.*

He noticed a light blinking on the console of his desk communicator. "Gavilán" he said, "I have another call."

His son frowned petulantly. "But, Father—"

"It is on our employer's direct line. I will speak to you later." He broke the connection, not without relief.

Gavilán's face was replaced by that of HTE's security chief. "Colonel Camacho," the *Mirza* said, "I hope I find you well."

"As well as can be expected, praise the Virgin. And yourself?"

"My health is excellent, Colonel, thank you. But I admit I've done better."

"What can I do for you, *Mirza?*"

"Have you heard the evening news?"

The Colonel smiled and shook his head. "My duties leave me little time to watch HV."

"Permit me to replay you a segment from this evening's broadcast."

When he had watched the piece about the spurious "breakthrough" at HTE, Don Carlos sighed heavily.

"We can expect a visit from *los ateos* soon, can't we?" he asked.

"I beg your pardon? I'm not familiar with that name."

"The atheists. The Word of Blake adherents." To pious Caballeros, the mainstream ComStar fanatics were no less atheistic, but the Colonel saw no need to explain that.

"Yes." The ascetic face studied him a moment. "Colonel,

duty compels me to ask a question that I find personally distasteful."

Don Carlos smiled. "I never hold the doing of one's duty against a man."

"Very well. You and most of your people are natives of the Free Worlds League. Many of your MechWarriors formerly held commissions in the Marik military. You yourself had a history of distinguished service to House Marik before you became a mercenary."

The thin lips compressed momentarily before the *Mirza* went on. "Captain-General Thomas Marik is practically the Word of Blake's Primus-in-exile," he said. "Colonel, is there any possibility of a conflict of interest here?"

Were my son listening, he would call you out for impugning my honor as a Knight of Galisteo. The thought came without heat; Don Carlos had acquired far more sophistication than he was comfortable with during his decades away from the quaint, archaic, and thoroughly insular Trinity. He understood full well why the *Mirza* had to ask the question. What he felt was consternation; before he could retire and hand the regiment over to Gavilán, the boy had a great deal to learn.

"Do you know why I left Marik service, *Mirza*?" he asked, all the while thinking, *I'll bet you do, you bloodless old cabrón.* He respected the *Mirza,* but he understood what he was.

Abdulsattah shook his narrow saint's head.

"Many years ago I backed Duggan Marik as successor to the Captain-Generalship. After he and his father Janos were killed by an assassin's bomb, I retired from Marik service. I knew that whichever surviving heir won power, Thomas or Duncan, neither would find my services indispensable."

Abdulsattah laughed softly. "You are a wise man, indeed."

"As to my people—" Don Carlos shifted in his chair in an attempt to find comfort. It sometimes seemed to him as if the weight of every one of the two thousand warriors, support personnel, and dependents who made up the Regiment—and for whose well-being he was responsible— rode directly on his shoulders. "Most of them are from the League, yes. And most are voluntary exiles. We of the Trinity—what most of the Inner Sphere calls the Southwestern Worlds—prize our autonomy above all things. As Captain-General, Thomas Marik has usurped more power than any of his predecessors. He is pressuring our people sorely back home, trying to bring them into line.

"And as for this business of his being set up to become Primus-in-exile, there are fears, back on our homeworlds, that he intends to approve the Word of Blake as the established religion of the Free Worlds League. We Caballeros are religious folk, *indios* and Protestants as well as good Catholics like myself. We have learned to live—mostly—at peace with one another's faiths, and over centuries of strife we have come to accept that the best way to protect our own freedom of worship is to respect the same right in others. If the Captain-General wishes to worship Blake, that is his concern. When his followers try to tell us that *we* must bow down before his false prophets, then we fight."

"Thank you, Don Carlos," the *Mirza* said gravely. "I am satisfied, and I speak for Chandrasekhar Kurita as well. I hope you understand that I did not ask the question lightly."

Colonel Camacho inclined his head. "I will begin recalling my troops at once," he said. "If it can be arranged, it might be best to bring them in at night, under cover on the river barges. No point in alerting our enemies to our preparations if we can avoid it, *¿qué no?*"

"Indeed not. If I might make a suggestion, Colonel?"

"I would be honored, *Señor* Abdulsattah."

For a moment a smile almost threatened to break out on the *Mirza*'s ascetic's mouth. Don Carlos noted again how it always seemed to startle these *culebras* that people from elsewhere in the Inner Sphere were as fond of ritual courtesies as they.

"It seems unlikely that we face a full-fledged BattleMech attack; for one thing, the ISF would hardly let 'Mech-equipped Blake fanatics loose on Hachiman. We can anticipate something more along the lines of a commando raid. It might be best if you recalled no more than one battalion, to avoid crowding your people. We don't have much spare housing within the Compound."

"I agree. I shall give the orders at once."

Abdulsattah nodded. "I'll speak to our transport office and arrange for the barges. I believe we have the bottoms available to begin operations tonight."

After an exchange of pleasantries the *Mirza* rang off. Don Carlos squeezed his eyes shut.

It was a mistake. He saw Patsy again, surrounded by

Smoke Jaguar OmniMechs, a coyote battling mastiffs. His old *BattleMaster* had been slow, too slow. . .

The door to his office opened. Marisol Cabrera entered, trim in her Marik-style uniform, her dark auburn hair, lightly dusted with gray, tied up on her head in a traditional Galistean knot. She carried a plastic tray, on which sat a white teapot of heavy Galisteo ceramic with two matching cups. All were painted in blue with scenes of great-horned Ranger bulls doing battle with *vaqueros* in AgroMechs. The set had been fashioned by craftsmen on Don Carlos' own *hacienda* of Vado Ancho, and had accompanied him and the Regiment on their many adventures throughout the Inner Sphere.

She set the tray down before him. He smiled at the minty smell of the steam.

"Yerba Buena," she said. "It will help you relax."

"You know just what I need, Marisol," he said. "What would I do without you?"

"Let me rub your neck," she said, moving around behind Don Carlos so that he would not see her smile of pleasure at his words. He nodded, then groaned in satisfaction as her small, strong fingers began to knead at the knots of tension in his neck and shoulders.

He closed his eyes, and this time his daughter's martyrdom did not rise up behind the lids. "I am getting too old for this," he said dreamily. "I should retire to Vado Ancho. My sister Marta grows old beyond her years with the strain of managing the place, but it would be a blissful rest for me."

And I'd be willing to take my chances that Thomas Marik no longer remembers which side a long-ago commander of the Free Worlds Legionnaires took in the succession dispute. And that we'll be permitted at least some of our ancient freedoms until I'm safely resting with Patsy and the Queen of Heaven. He crossed himself.

"What are you waiting for, Carlos?" she asked in his ear. "Why not give it over now? Surely you've fought as long as any man must. Not even Saint James the Moor-slayer did more."

And hand the Seventeenth over to Gavilán. He almost shuddered. There were certain young bravos, particularly in his First Battalion, who would like that. But the older hands—and wiser heads—might not be as ready to accept

the younger Camacho's leadership until he had shown that
he could truly bear the burdens of command.

Don Carlos sighed. *My son, my son, what have I done to
you?* He knew the answer all too well.

"I cannot," he said. "At least, not now. Have you heard
the news?"

"There was something about a scientific discovery here at
this very place," she said.

"It was a lie. A lie meant to cause trouble—to *cover* trouble. We are due to be attacked here soon. I have a duty to
our employer, and to my people. Surely, I cannot rest until
the danger is past and I have fulfilled my commission to
Chandrasekhar Kurita."

It was Cabrera's turn to sigh, though she did so inaudibly.
"You'll want to recall a battalion from the bivouac outside
town."

He nodded. "The First, I think."

"*¿Por qué?* They've had their turn here already. Third
Battalion has yet to serve its rotation in the Compound."

"Third is the greenest. First is our best Battalion."

"You must be so very proud of your boy, for what he's
made of them."

Or what they've made themselves, in spite of him. Still, it
would be good seasoning for the lad. "Yes," Don Carlos
said.

"I shall see to all the arrangements," Cabrera told him,
resting both hands briefly on his shoulders.

He reached up to pat her hand. "Dear Marisol. Ever the
perfect executive officer. You are a treasure."

Again she was glad that he could not see her face, could
not see the pleasure in her dark eyes, nor the pain.

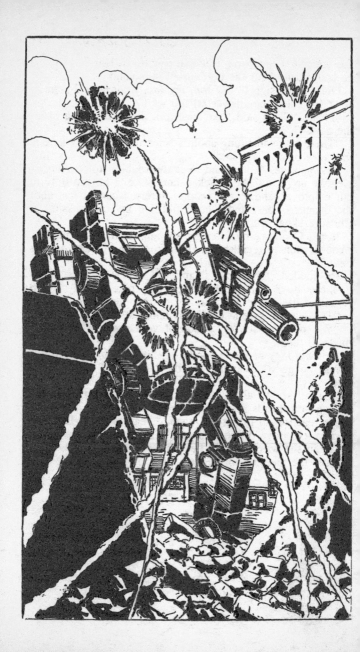

23

Between 2330 and midnight, workers arriving for the grave-yard shift thronged the Tubeway station beneath the center of the Hachiman Taro Compound. Those workers jammed into the first two cars of the East Rain train, which served the lower Middle Class and upper Laborer districts of Shin Kobe, Hangan, and Kim, north of the Compound, were aware of the presence of some two dozen *gaijin* in the pastel jumpsuits of the late-shift HTE employees. Politely, they refrained from questioning them, or even staring too openly. Foreigners or not, these people had evidently been accepted into Uncle Chandy's *uchi*. They were not altogether *tanin*.

Some of them carried gym bags with sporting-good company logos printed on them—several, in fact, from outside the Combine. This was not remarkable. Uncle Chandy encouraged fitness among his employees, and set aside a one-hour workout break for those who desired to run, perform calisthenics, or practice *kendo*. The foreign logos, having begun to appear openly in Combine markets only recently with Theodore's reforms, were already past their prime as status symbols in Masamori.

The foreigners did not join quite so enthusiastically as the *Masakko* in the rush for the exits when the train pulled into the HTE stop. They let the first quiet crush flow past them and out the doors toward the exit turnstiles, where the workers obediently queued to present their holobadge IDs to a pair of guards in sky-blue jumpsuits and helmets with a distinctive white stripe painted around them.

The first of the foreigners was a head taller than most of the *Masakko*. He wore a dark goatee and a Fab Three decal on his hardhat, indicating he worked on building controller boards for household appliances in the northern part of the Compound. His lemon yellow jumpsuit fit his lean frame loosely.

The guards glanced at the ID he held up, nodded. As he started through the turnstile, a metal detector began to shrill alarm.

From inside his baggy jumpsuit, the goateed man produced a compact semiautomatic pistol with built-in sound suppresser. Before either guard could react, he had shot both between the eyes.

From a news kiosk inside the concourse a voice shouted a phrase he did not understand as the whole situation went abruptly and totally to hell.

The words meant "*Get down!*" in Japanese. Unruly though they could be, the residents of Hachiman were amazingly docile and obedient by the standards of most of human space. When the voice of command told them to *get down,* they dropped unquestioningly onto their bellies—leaving two dozen *gaijin* Word of Blake terrorists standing with their teeth in their mouths.

From kiosks, from behind square structural columns, from maintenance closets, yellow muzzle-flashes flared. The tall man with the goatee had time to shout a defiant slogan in praise of Blake, trigger the preprogrammed emergency broadcast from the communicator he held in his left hand, and raise his silenced pistol. Then a score of bloody flowers bloomed on his chest, driving him back half a dozen steps even before he could fall.

The two dozen Aztechs stationed in hiding in the Tube way station were not MechWarriors. But they were warriors just the same, and none had served the Regiment with spanner and torch alone. Many had been blooded before ever leaving the homeworlds.

Most of the terrorist commandos were cut down as they were still grabbing for weapons concealed in their clothing or their gym bags. Four of them managed to break past the barriers, hurling grenades and firing full-auto. They reached the stairs that led to the surface, started up.

Her face bleeding from half a dozen grenade fragments, Staff Sergeant Belle, the diminutive Acoma woman in charge of the ambush, pressed a contact on the small black unit she held in her hand. It made a distinctive clacking sound.

The pair of Claymore mines had been placed so that they would fire their hail of steel marbles at an upward angle, over the heads of the obediently prone Laborers, and straight into the Word of Blake raiders, blasting them to shreds from the stairwell.

Sergeant Belle had not forgotten her first duty in the hot rush of action. She had hit her own panic button before opening fire herself.

Alarm klaxons had scarcely begun their rising-falling whine aboveground when a huge white flash came from the north wall of the Compound. The noise of an explosion rolled like a wave across the great enclosure.

With whining servos and the thud of great metal feet, the BattleMechs of the Seventeenth began to move. Don Carlos had been keeping a whole company at a time in their machines for four-hour shifts. With six companies within the Compound's walls nobody got a day off, but the Colonel believed that his MechWarriors were at their sharpest when they weren't in the cockpit for too long at a stretch, and twenty hours out of twenty-four was plenty of stand-down time.

Bronco was the hot company tonight—and suspecting that the terrorists might try to take advantage of shift change, Colonel Camacho had his watches staggered so they did not coincide with those of the Compound workers. The other companies, in stages of alertness ranging from ready-room to pulling rack time, began to race for their machines.

Cassie nodded to Zuma and Diana, bulky in their armor vests, who were overseeing noncombatants and dependents—mostly children under twelve, who were already streaming into underground air-raid bunkers. Whether Uncle Chandy had prepared for the inevitable time when the Clan truce ended, or whether he simply believed in preparing for any contingency, the Compound had been well-prepared to endure a siege before the Seventeenth ever got there.

She kicked her little Honda-Rheinmetall motorcycle into life and snarled off in the direction of the blast. A believer in stealth as the foremost virtue—over even mobility—she usually disdained any transport with a mill in it. But with sirens going off everywhere, vehicles racing in all directions, and BattleMechs rumbling into action, the noise of the bike's engine would make no damned difference. And not even Cassie's powerful legs could drive her MiG mountain bike across the vast Compound as quickly.

She snarled past the 'Mech assembly buildings, great, brightly lit caverns that seemed almost portals to other worlds. In front of her, a giant shadow strode purposefully forward. She felt a reflex twinge of panic at the sight of the all-too-familiar silhouette of an *Atlas*.

She felt a second twinge, then, because there was only one *Atlas* hot at this time of night. *Don't pull a Patsy on me, Lady K. These aren't* tigre *Omnis we're facing, but that doesn't mean they can't hurt you in your hundred-ton cocoon.*

Somehow she doubted her new friend was one to take anything for granted, which reassured her. The metal monster raised its right hand in greeting as Cassie swerved to pass it.

On the three-sixty display above her transpex viewscreen Captain Kali MacDougall saw the figure of a *Wasp* rising past the pagodalike Citadel, visible as a moving blot of blackness against starshot black, above the yellow light-dome cast by the Compound floods.

"Sabado," she said into the mike that curved in front of her mouth from her neurohelmet, "get your butt back down on the ground. Don't make yourself a target until we know what we're up against."

A double flare of jump jets as the jock clutched the gyros to tilt his machine back and brake his forward progress. "Affirmative, Lady K," came back into her ears. *"Lo siento."*

"Winger," Kali said, calling one of the two pilots patrolling the north wall. "You read me, Winger? Tecolote?"

"Teco here, Captain," came back the voice of Lieutenant JG Hector "Teco" Alvarez, piloting the Regiment's sole *JagerMech*. "There's a great big *puto* of a hole in the wall up here. Lots of small-arms fire coming in at the Blues holding out in the North Unit Fab buildings. I saw Winger's *Jenner* take a rocket right to the cockpit. His systems are all shut down."

"He punch out?"

"Negative, Lady K. *¡Ai, cabrón!* A whole boatload of rockets just missed *me*!"

"Well, use the buildings for cover and shoot back." Run-ins with Clan Elementals, and, ironically, having the obsessive and highly successful 'Mech-slayer Cassie Suthorn in the unit, had gone a long way toward eroding the Caballeros' smug MechWarriors prejudice that the only true threat to a BattleMech was another BattleMech. Lady K's people were nervous about facing infantry armed with anti-'Mech weapons and fanatical enough to use them—especially once they got in among the hardened buildings of the Compound. Restricted mobility and daggers-drawn engagement range made a built-up area like that perfect for just the kind of nasty ambush their own Abtakha so loved to spring.

"The cavalry's on the way," Kali assured Teco. And then she had time to think, *Sierra Foxtrot, this fandango's just begun and I've already lost a man.* A hell of a start to her career as a company commander.

There were voices in the back of her head, familiar voices, telling her she was bad and stupid and would fail. She set her jaw. She had long since learned to recognize those voices: *they* were the enemy. The hostile figures stealing through the night with their man-portable SRMs were nothing more than potentially lethal nuisances.

One good thing about being strapped into a BattleMech cockpit in the midst of a firefight, she thought. Makes it darned hard to break your sobriety. She'd talk to Zuma after this one was in the books. If they both made it through.

Right now she had to buckle down to the business of pulling her command through. She recited a prayer to herself and punched up the command net. "Bronco Company, we have a major breach in the north wall, heavy fire incoming, small-arms and anti-armor . . ."

It took Cassie less than ten seconds to decide the north wall attack was a feint.

It didn't *look* like a feint when she'd come skidding broadside out of the mouth of a Compound street near the river to look west along the avenue running inside the perimeter. The Blues, as the Caballeros called HTE's own security troops, were indeed trading an impressive volume of fire with a force trying to push through a breach fifteen meters across.

Awful big blast, she thought. *Van bomb, I'll just bet. Fertilizer and fuel oil.* She could see bodies sprawled in the opening, and on the far side a *Jenner* showing no sign of damage but also no signs of life. Just then she saw Teco's *JagerMech* step out of a street west of the breach and hose down the hole with the big autocannons in either arm.

The Word of Blake terrorists were as fanatical as advertised, answering the *Jag*'s barrage with an immediate swarm of SRMs that blew big chunks out of the cement-bunkered Fab buildings of North Unit. Cassie saw a couple of rockets flash off against the 'Mech's barrel belly before it ducked back.

They were burning man-portable missiles as if they were free and that was what clued her. Unarmored infantry could never hope to batter its way into a fortified compound against resistance from BattleMechs supported by ground troops, no matter how many SRMs they were willing to light off. What they *could* do was cause some hurt and make a whole lot of noise.

"Tiburón," she said into the mike in the commo headset she'd crammed on before peeling out. "Tiburón, this is Abtakha. Come in, Tiburón."

"He isn't on the net yet," came the dry, supercilious voice of Gordo Baird. "This is Colonel Baird. You can give your information to me."

"Is there anybody else on the command net?"

"Now, just a minute, young lady—"

"Lady K reading you, Abtakha, GA."

Imagine being glad to hear the voice of a 'Mech pilot. "I'm at the breach, Lady K. You around here?"

"Getting there. Dark Lady's a big-legged bitch and slow, but she's pure mean. Some of the other Broncos ought to be up with you, though."

"Lady K and any 'lleros listening: I think this is a fake. I say again, the attack up here's a diversion."

That brought a babble of excited comment, mostly from the Bronco 'Mech pilots who had come up to support Teco and the Blues. "That's ridiculous," Baird said, overriding the babble. "From all reports, this is a major raid."

"They're busting lots of caps, Gordo. That doesn't mean this is where they're taking their big shot."

"Abtakha, this is Badlands. We had a bunch try to come in through the Tubeway station. Zuma's people dry-gulched them, no survivors."

"See?" Baird said with hornet triumph. "This is a two-pronged attack. HTE security has already talked to a prisoner from the breach; the two attacks are all there are."

Cassie wheeled her bike and gunned it south, toward the dark approaching bulk of Kali's *Atlas*.

"That's all your bird *knows about*," she said, bent low over the bars. She streaked past the *Atlas*. "Badlands, I'm headed for the south wall. I want you to send Scout Platoon that way; they'll get there before me."

"Lieutenant Junior Grade Suthorn, this is desertion in the face of an enemy! Captain Powell, you are to hold your platoon in reserve until—"

"Cram it, Gordo," Badlands Powell snarled. "You're not in my chain of command. And try to remember to use callsigns like a real soldier. Abtakha, I will comply. Badlands out."

"Nothing up here Bronco can't hold," Lady K added. "And if the real action's down south, it'll all be over but the shouting by the time I leadfoot it down there, anyhow."

Colonel Carlos Camacho sat in the cockpit of Great White, his captured Clan 'Mech, and dreamed. Queries and situation reports crackled in his neurohelmet. They went unheeded; he was in a different time, a different place . . .

The Drac mining world of Jeronimo, facing the inexorable advance of the fearful tigres, *Clan Smoke Jaguar. The Seventeenth and their DCMS allies were falling back again, trying to gain enough space and time for DropShips to evacuate the battered units. Only the brutal terrain of the Contra-Pelagian Mountains into whose heart the Inner Sphere survivors were retreating kept the faster Clan Omnis from overrunning them—the terrain and the equally brutal ambushing tactics of the Caballeros.*

They had almost reached the broad caldera of a long-dormant volcano, a place where DropShips could put down to rescue the MechWarriors and their dependents. A Star of tigres *had lunged ahead of the pack and was pressing hard, even as the first ships were landing.*

Don Carlos well remembered the thrill of despair and terror as the first fast-striding Clan Puma *broke free of the rocks and raced down upon the laggard survivors. The rest of the mixed Star followed close behind, eager for the kill. And he recalled with pride and grief the way Patsy's* Phoenix Hawk, *la Capitana, suddenly flew out from between the knife-toothed lava cliffs, rich in metal ores, which had concealed it from the Clanners' better sensors. She had been firing her weapons point-blank into the* Puma's *head from above even before the pilot's gene-engineered reflexes could react.*

The Smoke Jaguar MechWarrior was probably dead before the Phoenix Hawk's *right foot smashed through the weakened top armor of his BattleMech's head. And then Patsy was in the midst of the Star's surviving four 'Mechs, which had been forced by the terrain to close their formation, and was slashing about like a mad thing. She was giving the* tigres *no chance for the one-to-one duels they favored—in particular, no chance for one of the enemy 'Mechs to engage her while the others raced to destroy the descending DropShip. She made them all fight her.*

She made them kill her.

Again Don Carlos relived the agony of his BattleMaster's *ponderous progress, watching as the Omnis blasted Patsy to pieces. By the time her* Phoenix Hawk's *cockpit was hammered into a smoking cavity, the rest of First Battalion was within range.*

Patricia Camacho was swiftly avenged. Don Carlos himself held the Star commander's Mad Cat *by the arm while he roasted the pilot alive, pressing the muzzle of his PPC against the transpex canopy and firing until his own heat soared well past the red line and his cooling system overloaded. He had been forced to eject to avoid being cooked himself.*

The overeager Star of Clansmen were slaughtered. The shell-shocked DCMS and Seventeenth survivors boarded the DropShip, carrying with them the mostly intact Mad Cat *as a final defiant trophy. It went a little way to assuage pride battered by their swift, inevitable defeat.*

But nothing could ease the loss of Patricia.

And nothing could ever lessen the pain of knowing why the Regiment's most brilliant pilot and beloved officer had chosen to die.

Don Carlos sat amid his thoughts in the compact but comfortable *Mad Cat* cockpit, and did not hear the voices calling his name.

Masamori, Hachiman
Galedon District, Draconis Combine
15 October 3056

The communicator's chime whipped Lainie Shimazu instantly from sleep. She rolled over and hit the button. "Shimazu."

"*Tai-sa*, this is the ready room. We're monitoring Civilian Guidance Control traffic down there. The *deka* report a major firefight in the Hachiman Taro Compound. Explosions and gunfire, perhaps missiles."

"So the Word of Blake is heard from." Lainie swung long legs off the futon and sat up. Chandrasekhar Kurita had denied the rumors of a new hyperpulse breakthrough, and indeed disavowed any interest whatsoever in hyperpulse technology. No one expected the Word of Blake fanatics to buy it.

Behind her bare back, her nocturnal companion stirred. She ignored him. Just now she couldn't even remember his name.

"Bring the Regiment to Condition Yellow. I want First Battalion hot and online. Everybody else stand by. I'm on the way. Shimazu out."

She stood up, looking around for her panties. Her partner was sitting up in bed blinking sleepily at her through his shock of black hair.

"What do you think you're doing?" the young man demanded. He was from a good Masamori family, long, lithe, and tanned. All of it, the tan, the muscles were a product of the gym, not the hard soldier's life. He was basically a toy.

"Out," she said, in no mood to explain. "Business."

"If I haven't worn you out too much for you to even think of leaving," he said, stretching so she could admire the play of muscles under his sleek expensive hide, "then get back here."

"I told you, it's business," Lainie said flatly.

He bounced naked to his feet, handsome face twisted in fury, one hand cocked to strike. Her eyes went from almost-black to maroon. He stopped, standing with his feet tangled in the bedclothes and his fist drawn back.

"If you hit me," she said, "I'll break both your arms and have my men throw you naked in the street."

"You can't talk to me like that, you whore! I have connections."

"Who will rapidly become disconnected if they learn you've been coupling with a no-class *eta* bitch." By the time the young man's impulse to violence had passed, Laine had pulled on her panties and gotten a white cotton tee-shirt from her drawer. Her heavily padded MechWarrior cooling gear stood by the wall like an ancient suit of samurai armor. It would not be the first time she'd driven her *Mauler* wearing nothing under it.

She pulled the tee-shirt over her head and faced the youth, whose name she suddenly remembered. "You were adequate, Yuki, but you were starting to become a bore. Run on back to your little rich girls and forget all about me. I'm an officer in the DCMS. Any kind of cheapjack juvenile revenge you try to run on me will only blow up in your pretty face. Cut your losses and go."

He glared at her a moment, then seemed to simply deflate. He turned away to find his own clothes.

She began to clamber into her 'Mech-jock suit. He had already ceased to exist for her.

"We've received word from HTE Security," Gordo Baird's voice came, smug and hateful, into Cassie's headset. "Their people on the south wall report no activity at all. You're leading our reserves on a wild-goose chase, Lieutenant Suthorn."

Cassie grunted. With the bike parked up against a fabrication building, she was on foot, peering up and down the perimeter road along the south wall. A few other scouts had arrived on their bikes and stood hunched over next to her.

Blue patrols were moving along the base of the wall. A four-man squad trotted toward the little knot of Scouts. They didn't seem to have spotted the mercenaries yet.

"Guess that's it, Cass," said Staff Sergeant Willard "Drygulch" Dix, a rangy blond Hillbilly from Galisteo. Even the Hillbillies' Cowboy brethren often dismissed them all as slow-witted. Dix had a drawling, deliberate mode of speech, but Cassie knew better than to make that mistake about him. "Best be getting back north."

"Mierda de toro," Cassie said. "Why would there still be so many Blues at the other end of the Compound from where the action is?" She shouldered her assault rifle, leaned around the corner, and fired a single shot into the middle of the blue-jumpsuited chest in the lead.

The security guard sat down hard, losing his rifle. The other three dove for cover in the shadows of the Fab building. A moment later, so did the one Cassie had shot.

"He ain't bleedin', Drygulch," Jimmy Escobar said.

"Body armor," the sergeant said. "Blues don't wear no body armor!"

Cassie switched circuits on her communicator. "All units, we have infiltrators coming across the south wall. Be advised some are dressed as HTE security. Challenge any Blues you see—if they're in body armor, they're ISF."

"Tiburón's still not responding." Gavilán Camacho had no sooner settled the neurohelmet over his head and shoulders than the words crackled in his ears. "We got us a situation at the south wall. Infiltrators breakin' in, some of 'em wearing Blue uniforms."

"This is Falcon," Gavilán said. "I'm assuming command."

That was a questionable call, since fellow Force Commander "Maccabee" Bar-Kochba had seniority on him. But Second Battalion was stood-down this shift, its people chowing, taking care of maintenance, or pulling rack time. The Rabbi was not on the net yet himself. He was probably still climbing the ladder to the cockpit of his *Warhammer*. He wasn't as young and spry as he used to be.

Taking no chances, Gavilán rapped, "All active 'Mechs, check in with me."

Responses rattled back with gratifying crispness. That was one thing about the Caballeros. They gave endless backchat under whichever of the good Lord's suns happened to be shining on them, but when the hammer came down, they got right to business.

Bronco was pretty fully committed to the north wall breach. Several of Cochise's 'Mechs were already engaged up there as well; incoming fire from the Blake raiders forted up in the workers' housing north of the Compound was rapidly beginning to slacken as the awesome firepower of a dozen BattleMechs was brought to bear on them. Second Battalion was only just settling into their 'Mechs. Most of Adelante was up, though, and ready to go.

I'm going to show them how it's done, Gabby thought. His father had been leading from the rear for too long. Gavilán would never dream of questioning his father's courage, and would call out anybody who did. It was just that the old man had grown too cautious of his children. He preferred to remain on top of the action as much as possible, instead of in the hot red core of it.

"Follow me," Gabby said, and set his *Shadow Hawk* into a run toward the south wall. The impact of the 'Mech's footfalls jarred his tailbone even through his seat padding; the *Shad* had a gait like a mule. No *Shadow Hawk* he'd ever been in had a smooth ride at running speed, but Red-tailed Hawk was worse than most.

The scouts who first spotted the ruse were hollering for help. The fake Blues had them massively outgunned and were driving them back. Worse, some of the intruders had already gotten past them into the Compound.

He came in sight of the wall. In his enhanced vision, muzzle flashes flickered like hyperactive fireflies from the inside of the ramparts. Too slow, he thought, then gathered his 'Mech into a crouch and jumped.

The roar of the jets filled his ears as the 'Mech soared forward over the low South Fab buildings. He bit his lip beneath his mustache, fighting to keep his machine steady in an unexpected crosswind. Bullets from the wall ahead of him ticked off the *Shad*'s armor like the beaks of hens scratching for millet.

Gabby wasn't terribly proficient at jumping a 'Mech. Probably because he didn't *like* jumping 'Mechs, except maybe for the fearsome ninety-five-ton Clan *Gladiator*. He liked *big* 'Mechs, the heavier the better. No like his sister, leaping all over creation in her *Phoenix Hawk*.

Only thing was, Daddy wouldn't let him drive one. Don Carlos insisted that his son should be a mobile commander. No *Atlas* for him, or even his father's old *BattleMaster*.

The SRMs that darted at him from the top of the wall took him by surprise. Coming into the net late, he wasn't expecting the intruders to fire at him with 'Mech-class weaponry. None actually hit him, but they did startle him into backing off the jump-jet trigger ever so slightly.

Enough so that he dipped down, caught a toe on the roof of a Fab, and flopped facefirst into the building with a rending crash.

"The public wants to see things blowing up, Archie," Mariska Savage said in a patient voice.

"The public also wants human-interest stories," Archie Westin replied, equally patient. The two had the most reasonable disputes any Southwesterner had ever seen; they were the wonder of the Regiment. The pair were with Zuma, Diana Vásquez, and a pair of blue security troopers, overseeing a score of the Regiment's children in the underground infirmary that was providing shelter during the alert.

"If the fight keeps up, or comes to us, we can get all the action your heart desires," Archie explained. "This is our perfect chance to humanize the Seventeenth for our audience, show that mercenaries are something other than coldblooded fighting machines like the 'Mechs they ride."

Diana smiled. She had a baby in either arm, and was crooning comfortingly to them. The older children sat calmly among the examining tables, playing with toys. They showed no sign of fear at the muted racket from outside; they were Caballeros too.

Zuma laughed and clapped his hands. "I like that, Arch. That's pretty good." The Chief Aztech had an autoloading shotgun tucked under his arm. Father of six kids, he, like Diana, spent a fair amount of his free time working in the nursery. His own children, along with Diana's son and most of the Regiment's other youngsters, were out at the Sportsplex. They would only be moved into the Compound if the whole Regiment transferred there.

"Archie," Mariska said in mock exasperation, "if you're going to wax poetical, at least wait till I get the audio recording up and running."

Archie laughed. "Why don't you do that? I'll see if I can remember what I said."

Grinning, the camerawoman was just unlimbering her holocorder when a pair of Blues, a man and a woman, came trotting down the steps. The two security guards already in the room glanced at them. The older one frowned, started to approach the newcomers.

The female raised her machine pistol and fired a brief burst into his stomach.

The noise was shattering in the confined space. Several children began to cry. Good Southwesterners, they were all flat on the floor before the tears began to flow.

"Consider yourselves hostages," the male newcomer said. He had blond hair and black eyes with pronounced epicanthic folds. "If you remain calm, no one will be—"

Zuma had let the shotgun slide down so that the pistol-grip fell into his hand. Now he raised it and fired one-handed, the blast catching the female fake Blue in the midriff and slamming her against a black-topped counter. Her head snapped back against a metal towel dispenser. She dropped to her knees.

Moving with mongoose reflexes the male intruder shot the remaining Blue as he reached for his holstered sidearm, then pivoted to hose bullets at Zuma from his assault rifle. The Chief Aztech ducked behind an examining table. It would be mere seconds before the jacketed rounds punching through the pedestal's thin metal found him.

Archie Westin hit the gunman in a creditable body slam and drove him back into the wall. The assassin dropped his assault rifle as Archie drove a fist into his belly.

The man's body bent only slightly in response; the ballistic-cloth armor he wore under the blue HTE Security jumpsuit absorbed most of the blow. He kneed Archie hard in the groin, then sent him reeling back with an elbow slam to the face.

Zuma popped up again and shot the man in the belly with the shotgun. The intruder roared; even with the body armor, the load of 00 buck had to cause incredible pain. He whipped out a *tanto*-style dagger, started forward.

The Chief Aztech walked three more blasts up the man's body. The final one struck him in the face and dropped his headless body flopping to the floor.

Archie had picked himself up again. He had one of the fallen Blues' sidearms in his hand.

"Don't move!"

The voice was a ghastly hiss between bloody lips. The female commando sat with her back to a wall and a pistol stuck in the ear of four-year old Lucy Aragón, who was in the main Compound for treatment of a bad case of measles.

The blue jumpsuit's belly had been ripped open to reveal a black DEST commando suit beneath. Her face was a mask of blood. The corner of the towel dispenser had opened her scalp, and she might also be bleeding from the mouth from the effects of Zuma's shotgun blast. But her blue eyes blazed with fanatical fervor to match any Blakie's.

"Drop your guns or the girl dies," she said.

Diana Vásquez stood up from behind a table, still holding an infant in her left arm. Her right arm was by her side. Her lovely Madonna's face was fixed.

The assassin looked at Zuma. "Do it," she said.

Diana Vásquez' right hand snapped up., The motion caught the commando's eyes. She turned her head to look.

The compact autopistol in Diana's hand fired as it came online, the bullet hitting the woman in the left eye. Her bloody head jerked back, the last dying barrage of neurotransmitters making her hand contract, spastically firing the pistol three times. But impact had jerked the gun away from Lucy's head, and the only damage was the chunks of white acoustic tile the bullets gouged from the ceiling.

Mariska Savage, who had recorded the whole scene, dropped her holocorder and ran forward to scoop up the hysterically crying Lucy. She turned accusingly to the two Caballeros.

"The children could've been killed!"

Diana lowered her pistol. "They shouldn't have threatened my babies," she said.

"But you put the children at risk."

While they argued, Zuma quickly examined the bodies to make sure the intruders weren't shamming. Then he hit the intercom button on the wall to report what had happened to HTE Security Central. Now he was kneeling over one of the two authentic Blues, shaking his head.

He looked up at the camerawoman. "We didn't risk nothin', Ms. Savage. If they had taken us hostage, Don Carlos would've pumped a couple hundred liters of gasoline in here and fired down a flare. Or somebody else would have."

Savage gasped and turned gray. "We don't negotiate for hostages," Zuma said. "We rescue them, or we bury them. Ain't no middle ground."

Savage looked at Captain Diana Vásquez. The other

woman was soothing the children, making sure none of them was hurt, but she caught the camerawoman's look. She nodded.

Archie had managed to pick himself up and stood with his back to an operating table, kind of bent in the middle and massaging a cheekbone that was already beginning to show a bruise. He looked at Savage and both shook their heads. It was obvious they shared a common thought: these Caballeros were in some ways as alien to their ultra-civilized Federated Commonwealth outlook as the Clans.

"SRMs incoming!" crackled into Cassie's headset. The Cowboy-accented caller didn't identify himself; usual commo discipline for the Seventeenth. "Falcon is down!"

"No lie," remarked Sammy Chato, ducking back as a long burst sprayed cement chunks from the Fab wall beside him. A moment before, the scouts had all been dodging a rain of debris from the junior Camacho's swan dive.

There weren't a lot of bad guys shooting at them at the moment. One bunch was atop the wall, but they had abruptly lost interest in the groundpounders while volley-firing anti-'Mech missiles at the jumping *Shadow Hawk*. The scouts were taking some rounds from street level. But either not many intruders had gotten off the wall, or most of those who had were loose in the Compound.

"PH coming," Private Patricio said, pointing into the sky to the west of them. A humanoid 'Mech was in mid-jump, raking the wall with arm lasers and its outsized laser rifle.

"Looks like Don Coyote," somebody else said.

Cassie glanced up. The rapid ruby pulses from the left arm had a bit of sputter to their cadence; the Adelante CO's *Phoenix Hawk* had been retrofitted with state-of-the-art beam weapons, but there was a control interface problem with the medium Martell pulse laser in its left arm. Definitely O'Rourke.

The 'Mech touched down lightly in the narrow street next to the building into which Gavilán's *Shadow Hawk* had fallen. The PH had taken no fire in flight—not even élite DEST commandos were eager to match small arms against extended-range large lasers. The instant the 'Mech's feet touched blacktop, though, and its knees flexed to absorb the shock of landing, so many tentacles of white smoke tipped by starbright SRM exhaust flares were streaking toward it that it looked as if a giant white-phosphorous round had gone off atop the wall.

The 'Mech became a giant human torch, standing in a lake of fire. "Sierra Foxtrot," Sergeant Dix said. "Infernos."

"I'm shut down," Captain O'Rourke said over the commline. The young black *norteño* sounded as calm as if he were taking his 'Mech for an afternoon stroll along the banks of the Yamato. Don Coyote was always cool, always in control. Those traits had advanced him rapidly in the Caballeros, where they weren't always in long supply.

Even if his voice didn't reveal it, though, he was in trouble. A jump and all that laser action had run his heat way up. Being doused with sticky napalm had pushed his 'Mech instantly past the red line. His *Phoenix Hawk* had *not* received double-capacity heat sinks yet.

"Punch out, Coyote," Lady K urged. "Nothing you can do, and if your ride doesn't blow, we recover her when this little fandango gets over."

Don Coyote didn't have his name for nothing. Despite being the most persistent of ranch pests, the coyote of ancient Terra had deliberately been brought along by the cranky, turbulent settlers who colonized the Trinity Worlds. The animal was a rasty, nasty, disreputable half-breed, outlaw to the core; so were the Caballeros. It was also noted for its cunning and unmatched survival skill. Alone of North American mammals, to say nothing of predators, the coyote's numbers had increased after the European colonization.

Captain O'Rourke was brave when bravery was called for. He also knew when to beat cheeks. That was *another* reason Don Carlos had given him a company to command.

The captain's ejection seat came shooting up out of the flames enveloping his 'Mech. The zero-altitude ejection system was supposed to propel you slightly backward—it was assumed that, if you had to punch out, there were likely Bad People in front of you. Unfortunately, so quick had been the inferno barrage and the overheating they caused that the *Phoenix Hawk*'s reactor had shut down with its torso still angled forward. O'Rourke was projected straight up. His parachute blossomed like a ghostly flower.

The breeze off the river caught it and carried it southwest—directly over the intruders. Muzzle flashes flickered toward the figure dangling from the chute, which was rapidly coming down in the street outside the wall.

The Ninth Ghost Regiment's BattleMechs stood in ranks beneath the floodlights of the base in Masamori's southern suburbs like an ancient Chinese emperor's statue army. Moving past them, Eleanor Shimazu strode toward her *Mauler*.

Just as she reached the foot of Vengeance, her ninety-ton war machine, a stocky figure stepped up to her and bowed. *"Tai-sa."*

It was Moon, the *Tosei-kai* yakuza who had long ago appointed himself her chief aide, shadow, and bodyguard. "Yes?" she said.

"We have received word from the Planetary Chairman, Colonel. He forbids us to move in support of Hachiman Taro Enterprises. The Civilian Guidance Corps is sufficient to the situation."

For a moment she stood with one hand on the 'Mech's retractable ladder and the other at her forehead, clutching a hank of red hair. She gazed off across the long-grass flat that led down to the rocky verge of the Shakudo, invisible now in the blackness beyond the lights.

There's treachery here, she thought. True to the traditions of soldiers and yakuza alike, she considered the *deka*—cops—little more than bullies with badges and guns. The Friendly Persuaders were well-armed, but there was no way they would be much use against what the Word of Blake would send against the HTE. The media would call the strike teams "terrorists" when the shooting was over, but they were in fact full-blown commandos, special-force elements of either the great army ComStar had assembled in secret before the Clan invasion, or their dreaded ROM secret police, both of which had fractured along with the religion itself after Precentor Martial Focht executed Primus Waverly for treachery.

That useless worm Percy. "What exactly do the honorable Chairman's orders say?"

"We are bidden to remain on alert," Moon said, "but no 'Mechs are to leave the base."

Lainie smiled slowly. "Very well. No 'Mech will move." She began to unfasten the clasps on her suit. "Get me a squad of volunteers and transport from the motor pool. Body armor and small arms; same for me."

She stepped out of the suit. The techs scurrying around the feet of the parked BattleMechs tried not to stare at the spectacle of their commander standing in the middle of the parade ground in her underwear. Physical modesty was not a big factor in the Combine, but Lainie was pushing the envelope here. As usual.

"Have somebody go back to my quarters and get me some boots," she said, handing her cooling vest off to a pair of gaping ratings.

Moon stood unmoving, gazing at her with heavy-lidded eyes. "And a pair of trousers, too," she added.

"The *cabrones* are shooting at him!" a scout yelled.

"Don Coyote." For the first time the voice of Colonel Camacho spoke on the commline. "Don Coyote, come in, please."

No response. There was a transceiver built-in to the captain's neurohelmet. It might have malfunctioned, of course. But with at least half a dozen assault rifles blazing at O'Rourke as his chute settled into the street, a darker explanation for his silence seemed more likely.

Like a monster from an ancient Japanese horror film, a *Shadow Hawk* reared from the wreckage of South Fab Nine. Seeing the intruders blasting Don Coyote as the MechWarrior hung helpless in his chute, Gavilán Camacho uttered a raptor's scream of fury as his *Shadow Hawk* lumbered forward, kicking the Fab's walls from its path, blasting the perimeter with everything it had: the autocannon in its left torso, the Doombud LRM launcher in its right, the Marty medium laser in its right arm.

Figures in powder blue jumpsuits exploded away from the Fab's collapsing walls like frightened quail as the 'Mech barged on through. The *Shadow Hawk* altered course slightly, its immense right foot coming down on two of them. Shrill screams sounded, then abruptly cut off.

Howling like wolves, the MechWarriors of the Seventeenth charged the south wall. It had been known since the Yom Kippur War almost twelve hundred years before that it was possible for infantry to hand armor a major hurting as long as they could afford to spend antiarmor missiles like firecracker strings. The problem that wrecked the Egyptians in AD 1973 was the same one confronted by the DEST commandos: they could carry only so many missiles. And the ISF strike force, traveling light, didn't have *nearly* so much logistical support.

Missiles, inferno and armor-piercing, hammered into the charging BattleMechs, but their numbers prevented the intruders from being able to concentrate their fire on any one target, the way they had on O'Rourke's *Phoenix Hawk*. The missile volley passed like a Cerillos gully-washer, and did about as much to the Caballero 'Mechs.

The DEST body armor had enabled a few of the commandos to overmatch the *gaijin* scouts and the authentic HTE troops who opposed them. But against the energy weapons and huge projectile launchers of the 'Mechs, it was no more effective than a man's thin skin.

The first battle of the Compound was over.

25

Masamori, Hachiman
Galedon District, Draconis Combine
15 October 3056

The fighting was done. The killing, however, continued through the night.

Some of the DEST force holed up on the ground floor of the office building directly across the street from the Compound's south wall, but the Caballero 'Mechs simply blasted them out. Skyscrapers on Hachiman were built to last, and Uncle Chandy owned that one. What damage was done could be repaired.

A bigger problem was the unknown number of ISF commandos who had actually gotten loose in the Compound dressed as HTE security. Chandrasekhar Kurita ordered the facility sealed. Then squads of mercenaries, scouts, support troops, and dismounted MechWarriors, supported by BattleMechs, swept the entire Compound. They scrutinized the IDs of every HTE employee inside the wall—paying particular attention to the security troops—checking them against the personnel department's computers.

All of which caused serious friction between regular HTE employees and the Caballeros. On three occasions legitimate Blues reacted with angry defiance when ordered to disarm and identify themselves by *gaijin* money-troopers. But the mercenaries weren't in a mood to play: three HTE security men died, and two got helicopter rides to Masamori Central Hospital with tubes in their noses. After word of these early incidents got around, everybody cooperated, cheerfully or not.

Eleven infiltrators were located. At least, eleven men and women were found wearing black DEST body armor, or could not be accounted for by the *Mirza*'s computer. All of them suicided, some by the time-honored expedient of biting down on a hollowed tooth filled with cyanide, others by offering resistance. These managed to take six more Blue troopers and five Caballeros with them, including two 'Mech jocks.

There was a momentary flap twenty minutes after the DEST commandos in the skyscraper were massacred, when a couple of light trucks loaded with heavily armed Ghosts turned up at the front gate offering to help. Abdulsattah was reluctant to let them inside. Captain MacDougall vouched for them, and Colonel Camacho, roused from his funk, supported her. The DCMS regulars were admitted and set to guarding the infirmaries where casualties were being brought.

The ID-checking operations were carried out carefully out of the line of sight of Colonel Shimazu and her MechWarriors. Neither Uncle Chandy nor the Seventeenth saw any reason to advertise possible ISF involvement, even to apparent allies.

The perimeter surveillance cameras' memory clearly showed the large panel van that drove, apparently innocently, down the street that separated the Compound from an upper-Laborer housing complex inhabited by HTE employees. It had veered up onto the sidewalk and detonated, presumably by a driver willing to die for the greater glory of Blake. It had been loaded with an estimated three tons of that old standby, nitrate fertilizer soaked in fuel oil. The blast had wiped out half a residential block as well as breaching the north wall, giving the heaviest casualties of the whole battle to unsuspecting Workers and their families.

Like the DEST commandos, the Blake raiders had quickly run out of rockets, which made their battle against Bronco Company notably one-sided. Some of the terrorists had faded into the housing complex, where the MechWarriors were reluctant to pursue them, not wishing to kill more innocents. By that point, though, with the outcome of the attack painfully apparent, the Civilian Guidance Corps had suddenly decided to take an active role in preserving the peace, and had moved in to mop up the raiders. They carried out the operation with their usual discrimination—firing at anything that moved—thereby causing many of the civilian casualties Uncle Chandy and the Seventeenth had tried so hard to avoid. But there was nothing the Compound defenders could do about that.

The DEST strike was another story. As the *Mirza's* investigators pieced it together later, the Dragon's Breath had gotten to one of the legitimate security men on duty on the south wall that night. While the personnel on duty at the surveillance video monitors in the central Citadel had been preoccupied with the abortive action in the Tubeway and the all-out assault in the north, he had apparently disabled his partner and lowered a rope to the street. ISF teams dressed in HTE Security jumpsuits came swarming in. That was surmise—when the fight turned against them, the commandos had executed all the legitimate Blues in their hands, including the theoretical turncoat—but the theory matched the available facts.

Several Word of Blake raiders were captured alive. Under interrogation they persisted in denying any knowledge of ISF involvement; they believed they had managed to smuggle themselves and their weaponry onto Hachiman *despite* the Combine's secret police. They had counted on their own scheme of infiltrating through the Tubeway. The van-bomb attack on the north wall had been designed as a fallback strike and as a diversion for the tubeway team if it were detected after penetrating the Compound.

Nothing could be learned from the ISF dead. Incendiaries

built into each DEST commando suit self-activated within minutes of the wearer's death, reducing corpse and equipment to a fused black mass.

For the ISF, the whole Word of Blake attack had, obviously, been no more than a diversion. The Blakies were expected to fail noisily—their goal, after all, was to destroy an entirely imaginary research project—while the DEST commandos broke in and murdered Chandrasekhar Kurita.

One more important question occupied the minds of everyone inside the Compound: would the failure make the ISF back off and reconsider its designs on HTE's owner and Chief Executive? Or would they try again?

The answer seemed painfully self-evident. The Dragon's Breath would be back. And next time they would hit *much* harder.

"You stick that probe in there, man," Zuma said helpfully, leaning over Astro Zombie's hunched shoulder, "she's gonna smoke." The two chief technicians had an access panel popped on the side of the head of Winger's *Jenner*, trying to figure out what had happened. It was not a good sign when a single SRM hit took down a medium 'Mech.

Cassie was up on a cherry picker in the mellow afternoon autumn sun. The breeze off the river still carried the stinks of burned insulation and human flesh. From up here the Compound showed little damage, save for the hole gaping in the north wall, and the smashed South Fab 9. She could just make out the burned patch where Captain O'Rourke's 'Mech had been hit by infernos. Ironically, it had not blown; it had already been recovered, having suffered mostly cosmetic damage.

She leaned back with her elbows propped on the safety rail, unconcerned at hanging almost ten meters in the air. Caballero causalities had been blessedly light. One Aztech died in the Tubeway station, Captain Juan Pedro O'Rourke bought it in his parachute, and casualties had been incurred in hunting down the DEST infiltrators. Funerals and a Mass of thanksgiving were scheduled for tomorrow.

One prominent non-casualty was Lieutenant JG Nelson "Winger" Blackbird. The missile that struck his 'Mech's head hadn't even penetrated armor. But it had broken circuits and knocked crucial chips loose, completely shutting down all the machine's systems. Even the ejection seat was knocked out.

The explosion also warped the hatch, jamming it so that Winger could not escape. He had spent the whole battle alternately screaming in rage and singing his death song, just in case the Blakies thought of firing infernos at *him*.

Astro Zombie reared back in outrage at Zuma's presumption. He pushed the taped bridge of his glasses up his nose. "Nonsense. I know what I'm doing. *I* have a degree in electrical engineering from the Atreus Institute of Technology."

"That's OK," Zuma said equably. "She don't know that. She's gonna smoke anyway."

Astro Zombie snorted and stuck the probe in. Sparks flew, followed by a bacon-frying sound and brown smoke pouring out. The lights on the Chief Tech's test board flashed once and died.

Cassie snickered. "I don't know what they teach you kids in school these days," Zuma said, mournfully shaking his head. "You oughta know that they build these things with just the right amount of smoke inside. You let some of it out—*whoosh,* she don't work no more."

Astro Zombie emitted a thin scream through his teeth.

Zuma tapped an open-ended wrench on the armor plate aft of the open panel. "This *mamacita*'s always been cranky," he said. "Shoot, I think she's probably one of the first *Jennies* ever built."

"Don't be stupid," Astro Zombie said. "I've been all over this machine. None of the serial numbers is anywhere near low enough."

"Oh, but see, she's just like my grandfather's old axe that had three new heads and six new handles. Everything's been replaced a couple times over, y'know?"

The Chief Tech threw up his hands and stilted as far away as the four-meter platform would permit. Zuma looked at Cassie behind his back and winked.

A call from the ground: "Yo, Cassie!" She twisted and looked down. Kali MacDougall stood on the ground, waving up at her.

"I'm taking a break from the infirmary," the MechWarrior said. "Want to walk?"

Cassie glanced around. She took an active interest in BattleMech maintenance and repair on the principle that if you knew what made them run, you knew how to make them stop running. But the lessons to be extracted from this particular set of circumstances—that the mightiest war machines in history could be startlingly fragile if something popped their chips from their sockets and interrupted their delicate control circuits, and that old 'Mechs were just as cranky as old people—were already pretty apparent. The finer points of the post-mortem and eventual repair were beyond her competence—or her interest.

She looked at Zuma. The Chief Aztech waved distractedly at her. "Later, *'manita*," he said. Astro Zombie paid no attention to her. That was Sierra Hotel by her; he never *did*. It was widely accepted in the Regiment that the Chief Tech didn't like girls. On the other hand, there was no evidence he liked boys, either. The more scurrilous-minded enjoyed speculating about Captain Harris and the giant humanoid machines to which he devoted his every waking moment, of course, but that was just talk. Probably.

"Be right down," Cassie called. She clambered down the ladder like a lithe brown monkey.

"I wouldn't have believed it," Archie Westin said, "but you Southwesterners still manage to amaze me."

The tables in the commissary had been covered with padding to serve as makeshift hospital beds for bandaged civilians from the housing complex. Mothers tried to comfort wailing children. Seriously injured patients moaned and tossed on the tables, prevented from falling off by straps or sometimes just duct tape. Dr. Sondra Ten Bears, *la Curandera,* the Seventeenth's chief medical officer, moved among them, examining them.

"What's eating you now, Arch?" called Cowboy, parking a dolly laden with boxes of painkiller syrettes by the wall.

The reporter gestured around the ward. The tall, heavily built *Curandera* was only one of many mercenaries aiding the HTE med staff.

"You're as proud a lot of MechWarriors as any I've encountered," he said, "and I've covered the Crucis Lancers and the Lyran Guards, as well as the Kell Hounds and Wolf's Dragoons. Yet here you are, playing nurse for civilians—civilians who were your mortal enemies not so many years ago."

Chuy Montoya, a *Wasp* driver from Cochise and no relation to Father Montoya, stopped and wiped a handkerchief across his forehead. He was helping to manhandle wounded and the dead onto stretchers, the living to be transferred to one of Masamori's hospitals and the rest to be laid out under tarps beside the building.

"We got families ourselves, *carnal,* you know?" he said.

John Amos Ames and his wife Raven came in. Ames was looking a little dazed. The 'Mech pilots broke off playing medical orderly to applaud him. He winced. Raven smiled her cool smile.

"Congratulations, Captain," Ten Bears said.

Ames shook his head. He was medium height, with long dark-blond hair, black eyebrows, and melancholy brown hound-dog eyes that belied his reputation for revelry. He waved his hands as if trying to bat the clapping away.

"Thanks, I guess," he said. "If I had my druthers, I sure wouldn't have got my second stripe this way." He had been promoted to succeed Don Coyote in command of Adelante.

"If he had his druthers," Raven said coolly, "he wouldn't have gotten the promotion at all. It might mean he has to take some responsibility."

FrenchFry folded his hands over his heart. "Sierra Foxtrot, honey, go easy on me. I didn't get me much sleep last night."

"So what else is new?" his wife asked.

Archie looked at Cowboy, who had stopped for a breather, leaning against a table on which a mountainously fat woman with both arms splinted lay snoring. "I never have figured out what 'Sierra Foxtrot' means."

"Santa Fé," Raven said. Sierra's capital city had come to epitomize the way outsiders saw the "Southwestern" worlds, the way its namesake had epitomized the American Southwest for *gringos* centuries before. Like their ancestors before them, the rural Caballeros were loudly contemptuous of Santa Fé and all it stood for.

"Shoot, Raven," Cowboy said, "It don't *exactly* mean that."

"It's close enough for Mr. Westin's viewers back in the Federated Commonwealth," Raven said. "FCNS is a family network."

"Zuma and Diana tell me he give 'em an eyeful last night when the bad guys tried to take the kids hostage," Cowboy said. "His little pal Savage got it all on disk."

He gave Westin a huge, folksy grin. "I guess they train you Stealthy Fox boys right, back in New Avalon."

= 26 =

Imperial City, Luthien
Pesht District, Draconis Combine
16 October 3056

Sitting in his garden in his powered chair, the light of Luthien's sun dappling him with welcome warmth through the branches of the young plum trees, the old man clutched the flimsy slip of yellow paper in a liver-spotted hand and felt an emotion almost alien to him in all his long years of life: fear for himself.

He felt a measure of fear for the Combine as well. If Chandrasekhar Kurita was truly treating with the Clans, the consequences could be almost incalculable. Yet should the knowledge that a member of the Coordinator's family was suspected of treason on a cosmic scale become public, the results might actually be worse.

But that was familiar fear. Subhash Indrahar had devoted most of his nearly ninety years of life to serving the Combine. His loyalty to House Kurita transcended even loyalty to any individual Kurita, as his long-time friend Takashi had learned when Subhash and his adoptive son had attempted to kill him. Most of his passions were reserved for the Dragon.

But now . . . he could not restrain the stirrings of purely selfish fear within his shrunken breast.

Even that in a way was for the Dragon, or so he told himself. His body had once been that of an athlete, lithe and strong. But he had outlived its power. For the past several years all that had kept him alive was the sheer indomitable force of his will.

He feared, yes. He feared the Clans. He feared the chaos that threatened to overwhelm the Inner Sphere, after a fleeting period of unity in the face of the Clan juggernaut invading from beyond the Periphery. He feared that the seeds of anarchy might have already been sown within the Draconis Combine. Theodore's liberalization had been forced by sheer necessity; the Combine was nearly out of resources, and its attempts to regiment the lives of its citizens ever more stringently had begun to increase entropy, not reverse it. Yet Subhash did not know whether the reforms would halt the process of decay, or accelerate it.

But of one thing he was certain: now more than ever the Dragon relied on the strength and wisdom and self-sacrificing courage of its Sons: the Internal Security Force.

For the greater part of a century Subhash Indrahar had *been* the ISF. Yet not even the Smiling One could continue to carry that burden much longer.

He yearned to be able to pass it on with an easy heart. Once before, he thought he had found a worthy successor. But Nakina Grandy, his chosen heir, had failed in a task, and taken his own life in expiation.

Now he had another heir, a successor who was even more worthy, if the rough edges could be sanded off Ninyu Kerai. But here was Ninyu confronting apparent failure. He might even now be contemplating the *wakizashi* with which he'd rip his guts out.

That was Subhash's fear. He had no more time to search for a new successor. And to leave the ISF without a strong leader would be to leave the ship of the Combine rudderless in the face of myriad storms.

It was not that Subhash lacked faith in Theodore. Many—most notably Theodore's father, then-Coordinator Takashi—had sold the younger Kurita short, doubting his ability and strength of character. They had all been wrong. To Subhash's mind, Theodore Kurita was as great a leader as House Kurita had ever produced.

But if the Coordinator was the captain, Internal Security was the helm. Without it, the Coordinator would lack the *means* to guide the state.

The Smiling One was not longing for a chance to retire. He longed to be able to *die*.

A curl of combustion-smell. Subhash let go the flimsy paper. The chemical reaction initiated when the printer ink came into contact with the special paper had run its course, culminating in flame. The message slip's mayfly span had ended in self-destruction.

It did not matter. The Smiling One had committed it contents to memory with a single glance.

Now he must compose a reply. The fate of the Draconis Combine—and perhaps the whole of the Inner Sphere—was riding on it.

"How you holding up, girl?"

Cassie walked with her hands stuck in the pockets of her baggy khaki trousers. She was kind of dancing around in her black sneakers, ostensibly in order to keep up with the taller MechWarrior's longer strides. She shook herself slightly, looked up.

"Fine. Just fine. I was helping Diana with the little ones— they're still pretty shook up by what happened last night. Captain Vásquez told me to knock off and get some rest. But I don't feel like resting right now."

"Still jazzed, are you?" Lady K asked. She was dressed in her usual off-duty garb of jeans, and a man's shirt with the tails tied up. Her blonde hair was clamped any which way on top of her head, a lank strand escaped and hung like a tentacle in her eyes. The blue eyes had dark circles under them, and there was a smudge on one cheek. Cassie felt a certain perverse satisfaction at seeing her glamorous new friend looking like something the cat dragged in.

"I don't know," Cassie said, wondering yet again why she felt the compulsion to be candid with this damned woman. "I feel *incomplete*. As if things're only half-finished somehow."

Lady K's brows drew together. "You're not feeling twitchy because you didn't actually get to kill anybody last night?"

"What the *hell's* that supposed to mean?" Cassie shouted. Rage spiked in her like a plasma jet.

"Pretty much what I said," Lady K replied calmly, "as usual."

"Are you trying to tell me how to do my job?"

"Wouldn't dream of it. I just want you to kind of think about things."

"I do my part."

"Nobody does more for the Regiment than you do, hon, and everybody knows it. But your job is to gather information. Killing people's secondary."

"It has to be done, sometimes. We're warriors, in case you're forgetting."

"I'm not. My job *is* killing people. But I worry about you."

Cassie had paced a few steps ahead of her. She turned now to face the taller woman. *"Why?"*

"You really want to get a taste for it?"

For a moment Cassie stood, face frozen in an angry mask. The rage seethed inside her like a storm on the surface of Hachiman's orange sun.

"What are you trying to do to me? Weaken me? Take away my edge?"

Lady K shook her head. "No, hon. Just trying to make sure you stay human."

Cassie spun away and hugged herself tightly beneath her small breasts. "Thank you too much."

She felt Lady K come up behind her, tensed, afraid the other world try to touch her. She didn't want anyone near her now.

But Lady K did not touch her. She merely stood, not quite close enough to crowd.

"What do you *want,* anyway?" Cassie demanded. To her surprise, the catch in her voice told that she was close to tears. Her eyes began to sting with the realization. "Why all this interest in me, anyway? What do you *want* with me?"

"To be your friend."

Cassie spun. *"Why?"* she almost screamed. Tears poured freely down her cheeks now. "Do you want to go to bed with me? Do you think it's a good idea to cozy up to me 'cause I'm such a Sierra Hotel scout? Why the *hell* do you want to get next to me?"

"Purely because of who you are."

Cassie glared wildly at her. Her eyes were almost the same pale blue as the sky. "Why? Who am I?"

"Somebody I'm proud to call my friend."

Cassie drew in a deep breath, a huge breath, a breath almost bigger than her whole skinny body. She was about to blast it right back at MacDougall, call her a liar to her fashion-model face. Instead she just swallowed it, turned around and stood there.

"Why do you find it so hard to believe somebody could like you just for you?" Lady K asked.

"Because I'm not worth it," Cassie said stiffly. "I'm street trash, a cheap little slut. A wanton killer."

"You're none of those things. But you could turn into them if you don't take a good look at yourself and make some choices. If we try to fight our nightmares too long, we turn into something straight out of them."

"Yeah," Cassie sneered, turning to face the MechWarrior. "I'm gonna metamorphose into a ten-meter war machine. Any goddamn minute now."

"You've wasted more 'Mechs than half our MechWarriors," Lady K said, "so I don't know as how that's so far-fetched. What you're *really* runnin' the risk of is turning into a killing machine, pure and simple. Instead of a woman who can be deadly when she needs—when she *chooses* to be."

Cassie stood with the sun hot on her face and her fists balled so tight the tendons of her forearms ached. After a moment Lady K let loose a quiet laugh.

"You can stand there and hate me if you want, baby doll," she said, "but *I'm* gonna hunt up some of the gang and hoist a few tall cool ones."

Archie's jaw dropped. In the sudden booming silence Caballero heads turned. Toward Cowboy. The lanky 'Mech pilot glanced around the half-circle of his comrades, then back at Westin. The reporter's handsome young face had gone a most unflattering shade of pale green beneath his freckles.

"I guess I went and stepped in it," Cowboy said in a small voice.

"That's a fair assessment," Raven said.

Westin drew in a shaky breath. "I think I need a drink," he said.

"Here come Cass and Lady K," Raven said. "Let's take a break and sort things out."

"When did you make me?" Archie asked. They were sitting in a rec hall with no locals about. The reporter was on his second Borstal Boy from the dispenser. He'd already been through the usual round of denials, which his companions had met with what for them was polite skepticism.

"First time I laid eyes on you," said Cassie with waspish relish. She seemed to be in an angry mood. Westin had never seen her like this, and wasn't enjoying it now. "You had *spy* written all over you."

"It's not really that bad, Arch," Lady K said. "Think about it: You got mercenary MechWarrior regiments going missin' by the job lot during the Clan War. One of 'em happens to be the Seventeenth. Your Inner Sphere intelligence services wondered what they hey happened to them. Then we turn back up—on a JumpShip bound for the heart of the Draconis Combine."

She shrugged. "And next *you* turn up the minute we break the jump point in-system, saying you want to cover us for your news service. And you stick with us for weeks."

"But your story is quite compelling—"

"Sure." she reached out and patted his hand. "But nobody gives a pinch of sour owl crap, hon, because we're not a glamorous outfit like the Dragoons."

"Nobody ever heard of us," Chuy said, "except the people who hire us."

"And the people whose butts they hired us to kick," Cowboy added.

"But I really *am* a journalist for the Federated Commonwealth News Service."

"Sure," Cassie said. "And your FedCom news services are notorious for rolling over when somebody with Davion or Steiner in their last names asks them nice."

Archie winced. "That's harsh. You make us sound as if we're puppets, like—like the Combine media."

Lady K shook her head. "Nope. There's a difference between a subservient but free press and an out-and-out puppet. We all used to be up on that kind of thing, back when the *Free* in Free Worlds League meant somethin' other than freedom to be Tommy Marik's personal play-toys."

Westin raised his beer, then lowered it again. His expression suggested it smelled like it had spoiled.

"So you've all been stringing me along, lo, these many weeks."

"Arch," Lady K said, "we like you. We really do."

"And we don't mind getting a little favorable publicity, now and then," Raven added.

"What—what about Father García?" The Jesuit had taken some EMT course along the way, and was off picking through the ruins of the housing complex, tending to survivors of the terrorist attack and the CGC "rescue." There was a certain potential for tension in letting a Catholic priest loose on the streets of a city in the Combine, where any Christianity other than dour Rasalhaguian Lutheranism was officially proscribed. But Father Bob was not exactly the proselytizing type, and generally wore a black turtleneck instead of a dog collar—and anyway, it wasn't reckoned anybody would be too eager to hassle a man with fifty friendly BattleMechs in whistling distance.

"He was spying on me, wasn't he?"

"He was just tryin' to keep you outta trouble, cousin," the new Captain Ames said.

"He really does like you," Raven said. "You're a refreshing change for him—a real live sophisticated F-C kinda guy, in contrast to all us scrubby provincial *coyotes* he's gotta live with."

Archie scowled. He had gotten no more sleep than the mercs had, which was none, and even a beer and a half were having an effect on him with his defenses down. He stood, swaying slightly.

"You have all been quite disingenuous in your dealings with me," he said.

"Hey, now, Arch, no need to go talkin' dirty in front of the ladies," Cowboy said. "Sierra Foxtrot, it's not like we wanta get *rid* of you. Davion might turn around and stick somebody on us we couldn't spot so easy."

Kali MacDougall lowered her forehead to the tabletop. Westin glared at Cowboy wildly and stomped out. Cowboy blinked around at his comrades.

"What'd I say? What'd I *say?*"

Raven put her sharp chin on her hands and looked at him with a marveling expression. "Cowboy," she said, "are you just naturally that big a butthead, or did you have to go to school to learn it?"

The room overlooked a twilight Shakudo Sea through a transpex wall. The floor was green marble, with an ornate Arkab carpet laid over it. The furniture was spare, with that understated elegance that made no compromise with the human form. Ninyu Kerai Indrahar, equally oblivious to either comfort or elegance, stood in the center of the room watching the dance of holographic puppets on the stage in the corner.

An earnest, clean-cut young reporter was standing in front of an apartment block, one of whose whitewashed walls had slumped into the street, exposing beams like twisted skeleton fingers. Smoke poured from the ruin. A squad of firemen played the stream from a hose into it.

"Terrorism and disorder," the young man was saying. "The twin scourges of the Inner Sphere have now disturbed the placid sanctity of the Dragon's realm ..."

"Of course, my Lord observes how we turn the story to our advantage," said Enrico Katsuyama, who stood slightly behind Ninyu. That in itself was irritating, but Ninyu would not show his discomfort by moving back to bring the obsequious little toad into his field of vision. "Shortly they will cut away to scenes of the current nationalist unrest in the Federated Commonwealth, establishing how very much more common this sort of commotion is there."

"The Federated Commonwealth is not our enemy," Ninyu said, "for the moment."

Katsuyama bobbed his head. "Indeed not, lord. But it is the Commonwealth lifestyle our people are most likely to envy. These events give us the opportunity to show that their ways are tainted with disorder."

Ninyu scowled. "But we're not trying to hide the fact that the attackers were Word of Blake terrorists—we're relying on that to mask our own involvement. What does the Word of Blake have to do with the Federated Commonwealth?"

"Why, nothing, lord. And what of it? We show the public one thing, and tell them another, and no one suspects a thing." His eyes shone. "It's a technique perfected by the early masters of the twentieth century."

Ninyu made a sound low in his throat and gestured at the display. A mercenary *Archer* was holding up its hand, while a trapped Worker woman with an infant in her arms stepped from the balcony of a shattered building onto its palm.

"They're making Chandrasekhar Kurita's foreign hirelings look like *heroes*," he said. "Did you clear this?"

"Why, yes, lord," Katsuyama smiled tentatively. "We will turn this to our advantage in the second phase of our operation."

The second phase ... The man said it so blithely. As if

last night's failure had been expected, deliberate even, merely a steppingstone along the way.

Ninyu paced to the window-wall. The sea's surface was black. The tips and the edges of the chop were gilded by the light of the setting sun, making the water look like the background of an ancient oil painting, laced with a craqueleur of flame.

What made it worse was that the lumpy little media doctor's assessment was reinforced by the hyperpulse message Ninyu's adoptive father had sent him that afternoon. *Think of it as a reconnaissance, my son,* Subhash Indrahar had written. *We needed to know the strength of our target's defenses. Now we do, at negligible cost.*

It had, in fact, cost the lives of more than a hundred Word of Blake raiders, which of course meant less than nothing to Ninyu Kerai Indrahar, or his father. But it was harder to write off the thirty-six DEST commandos lost. Ninyu understood that their lives were coins, to be spent without thought in the Dragon's service; it was even so with his own life, and that of his adoptive father. But it aggrieved him to waste so much for so little apparent gain.

They had inflicted scandalously few casualties on the barbarians, a fact that Ninyu experienced as bone-deep shame. Yet, despite the missile-launchers the ISF strike team had carried, it was never intended that they would battle toe-to-toe with BattleMechs. They were supposed to get in as quietly as possible, assassinate Chandrasekhar Kurita, and withdraw as best they could. The plan had been compromised, however, and the team members butchered by foes even they could not overmatch.

One way to expiate the shame that burned within him was suicide, of course. But his father's message precluded that option, making it very clear that *seppuku* would only be shirking his duty to the Dragon. Ninyu accepted that, as he accepted everything his father laid upon him.

So his option was rage. A rage that he would slake in full against that ludicrous fat fool Uncle Chandy. *And* his pet barbarians.

"Lord," Katsuyama said respectfully, "look at this."

Ninyu glanced at the holostage. The anchorwoman's face had reappeared.

"Just a few hours ago," she was saying, "the tragic and horrifying events in the capital city were overshadowed—or

rather, *outshone*—for residents of the southern hemisphere city of Hawthorne, whose nighttime sky was illuminated by a remarkable pyrotechnic display."

The image changed to a starry sky. Something resembling a giant meteorite—a flaming freight train, more like—blazed a lurid trail across it.

"The fiery spectacle was itself sign of tragedy," the anchorwoman said gravely, "the catastrophic re-entry of the DropShip *Peggy Sue,* off the Davion-registered JumpShip *Daisy Belle.* The DropShip was lost with all hands. Such accidents are extremely rare. . . ."

"Now where did *that* come from?" Katsuyama said.

Ninyu shook his head. He didn't care how many DropShips fell from the sky.

He had a fireworks display of his own to arrange.

27

Masamori, Hachiman
Draconis Combine
17 October 3056

The smell of humidity and potting soil hung like thick damp curtains in the greenhouse. "Well, daughter," Chandrasekhar Kurita said, "Ninyu Kerai has tested our defenses. And found them strong, thanks to you and your friends."

"He'll be back," Cassie said flatly.

The fleshy blooms of orchids surrounded them, like polychrome explosions frozen in time. Uncle Chandy tamped peat moss into a pot beneath an orange and black blossom, turned to Cassie, and smiled.

"Of course he will," he said, looking like Buddha in a gardener's apron. "The question is, what are we going to do about it?"

"Take the initiative," Cassie said.

Uncle Chandy laughed. "Truly, your presumption is wonderful, girl. Seizing the initiative from a man like Ninyu Kerai is like trying to snatch fresh meat from a starving banth."

In known space there were two dozen animals known as *banths*. All of them were predators.

Cassie tossed her head, flipping a loose strand of hair from her eyes. "It's that or wait passively for the knife," she said.

Uncle Chandy had picked up a trowel. He turned and stood gazing at her with those thick-lidded amphibian eyes, turning the implement over and over in his hands. Cassie was taking a risk in lecturing him, and knew it.

He smiled. "You are wise, my daughter," he said. "In your perceptions, if not always in your demeanor."

"You've got plenty of people to tell you what you want to hear."

He boomed laughter. "It is truly amazing how often the price of competent help is impertinence," he said. "How fortunate for us all that I—unlike so many of my peers—find myself willing to pay such a price. Otherwise how many valuable resources would be wasted?"

He gave the word *wasted* a certain emphasis. Cassie refused to quail.

He turned back to his plants. "What about the *Daisy Belle*?" she asked.

"The *Mirza*'s people are looking into it. It is of secondary concern at the moment."

"The Clanners—"

"Seem unlikely to pose as immediate a threat as Ninyu Kerai Indrahar, eh?"

Cassie bit her lip. She nodded.

"I have a specific task in mind for you," he said, reaching up to a rack above his head. "That is, if you are truly serious about seizing the initiative."

"My street contacts—"

"Will not suffice. What chance have we of defeating Ninyu in the long run?"

Cassie paused, calculating odds of survival. Her own, if

she told the unpalatable truth; the odds Uncle Chandy was inquiring about needed no calculation.

"In the long run," she said, "none."

Uncle Chandy took down a pot with an extravagant green, orange, and purple flower hanging from it. "This strain was developed in the late twenty-eighty century by Filbert Fujimori, who was subsequently put to death," he said. "Nothing to do with horticulture, as it happened; he wrote a scurrilous *haiku* about Coordinator Jinjiro—understandable, to be sure, but scarcely prudent. This orchid has always been a particular favorite of mine. I don't know why; it's in truly frightful taste. Perhaps I have a yen for the perverse."

He set it carefully on a long table with a metal-mesh top and set about repotting the garish plant. "What we need to do," he said, "is make Ninyu Kerai lose interest in us. You needn't bother protesting that this will not be easy; as long as he lives, he will pursue us, and should he die, his adoptive father will surely avenge him."

Cassie turned away. She did not want Uncle Chandy to see the sheen of desperate tears in her eyes.

"So what can we *do*?" she asked, the words nearly choking her. She was admitting powerlessness—and in the face of her new nightmare, the red-haired man. It was as painful a thing as she could remember since Patsy died.

"Demonstrate our innocence."

"I didn't think the ISF gave a damn for that sort of thing."

"The ISF assumes guilt from the fact of suspicion. Not the same thing, not the same at all. Neither the Smiling One nor his heir presumptive operates on a basis of animus. If we can show him the *real* culprit, he will turn his rage aside from us."

Cassie sat back against a shelf. "And who *is* the real culprit?"

"Tanadi," Uncle Chandy said. "Who else can it be?"

Someone ruthless enough to murder a DropShip crew to cover his tracks. "Do you know that?"

"The *Mirza* believes so, on the basis of what his inquiries have revealed."

Cassie shrugged. "Has he got evidence that will convince Ninyu?"

"Sadly, no. That's where you come in."

"You want me to get inside?"

The great smooth head nodded. Artificial daylight slid back and forth across it.

"What's the Tanadi CEO like?"

"Hardly the sort to slip a twenty H-bill note inside one of the red shoes that comprise the bulk of your costume at Torashii Gyaru," Uncle Chandy said. Cassie made a face at him. "Redmond Hosoya is a man of probity, after his own fashion. His vices, while deplorable enough, are carefully monitored by his security staff. He allows no one to get close to him without careful screening—more careful than we can prepare you to survive, given the limited time in which we have to work."

He turned to her, brushing black soil from his hands, and smiled. "Fortunately, not everyone at the higher ranks of our society is so discriminating."

"We must act quickly," Force Commander White Nose Pony told the officers packed into the Compound commissary set aside for mercenary use. "We need to move our remaining forces, and our dependents, within the walls of the Compound at once."

It was what the 'lleros called a Council of Elders. Such gatherings were called on matters of policy pertaining to the Regiment as a whole; strictly military concerns were dealt with by a Command Council. In the wake of the attack, with further trouble almost certainly in the offing, the more general voice seemed called for.

The council consisted of commanders from company level up, senior staff and support personnel, and people whose words for one reason or another commanded respect within the Regiment. Zuma was there, as were Diana and Dr. Ten Bears. The various chaplains were also present. So was Third Battalion *Crusader* pilot Teresa de Ávila Chávez, *la Guadalupana,* who—though a mere Lieutenant Junior Grade—was present because the Virgin of Guadalupe frequently appeared to her. The faithful back home in the Trinity avidly followed her exploits, particularly on Cerillos, where she was especially revered.

Tables had been pushed together to create one giant table with Don Carlos at the head and his officers flanking him down the sides, in order of descending seniority. That meant junior officers had to yell to make themselves heard. Caballeros were not backward about that sort of thing.

"That's lay-about-the-fort thinking," said Lieutenant SG James Kicking Bird, CO of Geronimo Company. A full-blood Comanche, he was perpetually disgruntled that his command was named for an Apache. "Relying on *walls* to defend you."

White Nose Pony turned him an impassive obsidian gaze. "We're contracted to defend the Compound, not the Sportsplex," he said. "This is where further attacks will come. That being so, is it wise to gather our warriors and leave our flocks and children exposed?"

Kicking Bird scowled. He didn't have much of a come-back to that. The Singer didn't say much, but when he did, he was hard to answer.

"So we concentrate our forces," said Captain Bobby Begay firmly. Singer did not look pleased at the apparent support. "That's decided. There's another question we have to face: whether Colonel Camacho is still fit to command us."

Silence fell like a toppled *Mauler*. "What are you saying, evil thing?" Singer asked.

Bobby the Wolf's handsome face turned to color of boot leather and he started to rise. Seated at his father's right, Gavilán Camacho leaned forward. "Take it easy, Bobby," he said quietly. "It doesn't mean a thing."

Glaring, the Cochise commander sat down again.

"I smell a setup," Kali MacDougall said.

Heads turned toward her. She sat back in her chair with a sour smile. "Looks to me as if some of our young Turks reckon it's time for a change."

A tumult of questions, comments, and arguments spread like prairie fire through the commissary. "Colonel Camacho failed us during the terrorist attack," Vanity Torres said loudly, trying to be heard above the noise.

"You behind this, Gabby?" Lady K asked.

The young officers were beginning to look uneasily at each other and then back at the tall, blonde Captain. Nobody was quite prepared to confront her.

"No one doubts my father's bravery," Gavilán said. "Not to *my* face, anyway. Yet his conduct in the last battle has raised questions nonetheless." He hesitated. "Even in my mind."

"He froze," Bobby the Wolf said. "He didn't command us when we needed him. He dwells too much in the past."

"We *won,* remember?" Lady K broke in. The dissidents glared at her. She kept asking questions they didn't want asked, making points they liked less.

The Colonel's head was hanging as if it had turned to lead. "You have reason," he said in Spanish. "I could not focus my mind in combat."

He looked up with visible effort. "Such behavior is unacceptable in a commander—"

"Don Carlos."

The noise quieted. Force Commander Bar-Kochba had not raised his voice. As usual he didn't need to.

"We are in a mighty dangerous situation," he said in his slow drawl. "You've pulled us through many a narrow time before, Colonel. I think we need your judgment and experience to pull us through this one." He gazed around the meeting chamber, eyes fierce. "If Colonel Camacho were to retire, I'd have to think mighty hard about joining him."

"Are you a coward, then, to turn your tail in the face of danger?" Gavilán flashed.

Deliberately as an *Atlas* twisting its torso, Bar-Kochba traversed his balding head until his eyes—so blue they were startling in the tanned and grizzle-bearded face—bore on the young Force Commander like PPC muzzles crackling at the brink of discharge.

"In the interests of the Regiment," the Rabbi said slowly, "and out of respect for your family, which has long been allied with mine, I shall pretend you never said that."

Gavilán went pale behind his mustache. The boy was no coward. Neither was he a total fool—quite.

Bar-Kochba was among the Regiment's most respected members for his calm wisdom under the most trying conditions. He was also respected for the nearly badgerlike savagery he could display with his back to the wall, and for his skill as a MechWarrior. He was not a man to provoke lightly.

Forbearance in the face of provocation did not come naturally to his people. Unlike many Jews of the time, his ancestors had *not* opposed the measures of Israel's militant regimes in the twenty-first century. They had rejoiced in their country's reputation for militant truculence, and generations after the great Reconciliation had carried it proudly with them to the outlaw Intendancy of New New Spain. There they were adopted into the Cowboy ethnic affiliation, took for themselves the defiant sobriquet of *Jewboys,* and settled into lives of happy piracy with the rest of the Caballeros. They still named their children for Moshe Dayan and Ariel Sharon and Golda Meir and other heroes of Israel's early days, and they worked hard to maintain that tradition of ferocity that in Old Testament times had inspired conquerors to plant Hebrew settlements along their borders to deter intruders, like hedges full of thorns.

Gavilán bowed his head and held his tongue.

"This was not an isolated incident," Regimental intelligence officer Gordon Baird said. He always sounded strained, as if he had to squeeze the words out of his throat. "Everyone knows I'm an old comrade in arms of Colonel Camacho; I yield to no one in my respect for him. But—" He sadly shook his immaculately groomed gray head, milking the elder-statesman role. "The fact is, he has been distracted and neglecting the Regiment's affairs for quite some time."

"It's true."

The quiet female voice from the Colonel's right hand could hardly have produced a greater effect had it been loud as a stun grenade. The rising clamor cut off. Everybody stared at the woman who now stood next to *el Patrón*.

"For some time Don Carlos has found himself unable to attend to his responsibilities. I have covered for him. Now I fear the situation has grown too grave to do so any longer."

The Colonel stared at Marisol Cabrera, dumbstruck. His expression of passive resignation had vanished. Now he looked angry.

He rose. For a full minute he stared at her, while the room seemed suspended in a cargo net of silence.

"Lieutenant Colonel Cabrera," he said, when his face had gone from white to red, "you are relieved as my aide-de-camp." He stalked from the hall.

La Dama Muerte's ironbound façade cracked like armor plate hit by a Gauss rifle round. She covered her face with her hands and fled weeping out the door.

The commissary erupted in wild clamor. Everyone was yelling. Half the 'lleros were on their feet. Some of them were squaring off, cocking fists or dropping hands to gun butts.

In the confines of the room, the crack of ionized air fleeing a laser bolt was grotesquely loud. Everyone shut up, listening to their ears ring and staring toward the table's head.

Captain Kali MacDougall holstered her laser pistol. "I'm sure glad these buildings are hardened," she remarked. "Hate to shoot somebody upstairs in the fanny."

She looked around. "I think y'all are forgetting one teensy little detail."

"And what might that be, Kali dear?" Vanity asked in tones of silken bitchiness.

"We're under siege, right here and now. For all we know, we might find this whole danged world outside the walls rising up against us. All we got's each other. We can't afford to go fighting amongst ourselves."

"But the Colonel—" Bobby the Wolf began.

"*Listen* to me, dammit! Don't you see we're in deeper than we were when up against the *tigres* on Jeronimo?"

"What are you talking about?" Gavilán demanded. "The Clan beat the Snakes as easily as they beat us."

She fixed him with eyes as clear and unyielding as blue sky mirrored in a transpex windscreen.

"This time, Gabby, there's no pickup," she said softly. "This one we got to win. Or that's it for all of us."

Kali sat with her back to the wall, smoking a cigarette. The mess hall was deserted; she was alone with her thoughts. They weren't congenial company.

Archie Westin poked his wavy-haired blond head in the door, peered around, saw her, hesitated, then came walking over.

"Might I join you, Captain?"

She sighed and spread her hands. He nodded, taking the chair across from her.

"If you're looking for Cassie," Kali said, "she's busy. And she's liable to be out of circulation for a while."

"Cassie?" he shook his head. "No. She's a lovely and fascinating creature, but I've decided I've spent quite enough time banging my head against that particular brick wall, thank you."

Kali cocked an eyebrow at him. "Might find it worth the effort to keep on battering. Even if it is a might tough on the old coiffure."

He grinned. "You're quite a rare specimen yourself, Captain MacDougall, if I may be bold enough to say so."

"I'll take that as a compliment," she said. "Otherwise I

reckon I'd just have to shoot you, and I got enough problems without having Davion's MI4 gunning for me."

Archie's lips tightened beneath his pencil-thin mustache. "They'd probably think you were doing them a favor. The head of MI4 is my uncle, you know."

"No foolin'?"

He shook his head. "It's no state secret; I'm really Archie Westin, and my mother really is the former Leticia Cromwell. A matter of record, back in the Federated Suns."

She looked at him, and he quickly corrected himself. "Federated *Commonwealth*, I mean. I'm afraid that *was* rather a sinister slip of the tongue, given the situation back home."

"May turn out to be accurate enough again, though, real soon now."

He sighed. "I hope not. I was raised to consider myself a son and servant of the Federated Commonwealth."

"Yeah, well I was raised to consider myself a daughter of the Free Worlds League, and look how that turned out." She leaned forward. "So how the heck did you wind up on secret assignment for your uncle Ian?"

He shrugged. "I always idolized him as a boy. Wanted to emulate him. Drove my mother crazy."

"So when you got old enough you signed up."

"Oh, yes." He gave his head a rueful shake. "Oh, I know I'm not too good at the cloak-and-dagger stuff so far. I started out as a rather more active type of operative, if you can believe that. Following in Uncle Ian's footsteps again; he also got his start in MI6."

"I noticed you keep yourself awful fit for a newscaster." She took a drag on her cigarette. "So you were a Rabid Fox. What happened?"

Archie sighed. "My mother. She's rather overprotective of me and badgered my uncle until he agreed to transfer me out. I was the only one to carry on the Westin family name, she said. A formidable woman, Dame Leticia."

"I see."

"This is my first go as a covert. After all, it is rather a low-priority assignment. With all due respect, the Commonwealth may be interested in where the Seventeenth Recon has been, and why it has so abruptly resurfaced in the pay of a Combine potentate, and an actual Kurita to boot. But it's not *that* interested."

"NBD, Archie. No big deal. We think high enough of ourselves for the whole darn universe."

They sat together in silence for a time. Then Kali sighed and put out her cigarette in her polymer coffee cup.

"So what's the deal, Arch? Reckon there's a reason you stopped making yourself so scarce."

He spread his hands. "You've caught me out again. You are a most perceptive lady."

"Save the soft soap for later; might find it comes in handy. Now, what's really on your mind, other than that pretty blond hair?"

He bit his lip. "I made a right ass of myself, the other day, Didn't I?"

"Yep."

"I accused you all of deceiving me. I know that's rather petty, given that what I was truly miffed about was my own utter failure to deceive *you*."

"Which you'll notice none of us was holding against you."

"Indeed. In any event, I wanted to look you up and apologize. Is there any way I can atone for my offense?"

She looked him up and down, a smile winching itself slowly across her face. "You could buy me dinner at the executives' lounge. Real steak. Drac mucky-mucks don't care a hoot what these half-converted Hindus think about eating cows."

Archie blinked. Then he grinned. "Dear lady," he said, "it would be my pleasure."

$$=== \mathbf{28} ===$$

Masamori, Hachiman
Galedon District, Draconis Combine
21 October 3056

"**W**ho's the ravishing creature with the Fat Boy?" the Right Honorable Percival Fillington, Earl of Hachiman, asked his trusted aide Gupta Yoritomo.

Without turning his sleek round head—temples shaved to the tops of the ears, the heavy brown hair above worn long and gathered into a ponytail—the shorter man glanced across the salon of the Citadel's penthouse suite toward their host. Decked out in his usual gaudy scarlet robe, Uncle Chandy had a huge brandy-filled snifter of Srinagar crystal in one hand and a gorgeous woman on his arm.

"His newest play-pretty, one presumes, milord," Yoritomo murmured, in a voice precisely calculated to carry above the burble of cocktail conversation to his master's ears, but no farther. Members of his family had served as personal aides to the Earls of Hachiman for generations; like so many of his kind, he had been bred for his post as well as schooled in its skills since birth. "One in a long line, but not one I'm familiar with."

Percy grinned with a schoolboy's frank enthusiasm. "One well worth knowing, I'd say." The stern detachment of the samurai did not come naturally to Hachiman's young Planetary Chairman. It hadn't come with long and grueling training, either, though he could fake it for state occasions.

It was widely accepted that Percy was a twit. His twithood, however, was considered beneficial to the State. Despite the centralization of state power on Luthien, which had been one of Theodore Kurita's less-publicized reforms, the Combine's individual Planetary Chairmen still enjoyed considerable autonomy. It therefore served the interests of the Dragon that the Earl of a planet as important as Hachiman be a twit.

Even a non-twit might have agreed with the young Earl's assessment, though. The woman was of slightly above average height for a Combine female, 165 centimeters or so, and almost boyishly slim—a far cry from the leggy, top-heavy blondes traditionally beloved of Kurita dignitaries, though her stiletto-heeled boots added to the apparent length of legs that were already long for her height, and immaculately sculpted. But there was a sinuous grace to the figure defined by a sheath of incomparable emerald silk from the Hachiman city of Kuranosuke. Her hair was a bold metallic red that clashed rather horribly with her escort's robe. Her eyes matched her dress. Her skin was pale, ivory rather than alabaster, which had the effect of setting off the distinctly Asian cast of her fine features in a way Percy found most fetching.

She caught him looking at her, then glanced up at her escort. Uncle Chandy was engaged in swapping insincerities with some of the lesser local nobility, completely oblivious to her; she was nothing but a woman, after all. It was almost surprising to see the bumptious Chandrasekhar displaying such classic Kurita virtue—and Percy felt a twinge of something akin to envy that the man *could* remain apparently indifferent to such a woman.

She looked back at Percy and smiled. It was a smile to induce arrhythmia. He swallowed hard.

"I shall run a check on her, if your Excellency desires," Yoritomo said.

Percy waved him off. "Not just now; can't be making indiscreet inquiries in the midst of mine host's castle." He shook his head regretfully. "Appalling to think of such a lovely young woman bound to such a gross pig as Chandrasekhar."

"Indeed, lord." Yoritomo gave him a quick *tsu's* smirk. Percy swallowed a sigh. His aide was a Kurita to the marrow; he was only thinking of the waste of such pretty meat, not the deeper tragedy of a beautiful soul such as Percy thought he saw in the brief flash of those eyes—green as the hardwood forests of the Trimurti foothills in May—trapped in the clutches of a despoiler like that slug of a Kurita.

For a moment, in his mind, the Planetary Chairman was a knight in armor—not a horn-helmeted samurai in colorfully lacquered steel on a scrubby little island pony, but a medieval European armored in articulated plate and chain astride a mighty white charger. It had been one of the dangerous romantic visions of his youth, and quickly suppressed. There was no place for dragon-slaying chivalry in the Dragon's realm. Besides, his childhood tutors—who were quite sophisticated, as was appropriate for a cosmopolitan world such as Hachiman—had made sure he read what Miguel de Cervantes had to say about the ancient ideal of knight-errantry.

Feeling peckish, the Chairman drifted toward the buffet. It was of course a masterpiece of extravagance, a sumptuous assortment of foods arranged with impeccable taste. Though the cult of the Dragon preached austerity, the nobility were supposed to live well, with a certain ostentation, to demonstrate the superior position they enjoyed in society. *That* was one responsibility attendant upon his name that Chandrasekhar Kurita did not shirk.

Fat Chandy's parties were the talk of all Hachiman—whose standards for festivity were themselves legendary. To celebrate surviving the raid on his corporate headquarters, the CEO of HTE had decreed a humdinger.

Percy was using a pair of ornately engraved silver tongs shaped like crane wings to place a purple crescent of melon next to some marinated sea scorpion when the scent of a perfume wafting toward him like a nightingale's song made him look up suddenly.

Standing beside him was Chandrasekhar Kurita's lovely guest. "What amazing fruit," she said. "Does it taste as lovely as it looks?"

"Indeed it does," he said, feeling his heart beat faster. "It's Tamerlane melon, imported from New Samarkand. Quite the delicacy."

He glanced at her sidelong. Up close she was breathtaking. "When one speaks of beauty, though, one might do worse than begin with you. And end as well."

She smiled, dropped her eyes. Long black lashes fluttered in pretty consternation.

"Your Excellency is much too kind," she said.

"My Excellency is merely truthful," Percy said. "Understating the case, if anything." He grasped her hand, lifted it to his lips.

She flicked a wary glance over a bare shoulder. Her escort was still holding forth in the corner.

"I'm Percival Fillington," he said. "It is my honor to serve the Dragon in the capacity of Planetary Chairman of the world of Hachiman."

"I recognized your Lordship," she said, lowering her eyes respectfully. "Only you are much more handsome than you look on holovid."

For a fact, Percy thought he cut quite a dashing figure, his rapier-slim form draped in the dark purple robe of his station, over a ruffled white shirt and bottle-green breeches, his wavy red-highlighted hair caught in a queue at the nape of his neck. He realized it was quite absurd to feel so flattered. *Careful, lad,* said a voice inside his head. *Don't fall too fast. She's only a woman.*

He had trouble accepting the latter part. Someone so lovely could never be *only* anything.

"Here, allow me," he said, and tonged a slice of melon onto the woman's carven-quartz plate.

She opened her mouth in a pretty "O" of surprise. It was an almost unheard-of gesture.

"Come, child, tell me your name," Fillington urged gently.

"Jasmine, my Lord," she said. "Jasmine Mehta, at your service. I come from the city of Srinagar."

"Many precious things come from Srinagar," he murmured with the air of one quoting ancient wisdom. "Come, sit with me and tell me about yourself."

Her face brightened, and as quickly clouded again in a look of alarm and consternation. Percy sensed a presence behind his right shoulder, turned.

Two obvious *gaijin* from Uncle Chandy's hireling regiment stood there. One was white and gangly, with ill-groomed dark hair and an adenoidally open mouth. The other was black and immense, a good two meters tall and at least that large around the middle. His bald head gleamed like polished mahogany in the light of the crystal chandelier. A furious frizzy black beard framed his moon face.

"The boss ast us to keep an eye on Miz Jasmine, here," the black thug rumbled in an earthquake voice.

"Yep," the skinny one affirmed, bobbing his head and chuckling as if his partner had made a joke. Percy suspected he might be slow-witted.

"Come along, little lady," the fat mercenary said. He enveloped the girl's upper arm in a giant black paw.

She went readily enough, but the single look she cast the Planetary Chairman over her bare shoulder spoke volumes.

"Your Excellency appears perturbed."

Percy jumped, turned. His aide had materialized at his elbow. "Dragon's blood, man, don't sneak up on me like that!"

"As your Excellency wishes," murmured Yoritomo, who had done it before and would again. "Is there something your Lordship wishes?"

Percy glanced at where Jasmine stood at the Kurita's side now, an abject and beautiful satellite to a bloated planet. She glanced his way again.

He willed his fists to uncurl. "Yes, there is, Gupta," he said. "But there are things even a Planetary Chairman cannot have."

On the way from the elevator across to his personal helicopter parked on the rooftop pad of Chandy's Citadel, Percy paused to put one polished boot on the parapet and peer out over the sprawling Hachiman Taro complex. Truly it was huge, a fairy city spun of traceries of light, the bronze towers of his capital surrounding and looming over it like light-encrusted mountains. He sighed.

It truly is grand, he thought. Pity it's wasted on Chandy, who disgraces his name and defiles everything he touches.

"My lord," said Yoritomo from behind him.

"I won't fall, you know," Percy said without turning.

"Not even your Excellency's exalted position confers immunity from the laws of gravity."

Percy grinned into the night wind, thick with the river smell, tanged with ozone from arc welders and the sting of methanol-induced formaldehyde smog. It was traditionally the prerogative of Combine majors-domo to speak bluntly, even impertinently, to their masters. It was also their prerogative to pay for that privilege with their heads when they erred—or should the whim happen to strike their masters. Percy Fillington had always enjoyed his aide's calculated snottiness. It was a game he had long mastered.

He sighed again, dropped his boot to the graveled rooftop. "The ancient King Canute, of old England on Terra, is often held up to ridicule as an example of megalomaniac folly because he sat his throne on the beach and ordered the incoming tide not to touch him."

"One imagines he got rather wet," Yoritomo said.

"Indeed he did. But the scoffers miss the point: the King was surrounded by sycophants at court, who professed to believe his majesty was so great that even the tides would obey his hest. His intention was to put paid to such silly talk; and look where it got him."

"Dead," Yoritomo said, "for several thousand years."

Percy laughed in surprised delight. "You're right, of course," he said. "And I suppose I shall be doing rather all right if I'm still spoken of two thousand years from now, even if it's as a figure of fun."

Before he could say more, a female cry breasted the night wind and brought his head around.

Uncle Chandy's escort, the magical Jasmine Mehta, was flying from the elevator housing. Her auburn hair was in wild disarray, the strapless dress was torn revealingly, and blood fanned from her nostrils across her lips and chin. She had kicked off the stiletto heels and was running for all she was worth.

She caught sight of Percy and darted toward him. A pair of armed guards in House Fillington livery moved from watch on the helicopter to intercept her.

"Your Excellency!" she cried. "You must help me! He's gone insane!"

Percy started forward. Yoritomo grabbed his arm.

The Chairman spun, face opening in shock. Even from his aide, that was a sizable breach of decorum.

"Don't get involved, your Excellency," Yoritomo said urgently. "He's a Kurita."

The guards were holding the distraught young woman by her fine bare arms. She struggled furiously. "He'll kill me!" she wailed. "He already tried."

"A grotesque fat parody of a Kurita, and one long banished in disgrace from court," Percy said stiffly. He did not add, *and one suspected of blackest treachery by the ISF*. His aide knew that well enough; no point in the indiscretion of committing it to sound.

"And I'm the Planetary Chairman," he added, taking his arm back.

The door to the stairway next to the elevator housing flew open. The two *gaijin* thugs burst out, glaring around. The skinny one grabbed the fat one by the arm and pointed. "There she is!"

They raced toward the girl, who uttered a despairing scream.

Her hand moved mongoose-quick to unsnap the safety strap on the holster of one of the guards who held her. Before anyone could react, she'd hauled out his heavy sidearm and had it pointed at the charging mercenaries.

"You'll never take me back to that monster!" she cried, and fired.

The huge black *gaijin* staggered as the bullets struck the mountain slope of his chest and belly. Dark stains blossomed on the front of his shirt. He clutched himself, staggered back, and collapsed moaning as the guards wrestled the girl to the rooftop and disarmed her.

The guard still holding his piece drew and aimed it at the nape of the sobbing woman's neck.

"Hold!" Percy exclaimed, stepping forward. He heard his aide protesting behind him, but his ears were closed. "Let her go. This woman is seeking my protection."

The guards gaped at him. "But your Excellency, she shot that man!"

"He was attacking her." The guards still looked blank; the right of self-defense was not exactly guaranteed to citizens of the Draconis Combine. "He was a *gaijin* attacking a Hachiman woman."

That smartened them up. *Tanin* were of course fair game if they stepped out of line. They let Jasmine go, stood and turned to face the mercenaries.

The skinny one was bending over his monstrous comrade, who wasn't moving. Skinny raised a rage-distorted face.

"You killed him, you *bitch!*" he shouted, so violently Percy half-expected blood and tissue to come flying from his throat and mouth. "You'll pay for this! No matter where you run, you can't hide from us! We'll track you down, we'll take it out of your worthless hide before we let you die—"

If the Earl of Hachiman had harbored any doubts, the psychotic threat-stream dispelled them. "Help me get her into the chopper," he told Yoritomo in a tone that brooked no further debate. Gupta rolled his eyes skyward, and did as he was told.

HTE security troops in powder blue uniforms had begun

to spill from the elevator. Several approached at a trot, machine pistols at port-arms.

"Your Excellency," one called, "you must surrender that woman to us. She has committed crimes against a member of House Kurita!"

Percy stood tall before them as Yoritomo bundled Jasmine into the ship. "She is under my protection now. Any man who lays a hand on her, or tries to hinder me, is a traitor!"

The HTE guards looked at each other in consternation. Percy climbed into the helicopter. His guards crowded in after, sidearms still in hand.

"Get us out of here," Percy told the pilot, "before Uncle Chandy decides to see whether his name will get him off for shooting down a Planetary Chairman."

The pilot didn't need to be told twice. The engine screamed, and the helicopter leapt up off the roof and into the night.

"There, there, child," the Earl of Hachiman told the sobbing girl, patting her shoulders through the cloak he had wrapped about them. "Everything will be all right."

Sitting there in her torn dress with a handkerchief pressed to her face, Lieutenant Junior Grade Cassiopeia Suthorn of the Seventeenth Recon Regiment was not concerned with her prospects for surviving this harebrained mission, nor even whether her allegedly long-term waterproof hair dye and skin tone and extended-duration contacts really were. What she was thinking was, *When I get ahold of Cowboy, I'm going to bust his nose* again.

The little group on the roof watched the Chairman's helicopter dwindle into the night, until it was just lights, and then nothing but a hint of throb above the pervasive city sounds.

As a general thing Lieutenant JG Earl Willie "Man Mountain" Carter considered it his life's misfortune to bear an astounding resemblance to the bearded black patriarch who was the trademarked symbol of a chain of barbecue restaurants, originating in fact on the Southwestern worlds, a chain that had spread throughout Marik space to Steiner and Davion territory. In fact, he loathed barbecue. His passion was French cooking; a sizable portion of what he earned as a *Locust* pilot for Adelante Company went to pay for a video correspondence course from a chef *cordon bleu* under whom he'd studied during a gig the Regiment had spent on New Avalon.

Tonight, though, his misfortune was to be one of the Seventeenth's people whose appearance seemed most calculated to intimidate Dracs.

With a groan, he climbed to his feet. He felt his expanse of belly gingerly, as if to be certain the red mess the front of his shirt had become was all the product of squib-charges and blood bags, and that none of the three rounds that hit him had actually penetrated his ballistic-cloth vest.

"If it had been anybody but that Cassie girl," he rumbled, "I'd never of gone for this. Lord, I think she busted some ribs."

Cowboy Payson was shaking his left hand in the air and shaking his head. Chandrasekhar Kurita had flatly declined to strike Cassie, so it had fallen to her comrade from Adelante to add the final touch of verisimilitude to her scam. Lieutenant JG Payson had been only too happy to oblige.

"You know what the *real* bitch is?" he asked ruefully, rubbing the knuckles of his business hand. "That skinny little runt took my best shot, and she didn't even go down."

29

Masamori, Hachiman
Galedon District, Draconis Combine
30 October 3056

The wind that swirled dead leaves across the terrace with a sound like insects skittering over the flagstones caught the sheer white folds of Cassie's muslin nightgown against her legs. The air was bladed with autumn chill, yet the sandstone beneath her bare feet was warm from the morning sun hovering over the distance-blued Trimurtis. She sipped strong native tea from a cup of china so fine you could almost read through it, and stood staring at the surf breaking on the rocks far below.

"Did you sleep well last night, Ms. Mehta?" Percival Fillington's voice asked her from behind her.

For a moment she stayed facing the turbulent sea so he wouldn't see her grimace. She hadn't heard him emerge from the villa. *Am I losing my grip?*

She turned, then, with appropriately downcast eyes, "Well enough, milord."

His mouth smiled, but his eyes were troubled. Even if her room wasn't bugged—and Cassie had to assume it was, with or without the Planetary Chairman's knowledge—she doubted that the soundproofing on the heavy door Fillington had permitted her to lock behind her was sufficient that he would not know her lie. Her screaming nightmares had, no doubt, been exactly what the young Earl might expect from a recent victim of Chandrasekhar Kurita's lusts.

The problem was, she wasn't acting. The nightmares had returned, the dreams that had haunted her since childhood, dreams of a dark and menacing figure pressing down on her—the dreams of the violated.

She could tell herself it was because she felt insecure being separated from Blood-drinker, locked in her quarters in the HTE Compound, there having been no way Fillington would accept Chandy's innocent play-pretty coming complete with a lethal-looking dagger as long as her forearm. Or that she was denied the meditation-in-motion of practicing her *pentjak-silat* forms.

Nor was her problem that she was walking unarmed and alone into the stronghold of the enemy, and that if discovered, a quick death would be the best she could hope for. Cassie was accustomed to deadly danger.

Those things helped push her off-center, certainly. But they alone couldn't account for the nightmares.

Rationally or not, she blamed Kali MacDougall. The tall blonde woman had gotten inside her defenses and in so doing had stirred up creatures from the murky depths—dislodged long-submerged fragments to come swirling up toward the surface of her mind, dark things, hidden things.

She felt Percy Fillington's warmth close behind her,

smelled the soap he had used that morning, felt one hand poised above the skin of her bare shoulder as if the fingers were heated red. She cringed.

The heat of near-contact hovered, was withdrawn.

"Mmm," the Chairman said. "Yes, my child. Would you be so kind as to join me for breakfast? We shall eat out on the terrace and enjoy what autumn warmth remains to us, if it pleases you."

She nodded, a touch spasmodically, permitted him to hold a white-enameled metal chair for her. She still marveled at the high-ranked Draconians she had met on this world. The world of Hachiman was a noted maverick, permitted to go its own way largely because it produced a significant percentage of what the Combine could boast in the way of positive economic balance, partly because its independent-minded citizens were notable pains in the ass when provoked, even for the dread ISF.

But the three important Dracs Cassie had dealt with most intimately since coming to Hachiman—the *Mirza*, Uncle Chandy, and now Planetary Chairman Fillington—had all treated her with respect and courtesy. Even on Larsha, where she'd been due consideration as daughter of a well-respected man who had died a warrior's death, the Combine exiles had not treated her as well.

She sat, then raised her weight again so the Chairman could make a properly gallant show of pushing in her chair. Her shudder of revulsion at his near-touch had only partially been acting, too. She had learned while still on Larsha to suppress that impulse when the scam required it. But only on rare occasions was she comfortable being touched, especially by a male.

The revulsion had diminished over the years. Now, like her nightmares, it had returned full-force.

It was strange, Cassie thought, as the Chairman seated himself across from her while silent servants in immaculate white tunics emerged to refresh their tea and set enamel trays of food on the table. Because, despite herself, she found herself wanting to *like* Percy. He was handsome enough, but more than that, there was an innocent enthusiasm to him, a little-boy quality, which she found appealing.

What's happening to you? her internal voice demanded. *When did you start liking marks? That's* dangerous.

And the answer seemed to be, ever since she had permitted herself to start liking Lady K, with her gentle insistent way of probing, of challenging without actually provoking. Not since Patsy had Cassie permitted another so far inside her defenses.

And see what happens? Patsy deserted you by getting her silly self killed by the Smoke Jaguars. And here that blonde bitch is trying to split you open like a steamed lobster!

She became aware of Percy studying her. An expression of sadness shadowed his smile. He reached to touch her hand. She let him.

"You must have been through a terrible ordeal," he said, withdrawing his hand with visible reluctance.

She nodded. "Yes," she said, in the taut tone of one barely keeping self-control. In truth, this was easier for her; she was slipping into her scam. Playing the role rather than dealing with her mark as a person.

"Can you tell me about it?"

She could, of course. Her younger brother was an electrical-engineering student in Srinagar. Their father had died while both were young. Their mother had been forced to make many sacrifices for them.

When she was old enough, Jasmine became a hostess in a bar, where she managed to earn enough to send her brother to school. But recently, with her brother on the verge of completing his studies, their mother had become very ill.

Though women were basically inconsequential in the Combine scheme of things, mothers occupied a special role. Even a samurai acknowledged his debt to the endless sacrifices his mother had dutifully made for him. In this the people of the Combine were much like the Caballeros, especially the *norteños,* for whom to make one's mother weep was among the greatest disgraces a warrior could incur.

Jasmine's younger brother had been trapped in a classic conflict of *ninjo* and *giri:* duty to the Dragon, which required him to complete his studies so he could serve in that capacity for which he was best suited, and his filial duty to help his mother—which, indeed, was a kind of *giri* as well.

Enter Chandrasekhar Kurita's boudoir talent scouts, who "discovered" the lovely Jasmine in her Srinagar bar. If she would agree to audition for Uncle Chandy's harem, they would not only employ her but guarantee her brother a position. Their mother, they assured her, would have no further worries.

Mother and brother were, of course, fictional. Yet the *Mirza* Abdulsattah had assured her that any investigation the Planetary Chairman might mount into her background would substantiate her story—at least, for as long as this mission was going to last; it was to be as quick an affair as possible, in and out, hopefully, before the ever-suspicious Ninyu could take much interest. Cassie knew that criminal investigation and forensic science were much less developed in the Combine than elsewhere in the Inner Sphere; punishment on suspicion was so much less resource-intensive. Besides, she trusted Uncle Chandy's security chief.

Or rather, she trusted his competence.

She stared at her plate. Despite her distraught condition—both real and assumed—she had eaten with her usual appetite. She was hoping the Chairman would chivalrously assume she had an uncommonly strong stomach.

"And now I have failed both my mother and Michael," she said in a lost little-girl voice. "But I—"

She covered her face with both hands and sobbed. "I couldn't bear to be with—*him*—any longer."

Fillington stared at her, drumming his fingertips on the damask tablecloth, white as a seabird's wing. Then he rose and strode a few steps toward the stone retaining wall around the terrace.

Cassie had a momentary vision of Chandrasekhar Kurita roaring uproariously at the lambent loathing with which she'd spoken of him. She was finding it hard to square her experience of the man with Percy's demonic vision of him. It was possible Uncle Chandy's hands were not as clean as they might be—probable, even. Yet Cassie was coming to suspect something else at work. Somebody had made an effort to inspire the Planetary Chairman with deep hate for his powerfully connected subject. Tanadi likely had infiltrators on his staff; perhaps they had poisoned Percy against Uncle Chandy.

Of course, if it was probable Tanadi had plants in the Chairman's household, it was certain the ISF did. It was only a matter of time before Cassie's arrival came to the attention of the red-haired man. She shuddered.

Fillington happened to glance back at just that instant. He

frowned slightly, then nodded; of course, she was feeling another spasm of revulsion at the memory of Kurita.

"You've done the right thing, Jasmine," he said. "Believe me. The Dragon can be harsh, but he does not demand of his children that they degrade themselves for—for monsters."

She bowed her head. "Your lordship is very kind."

"Call me Percy." He crossed to stand behind her. His hands hovered like birds above her shoulders.

"I must go back," she said. "I cannot permit my mother and brother to suffer the consequences of my weakness."

"Nonsense!" he said forcefully. "You're not going back to—back *there*."

She turned in her chair. "But what of my family?"

He smiled. "I am not without resources, dear girl. Permit me to see what I can do for your brother. The Dragon needs trained engineers in this time of crisis."

"Oh, *could* you?" She jumped up, squeezed both his hands, and fled.

Gupta Yoritomo tried to intercept Cassie's tearful dash for her chambers on the villa's second floor, his smooth round face set in lines of concern. Despite his initial concern about his master taking her in, he had become an avid supporter of "Jasmine." Cassie shrugged him off and shut the door on his solicitude.

She turned her back to the heavy carved wood and slid down to sit on the plush carpet. She felt exalted. As long as his Excellency kept taking hints, it looked like maybe this was going to work after all. Cassie was expert at covert hinting—and at nagging, too, if it came to that. They were two among the myriad skills useful for a skinny, brown-legged street girl trying to survive on the fringes of Larsha's all but nonexistent economy.

To take the edge off, in case the Chairman's obvious physical attraction to her overcame his pretensions to chivalry, Cassie was pretending to have her period. She was prepared to keep up the pretenses indefinitely—the Chairman's physicians could tell him, if he didn't know, that extreme stress could produce such a condition. It should keep him backed off. Combine males generally had a horror of "unclean" females.

Cassie had accumulated a bagful of tricks during her scamming days to avoid having to deliver on a mark's sexual expectations. In fact she never explicitly promised sexual favors; that was another of her odd points of honor. The mark's masculine imagination customarily supplied such promises, however, and she didn't discourage them until they tried to collect.

One of Cassie's juvie street criminal friends and sometime accomplices had once called her the only whore she knew who never went to bed with anyone. The remark was made half disparagingly, half admiringly.

Cassie had been provided a lovely, airy little bedroom, decorated all in white and yellow, complete with private bath and a closet full of clothes. The Chairman had radioed ahead from the helicopter the night before for proper preparations to be made to house his lovely fugitive. He had a good eye for women's sizes.

As soon as she locked the door behind her, Cassie went into the bathroom. It was stocked with the usual necessities, some of which had to be used to maintain her ruse.

She took out a packet from the cabinet next to the sink, prepared to tear it open. A small square of flimsy paper fluttered out. She stopped, stared at it, then stooped to pick it up.

It was a note. *We're keeping an eye on you,* it read. *What you need shall be supplied when the time comes. Watch those close to P. Leave return messages in the same location.*

The note had been hidden in one of the few places where even a moderately serious search would not have turned it up. She moistened her lips, swallowed, not without a degree of effort. Presumably it came from one of the agents the *Mirza* assured her he had on Fillington's staff. But what if it wasn't, what if it was from a *provocateur* trying to see if she would do the proper thing and turn the note over to the Chairman? She shrugged. She couldn't cover all bets. All she could do was roll the dice.

The note was rice paper, which, aside from being so generic within the Combine as to be untraceable, was readily edible. She crumpled it up, swallowed it, and went on with her business.

"Why do you hate *him* so?" Jasmine asked the Planetary Chairman. She was kneeling on a Persian carpet from Terra, dressed in a silken gown patterned in rectangles of wine-red and umber, stroking the Earl's long-haired white cat, Amadeus. The "Autumn" Concerto of Vivaldi's *Four Seasons* filled the drawing room from hidden speakers, nicely complementing the understated yet comfortable elegance of the drawing room. Besides that, it was, as Percy pointed out, *basho-gara:* appropriate to the circumstances.

Back from a day wrestling with the problems of administering his unruly planet, Percy Fillington stood dressed in a ruffled-front white shirt and tight indigo breeches, with one elbow on the mantel and a snifter of fine Arc-Royal cognac in his hand—a Lyran import still a favored luxury on Hachiman even though no longer contraband.

He frowned slightly. He obviously disliked for his houseguest to trouble herself thinking about her erstwhile "employer."

"I suppose it's because Chandrasekhar represents so much of what's wrong with the Combine," he said. "He's taken advantage of his family name to amass an unbelievable fortune. Yet he so blatantly lacks all the traditional Kurita virtues that he could be a poster boy for decadence."

Cassie nodded, directing her attention to the cat, who expected nothing less. In her experience the only Kurita virtues Uncle Chandy lacked were austerity and a reflex for belligerence. She wasn't here to enlighten young Percy on the subject, however. But she *was* curious to know just why the Chairman bore her employer such hatred.

"He appears to treat his workers well—upped their pay, shortened their hours, which gave fits to old Redmond, I assure you. But he exploits them, and ruthlessly crushes any dissent. And he's savagely repressed Sumiyama's attempts to organize HTE workers in order to protect their rights."

It was just possible that his Excellency was naïve enough not to realize that the Workers' Fraternal Protective Association sponsored by Sumiyama-*kai,* ostensibly a labor union, was in fact just another yakuza racket to extort money from the long-suffering Laborers. The Combine made much of its Workers' Associations, but of course true independent unions were not allowed; and the associations were inevitably dominated by the local yakuza organizations.

Not only was it possible that Percy was that naïve; he *was,* or so Cassie judged—and Cassie knew her marks. But it wasn't because he was stupid, or merely obtuse. She was finding him a genuinely intelligent man, with a rapid wit and agile imagination.

He was even a minor war hero, a trained MechWarrior who had distinguished himself in action in the early forties during the low-level but incessant skirmishing against both the F-C military and the Free Worlds League which followed the Fourth Succession War. At thirty-five standard years old, he was generally taken for ten years younger.

But like everyone else, he had been shaped by his upbringing. And it seemed that all involved, from his tyrannical grandfather, Rex, whose fierce, white-browed portrait glowered like a guardian demon from the wall, to entrenched local powers like Tanadi and the yakuza, to the Coordinator of the Draconis Combine, had an interest in grooming him to ineffectuality. Percy Fillington had been warped and stunted like a *bonsai* maple; and Cassie marveled that he could boast even as much poise and personality as he did.

She still couldn't help wanting to like him, a fact that continued to surprise and distress her. He was only a mark, after all. And if a con artist let a mark actually become a *person*—that was it. You lost your edge, lost your instinct for the jugular, and then you started making mistakes. In her youth Cassie had seen other scammers go that route, and get caught—or wind up getting scammed themselves. She'd vowed it would never happen to her.

"He's been after me constantly since the party, you know," the Chairman said, coming to stand behind her. "He's bombarding me with demands and entreaties day and night. He's all in a fever to get you back. Which I can sympathize with, surely."

Once more she could feel the desire to touch her beating from him like heat from a stove. It wasn't sexual—or not *purely* sexual. He wanted to hold her, comfort her.

Usually she took the same pleasure in such sensations as an angler took when a fish took his line. This time, Percy's behavior was upsetting and confusing her, even if it was all according to plan.

Master yourself, Guru Johann used to say, *and you can master every situation. Fail of self-mastery, and you control nothing.*

She turned, still kneeling, grasped one of his hands in both of hers. "Your Excellency is most kind to shelter me."

He pulled her up. "Here, now, don't worry yourself anymore about the monster. Don't even think about him."

She raised his hand, brushed it quickly with her lips, shied back as if terrified by the contact. "I am yours to command, lord," she said in her hollowest waif voice, keeping her fake emerald gaze downcast. "I am your humble servant."

He drew in a breath that shuddered like a sapling at the impact of a heavy body. She was skating the edge now. She felt an artist's fierce unalloyed pleasure as he raised a hand to touch her, advanced it, then stopped it as if Cassie were surrounded by an invisible force field. She was playing him now the way the long-dead musicians whose music filled the room played their instruments.

He dropped his arm like a dead thing. "You musn't talk that way," he said. "You're not my servant. You're—"

He frowned, searching for words. "You're someone who is becoming rather important to me. You're, ah, my friend."

"Your Excellency does me too much honor."

"Not at all."

She raised her face to his. "I am most grateful to my lord. But I am pained to be here, surrounded by such luxury, while my mother and brother suffer."

He raised a hand in an agitated gesture, let it fall again. "I'll see to that," he said. "I promise."

He turned, walked several steps away, turned back. He let his eyes travel down her slim body, which the loose gown alternately accentuated and hid in intriguing ways. For a moment she felt a thrill of fear, wondering if she had overplayed her hand.

He took a deep breath, gathering himself. "I must retire now, Jasmine. But, please, stay up as long as you wish. If there's anything you need, the servants will see to it."

He bowed and quickly left. She stood there a moment, tingling with accomplishment. And yet, down in the deep of her was a cold, unwelcome trickle of feeling, one she'd long been familiar with—but never in this setting.

I'm ashamed, she realized in a rush of anger and fear. She closed her eyes, rubbed them with the heels of her hands.

I'm losing it, she thought, wishing miserably that this mission was over. She had fought the battle for self-control so long and hard. To lose it here, in the midst of an assignment vital to the Regiment, her surrogate family, would be a punishment worse than any penalty of discovery.

She went to the bed chamber and locked the door. For half an hour she lay on her back in the dark, staring sleeplessly at the ceiling. When she realized she was actually missing the horrid pink stuffed bear Kali had given her, Cassie rolled over and surrendered to tears.

=== 30 ===

Masamori, Hachiman
Galedon District, Draconis Combine
30 October 3056

The drum of her horse's hooves on tide-wet sand filled Cassie's body with wild rhythm. The surf, whipped on by a storm invisible out across the Shakudo, pounded bass accompaniment. Clumps of tall, purple-tinted beach grass, bent by the wind, whipped her legs as she rode past.

In a thunder of hooves Percy Fillington's bay caught up and passed her—establishing the point at which normal Kurita attitudes took over from ancient Western chivalry. He reached the agreed-upon finish line, which was even with the main-mast stump of a long-foundered freighter a few hundred meters offshore. Wheeling his horse, he made the animal rear up to mark his triumph, then leaned over his neck, patting him as Cassie rode up on her dapple-fannied gray Arab mare.

"You're a quick study," he told her. "Already you're riding as if you'd been doing it for years."

"I've always been good with animals, your Excellency," said Cassie, who *had* been doing it for years. The once thoroughly urban street-trash girl had learned to ride a variety of more or less domesticated beasts in her pursuit of scout mastery. But it was a rough-and-ready form of riding, far from polished. Horsemanship was a prized skill among the Combine's upper classes; it was an appropriate pastime for warriors, it smacked of tradition, and, besides, there were plenty of planets within the Combine on which horses were the prime source of motive power. The Planetary Chairman rode better than Cassie, and had won without any help from her.

They continued down the beach at a sedate pace, feeling their mounts' sides pump like billows between their legs. The air was cool, but not chill; they were enjoying a final unseasonable spasm of warmth. Hachiman's larger moon, Yoshitsune, hung pink and swollen above the distant black serration of the Trimurtis. The last of the day lay like a spill of liquid fire on the opposite horizon. The smell of salt and wet sand and decaying sea-life and the endless, ageless surge of ocean wrapped them like blankets. Late season crickets trilled in the dunes above the beach. Nightgaunts seemed to brush their faces with soft-furred wingtips as they wheeled through the gloom, seining tiny insects in through widespread mouth-funnels and uttering dismal hoots. For the moment, the riders were content in one another's silence.

Which was either a good sign or a very bad one. That she could not be sure showed exactly how off-center Cassie was. Percy had been away tending to affairs of state for three whole days while she fretted and played mahjong and poker with Yoritomo, whom he had left to keep an eye on her. Knowing that somewhere a clock was ticking—that somewhere the red-haired man was preparing his next onslaught against Uncle Chandy and the Regiment—she had begun to feel trapped and hopeless. By the time Percy got back that afternoon it felt like her nerve ends had begun to curl up out of her flesh like twists of flayed skin.

Yoritomo had been a sympathetic if unobtrusive presence. There was a knowing quality to the way he looked at her, and she had just about concluded he was the *Mirza*'s plant in Stormhaven. Or one of them, anyway, and most likely the one who periodically left her hidden messages.

They rode a transverse trail up a steep hill, then followed the cliffs rising toward the manor's dark mass up on its promontory. Lights were just coming visible from within. Percy told her soft-voiced stories of official foolishness and noble pomposity as they rode, making Cassie laugh, readily and genuinely. He had a good way with an anecdote.

Down the hill from the big house they handed their

mounts off to solemn-faced grooms with bare brown feet, then walked up a trail of crushed seashells. "I rather missed you, I must admit," the Chairman said.

"I missed your Excellency as well."

He stepped in front of her, tucked a crooked finger beneath her chin and raised her face to his.

"Isn't it time you started calling me Percy?" he asked.

He kissed her. For a moment Cassie stood, accepting. Then she broke away and ran up the path.

He came pelting after, laughing. She found herself laughing too. His pursuit did not threaten her. She considered, briefly, letting him catch her.

At the top of the path she stopped dead. A small helicopter with obvious weapon trays bolted to the sides squatted in the midst of the broad, immaculate front lawn. The intrusion was like a blow to the face.

The Planetary Chairman stood behind her. He laid a gentle hand on her shoulder, was no longer laughing.

"Perhaps you'd best go in by the back entrance, my dear," he said quietly.

She looked up at him, putting horror on her face. He gave his head a slight shake.

"Don't be afraid, Jasmine. It isn't Chandy. It's just state business."

She nodded, started away, stopped. "Lord—Percy—about my brother . . ."

"Later! Later, I promise. And now—off with you."

"You kept me waiting," Ninyu Kerai Indrahar said when the Planetary Chairman walked into the drawing room.

"I was occupied."

"Indeed." The second in command of the ISF was dressed in his customary black. He stood with hands behind his back, studying the portrait of the current Earl's grandfather. He was still obediently cultivating his taste for beauty, though he did not yet grasp just what a sense of esthetics had to do with being an assassin. Here, for once, was something he could almost appreciate. The old Earl had obviously been a warrior, a Draconian to the core, with his intense hawk's eyes and uncompromising brows, his jaw set as if the painter had captured him grinding his teeth with fury at the foes of House Kurita.

Still, Ninyu felt a certain relief, as of a load lifted from his shoulders, when he could turn from art to business.

"Your new toy," he said. "She was Chandrasekhar Kurita's." It was a flat statement, not a question.

The Chairman nodded. He still wore his riding breeches and boots. "She was. And is no longer."

"How do you know she isn't a spy?"

"She shot one of Chandrasekhar's foreign hirelings with a gun belonging to a member of my personal guard. I hardly think even Chandrasekhar would go to such lengths."

"*Gaijin* mercenaries are easily come by."

"I've investigated her background thoroughly. She is what she seems, a simple victim of Chandrasekhar's appetites."

"I want her questioned."

"No."

Scarred brows beetled over black eyes. "I could take her."

"With respect, Assistant Director, what would be the point? She's not in a position to learn anything here that might benefit the Dragon's foes." He shook his head. "She's been through quite enough, poor child. I won't have her subjected to your interrogation techniques, even at their gentlest. You may take my word for it; she has as little use for Chandrasekhar Kurita as you or I or anyone on Hachiman."

For a moment those black eyes stared into Fillington's, Ninyu's face resembling a mask of scarcely controlled fury. A muscle in the side of the Chairman's jaw twitched, but his gaze did not waver.

Ninyu shook his head as if seizing himself by the back of the neck to do it. "It is of no consequence. I have come to tell you that we are ready to act." A pause, and then reluctantly, "Associate Director Katsuyama informs me that the climate of opinion is propitious."

Percy's smile included a touch of relief. "Capital. When do we move?"

"Tomorrow." The scarred lips sketched something like a smile. "And even if Chandrasekhar Kurita knew every detail of the plan, there would be nothing in this world or any other he could do to stop us."

Masamori was often described as the City of Bronze Towers. Tallest of its asymmetric Yamato-style skyscrapers was the administrative headquarters of Tanadi Computers soaring two hundred fifty stories above the congested heart of the city.

When a sleek blonde secretary announced the arrival of the Planetary Chairman, the Marquis Redmond Hosoya, Tanadi's Chief Executive Officer, was standing with his back to his surprisingly small office, staring out the window east toward the river—and the vast rectangle of the HTE Compound. Buttery morning sunlight filled the room, lending it an altogether spurious cheeriness.

"Ah, your Excellency," the Marquis said, turning after the carefully calculated insolence of a beat's pause. "So good to see you."

He bowed, then strode forward to shake hands. He was, like his office, compact but immaculately and expensively turned out. His hair, sideburns, and mustache were thick and white as the never-melting snow of the highest Trimurti peaks. He wore a dark suit whose very severity of cut and color was an almost strident statement—and a perhaps deliberate contrast to Uncle Chandy's perpetual scarlet robe.

The Marquis' bow was cursory, but Percy, who after all had been playing this game his whole life, beat him with one that was little more than an inclination of his elegant head. His handshake was solid as brick. For all Hosoya's bearing and costly manicure, there was something in the thick shoulders and barrel chest that suggested the nobleman might not be above trying to crush the Planetary Chairman's knuckles. In fact he knew better than to try; Fillington's slim pale hands had a grip like an *Archer*.

"Marquis," Fillington said, "permit me to introduce my friend Jasmine Mehta, of the city of Srinagar."

Hosoya's dark eyes flicked over her like the beams of a holovid camera. "She's lovely," he said, in the same tone he might use to speak of a new racehorse or perhaps an imported high-tech wrist chronometer.

He turned his attention back to the Planetary Chairman, and it was as if Cassie had become invisible. "To what do I owe the pleasure and honor of your visit?"

She was dressed as conservatively as the wardrobe selected for her would permit, which was extremely: a dark brown dress to the knee, above darker stockings and shoes, a brown pillbox cap with a hint of net veil clinging to the front of it, more shading than obscuring her face. It was striking in its way, accentuating the ivory of her artificially pale skin and green eyes, but it was not flashy, not the sort of thing to draw undue attention.

"My friend here, has a brother in Srinagar who, I'm assured, is a graduate electrical engineer of some accomplishment. He finds himself in need of employment. It occurred to me that you might do me the honor of considering taking him on."

"It is your Excellency who does me honor; he is well aware that Tanadi is relentless in its search for talented and dedicated employees. I thank you for your magnanimity."

At a gesture from Percy, Cassie had settled herself in a chair to the side, crossing her ankles primly, in the attentive posture expected from a good Combine consort. The flowery speech was so much white noise, of course; the Marquis would have thanked Percy as profusely for a brass paperweight shaped like a cockroach. As an ornament, "Jasmine" was supposed to look as if everything said held infinite fascination, even if it bored her cross-eyed. Appearance was everything in Drac culture.

She put a little extra spin on it, leaning forward and moistening her lips, playing her role of concerned sister and daughter. In fact, she didn't want to miss anything. It was unlikely either man would let any pearl of intelligence drop, even in front of something as inconsequential as a kept woman. But you didn't get to be the consummate scout by taking things for granted.

Subtly, Hosoya steered Percy away from his consort, toward the window looking off toward the Compound and the river. Most likely it was because he found it distasteful to discuss matters of consequence in the presence of a woman, even if she was little more than part of the decor. Still, there was something in the men's body language as they spoke, voices pitched too low for her to make out what they said, which indicated that something was indeed passing unspoken between them. Whether or not it had to do with what they were discussing now—presumably her mythical brother in Srinagar—they *looked* as if they were conspiring.

If Hosoya really is dirty, Cassie thought, *I hope Percy's not in on it.*

The thought took her by surprise. *Why should I care?*

She opened her purse to take out her compact and touch herself up. It was the sort of female gesture that a Drac male literally would not see. Then she put her compact away, reached down to adjust her skirt—and slipped the disk-shaped bug she had palmed from its hiding place inside the compact onto the underside of her chair.

One surface of the matte-black polymer disk was covered with a special molecular bonding adheres-instantly-to-anything patch, recovered lostech from the time of the Star League. She'd been warned to avoid touching the sticky surface at any cost once she activated the bug. Suddenly turning up with an audiovisual bugging device affixed to her hand could be tricky even for the Planetary Chairman's new *enamorata* to explain.

Cassie wasn't sure how the thing worked. She knew it was passive electro-optical, not holographic. She didn't want to be zapping lasers all over the Tanadi CEO's office for precisely the reason she hadn't wanted to do it in the warehouse where she'd watched Ninyu Kerai's meet with Sumiyama. *Mirza* Abdulsattah had assured her the bug was unlikely to be found. It had a low ferrous content and used almost no energy while inactive, and was consequently hard to detect. Moreover, the peculiar arrogance of Drac executives meant Hosoya was unlikely to deign to have his office swept for bugs—as he was too proud to submit to having surveillance cameras spying on him in his sanctum.

What it would do, she was told, was watch. And wait. When the tiny nanoprocessor inside—yet more lostech turned up in the frantic searches stimulated by the Clan invasion—spotted something it thought was significant, it would record it, compress it, and zap it in a microsecond burst to receivers hidden near Tanadi Tower. At that point it was almost certain to be discovered; the building would be blanketed with sensors seeking unauthorized transmissions. But it would have done its job.

Cassie has little faith in fancy tech, Star League or not, and had no idea how it would "know" if it had witnessed something significant enough to transmit or not. But it was their only chance to get the red-haired man off the trail of Chandrasekhar Kurita—and the Caballeros.

It was also the reason for her entire elaborate charade with Percy Fillington, Earl of Hachiman. As soon as Cassie had it in place, it was as if she were filled and drained at the same time. She felt both elated and let down.

Stay alert, she told herself, and concentrated on being the perfect ornament.

31

Masamori, Hachiman
Draconis Combine
30 October 3056

Cassie sat in a pool of afternoon sunlight on her bedroom floor with legs outspread and arms locked in front of her, leaning forward in a stretch. Hidden monitors would view obvious martial arts practice with suspicion. A noble's consort, however, was expected to keep herself in perfect shape.

After meeting with Hosoya, the Planetary Chairman had sent her back to Stormhaven in his personal chopper. From his distracted manner, he apparently had urgent business to transact, giving her no more than a perfunctory hug and peck on the cheek.

The tension in her gut told Cassie what that business was. She had no hard evidence. But she *knew*.

A small holovid played in the corner of the bed chamber. It was to supplement her bimbo image; Cassie had never had much taste for canned entertainment. As she leaned forward far enough for her chin to touch the carpet, she saw the HTE Compound recreated in miniature on the holo platform.

She reached for the remote control, turned up the sound. In the foreground a female reporter was asking towheaded Private Mangum of Scout Platoon, "Why do you fight?"

He rubbed the side of his nose with his thumb, spat, grinned moronically at the camera, and said, "For the money. Why else?"

Scenes were shown of Caballeros lounging in rec halls, playing pool, arguing, or standing and drinking and gazing bleary-eyed into the camera. Most of the faces displayed were white or black, primarily of ethnic Cowboys. While there were plenty of blacks and whites in the Combine, they weren't the majority, overall or on Hachiman. Most of the

Combine's population, in fact, didn't look all that different from the *norteño* and Indian contingents of the Seventeenth.

Cassie's heart fell. If she needed confirmation that the hammer was about to fall on the Regiment, here it was. The Masamori media were slanting this story hard to make the mercenaries look greedy, loutish, and alien: *gaijin*. Coverage of First Battalion's procession through Masamori to the Compound had been favorable; the media had paid the Seventeenth slight attention since then, except in the wake of the Blake attack, and that coverage had been positive too. The sudden change could only have been mandated from above.

You know who it is, a voice said in her head. *Percy.* Yet while Percy had probably approved the sudden smear against Chandy and his hirelings, she doubted he was behind it. It had to be Ninyu Kerai rearing his ugly red head.

With a jerk of her thumb the holo vanished. I've got to get back, she thought in something like panic.

The *Mirza* had to know that her mission was accomplished—or at least, had to know she'd had her one shot at accomplishing it. Her unknown friend on the Earl's staff had left the bug taped under her sink the night before, after all. She still didn't know if it was Yoritomo or not, but whoever the HTE plant was, he or she knew Cassie was to see the Tanadi CEO today. Persumably the spy also knew she was back.

She had asked Abdulsattah about extraction after the mission. Every extra second she spent in proximity to Fillington increased the likelihood of exposure. His spies—and perhaps Ninyu's—were still digging into her background. Sooner or later they'd undermine the foundation, and the whole façade would come crashing. Or she might slip. Cassie was sublimely confident of her ability to run a scam, but much as she hated to admit it, she wasn't perfect.

The *Mirza* had told her not to worry about it. They would come for her.

She wondered when. Irrationally she was convinced she'd be discovered any minute. Every possible little misstep she'd made since Uncle Chandy's party began to blare in her mind like klaxons.

And even if she wasn't caught, she couldn't bear the thought of any threat to her "family" while she was unable to help. The irony of her desperation to leave the present comfortable safety of the Planetary Chairman's villa for ground zero in the HTE Compound never occurred to her.

Control yourself, Cassie told herself. If you panic, you're done for. She made herself breathe deep, told herself she'd been in tight situations before. She was just reassuring herself that if Abdulsattah didn't extract her, she'd just have to find a way to get back on her own when an explosion boomed from the front lawn.

She jumped up and ran to the side of the sliding-glass doors that gave onto her little balcony, twitched the opened curtain aside slightly so she could peer out without much risk of being seen.

A troop-carrier helicopter sat on the lawn, main rotor slowing to visibility as dark-clad figures poured out the door, hunched over machine pistols.

The staccato boom of another rotor directly overhead rattled the glass. Cassie turned from the window. The intruders weren't wearing standard DEST commando drag, but that didn't mean they weren't ISF. Over the last few days she'd covertly identified a number of boltholes, ranging in location from pantry to basement to sundry broom closets. She intended to dive into one and not come out until she had a better idea who all these masked people with guns were.

Before she could do any of that, the door to her chamber opened. Gupta Yoritomo stood staring at her. Cassie had left the door locked, but her reaction on seeing him was relief.

"Gupta," she said grinning, "I'm glad it's—"

He raised his arm and she suddenly found herself looking down the big double bore of a holdout gyrojet pistol.

"I knew you were a spy," Gupta said in the same silky, slightly bored voice as always. "Now I'm going to kill you."

Cassie stood there flatfooted, gaping at him. She had just enough time to think, *What the hell's wrong with you, freezing like this?* His finger was tightening on the firing stud when suddenly the balcony's glass doors exploded inward in a hurricane of glass fragments. It was as if a naughty child had dipped a brush in red paint and spattered the front of Yoritomo's immaculate white tunic with it. He reeled back three steps, looking down at himself.

Then, face contorted as if in rage at the spoiling of his clothes, he aimed his sneaky cone-pistol at Cassie again.

This time she had the presence of mind to drop behind the bed. A tall figure stepped through the ruined door, releasing a rope from carabiners fixed to its harness with one gloved hand. The other held a compact Shimatsu 42 machine pistol, its barrel swollen by an integral suppresser. With a sound like a string of firecrackers going off, the intruder walked toward the Planetary Chairman's aide, emptying the magazine into his chest and blasting him right back into the hall.

In the doorway the figure stopped, gazed through its gas-mask at Yoritomo, now sprawled outside Cassie's field of vision. Then it nodded and dropped the spent box from its weapon.

As the masked figure took a new magazine from a harness pouch and slammed it home, he turned toward Cassie. A patch showing a blade-down broadsword emblazoned the front of his black woolly-pully sweater.

Word of Blake! she thought. The terrible inertia that gripped her when Yoritomo entered had evaporated. In *pentjak-silat,* if you couldn't run from a weapon, you rushed it. She snatched a pillow from the bed, hurling it straight into the masked face with the same motion. She followed it, diving across the bed, hitting the floor, rolling, coming up with hands clawing for the weapon and a knee targeted for the juncture of the black-clad legs.

The figure was pulling off the gas mask and laughing in her face. "Jesus boy howdy, Cassiopeia," Lieutenant Junior Grade William Payson said, dancing back into the hall and fending her off with the machine pistol, "are you that eager to pay me back for busting your beak back at Chandy's?"

She stopped. "You didn't," she said.

"Bull puckey."

She made an irritable chopping motion with her hand. "What the hell are you doing *here*?"

Cowboy laughed again. From somewhere downstairs came the ear-piercing crack of stun grenades and the duller thump of tear-gas bombs.

"This easy livin' sure is slowing you down, Cass," he said. "First you let that guy in the headwaiter suit get the drop on you. Then you can't even figure out as how you're being rescued." He shook his head. "Wait'll I tell Reb and Sawbuck. They'll never believe it."

"Why the hell are you dressed as a Blakie?"

Cowboy gave her his big goofy grin. "Sierra Foxtrot, Cassie, we don't want ol' Percy thinking Chandy went and grabbed you back. He might think of comin' after you."

* * *

Cassie slid into the copilot's seat of the chopper on the front lawn. The pilot was a big blond man who was not a member of the Regiment. He nodded to her as members of the strike team piled aboard, then jumped the ship into the air. As they veered away from Stormhaven, she saw that the other craft, the one that had dropped Cowboy Payson onto her balcony in the proverbial nick of time, had landed behind the house. It wasn't bringing its rotors up to speed for takeoff.

As the villa dwindled she felt a strange sense of regret. Then she balled her hands into fists and began to beat her forehead in a frenzy of rage and fear at the way she had frozen when Yoritomo drew down on her.

"So Yoritomo wasn't your plant," Cassie said flatly.

The *Mirza* Abdulsattah glanced aside at his employer, who sat surrounded by his cushions, leaning forward slightly like a vast, fascinated baby.

"No," the gaunt security chief said. "We suspect that he was ISF."

A cold wind blew down the corridors of Cassie's soul. Feeling sure the dreaded Breath of the Dragon was watching her and having it confirmed were different sensations entirely.

"Who was your agent, then?"

Abdulsattah smiled faintly. "Do you really need to know that, Lieutenant?"

"No," she said. "What makes you think the Planetary Chairman is going to buy this Word of Blake dodge? He's been expecting you to try something ever since I escaped from you."

"Fortunately, our raid on Stormhaven caused few casualties to either side," Uncle Chandy said. "We did, however, leave two dead behind. The Word of Blake terrorists captured by the Civilian Guidance Corps after the attack on the Compound will be able to identify them positively as former comrades."

She sucked in a breath. She knew Abdulsattah's men had caught some live terrorists during the attack. That meant this smiling Buddha figure had ordered them killed and left behind to lend verisimilitude to the notion that it was ComStar schismatics who'd attacked the villa.

It was no skin off any part of her anatomy—which had recently been returned to its normal coloration and was still prickling from the chemical bath. This fat and jolly-seeming man was still a Drac, still a Kurita, and he played by hard rules.

So did she.

She shook her head, sighed. The tapestry-hung walls of Chandy's sanctum seemed to be closing in, for reasons unconnected to nonexistent pangs of conscience over the fate of failed terrorists. "What happens now?"

Chandrasekhar Kurita spread his chubby fingers. "We wait. The next move is up to Ninyu Kerai Indrahar."

"He'll make it soon."

"No doubt," Uncle Chandy said unflappably.

"What about the bug I planted on Hosoya? Is it going to have *time* to turn up anything?"

"Only time will tell. *Insh'allah,* as the *Mirza* might say: it's in God's hands."

Cassie glanced aside at Abdulsattah, whose Grecoesque face showed no change of expression. Though the Combine's rulers found it expedient to compromise with its useful Arkab subjects, Islam was officially illegal. Uncle Chandy was in a puckish mood this evening.

"What do I do now?"

"You may return to your people," the *Mirza* said, "and wait."

"Yes," Uncle Chandy added. "There'll be a part for you to play in the climax of our little drama. Never fear." He smiled. "Now, go back and rest while you can. They've just begun to celebrate what I understand to be a three-day series of colorful folk festivals." He spread his hands. "Perhaps you can find ways to divert yourself until—"

Cassie kept her face lowered. It disappointed her that Chandy was trying to jolly her. She thought he knew her better.

When it became obvious that her employer had no more to say, she stood up to go. At the door to the elevator she turned back. "There's one thing."

"Yes?" Uncle Chandy said.

"Percy," she said. "That is, the Earl of Fillington. I don't think he's got anything to do with this Clan thing. I want him kept out of it."

Uncle Chandy scowled like an infant abruptly deprived of its toy. "Do you dare to make conditions with me?"

"Yes."

He laughed. "Excellent. I cherish those who remain true to their natures—especially when they are as adept at concealing them as you. Fly back to your nest, little bird, and rest assured that no harm shall befall your Earl that he doesn't insist on bringing on himself."

═══ 32 ═══

Masamori, Hachiman
Galedon District, Draconis Combine
1 November 3056

The helicopter appeared from the west, over the center of town on the crisp, clear morning of the Day of the Saints. The radar atop the Citadel picked it up as a matter of course, but the human operators monitoring the array paid it no mind.

When its circling took it within half a klick of the Compound wall, HTE Security broadcast a routine advisory to Third Battalion, which was on active perimeter guard. First was on standby, Second stood down.

Today that meant recovering from last night's festivities, and preparing for tomorrow's. All Saints' Day served as a buffer between two of the most riotously popular holidays in the Trinity Worlds: Halloween and *el Dia de los Muertos*.

Even as the message was crackling into the helmets of Third's MechWarriors, the chopper broke off and went into a shallow full-power dive toward the Citadel.

In the Draconis Combine that was tantamount to suicide. Corporate executives, to say nothing of the nobility, took their security seriously. Even if the mercs had not been primed for trouble on twenty-four-hour alert status, they would have been weapons-free in a case like this.

Lieutenant JG William "Deputy Dawg" Carson of Infante had his *Rifleman* up on the five-meter "Mech step" that ran around the inside wall like the *banco* in a Galistean hacienda's sitting room. Stationed a hundred meters north of the big double gates on *Tai-sho* Dalton Way, Carson spotted the helicopter banking into its dive. Carson's 'Mech was an older-style machine, with Imperator-A autocannons paired with Magna III heavy lasers in the arms, though it was slated for an upgrade when the Regiment got the money ahead.

Carson traversed the *Rifleman*'s torso left, leading the aircraft with his sighting pipper. As the helicopter flashed over the wall, he fired. The two laser beams didn't need to lead the target, and ionized air harmlessly in front of the helicopter. He had better luck with his autocannon burst, chewing off a chunk of the port stub wing and gouging the fuselage between cabin and tail rotor.

By that point half of Infante had opened up on the intruder. 'Mechs all over the Compound joined in, including Reb Perez' *Awesome*, emerging from the 'Mech barns where Astro Zombie and the HTE techs had just finished installing an improved sensor suite. HTE Security, in their white helmets and powder-blue jumpsuits, joined in with sidearms, as a matter of pride.

The chopper couldn't last long, and didn't. The yellow spear of a PPC beam intersected its rotor circle. As it stumbled in the air, a dozen other weapons found it, vaporizing skin and structure, knocking pieces off the tiny, fragile craft. It became a flaming hurtle, crashing like a meteor dead-center into the Compound and blowing up with a white flash and sky-splitting roar. The blast gouged out a shallow, thirty-meter-wide crater from the pavement; the chopper had been laden with explosives. Fortunately the attack occurred mid-shift, when there was little surface traffic within the Compound. The only casualties were several dozen ruptured eardrums and four Plant Maintenance techs who died when the stricken craft struck the golf cart they were riding.

First Battalion 'Mech jocks tumbled from ready rooms in their bulky cooling vests and skimpy shorts. Sirens blasted Second bodily from their racks and from the kitchen where, under the widened eyes of the HTE commissary staff, they'd been preparing trays of pastries shaped like tiny skulls and skeletons for baking. BattleMechs lumbered into positions around the walls as rescue vehicles converged on the enormous black pillar of smoke rising from the wreckage.

With electronically augmented senses, the warriors of the Seventeenth scanned the skies and streets surrounding the great Compound. There was no further change in the traffic patterns, no more sign of threat.

No man or woman of the Caballeros believed that would last.

The newswoman had straight blonde hair cut off even with her chin and light blue-green eyes with pronounced epicanthic folds. Behind her stood the great bronze gates on *Tai-sho* Dalton. Above them a black smoke tree rose into the darkening sky. In addition to explosives, the helicopter had carried a substance that kept the fire burning far longer than conventional fuel.

"After a tense half-day of waiting for answers from inside the grim, fortress-like headquarters of Hachiman Taro Enterprises," the reporter said, "at last hints as to the true situation have reached anxious city and planetary officials."

Viewpoint switched to an oblique telephoto shot from a helicopter orbiting well outside the defenders' comfort zone. It clearly showed mercenary BattleMechs patrolling inside the walls or standing by near the citadel. In the midst of the image the crater still smoldered.

"In the wake of the still-unexplained helicopter attack this morning," the reporter's voice said, "authorities have learned that elements of the offworld mercenary Seventeenth Recon have mutinied in a dispute over pay. The mercenaries have taken hostage HTE Chief Executive Officer—and cousin of our honored Coordinator—Chandrasekhar Kurita.

"No official word has come from Government House in Masamori, but it is expected that Planetary Chairman Fillington will soon order decisive military action to suppress the uprising and, if possible, free Lord Kurita. The Draconis Combine maintains an ancient tradition of refusing to negotiate with terrorists, no matter who their hostages might be.

"For MBC news, this is Miyako Tadamashi."

Seated in the white sterility of the meeting room buried

deep in the roots of the Citadel, the *Mirza* Peter Abdulsattah expelled a long breath. "So it has begun."

Chandrasekhar Kurita rubbed his palms slowly together. "At least the wait is ended," he said.

The holovision broadcast switched back to the regularly scheduled program, a class on the proper way to make *sushi* from Hachiman's varied sea life. Someone switched off the set.

"Send our people home," Uncle Chandy said, "except for yours, Peter-*san*. Shut down the Fabs and tell the off-shift employees to stay home."

"But, Lord Kurita!" an executive protested, "That will cost us millions."

"You think fighting a battle in the middle of my factory will not? I have a duty to my people. Besides, they can do nothing until the crisis is resolved. I will not subject them to unnecessary risk."

"They might risk being taken hostage if we send them outside the walls," Abdulsattah pointed out quietly.

"My enemies evidently believe I am a poor kind of Kurita," Uncle Chandy said equably, "but they cannot neglect that I am, still, Kurita. I care for my people, but I'll not treat with hostage-takers, either."

The *Mirza* inclined his long head in acknowledgment.

"You will inform Colonel Camacho that as of this moment we may expect a full-scale assault at any time. He should dispose his forces accordingly."

"But who will attack us, Lord?" another executive, smooth face glossy with perspiration despite the air conditioning, asked. "The—the ISF?"

"They've taken their try at us, and failed," Chandrasekhar said, "though it may be they will play a part."

He paused, and his great moon-cheeked face looked more sad than fearful.

"Gentlemen, as to who will attack us, I fear there can be only one answer."

"I don't believe it," *Tai-sa* Eleanor Shimazu told the Planetary Chairman. They faced each other in his office, which was cluttered with bric-a-brac from old Terra. He was standing to face her as he delivered her orders. She was in no mood to appreciate the honor.

"I beg your pardon?" Fillington asked, head tipped back

to look the Ghost commander in the eye. He was a good four fingers shorter.

"With all respect, your Excellency, I cannot accept that the Seventeenth Recon would mutiny against their employer. I *know* these people, Lord. They take their loyalty as seriously as we."

"You know *some* of them, Colonel. Yet you cannot know them all. Our intelligence is beyond dispute. Some of them, at least, have risen in revolt. It's up to your people to put them down."

Lainie ground her teeth, but made herself face him. She knew full well it was a lie.

But she had no choice. The Earl had the power to order her. He had done so.

"What support shall we have, milord?" she asked, her voice rasping.

"You are the sole 'Mech unit currently on-planet, as you're aware. The Masamori Civilian Guidance Corps will be mobilized to assist you as infantry forces."

Lainie's lips compressed to a line. She would pit a company of Ghosts *or* Caballeros against all the Candy Stripers on Hachiman.

"Your Excellency was a military man," she said, "once. No doubt he is well aware that generally accepted military doctrine holds that an assault against a strongly held position requires an attacking force at least three times as great as the defenders in order to achieve a reasonable chance of success."

For a moment the Earl's eyes blazed, but he controlled himself with visible effort. "They have ninety-five BattleMechs. With the addition of half a dozen machines that Tanadi has been fitting with Cat's Eye targeting and tracking systems and that the Marquis had agreed to release to our service for the duration of the emergency, your Regiment has its full paper complement of one hundred and eight machines. For the first time in its life, I expect?"

Glaring, Lainie nodded.

"You are battle-hardened veterans who have served together for years. You are also DCMS. Your opponents are foreign hirelings of a degenerate who disgraces his name."

"It gladdens my heart that your Excellency feels the mystique of the Dragon renders His servants invincible."

Fillington tipped his head back again. *"Tai-sa,"* he said, in a dangerous-quiet voice, "do you tell me that you feel unable to discharge your duty by leading your troops into battle against Chandrasekhar Kurita's money-soldiers tomorrow morning?"

Lainie snapped to attention. "All that I am," she said, staring fixedly at a point well above the Planetary Chairman's head, "I owe to Coordinator Theodore Kurita. My life is his to claim at any time."

She lowered her eyes to his. They were black as jet beads. "In this matter, you speak with his voice. And so I will obey."

He nodded brusquely and transferred his attention to the screen discreetly inset in his desktop. She remained at attention.

"Does his Excellency know what the *gaijin* mercenaries call tomorrow?"

He looked up at her in annoyance. "No, *Tai-sa,* I do not."

"They call it *el Dia de los Muertos,*" she said. "The Day of the Dead."

Lainie's eyes burned and her stomach roiled with nausea as she pushed out the glass doors of Government House; the seethe of helpless rage within literally sickened her. In contrast to what would have greeted her in the Federated Commonwealth or even the Free Worlds League, no media minions thronged the broad steps to stick microphones and holocams in her face and demand to know every detail of the coming operation. The Combine press would wait patiently for whatever its masters chose to feed it. The nighttime street was nearly deserted, though flashing lights and bullhorn voices a few blocks away marked an evacuation route out of the Murasaki district, tomorrow's redzone.

Still, she was awaited. A white stretch limousine was parked behind the light utility car that had brought her. Emma and Sutton, personal bodyguards to the *oyabun* of Masamori, lounged beside it.

"The Father Figure wants to see you, Cinnamon," Sutton said, straightening.

She glared at the two. "Are you out of your tiny minds? I'm a DCMS officer, and this is a military emergency. You lousy *chimpira* don't dare lay a finger on me."

Emma growled and puffed himself up like a giant spitting

toad from the swamps south of Funakoshi. Sutton cracked his knuckles and laughed.

"Funny," he said. "That just what *he* said."

He nodded his head toward the rear bumper of Lainie's vehicle. The stocky form of her faithful *Tosei-kai* shadow, who had driven her to the meeting with Fillington, lay face-down in the gutter between the cars. He wasn't moving.

"Moon!" she exclaimed, starting forward. The vast *sumitori* barred her way.

"Is he all right?" she demanded.

"He just took a little knock on the head," Sutton said, "to teach him to be reasonable. He'll be fine—just as long as you come with us."

Lainie reached up to grab a hank of red hair and glared at the two enforcers. There were other men moving on the street, strolling casually to flank her. Men wearing dark glasses and shoulder-padded, dazzle-pattern, *zaki* yakuza sports jackets with bulges in the armpits.

She bared her teeth, nodded convulsively. "Very well," she said. "Let's go."

33

Masamori, Hachiman
Galedon District, Draconis Combine
1 November 3056

It felt strange for Cassie to be cocooned in the safety—however temporary it might prove when the Ninth Ghost Regiment came to call—of a deeply buried bunker while her friends prepared to fight.

"What am I doing here?" she asked the *Mirza* flat-out. "I

need to be up top with the Regiment, figuring out how we're going to stop the Ghosts."

"You have a mission," the security chief said, "that I think you will agree transcends the importance even of pursuing your personal vendetta against BattleMechs."

"What is it?" Cassie asked testily, in no mood for deference.

"The seed you planted in Marquis Hosoya's office," Abdulsattah said, "has already borne fruit."

She stood in the bare underground briefing room and felt heat prickling the surface of her skin, even as the hyperactive air conditioning raised goose bumps on it.

"So quickly?" was all she found to say.

He nodded, watching her closely. "Fortune has smiled upon us. It is no more than we deserve, I think, given what we are up against."

"You have the goods?"

"The Marquis is consorting with individuals who are unmistakably Clanners." He smiled. "As an added bonus, none other than Kazuo Sumiyama was also in attendance."

Her heart missed a beat. "And the Chairman?"

Abdulsattah shook his head gravely. "Nowhere in evidence."

She drew in a great breath, expelled it with a sigh. *Why should I care?* But she did.

"What now?"

"Ninyu Kerai Indrahar has established a command center in a hotel being built a kilometer northwest of the Compound," the *Mirza* said. He smiled. "Our efforts to maintain cordial relations with our neighbors continue to prosper: one of the construction crew tipped us. We have irrefutable evidence demonstrating that Hosoya of Tanadi is guilty of those crimes of which Chandrasekhar Kurita is suspected. It is your job to place that evidence before Ninyu Kerai."

She smiled humorlessly. "I just walk in and ask for an appointment, right?"

"You fight. There are at least fifty DEST operatives gathered in the building with him."

The red-haired man hadn't struck her as the sort to hide behind a phalanx of bodyguards. "A strike team."

Abdulsattah nodded. "Ninyu may expect the Combine military force present on Hachiman to overwhelm your troops, although the odds favor only a protracted slaughter ending in bloody stalemate. Our assessment is that he does not care. He regards the Ghost Regiment assault as little more than a diversion—the Word of Blake attack on a grand scale. If they can breach the walls and allow his men to slip in unhindered to murder Chandrasekhar Kurita, he will be satisfied."

"And we're not strong enough to keep the Ghosts out," she said bitterly.

He inclined his head. "Indeed. Many will die today, to no purpose." He raised his face and stared deep into her eyes. "Unless you can win through to Ninyu and force him to look at the evidence that clears us."

She inhaled unsteadily. "When do I go?"

"You won't move out for several hours yet. The Ghost assault will be your best cover, too." He touched her arm. "We'll tend to the preparations. You'd best get some sleep."

"Cassie."

She set her jaw and kept walking. Around her, floodlights had turned midnight to day to light the purposeful confusion of a camp preparing for battle. The night had gone deadly chill. It was full of shouts and hammering and the sputter-spark of arc-welders as the techs and armorers made last-minute adjustments to the mighty, man-shaped war machines. Carts rumbled by, pulling trailers riding low on their suspension under stacked missiles and bins of autocannon ammunition to designated resupply points within the Compound. Uncle Chandy had been most generous when it came to stockpiling munitions. The Regiment had enough reloads to fight a major war. Which was approximately what it faced.

"Cassie, damn it, talk to me. Please?"

She stopped, whirled. Captain Kali MacDougall was striding up behind her, bundled in her cooling vest.

"What do you want?" Cassie shouted with a vehemence that surprised her. "I let you slip past my guard. And now I'm falling apart!"

"Are you falling apart," Kali asked levelly, "or coming together?"

"I'm losing my edge. Is that what you want? For me to lose it and . . . and *die* out there?"

"I want you to make a choice."

"What's that?"

"To be human."

Cassie turned away. "I can't. I'll weaken. I won't be able to do what I need to do." She spun to face Kali again, and her eyes glistened with tears. "It's already started, damn you. Already almost got me killed."

Lady K was shaking her head. "You don't understand, Cassie. You can do what you need to do without becoming what you fight so hard against: a soulless robot, a killing machine."

"You're just like Father Bob. Is that it? You think I'm just a sociopath?"

"No," Kali said, "but I think you might turn into one."

"Fine! Let me be a sociopath then! It's the only thing that's going to save us."

"Cassie," Lady K said, "when are you going to start believing in yourself?"

"What the *hell* are you talking about? I don't have time for this!"

"The skills you've got are yours, Cassie. You're the best scout in the Inner Sphere—*you* are, not some . . . some robot monster. You can be a human without giving up anything you've fought so hard to gain."

Cassie stared at Kali as if any moment she might leap at her and tear out her throat with her teeth. "I don't believe you."

"Then believe this." The taller woman laid a hand on her shoulder. "I know what happened to you, Cassie. *And it wasn't your fault.*"

Cassie felt as if Kali had punched her in the stomach. The breath left her, and the strength flowed from her knees. Her vision grayed-out at the edges.

"The same thing happened to me, Cassie," Lady K was saying. "My father—but the details don't matter, not right now. We'll talk it out when all this is over, if you want. The point is, you're not soiled, you're not guilty, you're not bad. Because you didn't do anything wrong."

Cassie felt as if she had been made from porcelain, and been dropped, and had cracked. "Why are you telling me this now?" she whispered. "You're killing me."

"No. Because I'm not what's been trying to get you killed."

She touched a gloved fingertip to Cassie's sternum. "It's in here. Something inside you wants you to self-destruct, be-

cause it can't live with the fear any longer. It's the fear of
what you did wrong, and the punishment that's coming.
You're tired of waiting for the blade to drop, for punishment
to overtake you. But it isn't coming, Cassie, because you
didn't do anything wrong."

Tear-blind, Cassie turned and fled.

"It pains me, Eleanor," Kazuo Sumiyama said in tones of
infinite sadness, "to tell you how disappointed I am in you."

Lainie stood in the yakuza boss' office. Because the walls
were glass and the lights were low, it was as if she stood in
the open, surrounded by blackness and towers of light. The
light-worm of the evacuation wound through the night's
bronze canyons below. She had nothing to say, and said it.

Sumiyama shook his wizened turtle head. "These are
gaijin . . . tanin. More than that, they're mercenaries. Yet
you chose to keep company with them, despite my express
disapproval."

I'm not your captive whore anymore, she wanted to shout
into his face. *I'm not one of you anymore at all. I'm a soldier of the Dragon.* Yet this wasn't the time or the place to
say it. Because right now Sumiyama had the power to make
sure she never walked out of this room alive. And if her regiment had to go into battle against the Seventeenth, she
would trust no one else to lead it.

"Even as among our samurai brethren, *giri* must overcome *ninjo,*" the yakuza leader said. "We have our traditions
of *ninkyo,* nobility, to maintain."

You mealy-mouthed old fraud, she thought. *How dare you
call the samurai our brothers? If there's honor to be found
in our yakuza history, it's in our roots as* machi-yakko, *the
neighborhood self-defense bands who fought the samurai.
Now you and your kind wrap yourself in the traditions of
our ancient foes. Foes to whom we are still nothing but* eta:
filth and gatherers of filth.

"My Ghosts yield to no one in matters of honor," she said
stiffly.

"Ah, but you must learn to yield, my child. That is the
problem with you young ones: you think you know it all,
and seek to oppose your will to that of your elders. This is
not in accord with the Dragon's ideals of harmony."

He shrugged. "And see what happens? You have made the

Organization lose much face, consorting with these *koroshiya*."

Lainie didn't bother to point out the irony of his referring to the Seventeenth as "hired killers." She knew with sick certainty what was coming next.

"*Hazukashii*," the *oyabun* intoned. "I am ashamed. Your behavior has brought this shame upon me."

She felt Sutton and Emma looming suddenly on either side of her, crowding her. She swallowed. Her throat was dry.

"I trust you will follow the course *jingi* requires." *Jingi*: the yakuza concept of righteousness.

Her lips peeled back from her teeth. "I'll do what must be done."

He nodded. He pulled open a drawer, reached into it, brought forth a *tanto* in a black sharkskin sheath.

Sutton leaned past Lainie to spread a white towel across Sumiyama's desktop. Smiling, he held out a strip of white cloth to her.

She took it, wound it around her left hand. Wound it cruelly tight, to restrict the circulation as much as possible.

She held the dagger up before her eyes, pulled it from its scabbard. She placed her left hand palm-down on the towel, fingers splayed wide, and leaned onto it.

"Through my actions I have brought disgrace upon my *oyabun*," she said through clenched teeth. She laid the edge of the knife on the base of her left little finger.

"In this way I shall atone."

She pressed the dagger down with a quick decisive motion. Sumiyama drew back blinking as her blood spattered his face and the front of his suit.

Sutton handed her another bandage, with which she quickly bound her bleeding hand. Sumiyama smiled up at her.

"It is good to see you display the proper respect."

She gestured toward her severed finger, lying on the bloody towel like a snack before him.

"Keep it packed in dry ice," she gritted.

He laughed delightedly. "And so I shall." He looked at his two retainers. "A wonderful idea, is it not? And when you redeem yourself by crushing your former associates, you can have it back. You'll have earned it, certainly."

"That I will," Lainie Shimazu said. "That I will."

* * *

In the dark of her quarters, Cassie clutched the stuffed bear to her chest and cried. She had often cried before, alone, in the dark, but never like this. It was as if the grief were being squashed from her by a great hydraulic press; as if someone had taken a big steel hook on a hawser, fed it down her throat, hooked it to her grief, and was reeling it out of her with a power-winch. She moaned and writhed and streamed tears like a hydrant.

At some point, she simply passed out, without marking the transition from consciousness. When, less than two hours later, a Scout Platoon private came to rouse her from sleep, she came awake feeling entirely refreshed and filled with the warmth of purpose.

Part 5

Day of the Dead

34

Masamori, Hachiman
Galedon District, Draconis Combine
2 November 3056

The last stars of night hid themselves behind low, sullen clouds. Winter had swooped down on Masamori like a Clan invasion, the air become brittle and sharp as a shard of glass.

A few flakes of snow drifted down between raked bronze towers, dusting the heads and shoulders of BattleMechs ranked along deserted avenues. *Tai-sa* Eleanor Shimazu's *Mauler* straddled the fountain in the traffic circle where *Tai-sho* Dalton Way met four other streets. Around her, First Battalion gathered for the assault.

One way in which the largely yakuza Ghost Regiments resembled those other *eta* of old, the ninja, was the service they provided the samurai: they could fight dirty without impairing their honor, since in *buke* eyes they had none.

It was universally, if tacitly, known that that was why Theodore Kurita had formed the Ghosts. While the *Dictum Honorium* was less restrictive than the Clans' code of honor, there were some things the DCMS couldn't do, at least not without a crisis of conscience. And while *giri* always overcame *ninjo*, at least in theory, *giri* versus *giri* conflicts could produce deadly hesitation.

Lainie grimaced. She had her own codes. Duty bound her to fight, but she would do it her way.

She clicked her communicator to the standard HTE frequency. "Attention, men and women of the Seventeenth Recon," she said in English. "I am *Tai-sa* Eleanor Shimazu, commanding the Ninth Ghost Regiment."

She paused. Her mutilated hand throbbed inside the thick insulated glove. She ignored it. Ignoring pain was no novelty to her. What hurt was saying the next thing.

"If you do not lay down your arms, immediately vacate all BattleMechs and defensive positions, and surrender, we shall be forced to attack and destroy you."

"This is Colonel Camacho." It was the voice of a man old beyond his years, aged by worry and loss and pain.

"Colonel, I greet you. Now I must ask you for your surrender. You will be treated honorably."

"Can you guarantee that, *Tai-sa*?"

Lainie clenched her teeth. *No. I can't. Not with that devil Ninyu here.* She regretted that her Ghosts had kept such contemptuous distance from their street-yakuza brethren of the Sumiyama-*kai*. She had only just discovered what the *kobun* had known for weeks: that the Smiling One's heir was on the ground in Masamori, playing an active role in this lethal farce.

"Your hesitation speaks eloquently, *Tai-sa*," Camacho said. "It does not matter. We have our duty. We have taken Lord Kurita's coin, and we will protect him to the death."

At this juncture Lainie was supposed to make noises about how the Ghosts were coming to rescue Chandrasekhar Kurita. Stuff that, she thought. What can they do? Shoot me?

"I have no enmity toward you personally, Colonel," she said formally. "You are men and women of honor. But *giri* obliges me to take your lives."

"I thank you for your polite words," Don Carlos said. "Let us proceed."

There was a click as he signed off. Lainie switched to the Ghosts' general freak.

"All Ghosts," she said, "this is Red Witch. It's time for the *chi no matsuri:* the festival of blood."

With a moaning of servos and a shuffle-thud of heavy metal feet, the 'Mechs of the Ghost Regiment swung to the attack.

"The *culebras* are approaching, Cassiopeia," Colonel Camacho said. "The attack begins. Time for you to go."

They were alone in the Colonel's office. Cassie had heard the exchange with the flame-haired Ghost commander.

The *Mirza*'s outfitters had made a wide range of equipment available to the hand-picked squad of scouts who would accompany her on the raid, including assault-armor vests combining ballistic cloth with steel-ceramic inserts that would stop almost any conventional small-arms round. Cas-

sie Suthorn preferred to go to battle unencumbered, as near
to frankly naked as possible.

To her mind, mobility was life to a scout, and all else was
deadly illusion. Today, because there was going to be a lot
of particulate pollution in Masamori's comparatively clean
air—mostly fast-moving chunks of lead and occasional grenade and shell splinters—she'd consented to wear a simple
ballistic-cloth vest beneath a black woolly-pully sweater.
Loose black trousers and black athletic shoes rounded out
the outfit. As a final touch she had tied a black silk strip
around her forehead in imitation of the *hachimaki* headbands
many of their opponents would be wearing today, simply because she liked the way it looked.

She also wore a ripstop vest of many pockets, for magazines and other useful items. Blood-drinker hung diagonally
across her chest, hilt-down to the right, the way the Rabid
Foxes wore their combat knives. She had a bullpup machine
pistol slung over her right shoulder and a big Nambu-Nissan
autopistol holstered beneath the left, both firing the same
10-mm rounds. On her back she wore a light ruck containing
the all-important disk and a player-projector, along with
more ammunition. She looked like a little girl got up to play
terrorist at a costume party.

Don Carlos held out his arms. "Come to me." As they em-
braced, he said over her shoulder, "You have been as a
daughter to me, Cassiopeia. Be most careful. Strange times
are coming to the Inner Sphere. The Regiment may need you
more than ever once . . . once this thing is done."

They broke apart. She frowned at him. "It doesn't sound
as if you're planning to survive this fight, *patrón*."

His eyes fell away from hers. "I failed my people in the
terrorist attack. Bobby Begay and the others—Baird, Vanity,
Marisol—are right. My time is past."

"If that's the way you feel, why not retire back to the hacienda, the way you always said you would?"

He shook his head. "It's no good."

"What do you mean? You're not going out there to get
yourself killed, are you?"

"I killed my daughter," he said quietly. "I can no longer
bear that burden."

"Sierra *Foxtrot,* you killed your daughter! Patsy killed her
own stupid self!"

For a moment life returned to Don Camacho's eyes in the

form of rage. He raised a hand as if to strike her, and Cassie raised her face to accept the blow.

He sighed and dropped his hand. "I made her do it. She wanted to please me, but the harder she tried, the worse it became, the worse she made her brother look. I could not accept that she was the greater MechWarrior; my son must be *numero uno*. And so I forced her to die, and forced Gavilán to spend the rest of his life trying to match her."

"Forced her? You *forced* her?" Cassie's strident, unbelieving laugh rang like a trumpet in the tiny room. "When in her life did you know anyone to *force* Patsy to do anything?

"Colonel, listen to me, please. I honor your daughter's memory. I loved her as much as you did. She was my only *friend,* dammit! But face the truth: she chose to throw her life away against the Smoke Jaguars. There was nothing you could do about it then. There's less you can do about it now!"

He covered his face with his hands. *"Patricia—"*

"You don't have the luxury to be a martyr now, Don Carlos. The Regiment needs you. If you go out there to die, you'll be throwing away the lives of all of us."

She grabbed his shoulder. "Let it go. Let *Patsy* go. If you don't, everything you've done—keeping us together, keeping us *alive*—it all goes up in flames." Tears poured freely down both their faces. "Don't you *understand*?"

He drew a breath, nodded.

The door opened. The young *norteño* staff officer who had served as his aide-de-camp since Cabrera's banishment stood blinking nervously at them.

"Sir," he said, "Adelante reports contact with the enemy."

Cassie kissed Don Carlos quickly on the cheek. "I have to go." She looked a question at him.

"I will do my best to survive, *mija,*" he said. "For the Regiment and for you."

A faint smile raised the corners of his mustache. "But it may be out of my hands. Out of all our hands."

Fifteen men and women of Scout Platoon stood or sat in clumps in the pumping station, bristling with weapons and swollen with body armor. The small square structure concealed an entrance to the Masamori sewer system that Uncle Chandy had instructed his architects to build in. A foresightful man was Chandrasekhar Kurita.

Cassie looked around. The scouts responded variously, some with smiles of confidence, some with militant scowls, others with sullen stares. All masks they wore to cover fear.

Cassie was afraid too. Yet somehow she wasn't. She had the adrenaline edge honed to her senses, but deep in the center of her, where storm clouds of fear had raged almost all her life, were only clear skies and calm.

She had no time to contemplate her unfamiliar emotional state. Now was the time to number the odds, which weren't encouraging. Fifteen was either too many for the job at hand or too few. But there had not been much time to plan. In any event, three of them—Scooter Barnes, accompanied by his spotter and security woman, and with his huge Zeus sniper rifle slung over his shoulder—would be peeling off well short of their objective to take up station in a building facing Ninyu's command post to provide long-range covering fire. The remaining twelve would go in with Cassie.

Muffled by distance and the station's cinderblock walls, the unmistakable sizzle and crack of big energy-weapons sounded. A moment later, from closer by, came the whoosh-roar of Diana's *Catapult* firing its big Arrow IV homing missiles.

Cassie looked out the door to the west. All she could see was the wall, but in her mind she looked beyond.

I didn't get to say good-bye, Lady K, she thought, *but I wish you luck, my friend. I accept the gift you gave me.*

Cassie only hoped it wasn't a parting gift.

A single tear rolled down her cheek. She brushed it away. "Let's go," she said.

Sunlight lances stabbed down among the towers of bronze like PPC bolts. As Lainie's *Mauler* crested the rise east of the traffic circle, the tip of the primary's molten-copper disk was just rising above the walls of Hachiman Taro Compound, almost two kilometers away.

Broad *Tai-sho* Dalton Way was eerily deserted. So were the side streets and alleys. The street-level businesses were shut down, shuttered and dark. The Earl of Hachiman had sealed off everything east of the river within two thousand meters of the Compound—all of Murasaki and beyond, a gigantic bite out of the very heart of Masamori's business district. Win or lose, this would be an expensive day.

Economics were not Lainie Shimazu's concern. Tactics

were. Even without taking her little side-trip to humiliate herself and amputate her own finger without anesthetic into account, she had been given insufficient time to plan a detailed or subtle assault. If there *was* a subtle way to assault a giant urban fortress.

The ten-meter walls of the Compound didn't mean that much in a clash of 'Mechs, not with jump jets and heavy weapons. Mounting the firing-step did give added protection to defending BattleMechs. But mainly what the walls did was guarantee that any attack would be a frontal one: the worst possible for the attacker.

She had done what she could. Second Battalion she had sent around to attack from the south. The north, with its complex housing HTE employees, she was leaving severely alone.

Her perception of Chandrasekhar Kurita was much closer to street-level than the Planetary Chairman's or Hosoya's, and untainted by personal hatred, unlike Sumiyama's. She did not dismiss him as a sybaritic fat fool. Her assessment of the semi-disgraced Kurita was that he was a tough, shrewd, and thoroughgoing bastard, who missed damned few bets. If *she* were the HTE chief, she'd have had the Workers' housing salted with pitfalls, tanglefoot 'Mech traps, and missile infantry.

Such measures could not hope to stop a 'Mech assault, but Lainie knew she was operating on the razor edge of absurdity as it was. A handful of commando teams firing man-portable SRMs at back armor or vulnerable leg actuators could cause confusion totally out of proportion to the damage they inflicted—and she couldn't afford the damage to her BattleMechs, either.

Third Battalion was being held back in reserve. The exception was I Company. Supported by a pair of LRM-firing *Stalkers*, already in position in Sodegarami across from the HTE Compound, they would try a probe from the river itself. With heavy irrigation upstream, the Yamato was not terrifically deep or fast this time of year, but the complex tidal system made a riverine assault tricky. Nonetheless I Company would wade up from the south to test the eastern defenses, in the distant hopes of taking the mercs by surprise. If anything favorable developed, she could commit the rest of Third, and even detach some of Second.

First Battalion, under her personal command, was going

in by the front door, screened by lances of *Locust*s and *Jenner*s to act as tripwires in case the Caballeros wanted to try forward defense instead of sitting passively behind their walls.

And that was exactly what the *gaijin* wanted. A beak-snouted *Raven,* looking smaller than its 35 tons, popped out of a side street to the right, 700 meters ahead of Lainie in her Revenge, and launched a pair of missiles right over the heads of the leading Ghost light 'Mechs. One of them crashed through the third-story of an office building. The other hit an A Company *BattleMaster* on the left front glacis, right below the laser mounts high on its torso. The huge BattleMech rocked back slightly at the impact, but no explosion ensued.

"Narc pod!" Lainie exclaimed. "Taifun, get off the street! Now! *Now!*"

The whole lead company opened up on the *Raven,* muzzle blasts from heavy autocannon punching in windows like invisible fists. Glass and structural steel puffed away from laser and PPC caresses in vapor; brick and granite blew apart in blossoms of dust.

The mercenary 'Mech had already ducked back out of sight. The point-walking light lance pounded in pursuit.

The *BattleMaster* pilot had turned her machine and was trying to get back to the nearest cross street, hoping to interpose a skyscraper's bulk between her 'Mech and what was coming. By luck or design, her 'Mech had been caught in mid-block. The big machine had to get around its brethren to find cover, and it was not agile.

Away in front, two vines of white smoke rose up into the dawn haze from beyond the walls. "First Battalion, two missiles incoming, oh-nine-five, engage now-now-*now.*"

The Ghosts opened up with everything they had as the two missiles nosed over and streaked down toward the lumbering *BattleMaster*. The Ghosts were hoping to put enough lead and energy into the sky for a one in a thousand hit against the missile. Desperate, but sometimes desperation wins out.

One missile was hit and went ballistic. Slewing off course, it crashed sideways into the seventh floor of a Middle-Class apartment complex. The warhead didn't detonate, but unburned propellant spilled out and ignited a raging fire.

The other struck the BattleMaster square on the left shoulder. Head and actuator vanished in a white flash.

"I want trajectory data on those missiles fed to my onboard computer now," Lainie was ordering even as the missile stuck home. Gloved fingers jabbed buttons as messages danced in her heads-up display, indicating the figures were coming in. "*Dai-kyu* One and Two, I'm forwarding the data to you now. Get that launcher triangulated. I want counterbattery fire on the way before the *chikusho* moves." *Dai-kyu*—the asymmetrical Japanese longbow—was the callsign assigned to the *Stalker*s firing long-range missiles in support

A weird cry rose in Lainie's neurohelmet, a savage trill climaxing a coyote yips: "*Trrrreeeee-ya-ha-ha!*"

Other *gaijin* voices answered. "*Presente la Super Cadena, Radio KATN!*"

"Kick Ass—"

"—and Take Names!"

Lainie felt anger surge. The foreigners were gloating over the death of her friend, the warrior in the cockpit of the *BattleMaster*. She knew better than to let rage get the better of her. But the edge it imparted was good. Made it easier to do what needed to be done.

She sent B and C Companies winging off right and left. She and A kept going straight up the middle.

The *BattleMaster* had frozen in place, rocking gently back and forth, bleeding smoke from its cratered upper torso. Lainie had served with *Chu-i* van Doorn for six years, through the hell of the Clan invasion. A Middle-Class girl, not an outlaw born, Misty van Doorn had nonetheless chosen to accept the *irezumi* that marked her irreversibly as a yakuza and a Ghost. Lainie had held the other woman's hand during the painful tattooing process—and again, later, when van Doorn gave birth to her son Theodore, now the first in the Ninth Ghost's new generation of orphans. But Colonel Shimazu refused to acknowledge the new hole that had been excavated in her soul.

We're all dead, she thought savagely. *What does it matter whether we lie down now, or later?*

Masamori, Hachiman
Galedon District, Draconis Combine
2 November 3056

"It has begun, Assistant Director."

Standing by the window, gazing southeast toward the stronghold of the renegade Kurita, Ninyu Kerai Indrahar bit back a caustic response. Any fool would know the fighting had begun. Had he no ears to hear? But he said nothing, because technicians were not warriors, much less ninja. They saw no shame in chattering to cover their nerves.

The penthouse of the grandly and presumptuously named Coordinator's Rest Hotel occupied the entire top level, sitting like a cap atop the hundred-story atrium. At the moment it was all one huge chamber; the partitions had yet to be installed. The hotel, which was nearing completion, was being built to the design of a Free Worlds League architectural team, under the supervision of FWL construction experts. Rumors—which the tall, red-headed man happened to know were true—held that most of the money came from a consortium of mainly Lyran investors in the Federated Commonwealth.

To allow one's enemies to build up the Combine's economic base with their investments—that was one aspect of Theodore Kurita's far-reaching reforms for which Ninyu could understand his adoptive father's enthusiasm.

He was having a bit more trouble dealing with the directive implicit in his father's last hyperpulse message, which was keeping him cooped up in this aerie instead of where his warrior's blood told him he belonged—down on the ground floor waiting with the fifty-man assassination team for the Ninth Ghost Regiment to break into their target's stronghold.

The message had come in the form of a haiku:

The wise leader knows
That even great courage must
Kneel before giri.

The meaning was clear enough: Ninyu's place was overseeing the battle from a suitable perspective, not leading the troops with sword in hand. He might have pointed out that both he and the Smiling One had personally accompanied the DEST team they'd chosen to assassinate the late Coordinator, Takashi, an attempt that had culminated in the Coordinator's own *seppuku*. But that was different. Takashi wasn't just a Kurita, he had been *the* Kurita, ruler of the Combine, not to mention a lifelong friend of Subhash Indrahar. He had also been, despite his age, a formidable foe, formidable enough that he had managed to kill several of the elite ISF commandos come to assassinate him. Uncle Chandy was a fat fool, a Kurita in no more than name. The situations were not to be compared.

But understanding it didn't mean Ninyu had to like it. He would follow the battle as closely as a sophisticated communications suite emplaced in the unfinished penthouse would permit, choosing the most propitious moment to commit his team, and then to monitor their progress. He had promised himself that, should things go wrong, he would personally intervene. Only to make sure that the job was properly done, of course.

Raven's *Raven* skittered down the sidestreet like a frightened quail. The buildings were squashed together here in the guts of the capital; lordly showcase thoroughfares like Dalton were big enough to permit a light lance to walk in vee-formation without crowding—as the Ghost's point unit had been doing—but a lot of the lesser streets were little bigger than alleys. The housing of her two right-arm Ceres lasers scraped along the bricks of a building as she went, dragging a tail of sparks behind her. She was a true Caballera, born to pilot a 'Mech.

It was in marksmanship that the Caballeros tended to fall down, though Raven hadn't fared too badly. She'd made sure to tag the big *B-Master* with at least one of her Narcs; the Bronco light 'Mechs crouched in concealment farther down Dalton had then called a direct hit on the big 'Mech, proving her right.

The downside was that she'd popped out practically in the faces of the leadoff Ghost light lance. Before she could get clear of the buildings, a *Locust* came skidding into the three-sixty strip's view behind her. Its jock wasn't as sure at the controls as Raven; the little scout 'Mech banged off a building-corner already cratered by laser and PPC fire. But it righted itself instantly and came jolting after her in an angry-bird run, its lasers stabbing for Raven's tail.

The Caballera felt the heat spike upward in her heavily air-conditioned cockpit as the *Locust*'s medium Martell sublimated armor off the rear of her machine. Rear armor wasn't the *Rave*'s strong suit. *Can't take much of this!*

Seeing a *Jenner* poke its blunt nose into the alley behind the first Ghost 'Mech, Raven caught a dumpster with her 'Mech's right foot, spun it into the air. In the ensuing snowstorm of whirling paper she bounded out the end of the alley, ducked away from the charging *Locust*'s line of fire, then instantly pirouetted back to face the alley-mouth. Steel screamed on pavement as her feet skidded, but she kept the 'Mech upright.

Almost at once a tone shrilled in her neurohelmet, and a red warning flashed in her HUD. Two hundred meters west a pair of pointy-headed *Whitworth*s were dropping into the street, having found a four-story building to jump over. They were both lighting her up with their own Artemis-IV fire-control systems. It hardly seemed fair, somehow; that was *her* job.

Since she was facing that way, Raven pumped a shot from her two Ceres at the descending 'Mechs, but she had already clutched-in her gyros for a quick spin clockwise. "Adelante," she yelped, "this is Raven. I'm on Mitsui, and I'm in a world of hurt, here."

Across Mitsui Avenue stood a gym with a mostly glass entrance and a bottom floor that was extra tall to accommodate a basketball court. Not omitting a mental thank you to Cassie and Scout Platoon for doing the thorough survey of the area that Gordo Baird had considered so unnecessary, she bashed straight into the foyer in a shower of glass.

Not a particularly tall BattleMech, a *Raven* could run down the central corridor without barely stooping at all. But Raven inside her cockpit couldn't help reflexively doing so. Behind her the entryway erupted in orange holocaust as the double volley of Longbow long-range missiles from the *Whitworth*s spent themselves in futile fury.

"We got you covered, *güerita*," came the voice of Macho Alvarado. Raven grinned at the consternation the Drac medium and light 'Mech pilots must be feeling as Macho's *BattleMaster* swung into view down Mitsui and lumbered up the block toward them.

From the garbage she was getting on her Beagle Active Probe, Raven knew there was no way the *culebras* could keep track of her now that she was out of their sight. With all the structural steel and just general *mass* around, Beagles weren't much use in an urban center. She could keep cruising if she wanted. Her Ceres medium lasers were more than sufficient to take out the gym's back wall and let her into the next street *right now.*

Instead she turned around and hunkered down in the gloom to wait in case one of the Drac lights wanted to emulate her and duck into the gym to escape the *BattleMaster.* Raven had no problem with the hop and pop, shoot and scoot type of warfare mandated for First Battalion's forward-defense mission today. It was the 'lleros' preferred style, and the right way to fight a little light-armored *Raven* anyway. But if somebody wanted to give her a free crack at them. . .

The 65-ton mass of Diana Vásquez's *Catapult* rocked slightly forward as the LRM salvo from across the Yamato slammed into the Compound. Had she been on foot, the blast waves would have torn her to pieces. Her 'Mech's tons of armor shed shock and debris like light autumn rain.

The *culebra* commander had been on the ball, triangulating her so quickly. But the Seventeenth's arty 'Mechs practiced hit-and-run warfare too. The Huntress was rumbling into motion the instant her two Arrows cleared the racks.

And now for their trouble, the Ghost support 'Mechs across the estuary in the *ukiyo* were taking counter-counterbattery fire from two of the Caballero *Stalker*s. In contrast to the Drac BattleMechs, which were positioned shoulder-to-shoulder in classic artillery-battery style, none of the Seventeenth's 'Mechs was in sight of any other.

The way they saw it, it didn't matter where the heavy mail went *out* from. Just where it got delivered.

The fire-mission-request indicator lit on her HUD. Somebody had tagged another attacking 'Mech with a Narc. It was Lieutenant JG Silas García's turn to take the call in his *Catapult*. Almost at once the mission-request flashed green, indicating his Arrows were on the way.

Diana hoped no more calls would come in for a few seconds. It took time to shift the big artillery 'Mechs from one firing-position to the next. When things got hot and heavy they would be pinned in place, forced to fire continuously from the same location to support their distant friends. She said a brief prayer to the Virgin of Guadalupe to guide the *Stalkers*' aim in their duel with the Ghost artillery.

Then she said another, to keep her son and all the Regiment's other children safe, huddled in the vast bomb-shelters deep beneath the Compound along with HTE personnel who hadn't managed to get off-site. Keeping them safe wasn't really up to the Virgin; it was up to the BattleMechs of the Seventeenth and their pilots. But Diana prayed anyway, because the Brown Virgin was patroness of the Caballeros, and it didn't hurt to let Her know they were thinking of Her.

She reached her site before the next call came in, and promised to light a candle of thanksgiving.

Ahead of Lainie and A Company, Dalton Way stretched wide, open, and inviting right up to the gates of HTE Compound. Though she couldn't as yet even spot defenders on the wall, she knew they were there, crouched low on the 'Mech firing step or standing on the ground waiting to pop up and shoot.

Lainie took for granted that she was walking into an ambush. But that didn't bother her. If you took the offensive in a city fight, you got ambushed. Her concern was to be ready when it came.

She had called her light lance back to walk point down Dalton well in advance of A. Let B Company deal with the pesky Narc-firing *Raven*—not to mention the *Battlemaster* that had come to its aid. As it was, the lance was reduced to three. The *BattleMaster*'s PPC had burned off the lead *Locust*'s right leg before more of B Company joined the two *Whitworth*s and forced the merc assault 'Mech to withdraw in swarms of LRMs.

The *Heruzu Enjeruzu* were seriously deficient in artillery support, a problem endemic to all Ghost Regiments. That was because the DCFS High Command wanted them in there slugging it out with the foes of the Dragon, not standing off and bombarding them from safety. She had all of three *Stalker*s, the two across the river in Sodegarami and one trailing well behind A Company. The *gaijin*—better to start thinking of them that way—had four *Stalker*s and two 'Mechs mounting the lethal Arrow-IV missile launchers to her none.

As she entered an intersection, the three-sixty strip above Lainie's viewscreen showed sudden movement to her left. Something *big*—

"*Ambush!*" she shouted. "Left side!"

She turned her *Mauler*'s torso. A *Quickdraw* and a *Griffin* had appeared in the side street. Even as she turned, the yellow hellglare of the *Griff*'s PPC lit up the buildings to either side. The big *Mauler* rocked from the recoil effect of New Samarkand's finest ferro-fibrous armor jetting away from the beam in the form of plasma. The massive radiation discharge made her 'Mech's electronics scream in her ears like wounded children.

Hanging behind her 'Mech's left shoulder was the ever-faithful Moon in his *Rifleman*, a pad bandage wrapped around his skull under the neurohelmet. He flayed the medium 'Mech with the heavy laser and autocannon duos mounted on either arm.

The ambushers were already pulling back. Autocannon hits sparking against the *Griff*'s front armor, the 'Mech sidestepped into the alley mouth to its left. The heavier 'Mech tried to dodge right, but it was slower-footed. Moon's *Rifleman* shifted fire. The short-range impacts of its two Imperator-A autocannon rocked the *Quickdraw* back against the corner of a department store that backed on the alley.

Already traversing her 'Mech's torso counterclockwise, Lainie pivoted Revenge on its feet to bring her weapons to bear. The range was too short for the Shigunga LRM racks flanking the BattleMech's head to be effective. But the big Victory lasers that formed the 'Mech's either forearm were good to go.

The *Quickdraw* had the same trouble for which the *Rifleman* was so notorious: it was underarmored for a savage slugging contest at close quarters, and its chest armor was even thinner. Moon was lighting him up there, working the body like the good boxer he was, driving the heat up in his own cockpit by blasting with his torso-mounted medium Magna lasers as well as their larger cousins in his arms. A minivan-sized splotch of the *Quickdraw*'s inadequate front armor glowed cherry-red.

Lainie let the little smoothbore Imperator autocannon quad in her belly add to the punishment the off-balance BattleMech was taking to the torso. But her big arm lasers thrust red lances straight into its viewscreens. The *gaijin* heavy was blasting back for all it was worth with its own lasers, and the SRM pack on its chest managed to uncork its single salvo before Moon slagged it. But it was out-gunned, out-armored, and generally out of luck.

The *Quickdraw* gathered itself, tried to jump. Too late. Lainie's big lasers burned through its faceplate. It threw up its arms in grotesque mimicry of a human as filters failed and the hellglare of the twin lasers blinded the pilot an instant before they incinerated him and blew the *Quickdraw*'s head apart in a shower of glittering transpex and metal fragments that gouged bright scars on the two Ghost 'Mechs' frontal armor.

"One for us, *Tai-sa*," said Moon. Matter-of-fact as always, he might have been discussing the light snow now beginning to dust the streets.

"Yeah," Lainie said, feeling the hot flush in her cheeks a kill always gave her. *Hold onto that feeling,* she told herself, *and don't let yourself think who you're killing.*

"B Company," she demanded, "what's going on? Why aren't you watching our left flank?"

"No excuse, *Tai-sa*," *Tai-i* Iyehara, B's CO, responded. "But we just got hit hard from the north. It appears to be a company-sized attack."

Almost immediately other reports crackled in her neurohelmet. On her right, C Company had run up against fierce resistance to its front. Lainie felt a hard, dry smile stretch her lips. Felt herself move out of herself, into the larger role of battle commander.

At last, she thought, *the game becomes interesting.*

Chu-i Sammy Ozawa had not seen the Caballeros' wargame by the Yamato, and hadn't really believed the reports of those who had.

He had been working his 35-ton *Panther* east down an alley, guarding the north flank of B Company, as that company guarded A's. The *gaijin* thrust from the north had swept past him without even taking note of him.

The *Panther* was slow for a light 'Mech, even at the weight class' upper end. It compensated with an Artemis-IV augmented SRM battery in its chest and a seriously evil Lord's Light PPC in its right arm. When Sammy saw the gigantic *BattleMaster* cruise obliviously past the end of the alley, a plan had instantly formed in his mind.

Like most light 'Mech pilots, he dreamed constantly of humbling an assault 'Mech. Assault jocks thought they were the Dragon's gift to the Inner Sphere, kings and queens of the battlefield. His extended-range PPC was actually at a disadvantage close-up—it took a hundred meters or so for the beam to focus—but he was sure it and his rockets would be enough to fry a knee actuator and take the *Atlas* out of the fight in one quick stroke. And then the decent jump capability of his Lexington Lifters could bounce him out of harm's way before the monster's comrades could retaliate.

The *Atlas* was scarcely fifty meters from him when he slipped out of the alley and began blazing up its right knee from behind. Quick as a *Locust,* the *BattleMaster* wheeled and lunged for him.

Impossible! Sammy thought. For a moment he stood and fought, volleying SRMs into the center of the monster's chest and bringing up his PPC, firing as it rose. He scarcely pitted the *BattleMaster*'s frontal armor.

Belatedly it dawned on him to jump. As he rose up, the behemoth grabbed him by the foot. Against the full power of his jump jets, it reeled the *Panther* back down. Sweat streaming down his face, overheat warnings shrilling in his ears, Sammy tried to fire his PPC into its hideous, skull-like face. Instead, the emergency override shut him down.

Too stunned to punch out, the last thing Sammy Ozawa saw was the *BattleMaster*'s fist filling his viewscreen like a knuckled moon.

Natural athlete though she was, Lainie Shimazu wasn't much more than a competent BattleMech pilot. It was as a tactician that she excelled, the ability to fight her big machine and her regiment effectively at the same time.

In a flash she assessed her situation. The mercenaries were obviously launching spoiling attacks, trying to damage and disorganize her forces as much as possible before they reached the Compound. She guessed that most of their strength was waiting behind those blank stone walls.

She judged that the opposition reported by C Company was a screen; her gut told her the real stroke was landing on B from the north. She had two thirds of Third Battalion following in reserve. It was not yet time to commit them. Directing C to halt its advance and wing out to its left to lightly cover A's front, she also ordered A Company to wheel left to support B.

As far as Lainie was concerned, she was on no set schedule. She had no intention of pressing the attack against dug-in BattleMechs with enemies in her backfield. She would deal with the flank attack, and then she would ram the screening force back against the wall, and *then* she would assault the Compound proper. And if the precious Earl of Hachiman complained about the time it took, *he* could clamber into a BattleMech and stick his own pale fanny on the firing line. Until she was killed or relieved, Lainie would fight her own battle.

It was a gamble, of course. The risk to her career never entered her mind. But she was well aware that the attack from the north might be a feint, with the *real* stop-thrust about to smash through C's thin front to take her counterattack in flank. Or the mercs might get supremely bold, and sally forth from the Compound for a flank stroke.

Setting her *Mauler* in motion up the side street from which the *gaijin* 'Mechs had ambushed her, Lainie Shimazu smiled in grim amusement. She could give the defenders behind the walls something better to do than plague First Battalion. The tidal bore, driven by Hachiman's moons, was in full booming progress, routinely cresting in five-meter waves. Until that calmed, the Third Battalion company would have to wait to enter the water for the river assault. But Second Battalion had worked its way into the business district south of the Compound. Lainie ordered them to attack at once. *That* should make the mercenaries keep it in their pants.

Lainie was a yakuza, and had the heart of a gambler. She was betting on her judgment and on the ability of her hard men and women to smash the current threat before the mercs could pull another trick out of their cowboy hats.

Masamori, Hachiman
Galedon District, Draconis Combine
2 November 3056

The attack from the north was no feint. It was Bronco Company, and they came to kill. Within the first sixty seconds of contact, Lady K's command left five Ghost 'Mechs smoking at a cost of two of their own.

This was Kali MacDougall's debut commanding a battle of 'Mechs. She knew in an intellectual way that the exchange had been a good one for the 'lleros. But tell a mother the loss of two children is a small price to pay. . . .

Firing, she walked Dark Lady past Quicksilver, Joey Sosa's *Hermes* II. The medium 'Mech was burning fiercely, its autocannon ammo cooking off in fire-tipped lines of smoke sprouting from its back like the fin-spines of an exotic fish.

No one said this would be easy, girl.

"*Tai-sa!*" came the voice of the Ninth Ghost's top recon driver, Otenkinagashi, whose callsign meant "weather criminal"—*ingo* for lookout. He was a thin and quiet little yakuza whose *irezumi* covered his legs, arms, and torso like an outrageous, swirled body suit. He piloted the other *Locust* of the light lance that had been walking point and was now covering A Company's right as it marched to support B. "We're being attacked from the northeast!"

Lainie hauled Revenge around the corner, just in time to see a *Hatchetman* stove in the little recon *Locust*'s head with a blow of its namesake weapon. The mercenary 'Mech stood over its opponent as the now-uncontrolled *Locust* toppled to the ground at its feet. Then it stalked up the street toward the Ghosts.

Behind it the street filled with more BattleMechs. Missiles arced over its shoulders. *"Mattaku,"* Lainie said, "Damn! Samurai, take them. I'm backing you."

"Hai!" exclaimed the youthful officer leading a mixed medium/heavy lance from the cockpit of his *Grand Dragon*. From his tone it was clear he thought this was the ideal opportunity to redeem the disgrace that had driven him from home and forced him to serve with lowly *eta*.

Well, go for it, Lainie thought.

At last the cowards stand and fight! the young samurai exulted inwardly. Confidence bolstered by his double-capacity heat sinks, he was hammering the advancing BattleMech with his full forward-firing armament of PPC, heavy laser, and chest-mounted LRM cluster. The other 'Mechs in his lance were also focusing fire on the *Hatchetman*. His audio pickups bristled with the crack of laser beams and supersonic autocannon rounds.

Another sound also reached his ears, a guttural chant booming from the advancing machine's loudspeakers. He did not recognize it for the death-song of a warrior of the *Chihené*, the Red Paint People of the Chiricahua. He thought it was mere barbarous babble.

The *Hatchetman* was firing back with its Defiance LB-X autocannon and its three medium pulse lasers. But it was hopelessly overmatched, and blocking effective fire from its comrades behind.

"Chu-i," the Ghost in the *Whitworth* to the samurai's left said, "what does he think he's doing?"

"I don't know." What the *gaijin* was doing was dying. Projectiles knocked man-sized chunks of metal from the mercenary 'Mech's torso. Ferro-fibrous armor puffed away from energy-weapon hits in glowing vapor, ran in molten yellow streams from its wounds, like lava, like blood. Still the *Hatchetman* came on, irresistibly closing the range, two hundred meters, one-fifty.

The autocannon ammo stored in its right torso detonated, its CASE system venting the force of the blast out its back in a sudden gush of yellow flame. And still the BattleMech kept coming.

It had already gone past the point the young officer would have imagined possible. *Surely it must fall soon!* he thought. Its autocannon and lasers were slagged. With almost all the armor burned from the 'Mech's legs and left arm, the exposed myomer muscle bundles were beginning to curl and smoke.

At fifty meters the *Hatchetman* cocked its right arm and threw its hatchet. As it released, the arm fell off. The BattleMech then stumbled to its knees and fell forward in the street, swathed in smoke.

"Masaka!" the samurai exclaimed as the hatchet grew larger in his sight. It was pierced and jagged from the fearful barrage—but still a lethal three-ton projectile. "I don't believe it! These *gaijin* do know how to die!"

And so did he, because a heartbeat later the hatchet smashed through the low domed skull of his *Grand Dragon* and crushed him to red jelly.

As the samurai joined the *Hatchetman* pilot in death, a horizontal storm of fire blew up the street into the faces of Lainie and A Company. Realizing how seriously she had misjudged the mercs' valor, Lainie now knew that her First Battalion was caught in a vee-shaped trap. She made a fast, tough call.

The military pundits of Sun Zhang MechWarrior Academy considered it poor form to commit reserves early in battle, subtracting major points if an officer did so in exercise. But this was no exercise, and as far as Lainie was concerned, the only referees were Victory and Defeat.

"Third Battalion," she ordered, "advance to support B Company. Sideslip two hundred meters north; try to catch the *gaijin* on the flanks. A Company will attack to the northeast."

"Who-ee," Staff Sergeant Willard Dix said, peering out the crack of the manhole cover he was holding open with one hand. "That's one mighty expensive bonfire they got goin' out there."

Reeking, frozen, and tired, Cassie's little commando team had managed to make it a little more than halfway to their objective before running out of sewer pipe both big enough to negotiate and headed anywhere near the hotel where Ninyu Kerai Indrahar had his command post. As it was, they had been forced to duckwalk in shin-deep filth the last two hundred meters. Even Cassie felt as if her thighs were about to split open, which she attributed to the inability to maintain the customary pace of her workouts during her stint as the Earl of Hachiman's house guest.

Monkey-like she swarmed past Dix up the side of the manhole's steel-rung ladder to peer out. The overcast morning light seemed blinding after the sewer darkness. Blinking into the glare, Cassie could see that the sergeant was right.

The heart of Masamori was ablaze. PPC beams, shellbursts, lasers, and missiles had set off scores of fires. Though Hachiman's capital had been built to be fireproof, a quick glimpse showed Cassie a half-dozen buildings fully swallowed up in infernos, including a hundred-story bronze behemoth. Down below several of her troopies coughed as the amazingly varied smokes of urban battle rolled in through the manhole opening. There was the nose-pinching smell of burning rubber, the astringent chemical stench of burned plastic and polymer, the husky smells of paper and furniture burning in habitations and businesses. Overlying everything was the sweet, down-home barbecue tang of burning human flesh.

The noise was mind-numbing. It seemed to stab in between the lip of the manhole and its cover like blinding sunlight through cracks in a wall. There was no sense to the din, no sense of the individual noises that composed it. Just a constant roar beyond white noise, rising and falling to the rhythmless beat of heavy-metal battle. If not for the bone-conduction speaker taped behind her ear, Cassie would never have heard the sergeant's comment.

She slapped Dix's shoulder, pointed. He nodded, flowed out onto the surface like oil in reverse. For reasons best known to themselves, the Masamori city planners had put their manholes dead in the middle of intersections, at least in this part of town. Dix raced for the intersection's northwest corner, where mannequins dressed in the latest fashions watched the battle from behind glass, frozen into postures of synthetic gaiety. Cassie came right behind.

The rest of the squad was close on their heels. Barnes and his sniper team had already split off. The other eleven sprinted in ones and twos to join their fellows crouched on the sidewalk, with the largely illusory protection of the building corner between them and the battle.

They were way too close for comfort. Cassie could see part of the Adelante force that had taken Colonel Shimazu by surprise, slugging it out with Ghosts less than half a klick distant. There were 'Mechs down; rising from one smoldering pile of ruin she could just make out the finned-banana shape of what she feared was the head of Benito Delshay's *Hatchetman*.

Adelante seemed to be trying to fade back. Cassie saw Gabby Camacho's *Shadow Hawk* riding high on its jump jets, soaring away over a three-story structure as lines of fire converged on it. Reb Perez' *Awesome* stood square in the street, apparently covering its mates' withdrawal. His slab-fronted assault 'Mech was taking a beating, drooling smoke from its flared shoulder housings. But the defiant Cowboy was giving his twenty double-capacity heat sinks a workout, blasting with his fearful main armament of three extended-range PPCs and a medium pulse laser as fast as the weapons would cycle.

Down the street a Drac 'Mech exploded. Overhead glass shattered as a freak blast-wave reflection slammed upper-story windows. The fragments fell among the Scouts like razor snow. Cassie looked in horror at the great display windows directly above her; if they went, the resulting sheets of sharp glass would fall directly on top of the little clump of Caballeros. It would be like a mortar round going off in their midst.

The big windows shivered and boomed with musical-saw dissonance, but held. The rising popularity of *dekigoro-zoku* gangs, youngsters who roved the streets in search of opportunities for vandalism, smash-and-grab theft, and the occasional head to crack, had made it expedient for street-level shop owners to shell out for transpex windows.

It was the sort of battle that contributed so greatly to the thirty-first-century footslogger's sense of helplessness in the face of the armored leviathans who ruled the battlefield. Even if the Scouts had been participants, instead of unwilling spectators, in the combat, the BattleMechs wouldn't have deigned to pay attention to them.

But even without intention, 'Mechs were lethal to puny humans. As the last scouts emerged from the manhole to dart for cover, the Ghosts charged, firing furiously at Perez' stricken *Awesome*. One heavy laser missed the 'Mech and brushed the running scouts like the wings of the Angel of Death.

Contreras the *truchaseño* simply exploded like an insect that had blundered into an electronic bug zapper. Billy

Huckaby, the Black hillbilly who was the baby of the platoon, fell down screaming, hair and jacket on fire, polymer armor melting to his flesh.

Petie McTeague, who came from a non-landholding Cowboy clan and so was regarded as just as no-account as any hillbilly, started forward to help. Cassie grabbed the pantsleg bloused above his right boot and tackled him.

"You can't help him!" she shouted, though she knew he couldn't hear her.

Overshot autocannon-fire splashed the intersection. Billy Huckaby's body was torn to pieces as though by invisible fingers. McTeague turned and rolled back into cover, sobbing and holding his face, which had been peppered by fragments.

The *Awesome* exploded. Perez didn't eject.

Standing in a side street, Cowboy Payson saw his sidekick's 'Mech go. Bellowing rage, he started his little *Wasp* back toward the fight.

His other pal Buck Evans blocked him with the medium laser that made up his *Orion*'s right forearm. "Nothin' you can do now," the older MechWarrior said, " 'cept throw your life away. Just tell yourself it don't mean nothin'."

Payson's 'Mech almost seemed to sigh. "Yeah," he radioed back in a jagged voice. "It don't mean nothin'."

They faded north. They weren't done fighting yet.

Cassie glared at the approaching Ghosts in hatred so fierce it seemed to squeeze from the pores of her skin like oil. *Arrogant bastards! They think the only infantry that can hurt them is Elementals!*

She would show them. Cassie had nothing but disdain for the outsized Clan foot soldiers that the warriors of the Inner Sphere had nicknamed "toads." What Elementals only dared to do wrapped in their massive powered armor, she dared do naked—and had. These Dracs would see—

A touch on her arm. "Cassie," Dix said. "C'mon. It ain't our fight."

She shook herself. The sergeant was right. The driving need to punish BattleMechs and their arrogant pilots faded within her like the voice of someone falling down a well. She wondered whether that was a result of Lady K's counsel, or of the fact that she had an appointment with the red-haired man.

The Ghosts had started taking flanking fire from the north, were facing left to deal with it. The din of battle dimmed.

Cassie looked at her squad. "Listen up, people. I'm a hunter, a lone-wolf killer, not a leader. Win or lose, I'm going to get most of you killed."

She took a breath. "If you want out, go now, any or all of you. I'll go in alone if that's what it takes."

Yvonne Sánchez, the blocky little blaster from New Acoma on Sierra, grinned at her. "Shoot, Cass. You can't get rid of us that easy."

Cassie looked around at the others. One by one they nodded.

"Your funeral," she said with a shrug, and led off to the northwest.

Force Commander Gavilán Camacho screamed like his namesake in helpless rage.

Deep inside he still burned with shame for his failure during the fight with the terrorists. Even though the young-Turk faction called him the hero of that action, what *he* remembered was going face-first into the Fab building.

And during the abortive coup against his father—when the core group had come to him, Vanity and Bobby the Wolf and Baird and, astonishingly, his father's faithful shadow *la Dama Muerte*, he had bravely professed a total lack of desire to supplant his father. That was a lie, of course, and he had proven it by not telling them straight out to forget it. He had betrayed his father in his heart. It was a sin he had not dared confess even to Father Montoya, who was, after all, also his father's confessor.

Patricia would never have crashed her 'Mech. And she would have cursed Gordo and the rest for the faithless dogs they were. Don Carlos was right, Gabby knew, to have favored her all those years. Though she was only a woman, he knew miserably that she had been twice the man he was.

But he could redeem himself, in his own eyes and—with the help of the saints—his father's, if he could only prove once and for all that he was a worthy MechWarrior.

In Adelante Company's slashing attack in conjunction with Bronco, he had killed two enemy 'Mechs, an *Urban-Mech* and a *Whitworth*. But he had paid a price, blazing off

the whole ammo load for his *Imperator* Ultra autocannon.
The Martell medium laser mounted on his right arm had
been burned off, and a swarm of SRMs had pounded the
Shadow Hark's head and upper torso, filling his cockpit with
sparks and the stink of burning insulation. Now all his
weapon-control systems were dead. He couldn't even get a
display to tell him the *Imperator* had run dry.

"Gavilán," his father's voice said. "What is it, my son?"

Gabby ground his teeth so hard they creaked. "My weapons have all been knocked out, Father."

"Then return within the walls at once. Captain MacDougall will take over the battalion."

"No!"

"Do it, for God's sake," came the voice of Lady K. "No
point in you getting killed."

Gabby's lips curled in a soundless snarl. Part of him tried
to believe that the tight-assed *bolilla* bitch was trying to grab
his job, but his heart knew that wasn't true. If he stayed in
the fight unarmed, he'd be a liability, not a hero.

He punched up the general freak. "Attention, First Battalion. This is Force Commander Camacho. My 'Mech is disabled." A pause. "I'm turning command of the Battalion
over to Captain MacDougall and returning to base."

37

Masamori, Hachiman
Galedon District, Draconis Combine
2 November 3056

"**C**aptain, the tidal bore has passed."

"I can see that," *Tai-i* Roger Hanson said. He rubbed his
sandy-bearded chin and slowly grinned.

It had been a nervous time waiting among the godowns of
the seedy Two Moons district southwest along the Yamato
from HTE Compound. Now that the brutal flood tide had

passed, the wait was over. Hanson felt relief and a warm spreading prickle of anticipation.

The bottom of the Yamato was soft; his special company consisted of most of Third Battalion's light and medium 'Mechs, none heavier than his own fifty-ton *Trebuchet*. He would lead twelve machines wading laboriously upstream, with nothing approaching cover once they got in sight of their objective. Facing them would be elements of a regiment of mercenaries already aroused by the efforts of the rest of the Ninth and firing from defilade.

What he was so eager to commence looked like suicide.

The *Trebuchet* had the appearance of a stout man wearing an ancient sallet helmet. It waded into the chill, now-sluggish water with a certain gingerly air, like a middle-age *sarariman* who belonged to a polar bear club, out for some frigid skinny-dipping. The other 'Mechs followed, clambering or jumping down from the crumbling cement docks.

Captain Hanson, who raised prize salukis in his spare time, was not much daunted by the ordeal awaiting him. He had been through the hell of the Clan invasion, and had won a challenge death-duel with a Ghost Bear in a *Fenris*. The upside of his desperate mission was that if he could catch the *gaijin* paying too much attention to the assaults from west and south, his little force might effectively take them by surprise in a rear attack, with the usual devastating morale effects.

Besides, he'd been through his share of city fighting. From almost three klicks away he could actually see flames pouring from the windows of a burning skyscraper, saw the heat-shimmer above what seemed the whole of downtown Masamori. He knew his lightweights were lucky to be out of that.

Leaning his *Trebuchet* forward against the slow roll of Yamato-*san*, he led his troops to the attack.

The arrival of the Ghost reserves caught Lady K by surprise as she was accepting command of the battalion from Gavilán.

Bronco's western flank was anchored by Lieutenant Annie Sue Hurd in her *Rifleman*. Kali had been holding Hurd back out of the thick of the savage streetfight for medium and long-range firepower support. As a result, when the Ghost Second Battalion's lead lance of four heavy and assault

'Mechs came over the rise from the traffic circle, Hurd was the first Caballero they encountered.

"This is Avengin' Annie," Hurd broadcast. " 'Mechs attacking from the west; I see a *Marauder,* a *JagerMech,* a *Charger,* and an *Atlas.* There are others coming on behind. I call it at least a company."

"Clear out of there, Annie," Lady K ordered.

The rest of Bronco was already hard into it with the Ghosts. If the new assault couldn't be delayed, it would roll right over them. Hurd turned her Little Sure Shot to face the advancing BattleMechs.

"Sorry, Lady K," Hurd said, "Cannot comply."

She concentrated the fire of her paired autocannon and large lasers against the legs of the *JagerMech,* the least threatening of the lead lance. It was also the lightest armored, and consequently the one she judged the most likely to get hurt in the time she had.

The borders of Lainie's HUD abruptly turned red. "I'm being painted," she said over the company band.

A Company was pushing east toward the walls again, driving the *Gaijin* before it. After a brief but brutal slugfest, the mercenaries had pulled a fast fade. Several of the more impressionable Ghosts had hooted triumphant derision, believing the foe to be on the run.

Lainie shut them up in short order. The Caballeros were retreating rapidly, but they were still sticking and sniping as they went. Her people had hurt them bad, but had taken a mauling in the process. As far as Lainie could see, the *gaijin* remnants to their front were retiring in good order, having accomplished as much as they could have hoped to.

And they hadn't taken themselves out of the fight yet. Shifting her *Mauler* against the buildings on the south side of the street, for what shelter they might give, Lainie searched the surrounding streets and buildings with both her eyes and 'Mech sensors. She saw no enemy machines at all. In truth there weren't a lot of places on the wide business-district thoroughfare for something the size of a BattleMech to *hide.* But someone was unmistakably lighting her up with a TAG infrared beam—and she was caught mid-block the way van Doorn had been.

"Tai-sa," Moon said, "you must withdraw."

"Negative! Company A, prepare for antimissile defense, and *find me that spotter!*"

"Arrows incoming," Usagi reported from his *Javelin*.

Lainie saw the smoke vines rising from behind the walls and frowned. It was unacceptable to be taken out of the fight at this stage. Fate had betrayed her.

The Ghosts fired ferociously as the mercenary missiles streaked down toward their commander's 'Mech. This time they missed altogether.

Shig Hofstra's *Kintaro* darted in front of Revenge and leapt. Lacking jump jets, the 'Mech used only the strength of the myomer pseudomuscles in its legs. That sufficed. Both big enemy missiles struck it in the chest, blew it open, and sent it smashing back into Lainie's 'Mech.

Lainie fought but couldn't stay upright. Her *Mauler* fell onto its back, buckling the blacktop, the impact knocking her senseless despite the protective cushions around her.

BattleMechs clustered around her. "*Tai-sa—*" Moon said.

As Lainie came back to herself, a shape that had tugged unacknowledged at the periphery of her vision resolved itself suddenly in her mind. "The parking garage!" she exclaimed, struggling her 'Mech to its feet.

"*Tai-sa?*" That was Buntaro Mayne in his *Phoenix Hawk*, whose left arm had been blown off.

"Parking garage, third floor!" Lainie pointed her right large laser at a ten-story structure seven hundred meters northeast. By chance none of the Yamato-style skyscrapers had been built in its immediate vicinity. It commanded an excellent view both of the Compound and the streets approaching it. "Don't stand there gaping, you fools, *look.*"

They did. Just in time to see the drooped beak of the pesky *Raven* ducking back out of sight. The beam Lainie squirted at it just missed.

"*Tai-i* Mayne!"

"*Hai!*"

"Take three light 'Mechs and get me that damn *Raven.*"

The *Atlas'* large laser penetrated the armor of Little Sure Shot's head, filling the cockpit with terrible ruby glare. Strapped into the passenger seat, Bunny Bear burst into flames. Avengin' Annie cried out, more in grief at the loss of her beloved friend than from fear for herself.

The *Marauder's* PPCs followed up the laser hit. Lieutenant SG Annie Sue Hurd vanished in a painless flash, before she could register that the smell in her nostrils was her own flesh burning.

"Uh-oh," Raven said—to herself, thumbing down the suppress button on her radio. That red-haired witch had more lives than the old three-legged tortoiseshell tom on her daddy's ranch. And like that venerable barnyard scrapper, the Ghost commander didn't have any quit in her. She came up brushing away what was left of the *Kintaro* that had saved her and then pointed straight at Raver.

Raven wheeled, bolted, the ferro-fibrous bird feet of her machine striking keening sparks off the cement floor of the parking garage.

A pink flash lit her display. From behind her came a bang, followed by big lumps of cement raining down on the back of her 'Mech. That damned Shimazu woman had taken a potshot at her for good measure.

Raven grinned tautly under her neurohelmet. Hell, she'd *liked* the Drac colonel and the other Ghosts she'd met; so did most of the 'lleros. But Caballeros lived by a simple rule: *Come to hurt us, you'd best be prepared to tussle, 'cause we'll try our damnedest to hurt you first and worst.*

She ran between squat cement pillars toward the down ramp. No more than a scattering of cars were parked on this floor, most of the garage's patrons being day shift Middle-Class types who'd been caught home by the sealing-off of the Murasaki district. Raven hoped they were insured.

She heard a thump behind her, saw movement to her rear in the viewstrip. She wheeled, with the two medium lasers in her right "wing" snapping.

A Ghost *Jenner* had jumped onto the open deck of the garage. It stood with knees bent so that the missile launcher above its forward-thrust head would clear the ceiling. Its own medium lasers flared back. Raven's viewscreen automatically dimmed. When it brightened, a fresh furrow glowed white in Raver's beak.

The *Jenny* was no heavier than Raver, and its frontal armor wasn't quite as good. But with four Victory medium lasers and a Telos SRM quad launcher, it boasted substantially better firepower than Raven had, though her six-pack launcher was Narc-assisted. Much of a *Raven*'s 35 tons was taken up by fancy sensing, sighting, and target-designation electronics. It was not a dedicated hassler like the *Jenner.*

Besides, the *Jenner*'s presence proved that the Ghosts knew where she was. Others would undoubtedly be looking to enter the garage at ground level. They'd take her from behind if she tried to slug it out.

For luck, she fired an SRM salvo at the enemy 'Mech, then wheeled and ran. Her 'Mech had poor rear armor—with some divots knocked out of it already—and was slower than a *Jenny* to boot. But Raven O'Connor had been herding giant, long-horned Rangers in an AgroMech since the age of nine. She'd pit her shiftiness on the concrete floor—slick to metal 'Mech feet even where it wasn't smeared with grease from notoriously leaky Drac crankcases—against the Ghost's laser wattage and speed any day.

Besides, she had an ace up her sleeve. If she only got a chance to play it.

Darting, weaving, skidding madly around cement pillars while laser beams cracked past her ears, Raven raced for the ramp.

"Don Carlos?"

The commander of the Seventeenth Recon sat in the cockpit of his command *Mad Cat,* standing before the steps of Uncle Chandy's Citadel. The C3 displays kept him as informed as possible of the chaotic passage of the battle. He had just directed Captain MacDougall to bring what was left of First Battalion back inside the Compound. His mind was lucid today; he felt none of the terrible lethargy that had gripped him during the Word of Blake attack.

"Yes, Zuma," he replied over the communicator.

"*Coronel,* Lady K has asked me to give First Battalion a song."

Camacho nodded. It was not an unusual request. The 'lleros often asked their chief balladeer and master-of-trades to bolster morale with his songs in tough situations. The Chief Aztech was already at work repairing Second and Third Battalion 'Mechs damaged by the Ghosts hitting the south wall. But he could have his assistants rig up a mike, and sing as he worked.

"Of course, Zuma," he said, mildly surprised. "You don't need to ask."

"But *patrón*," Zuma said, "there is a particular song which I wish to sing them."

"Which one?"

"The one I've written in honor of your daughter, Patricia."

"No. I am sorry, but that I cannot permit."

A pause, crackling and singing with distant energy-weapon discharges. "Very well, *patrón*. Zuma out."

Don Carlos sighed. He drummed thick-gloved fingers on the arms of his narrow command couch. He was impatient for the *culebras* to come and get on with it.

Because there was a reason for his return to mental clarity. He had finally come to terms with his grief and self-doubt.

Despite Cassie's harangue, he had decided that today was a good day to die.

Her darting, erratic progress having frustrated the *Jenner* jock into standing stock still to try to put some solid hits into her, Raven had actually managed to extend her lead a hair by the time she reached the second floor. Instead of coming down the same ramp, she lit out across the echoing chamber for another.

As the *Jenner* pounded down the ramp behind her, Raven eased off the throttle until she saw the Ghost 'Mech's feet come into view. Then she thumbed the trigger hard.

At the foot of the ramp the *Jenner* tried to turn too quickly, skidded, almost fell over the rail out into the street. But Raven wasn't quite that lucky, nor was she in any position to help the *Jenny* along with a short-range missile or two. The Ghost jock regained control of his machine and came drumming in pursuit.

In the rearview portion of her three-sixty strip Raven kept a careful eye on the *Jenner*'s progress. When it passed beneath a cement joist with a yellow bar painted on it, she uncovered a button on a special unit taped to the arm of her seat. When the enemy reached a blue marker, she hit the button.

Sixteen shaped charges strapped to a four-by-four array of cement pillars went off with a rippling *crack*. At the same time other precisely placed charges cut joists and steel beams in the ceiling.

The *Jenner* vanished in an earthquake rumble and a cloud of dust as a several-hundred-ton section of the third floor fell on its head.

* * *

Raven hit the ground floor at a run. At the base of the other ramp, a *Javelin,* a *Locust,* and a seriously hunched-over, one-armed *Phoenix Hawk* stood in a clump peering up, as if trying to figure out what the awful racket was.

Twenty-five meters away an exit opened to the street. Raven went for it. The three Ghosts reacted quickly and smart, just shooting, not chasing. Raven felt hits rock her 'Mech, saw red lights spray across her boards like self-luminous paint. She gritted her teeth, keeping Raven upright through sheer force of will.

She had just reached the striped wooden barrier when a shot from one of the *Phoenix Hawk*'s lasers fused her right hip actuator. Inertia sent Raver hurtling forward to shatter the barrier and plow a furrow in the street outside with its beak.

The hammered remnants of Adelante and Bronco collapsed back on the Compound. Battalion commander MacDougall faced a final problem: getting non-jumping 'Mechs, including her own *Atlas,* safely inside.

At the base of the wall First Battalion turned and lashed out at its pursuers. The Ghosts, who thought they had finally broken their enemy's spirit, faltered and halted.

While Bobby the Wolf was out doing a little headhunting, his Cochise had for the most part done little but engage in a staring match with the Ghost C Company. Now, while the huge gates opened with glacial deliberation, he led the surviving jump-capable 'Mechs of First Battalion in a whirlwind attack to keep the Ghosts off-balance.

Stalled several hundred meters from the Compound, the Ghosts concentrated their fire on the gates, but Bobby's slash at their flanks quickly broke up that concentration. Kali MacDougall's Dark Lady was the last machine to lumber out of the firestorm into the temporary shelter of the Compound. Then, as the gates wound shut again, Bobby Begay's impromptu combat team soared over the wall.

With a hiss of heated air, the fallen *Raven*'s hatch popped open. Raven O'Connor clambered out, yanking off her neurohelmet. She tossed it aside and sprinted for the shelter of a shop whose windows had been melted out by a grazing strike from a PPC.

The one-armed *Phoenix Hawk* emerged behind her, straightened, then stood gazing down at the fallen BattleMech.

A whistle of jump jets. A *Wasp* with yellow and black stripes on its chest and its right-arm laser sheared away dropped onto the *Phoenix Hawk* from above. Armor buckled, and the PH went sprawling.

Buntaro Mayne rolled the PH and tried to bring his large laser "rifle" to bear on his attacker. The *Wasp* lashed out with a foot, destroying the weapon in the *Hawk*'s grasp.

"Better pack it in, good buddy," came a voice from the Caballero 'Mech's loudspeakers. "I got the drop on you."

"Cowboy?" the *Phoenix Hawk*'s speaker boomed. "Cowboy Payson?"

"Buntaro?"

Buntaro Mayne laughed. "I guess you still haven't learned your lesson, Cowboy," he said, and launched his 'Mech in a charge against the other warrior's machine.

As the Ghost Second Battalion and the battered First advanced on the wall, Lainie ordered the Third's two companies to step up the attack in the south. Not as surprised by Caballero *seishin* as the young samurai had been, she felt—briefly—in her gut the need to squeeze any advantage she could grab until the blood ran out.

She had the *gaijin* withdrawing—fine. Even if the maneuver was planned, the fact of retreat had a marked effect on morale. She would jam the attack to them as hard as she could.

Beaten bronze evanesced into plasma at the first kiss of PPC beams. Beneath the veneer, however, the gates were hundred-ton slabs of ferro-fibrous armor plate. From either side heavy weapons-fire flayed the advancing 'Mechs—all the more reason to throw everything she had into the defenders' faces. She had to make them flinch back from the walls. Then she could jump 'Mechs inside, including assault-class *Victor*s and *Katana* and one lifter-equipped MAD-5D *Marauder.* Her earthbound heavies could rumble through as soon as the gates or walls were breached.

And if the scratch company wading up the Yamato happened to arrive at a propitious moment—she actually smiled, despite the pain in her soul and mangled hand. Even the bravest troops had been known to shatter like a dropped sheet of glass when caught from behind while locked in battle.

The *Wasp* brought its elbow down hard on the *Phoenix Hawk*'s round head, denting it and jarring Mayne enough that he relaxed his grip. Then Cowboy pulsed his Rawlings jump jets to lift him off the pavement, clutched-in the gyros to snap him upright.

The *Phoenix Hawk* started to climb to its feet. "You can't win, Cowboy," Mayne said over his loudspeaker. "My machine's twice as heavy as yours."

The *Wasp* cut its jump jets and landed feet first on the other 'Mech's head. "It ain't the meat," Cowboy said, "it's the motion."

The *Phoenix Hawk* rose straight up on its own back-mounted jump jets, not quite so flash a maneuver as Cowboy's, but enough to get it back on its feet. Its right fist lashed out and caught Yellowjacket in the face.

It was Cowboy's turn to be stunned by a blow, his 'Mech staggering back under it. The backs of its legs fetched up against the wrecked *Raven*.

As Mayne lunged for him, Cowboy jumped straight up, soaring with the full force of his jump jets.

Face to face they rose, straight up, rising high among bronze towers. The *Wasp* kept striking down at the PH with its fist while Mayne got his machine's remaining arm around the smaller 'Mech's waist and snugged his head against its hips.

As the two 'Mechs reached the apex of their vertical jump, they began to fall back to earth, both pilots continuing to wrestle while braking their fall with pulses of their jets.

It was an inherently unstable system. Fifty meters above the street the writhing machines fell off the thrust-columns of their jets. At that point they had the glide characteristics of, say, a dropped anvil.

Fortunately, they did not fall the whole fifty meters back to the street. There was a four-story brick building under them to cushion their fall.

More or less.

"What do you mean you're taking my ride?" Lieutenant JG Alberto Jaramillo demanded. His voice echoed off the tiles of the deserted Tubeway station, which had been scrubbed clean of most of the bloodstains from the Word of Blake raid.

"Just that, Berto," Gavilán Camacho said. "I'm commandeering your 'Mech." It wasn't something anybody in the Regiment would exactly have predicted. The younger Camacho was known to aspire to bigger 'Mechs than his *Shadow Hawk*—whose weapons systems could not be repaired in time to get him back in the fight, no matter how loud the young Force Commander yelled at Zuma, Astro Zombie, or Chief Armorer Bogdan Michael "Stacks" Stachiewski. Yet here he was pulling rank to get into the cockpit of a *Scorpion*. Not only was the 'Mech the same weight as Red-tailed Hawk, it was also the least popular 'Mech in the outfit.

With the help of Abdulsattah's people—and even more, well in advance of the fact, from Uncle Chandy and his designers—the Seventeenth was preparing one final surprise for the Ghosts.

Though the gate was burned through, no Ghost 'Mechs had forced an entry. It was, of course, only a matter of time. Once they got inside, they would still face a bitter fight in the city-in-miniature that was the Compound, but they would have grabbed that much more of the initiative.

In planning his stronghold Chandrasekhar Kurita had considered that one day he might wish to have a way of getting 'Mechs in or out of the Compound without their being seen. Secretly, the underground Tubeway station had been roofed with a movable cement slab. Slid back it revealed a BattleMech-sized opening into a tunnel large enough to allow 'Mechs passage if they could keep low enough. Of course, the only ones able to do that were in the 30-ton and lighter class.

With one exception. The 55-ton *Scorpion* was one of the few four-legged BattleMech designs ever built. It was ugly as sin and had a horrible, kidney-jarring, single-footed gait like a mule. But it mounted a highly respectable Magna Firestar extended-range PPC. And most important, it was low-slung enough to pass through the Tubeway tunnel under the Compound.

It was an obvious choice to lend some muscle to the twelve light 'Mechs from Second and Third Battalions assigned to exfiltrate through the Tubeway and jump the Ghosts from the rear.

"But I'm supposed to lead the attack!" Jaramillo complained. An edge of whine crept into his voice, for which it was hard to blame him. It wasn't often that Lieutenants Junior Grade got to command a company.

"Not any more," Gavilán Camacho said.

"Go easy there, big fella," Cowboy Payson said as Buntaro Mayne hauled him from the wreckage of his *Wasp*. "I think my leg's busted."

The Ghost captain dragged the mercenary against a still-standing wall. The two BattleMechs lay entwined in a giant mound of rubble at street level, the fight obviously over for both.

Cowboy shifted his butt, trying to get comfortable. From the pallor of his face and the way sweat glued lank hair to his forehead, it was obvious he was in pain.

He looked at Mayne, who seemed to be uninjured, except that his good eye was blacked. "I'm not gonna have to hurt you, am I?" the mercenary asked.

Mayne laughed. "If I was a DCMS regular, honor would require me to kill you, no matter what shape we were in. Fortunately, I'm nothing but a low-down yakuza."

He sat heavily down. "And to tell you the truth, I feel like I've done enough for one day."

Cowboy was staring at a mound of rubble that did not quite conceal an elaborate musicbox.

"Say," he said, "do you realize where we *are*?"

The Ghost shook his head.

"Son, we went and fell through the roof of the old Permissible Repose."

Mayne was studying something he had pulled from the rubble: a little blue figure of Krishna playing his flute. "So we did."

"You know what that means?"

The one-eyed yakuza nodded. "It means," he said gravely, "that the drinks are on the house."

38

Two ISF commandos stood flanking the main doors of the Coordinator's Rest Hotel. As usual, they had straight-bladed ninjato swords strapped point-down across their backs, and held unslung Shimatsu 42s in patrol position, diagonally before their waists. In a little noodle shop across the street, Cassie and three members of her squad crouched behind the counter, insulated black balaclavas pulled down over their faces.

For all the fancy sensory gear built into the black suits, the DEST team were unlikely to spot the four unless actively looking for them. Cassie fervently hoped they'd given them no reason to do so.

Besides, there was plenty of incentive to look elsewhere.

The battle-clamor had died to a dull thunderstorm roar from somewhere behind them. The 'lleros were falling back into the Compound. That was all according to plan—as long as they had laid sufficient hurt on the Ghosts. From a few impressionistic glimpses, Cassie guessed the Seventeenth had inflicted a few more casualties than they'd suffered.

In this bizarre battle, that was victory. But it was transient.

The knowledge almost crushed her, that ultimately her MechWarrior comrades *couldn't* win. Only she could win; and if she failed, it would doom the Seventeenth to destruction no matter how they fared against their erstwhile friends of the Ninth Ghost Regiment. Because as long as Ninyu Kerai Indrahar and his father believed Uncle Chandy was a traitor to name and Combine, they would continue to hurl the Dragon's might against him in ever-larger doses, until the Caballeros drowned in a torrent of steel, fire, and blood.

She glanced at her companions. They nodded, looking like photonegative raccoons in the gloom. She reached up and turned on the communicator sewn into a pouch on her vest. They had shut down their radios at a point perhaps half a klick from the uncompleted hotel, taking for granted that the ISF had sophisticated RDF gear inside that could detect sets that were turned on, even without their transmitting.

Very soon now the Dracs would know the Scouts were there anyway. She broke squelch with her thumb, three clicks.

Five heartbeats later the right-hand sentry flew backward through the plate glass window into the lobby.

As with their sensors, there were tradeoffs to the environmentally sealed suits the DEST killers wore. Protection cost them flexibility, and like Cassie, the ISF agents opted for agility, wearing lightweight armor instead of bulky assault vests with steel-ceramic laminate inserts like the ones several of Cassie's team wore.

Of course, not even an armored assault vest would withstand the impact of a Zeus sniper's round the size of Cassie's little finger traveling five times the speed of sound. The bullet went clean through the DEST commando and shattered the supposedly bulletproof glass—not transpex—behind him.

The other sentry reacted just the way a DEST member would in the holos, dropping to one knee and bringing her Shimatsu up without an eyeblink's hesitation. Cassie, Elizondo, McTeague, and Absalom Sloat already had their machine pistols leveled over the counter.

In the action holodramas people were always doing things like knocking out windows with the butts of their weapons before shooting. That always made Cassie crazy; if you could *bust* it out, why not just *shoot* it out and drop your target at the same time? As near as she could tell, it was generally done so that the heroes would have the sound of breaking glass to warn them, instead of starting to spring leaks before they knew anything was wrong. Just as movie ninja—DEST and traditional—always blew their whole game plan by uttering a chilling scream before attacking their victims from behind. *Dumb.*

The noodle shop's window was not bulletproof. Supposedly that didn't matter; Uncle Chandy had provided bootleg 10-mm ammunition that would allegedly defeat most bulletproofing shy of actual armor plates. Not even DEST used such ammo, at least not within the Combine. For one thing, Combine citizens were not permitted body armor, and it also reduced the risk of the ISF operatives injuring each other in those embarrassing crossfire situations that so often developed in the heat of combat.

The window blew out satisfactorily as the scouts opened up. The kneeling DEST agent went over backward without even getting off a shot. That might bode well for the effectiveness of the ammunition—but with flexible armor, a dozen close-range torso hits would almost certainly put you down from broken ribs, if nothing else, even if they didn't penetrate. But the hotel window broke on that side too, which was a positive sign.

At the sound of shooting the rest of the commandos were supposed to switch on their radios. "Let's go," Cassie subvocalized into the mike-patch taped to her larynx. She vaulted the counter and ran for the street, the others close behind.

" *'Mechs!* José y María, *they're coming out of the river!"*

Slowly and inexorably, the Dracs pushed into the Compound from the west. From Great White's cockpit Colonel Camacho was fading elements out of the fight at the south wall, where the assault was not being pressed as single-mindedly, and throwing them into the breach.

He had not yet committed his own 'Mech to action. He wanted to choose his moment to die. Besides, despite the pain of knowing that his sons and daughters, the MechWarriors of the Seventeenth, were suffering and dying under *culebra* guns, he was rather having fun.

The warning cry jolted him from command mode to combat mode. He kicked Great White into motion, moving around to the south side of the towering Citadel.

As he rounded the corner, he saw them. A *Trebuchet* had already touched down inside the grounds. Other 'Mechs were descending from the clouds—like angels, he thought.

He smiled inside his helmet. These manifestations were definitely on the wrong side to be angels. Lieutenant Teresa Chávez would rag him *forever* if she knew he was harboring such heretical thoughts.

Across the river the snow fell heavily upon Sodegarami.

In fact, snow was falling to all sides. But none fell upon the blazing heart of Masamori.

It says much about our sins, Don Carlos thought, that God suffers His pure white snow to fall upon the Floating World, but not upon us.

Slowly he walked his *Mad Cat* to meet the intruding 'Mechs. He understood too well what had happened. The *Mirza*'s blue-jumpsuited security troopers were very good at what they did. But taking the brunt of a full-out assault by an entire veteran regiment of BattleMechs was not in their job descriptions. They had all gotten caught up watching the terrifying yet exhilarating display of *Tai-sa* Shimazu's forces gnawing their way to the heart of Hachiman Taro Compound, and had forgotten to keep an eye on the river.

As the enemy 'Mechs landed, they winged out to both sides until they faced Great White in a rough semicircle.

"Not too many captive *Mad Cat*s in the Inner Sphere," boomed the *Trebuchet*'s loudspeakers, "much less with that shark smile painted on the snout. Colonel Camacho, I presume."

"*Sí*. Whom have I the honor of addressing?"

"*Tai-i* Hanson, of the Ninth Ghost Regiment." The *Trebuchet* gestured with its left hand. "I'm calling on you to surrender, Colonel. This game is over. I know you're riding a *Mad Cat*—which means you were man enough to take it from the Clans in the first place. And we're just little guys. But we're twelve to your one."

Indeed, Don Carlos thought, and what a glorious song Zuma can make of my passing. He felt shamed, then, for not permitting the Chief Aztech to sing the song he had composed for Patsy. It was sheer pettiness, a last lingering hurt committed by an unworthy father. But Zuma was wise; he would know to sing Patsy's song at Don Carlos' funeral.

If any of Caballeros survived. But what more fitting way for their Colonel to die than fending off this attack in the rear long enough for a counter to be mounted?

"I regret," he said, "that I must decline your kind offer." Deliberately, so as to make his intentions abundantly clear—for he would die an honorable man, as he had tried to live as one—the Colonel raised the big PPCs that tipped either arm.

A shadow passed over him. He looked up through the canopy's top panel to see the unmistakable form of his son's

Shadow Hawk sailing overhead. Straight for the enemy company.

"Gavilán, *no!*" he screamed. "You're unarmed!"

Red-tailed Hawk touched down in front of him. It wobbled, then bent its legs and jumped at Hanson's BattleMech.

The Ghosts opened fire. Sensing wounded prey, they ignored the Colonel's *Mad Cat* to concentrate on the airborne *Shadow Hawk*.

Red-tail's armor was already shredded from the pounding it had taken in the streets of Murasaki. For one soul-tearing moment Don Carlos watched his son's machine hang against the clouds, crucified in fire.

The next moment the 'Mech blew apart in midair. There was no parachute.

"*No!*" Don Carlos screamed again. He tipped the *Mad Cat* forward into a run at its terrible, full OmniMech speed.

He no longer intended to die. Indeed, his own survival or otherwise had become immaterial to him.

His whole intention was to kill. His only remaining child had been slaughtered before his eyes.

He would wash those eyes clean in Drac blood.

Lieutenant SG Teresa de Avila Chávez—*la Guadalupana*—died leading a charge into the flank of the salient the Ghosts had driven like a spear into the Compound's side. No fewer than five MechWarriors swore later that in the flames gushing upward from her *Crusader* they saw angels swooping to cover the stricken heroine with their wings and bear her bodily up to Heaven.

Muzzle flashes flickered inside the hotel, bright in the unlit lobby. At Cassie's side Sergeant Dix grunted but kept running as he took a body hit. From behind she heard a wail; another one of her people hadn't been so lucky.

She had a grenade in hand, lobbed it underhand through a blown-in window. Then her whole squad went face down on the blacktop. An explosion, followed by tendrils of white smoke and screams.

On their feet again, the squad charged, firing as they ran. The gunfire that took out the two sentries had solved one problem: how to get inside. Both the electric-eye door and the revolving door were surely locked. Cassie had feared that valuable seconds would be wasted blasting a way in with door-knocker charges—and she knew that every second she gave the black-clad Dracs within would pare down her already razor-thin chance of success.

She leapt through into a hell of screaming, thrashing figures. Each seemed to be dusted with tiny stars.

The only three kinds of hand grenades in common use among the warriors of the thirty-first century were fragmentation, stun, and nonlethal disabling gases, for only a suicidal zany would loose lethal agents like tear, nausea, or hallucination into air he might be forced to breath himself. The ISF's commando suits protected them against fragments and the dazzling flash and bang of stun bombs, and were sealed against aerosols as well.

What Cassie used was a humble smoke grenade—or what was still by common courtesy called a smoke grenade more than a millennium after its introduction. White phosphorus was actually a pretty poor smoke round, tending to produce a forest of wispy spires of white smoke that seldom obscured much of anything.

The *real* point to Willy Peter was what produced those smokes-spires: hundreds of tiny pieces of phosphorous that clung tenaciously to anything they touched, burning at 2400 degrees Centigrade. They could etch ferro-fibrous armor, and ate quite greedily through the black DEST body suits. Which, as the suddenly frantic operators found, were very hard to get out of in a hurry.

Most of the hit team waiting to take down Chandrasekhar Kurita was assembled in a large auditorium and holotheater off the lobby of the Coordinator's Rest Hotel. The soundproofing was very effective; only the half-dozen nearest the exit heard anything when the sentries went down. A fact that proved most unlucky for them, because they were currently locked in an agonizing dance of death with phosphorus for a partner.

Their gunfire, the grenade blast, and the ensuing screams alerted the rest. Black-clad forms were beginning to pour into the lobby as the Scouts stormed in.

Yvonne Sánchez rushed past Cassie, holding a satchel charge to her chest with one hand, firing her machine pistol with the other. Her body protected by the bomb and her assault vest, she charged straight into the commando who stood in the auditorium door shooting at her. Blood sprayed from an arterial hit on her arm. She kept going.

She hit the commandos like a running back, trying to bull her way through. Several dropped their Shimatsus to draw swords, slashing at her arms and face.

The scouts were screaming at her to come back, hopping around as they tried to get a clear shot at her attackers without hitting her. Cassie just headed for the elevators. On this mission there was no time to deal with wounded. Poor Yvonne was dead.

The Coordinator's Rest was a towering hollow cylinder, terraces rising up an atrium a hundred stories high. The elevators were spindle-shaped pods that rose up tracks on the inside of the atrium. Illuminated only by work lights, it was a weird echoing vastness, like some surrealistic mine.

Behind Cassie came gunfire, more screams, and then a blast that shook the whole structure. Sánchez had forced her way into the auditorium and with dying fingers had triggered the five kilos of plastic explosive in her satchel.

Dix and five others reached the nearest elevator with Cassie. They crowded inside, hit the express button for the top floor. The doors whispered shut. Acceleration pressed them down as the pod sped upward.

Through the transparent elevator walls, Cassie saw muzzle flashes blossom below like fire-flowers as the DEST team fired up at them.

A bang. Patricio clutched his thigh and slid to the floor, leaving behind a red smear on the glass.

As commandos, the DEST agents had been trained since recruitment to think in snaky terms. The habit of deviousness was hard to break, which was probably why the elevator was passing the sixtieth floor before anybody thought of cutting the power.

The red floor indicator had just flickered past seventy when it died. The pod's overhead light went out. For a moment the only illumination came from strands of trouble lights that trailed down the atrium like self-luminous, deep-sea life forms.

The overhead came back, dimly, as the pod's emergency backup battery came online. Cassie looked at her five comrades still on their feet. Then she looked down at Patricio.

The young White Mountain Apache shook his head.

* * *

While his hit team cooled their heels on ground level, twenty commandos waited with their master on the upper levels. It was not that Ninyu felt the need of bodyguards; if anyone wanted trouble with him, it was his intention to fully accommodate them, a sword in his hand, a smile on his scarred lips. But his people *wanted* to guard him. In accordance with his laborious attempt to learn the unfamiliar, human skills—*ninja* skills—at his father's behest, Ninyu permitted them to do so. They took it as high honor.

Warned by communicator of what was on the way, five DEST agents were waiting outside the elevator when the pod finally coasted to a stop on the eightieth floor. The door slid open. All five DEST operatives fired their leveled Shimatsus instantly.

Their magazines were empty before they realized that only a single terrorist was in the pod, sitting on the floor. He was thoroughly riddled, and thoroughly dead. From his face he might almost have been Japanese.

The five crowded into the pod, scrutinizing it as if expecting to find the other reported terrorists somehow concealed in the tiny space. Then one of them pointed upward to the hatch open overhead.

They were all craning to look up when a black-clad foot brushed Patricio's arm. His hand turned over, and his dead fingers released the safety lever of the white phosphorus grenade they had been clutching.

Masamori, Hachiman
Galedon District, Draconis Combine
November 2, 3056

Clinging like baby opossums to the outside of the pod, the Scouts rode the elevator to a stop. DEST commandos on a higher floor spotted them and began to fire. Absalom Sloat, the unparalleled tracker who had never adjusted to the Regiment's urban surroundings, slipped away and vanished into the abyss below with a despairing diminishing cry.

The others swarmed quickly over the rail onto the floor above and vanished in the shadows.

Caballero Second Battalion MechWarriors on the Compound's south side spotted the fight by the river wall. Force Commander Bar-Kochba sent Lieutenant JG Bodine leaping to the rescue in his *Jenner.* The rabbi's own *Warhammer* and Marsh Waits' *Marauder* came rumbling after.

By the time Bodine's *Jenner* jumped over the leafless maples that rimmed the plaza before the Citadel, Great White's left arm had been blown off and its left knee actuator frozen. But the *Mad Cat* stood among the smoking hulks of four attacking 'Mechs, and its pilot was truly the *Tiburón* of old, spinning the 'Mech's torso this way and that, flipping its good arm over its back to keep pouring fire on the antagonists circling it like jackals.

The three-sixty view strips gave the Ghost 'Mech pilots eyes in the backs of their heads. But when a massive battle—into the blazing guts of which you might be ordered at any moment—was raging to your front, you tended to keep your eyes on the action.

The rearmost BattleMech of the forces assaulting from the

west was the Ghosts' lone and lowly *UrbanMech*. The first its pilot knew of the mercenary force that had blasted its way out of the Siriwan Kurita Opera House Tubeway station six minutes before was when Alacrán's PPC bathed his machine in yellow ion fire from behind.

With the arrival of Modine's comparatively intact *Jenny* and the two big 'Mechs from Bar-Kochba's Second Battalion, and several other Caballero machines pulling back from the battle in the west to counter the new threat, the assault off the Yamato was quickly broken up. Three Ghost light 'Mechs broke away into the Fab buildings near the 'Mech barns to the north to continue the fight until they were hunted down. The rest just smoked.

With a tortured groan of heat-warped metal against impact-deformed armor plate, Colonel Carlos Camacho turned Great White's cratered fuselage to face Bar-Kochba's Hammer of God.

"Why did you interfere, Rabbi?" the Colonel asked quietly over the commlink. "My son is dead."

"Your sorrow is mine," Bar-Kochba said. "Father Montoya will say Mass for your boy, and I shall say Kaddish. But you must go on. The Regiment needs you."

Don Carlos sighed. He no longer wished to die. All he wanted was the chance to weep and light candles over his son's body, and then to sleep.

"You're right," he said. "I have a duty to the only family I have left."

He punched up a different circuit. Zuma's rich baritone filled his ears, singing *El Camino Real de Guanajuato*.

"Zuma," he said. "Forgive me for interrupting your song."

"Yes, *mi coronel*. What do you wish?"

Don Carlos drew in a shuddering breath. "Sing for me, Zuma," he said, trying to keep his tears from choking him. "Sing Patsy's song."

The red glare of emergency indicators filled the cockpit of *Tai-sa* Eleanor Shimazu's *Mauler*. Not all the glow came from the warning lights; she could smell her hair beginning to smolder in the heat that filled her cockpit. She was engaged with two Caballero heavies at medium range, and the only thing holding her 'Mech upright was the futile anger inside her. Anger that she desperately wished she could vent against the mercenary warriors who had been her friends.

It's Sumiyama whose skin you want to watch crisping in plasma fire, she thought. But the yakuza boss sat smug in his distant tower, above it all, laughing. Untouched, untouchable.

She already knew the river assault had failed. The warning cry from her Second Battalion—"Gaijin 'Mechs in our rear!" was still reverberating in her ears when Unagi called her.

"Tai-sa," the light-'Mech pilot said. "Tune to the Ca—the *gaijin* general freak."

She did, in time to hear the Chief Aztech's voice ring out, bold as a trumpet: *"Presentando Patricia Camacho, ¡la Capitana!"*

He began to sing, of another cloudy day, in the mountains of a world named for the Christian Saint Jerome.

"Isn't that the song their Colonel would never let them sing?" Unagi asked.

"Yes," Lainie said, almost inaudibly. "It is."

A single tear rolled down her right cheek. She imagined she could hear it hiss away as steam when it fell below the rim of her neurohelmet.

Unagi's voice was saying something. She didn't hear. All she could hear was Patsy's song.

It was the funeral dirge for the Ninth Ghost Regiment. Whatever befell the Caballeros from here on, her brazen, brawling, shameless yakuza boys and girls could never beat them.

Only one thing remained to her to do.

Cassie thought her team had finally run into luck. No DEST commandos in black suits appeared above them to toss grenades down on their heads as they raced up the stairwell.

She soon found out otherwise. The stairs ended at floor 99.

"Damn!" she said.

The others looked at her. Dix was still with her, as were Jimmy Escobar—barely breathing hard—McTeague, and the rangy white-blond Mangum.

She gestured at the door with her machine pistol. "They'll be ready for us."

Mangum chuckled. "Who wants to live forever?" Escobar muttered something in Zuñi.

"Well, I was plannin' on taking a shot at it," Dix said, "but plans change."

Cassie took out another Willy Peter grenade. She pulled the pin, held it for a conservative two count, popped it out the heavy metal fire door, and slammed the door again.

The moment the grenade went off, rattling the door in its frame, Cassie bounced the opening bar with her rump and spun out, MP ready.

She was just in time to watch a blazing DEST agent pitch over the rail and plummet down through the atrium like a meteorite.

"Now, that's something you don't see ever' day," Mangum said from behind her.

The others burst out of the stairwell and spread out. The darkened terrace around the door glimmered with a galaxy of blue-white phosphorus stars. Cassie was cautious not to touch any of them. The white smoke they gave off seemed to claw at the lining of her nose and throat.

From the far side of the abyss muzzle flashes bloomed.

The rooms of each floor of the Coordinator's Rest radiated outward from a walkway that ran around the atrium. Cassie charged clockwise along it. Behind her Dix, Escobar, and Mangum traded shots from the cover of the elevator stage with the DEST commandos across the well of blackness. McTeague ran with Cassie toward the stairs on the far side, hoping they led up.

Halfway around, a door flew open as they passed. A blade flashed in the ghostly utility-light glow. McTeague screamed and fell with his head split open and Cassie's machine pistol was kicked from her hand the instant she brought the weapon to bear.

A pair of black-clad commandos slid out, splitting to prevent her from breaking either way along the catwalk. Both wore pistols in shoulder holsters. In true *ninja* fashion, they preferred to use their swords.

Anticipating their taste for swordplay, Cassie had come prepared. She reached behind to the light ruck on her back, pulled open a zipper on an extra pouch affixed to the bottom. Five kilograms of steel ball bearings fell thudding and clinking to the floor.

The DEST members refused to be daunted by any such childish trick. Both charged. The female's feet immediately flew out from under her. She sat down hard.

Slipping and sliding, the male got close enough to Cassie to aim a wild diagonal swipe at her. She simply sat down beneath it, folding herself to the carpet amid the dully shining metal marbles.

He recovered and lunged at her, raising his sword for an overhand stroke. The split-toed foot of his DEST suit came down on ball bearings. He overbalanced and began to topple forward, windmilling his arms for balance as he ran helplessly toward her.

She grabbed the front of his suit, put a hand in his crotch, and, adding ever so slight a set of vectors to what he already had, helped him to the waist-height guardrail and up and over it.

The firefight was still in progress, and quite one-sided, if volume of fire was any indication. But the Caballero scouts were raised to hunt the way their MechWarriors were raised to ride. Hillbillies, Dispossessed Cowboys, truculent hill *norteños,* Pueblo Indians, outcasts despised by their proud equestrian cousins, they hailed from the poorest regions of hardscrabble planets, where stalking skill and the ability to bring down game with one well-placed shot often made the difference between survival and starvation.

Unlike most footsloggers of the Inner Sphere—including the vaunted DEST super-commandos—the Seventeenth's scouts didn't like a free for all, at least when it came to gunplay. They liked to pick their shots, and they didn't like to miss.

The female commando had found her feet again and was circling with her sword held out in front of her. Body language made it clear that her view of reality had been seriously compromised. A lowly *gaijin* woman, an honor-lost money soldier at that, was not supposed to take on one of the Dragon's finest armed with a sword—the soul of any true Draconian—with bare hands and win.

She dropped into a low stance, as if figuring that would help her cope with the treacherous footing. Cassie drew Blood-drinker. Sitting, she spread her legs wide in a split-stretch, leaned forward between them, the *kris* held crosswise in her right hand, the left hand forming a tiger claw: *harimau.*

The DEST woman faked an overhand cut, whipped her sword into a backhanded transverse slash. The *ninjato,* hand-fashioned in alternate layers of soft and brittle steel according to nearly two millennia of tradition, could slice through Blood-drinker like rice paper. The wavy blade was not of the finest steel.

But it was never Cassie's way to oppose edge to edge, strength to strength; her lifelong obsession with hunting 'Mechs had taught her the futility of that approach. Instead, Blood-drinker caught the commando blade flat to flat, guiding it over and past Cassie as she ducked into the stroke. Her left hand caught the woman's arm and spun her hard into the safety wall.

The commando was good. She kept her head, and her recovery time was near-instantaneous. The dice rolled her way; the rubber soles of her soft black boots found bare carpet beneath. She turned with her back to the wall and her swordpoint toward Cassie.

From her cross-legged position Cassie unwound herself to come upright, then twisted into a stance facing her opponent as she began to circle her counterclockwise. The swordtip dipped briefly, then came up to point again at her eyes.

"Your tricks won't help you, *gaijin,*" the woman said in a voice muffled by her faceplate. She pivoted to keep facing Cassie. "I'll cut you to pieces."

Cassie had orbited until she stood with her right shoulder against the safety wall running around the outside of the atrium, from the depths of which urgent, confused voices echoed. She expected to be shot at any time, but right now that was out of her power. She was focused wholly on her foe.

The woman in black rushed her. Catlike, Cassie jumped back. Blindingly fast, her opponent cut for her face with a one-hand wrist-flick.

Cassie felt something like a fingertip brush her left cheek. Then there was the sting of air invading an open wound, and wetness down her chin.

There were steel balls underfoot, rolling. She rode them, let them add distance between her and her foe. Then she went down on her butt, all asprawl.

With a triumphant scream the DEST woman launched herself at Cassie, stepping straight onto the ball bearings. She lost her balance, flew forward.

Cassie's fall was faked. She caught the woman with a straight-legged stop-kick to the solar plexus. Even with the body armor it doubled the DEST woman over. Cassie let her hip play hub and the commando play wheel, rolling her opponent on over her and hard onto the floor.

With the air knocked out of the woman. Cassie leapt on her like a tiger. Her opponent was somewhat larger and stronger, but that didn't matter. Cassie strode her, grabbed her faceless head, and pounded it three times against the outer wall. Then she twitched the sword from feeble fingers, pitched it over the rail.

A black-gloved hand clawed for her eyes. Cassie caught the wrist, rolled off the woman, used her body mass to lockout the elbow, then broke it with an elbow smash of her own. The woman in black grunted.

Stoic though she was, the pain-shock momentarily immobilized her. That gave Cassie a chance to get an arm around her neck and drop her into unconsciousness with a sleeper hold.

She pulled the heavy autopistol from the commando's holster, stuck it down the front of her pants. She stood up, quickly spotted Blood-drinker, recovered it.

She tucked the *kris* back in its sheath and drew her Nambu-Nissan. The shooting from the stairwell had inexplicably ceased. Now there was a sudden loud flurry of shots from the stairs she had just left, the flash and crack of a grenade, and screams.

Figures ran toward her. She raised the pistol. "Don't shoot, Cass," a voice panted.

"Dix?"

"You got it." His tall form resolved out of the gloom. The even taller shape of Mangum materialized right behind him, dragging his right leg.

"DEST fellers across the way pulled back up the stairs," Dix said. "Jimmy bought it." He looked at her face. "You're losin' blood."

"Either I'll have a chance to make more," she told him, "or it's all gonna come out. Either way, I can't worry about it now."

"Don't wanta break up the party," Mangum said, teeth clenched behind smiling lips, "but all the DEST commandos in the world just came crawlin' up our buttholes. Don't reckon our old pal Willy Peter'll hold 'em forever."

Cassie pointed to the operator, who was beginning to stir and moan. "Bring her," she said. "And watch the ball-bearings."

Dix frowned. Then he shrugged and slung his piece. Leaning down he pounded the woman's head once against the floor for luck. Then he hauled her arm back in a hammer-lock and picked her up bodily.

Cassie led off toward the far stairs. Five black-clad forms were strewn around it like discarded dolls, testimonials to the efficacy of aimed fire.

She moved to the side of the door, turned the handle and threw it as far open as it would go. Light streamed out, but no gunfire. As the door swung back she dropped to the floor and rolled across the dwindling opening with her pistol held out before her.

The stairwell was empty. Apparently the defenders had decided to await them in the penthouse itself.

A burst of gunfire sent stucco dust spouting from the wall beside the door. "In here," Cassie said, jerking her head at the stairwell. Dix yanked the door open and propelled the unmoving DEST woman onto the steps. The three crowded inside.

For a moment they crouched, panting. Cassie pointed to Mangum's trouser leg, which was shiny and sodden with a dark stain. "How about you?"

His grin was mostly snarl. "Shoot, I always wanted to be that one-legged man in the proverbial ass-kickin' contest."

"I didn't know you knew any words that long," Dix said.

"What? 'Shoot?' "

"Can you two hold here?" Cassie asked.

Dix looked at Mangum and shrugged. "Till they pry our cold dead fingers off the triggers, anyhow."

"One way or another," Cassie said, "this won't take long." She grabbed the woman by the empty scabbard still slung across her back and dragged her up the stairs, looking like a cat carrying home prey bigger than it was to show the folks. Her comrades stared but didn't ask what she was doing. Exactly like a cat, Cassie walked her own way and gave few explanations.

"They're all just waitin' on you up there, hon," Dix warned.

"I know," Cassie said. She drew the woman's pistol with her left hand. Then she stooped, fed her hands under the unresisting commando's arms from behind, and stood up, holding the now semiconscious woman in front of her by the armpits.

"That's why I brought a friend."

40

Masamori, Hachiman
Galedon District, Draconis Combine
November 2, 3056

With the ballad of their lost heroine ringing in their ears, the Caballeros rolled to the attack as if by a single accord.

The bold stroke led by Gavilán Camacho wasn't capable of doing much actual damage—but Napoleon Bonaparte had not been blowing smoke when he said that, in war, the moral is to the physical as three is to one. In fact he'd been committing one of his rare understatements.

Such elements of the Ghost Third Battalion as had not already been thrown into the pot just shattered. The Drac MechWarrior knew, intellectually, that there was no way a reinforcing BattleMech army could suddenly turn up to aid the besieged *gaijin*. But rationality vaporized when 'Mechs appeared in the rearview with guns blazing.

Deru kugi utareru, ran a Japanese proverb much beloved of generations of Coordinators: "The nail which stands out shall be hammered down." The yakuza lived by a simpler creed: "Better to be the hammer than the nail." In their hearts, the Ghosts could not help but magnify the pitiful handful of *Locusts* and *Stingers*—and one *Scorpion*—into God's Own hammer.

In an army in combat, panic spreads like flame across spilled gasoline. South of the Compound Ghost Second Battalion MechWarriors saw Third Battalion flying west as fast as their jump jets would carry them. When the mercenaries suddenly came swarming over the wall at them, they could think of no good reason to stay and be slaughtered.

The battle rests in the Virgin's hands, now Don Carlos thought, as the reports of Ghosts on the run came flooding in. He popped the seal on his canopy, undid his safety harness, and climbed down his 'Mech ladder to the ground.

Hachiman Taro EMTs in oddly flat metal helmets were just prying the pilot from the wreckage of his son's *Shadow Hawk* with giant hydraulic jaws of life especially designed for use with BattleMechs. Don Carlos broke into a clumsy, weeping run.

He stopped just short of the party of medics. The shattered form they were laying on a gurney was much too small to be that of his son.

A female medtech with an untended shell-splinter gash across one cheek gently lifted off the helmet. Gray-shot red hair spilled out.

"Marisol?" Camacho whispered.

Lieutenant Colonel Cabrera reached out for him with bloody fingers. "Carlos?" she said. She choked, coughed blood. It poured over the front of his cooling vest as he gathered her in his arms.

"Sir," the injured medic said, "she's badly hurt—"

Don Carlos glared her back. "Marisol, what are you doing here?"

"I—could not let you throw your life away. I wanted to atone for what I did to you."

He huddled her head against his chest. "There, now. Don't talk."

She clutched his arm, pulled herself up to face him. "I betrayed you, Carlos," she said, "but I did so out of love. I knew if . . . I didn't do something, you'd never—"

Her voice began to fade, and as it did she began to slump back onto the gurney.

"Knew you'd never . . . retire and take me back to . . . Galisteo with you."

Her fingers began to lose their grip on his sleeve. "Carlos, I love you," she whispered. "Kiss me, *mi amor.* Kiss me and say you forgive me."

"I forgive you, Marisol," he said. "I love you."

He leaned down to kiss her blistered lips. When the kiss ended, so had her life.

A hell of fire gushed at Cassie like a volcano's glowing cloud when she kicked open the door. The DEST woman's body jerked to sledgehammer impacts. Cassie leaned into the firestorm and drove herself forward with strong legs and willpower.

Because the stairs ran up the outside wall, there was no way for the half-dozen commandos waiting for her to surround the door. That was what kept her alive long enough to fight back.

They hadn't used a lot of subtlety; aside from the odd pillar there was no cover in the half-finished penthouse. They had ranged themselves standing or crouching at various distances from the stairs, Shimatsu 42s trained on the door.

One stood not three meters ahead and to the right. Cassie raised the Nambu-Nissan and squeezed off the instant the three big white sight-dots appeared before her eyes.

A blacker dot appeared dead-center of the black-suited man's faceplate. The Mirza's armor-piercers worked as advertised, she was gratified to note.

Another DEST member fired at her up from the left front. She shot him in the chest, once, twice, again. ISF bullets would not penetrate ISF armor. But they drove him back. His flexible ballistic cloth did stop the slugs, but not before they punched a good distance into his body. He went down.

Keeping her face ducked down behind her human shield's lolling head restricted Cassie's field of vision. Feeling as though she were moving in slow motion, she concentrated on keeping her awareness unfocused, seeking targets with peripheral vision. She was aware of a tall solitary presence, dressed all in black like the commandos but with red head bare. The figure stood at the far side of the huge room with its back to the windows and a bank of electronic gear. White-smocked technicians cowered behind him.

The Gestalt flash showed him in a posture of poised watchfulness, not threat. Good, she thought, don't make me shoot you. That'd only complicate things.

Another DEST commando knelt to her right, trying to sight on her head. Barely able to see him past her shield, she pointed the Nambu-Nissan at him and sprayed shots. She saw blood mist behind his left shoulder, thought another round struck him mid-body. He went flailing over backward.

Another commando ran around her left side, trying to get a shot at her behind his slumped comrade. Cassie pivoted counterclockwise as far as she dared. The woman's dead weight dragged down her arms. She emptied the ISF pistol at the running man's leg, hitting his knee from the side. That shot didn't penetrate either—but it smashed the joint just the same. He went down howling.

Two final commandos blocked her shoulder to shoulder, their guns chattering thunder at her like Indra's own teletype. Cassie dropped her left-hand pistol and rushed them, feeling her human shield seeming to convulse in her arms. But it was only bullet hits; through her arms Cassie could feel that the woman's ribcage had gotten a kind of soggy, mushy feel to it.

When she was almost on top of the pair she put a hand between her shield's shoulderblades and propelled the body toward the one on the left. Herself she hurled to the right, thrusting her own sidearm toward the man on that side and pumping the trigger frantically. Muzzle flash seared away her left eyebrow; primer residue stung her cheek. The noise of bullets rushing past her head at twice the speed of sound was like the crackling ripple of rebar popping in a highway bridge failing beneath at *Atlas'* weight.

She landed to the side of the kneeling DEST commando, pistol still bearing on him, still firing. He was starting to look as if moths had been chewing up his tight black suit. Moths with red saliva.

Her Nambu-Nissan clicked empty. The nearer commando was still kneeling, but something in his posture suggested that nobody was home anymore. He began to topple toward her as his comrade writhed out from beneath the dead woman.

Cassie leapt up and ran at the last commando. She tore the sword from the nearer one's back scabbard in passing as he fell. She raised it above her head, point-down.

The remaining opponent had fumbled his own sidearm from his shoulder rig. As he brought it to bear, Cassie brought the *ninjato* down with a piercing scream.

Japanese blades were renowned for their ability to penetrate armor. The Smiling One did not equip his elite minions with pot-metal imitations from Sian. The swordtip punched through the armor atop the commando's head, through skull, brain, palate, jaw, and through armor again to jut three bloody centimeters below his chin.

She let go the cord-wound sword hilt and let him fall, turning to face the tall man. He still had not moved. She unslung her rucksack, took out the compact holoprojector. Holding it before her in two hands, signifying intent by deliberately making it difficult to reach a weapon, she walked toward him.

As she got closer she felt his dark gaze pushing at her like beams of force. Almost she turned and ran. Almost; but the Regiment was counting on her, and she had never let them down.

Short of death, she never would.

"You've come all this way," the red-haired man said, sounding almost amused, "to blow me up?"

"Lord Kerai-Indrahar," she said, kneeling before him, "this is no bomb. It is evidence that irrefutably clears Lord Chandrasekhar Kurita of the suspicion of treason which has unjustly fallen on him."

She bowed her head and held the projector forth. "I and my comrades have shed our blood to bring this evidence to you. Now I throw myself upon your mercy, and pray that as an honorable and magnanimous man you will view it before you pass judgement on my Lord Kurita or upon my humble self."

Ninyu Kerai Indrahar smiled with a warm sincerity that he knew would bring joy to his adoptive father's spirit, if only he could see it.

"Indeed, my child," he murmured, "it is I who am unworthy of the honor you do me." *And that's true, too,* he thought as he slipped a tiny two-shot cone-gun out of his right sleeve.

The next thing he knew his gun-arm was being twisted up behind him in a painful joint-lock and the impertinent young woman was clinging to his back like a monkey, with the tip of her wavy dagger jammed under the corner of his jaw hard enough to let blood out of him.

"I don't swallow that samurai honor noise any more than you do," she hissed in his ear, "but I'm tired of seeing my friends fry and die. Now, shall we take it again from the top, you lowlife ninja son of a bitch?"

* * *

Striding alone between burning buildings, Lainie found she could no longer move Revenge's left arm. She kept her large right-arm laser hosing a *Grasshopper* sixty meters away while the heat rose up and up around her. Just before her reactor redlined, the *Grasshopper* pilot punched out. Half a heartbeat later its ammo blew.

She felt no exhilaration at the kill. She barely noticed. Her being was focused on the Citadel rising before her. She intended to die upon its steps.

She came to the great open space before the administration tower. The trees were as colorful as spring come early, but their branches bore flames, not blossoms.

A figure resolved out of the smoke before her, a figure large enough to claim her attention. An *Atlas,* battered and grim.

"Lainie," a familiar foreign voice said over her general freak, "you look like hell."

The Ghost commander managed a croaking laugh. "You should see yourself, Kali. Your 'Mech looks like Benkei's meteor-battered backside."

"You know as well as I do that this fight's over," the *gaijin* said. "Go back."

"I must pass."

"I can't let you."

Lainie pounded the arm of her seat in rage. Heat-softened, the synthetic covering split and the interior padding began instantly to smolder. "Why must we kill each other? Why?"

"I guess because we're so much alike, doll," the other said, " 'and 'cause we can't kill the people who made us what we are."

The tears were pouring uncontrollably from Lainie's eyes. "Kali," she said, "good-bye." And she raised her 'Mechs good right arm.

"Attention, all units of the Ninth Ghost Regiment," a brisk, dry voice said on the general frequency. "This is Assistant Director Ninyu Kerai Indrahar of the Internal Security Force. All Combine forces are to cease hostilities at once, on my authority. I say again: Cease fire."

Epilogue

Patsy's Song

41

The Marquis Redmond Hosoya, CEO of Tanadi Computers, did not know the reason for Ninyu Kerai's inexplicable broadcast. But he knew what it meant. Life had a brutal simplicity in the Draconis Combine—that was one of the traditions he was so fond of, after all. A wind that blew fair for your enemy inevitably blew foul for you. If Chandrasekhar Kurita's fortunes had reversed, it followed with relentless logic that his had as well.

He called for a helicopter to land on the roof of Tanadi's proud bronze tower and whisk him away through the snowstorm to Rex Fillington Memorial Airport. There he boarded a small private jet with reverse-raked wings. He ordered the pilot to fly east with all due speed.

He sat alone in the spacious cabin, drumming nervous fingers on the arm of his seat and ignoring a cocktail a steward had brought him. He watched the Trimurtis grow larger by the moment. They looked especially huge with the eerie light of sunset glowing in their cloak of fresh-fallen snow, and that heartened him.

He was a prudent man, and he knew well how quickly fortune's wind could back and veer. He had made certain preparations to disappear into the great mountain range, to a subterranean hideout even satellites couldn't spot. He would bide there in perfect comfort and wait for the wind to turn again.

As he comforted himself with these thoughts, a black, unmarked *Sholagar* aerospace fighter dropped from orbit. It rolled out level twenty-five kilometers behind the fleeing jet, well out of the unsuspecting pilot's visual range.

The fighter's pilot switched on his radar. If the jet pilot detected it, he would think merely that it was the sweep of the traffic control beam from the popular resort town of Varner, fifty kilometers southeast. The *Sholagar* jock painted the jet just long enough for the seeker heads of four long-range fire-and-forget missiles to see their quarry and commit their destinies to it. Then he switched it off, pitched his nose up, and thundered back up into infinite night.

The Board of Inquiry from the Hachiman Aeronautic Authority never found a cause for the tragic crash which claimed the life of the esteemed Marquis Hosoya. They chalked it up to pilot error.

The dune grass already seemed brittle and winter-scorched. The sun had sunk from view in the Shakudo, and the wind off the sea was bitter. Cassie found it hard to believe she'd been riding horseback in the surf just a week ago.

"Everything about you was a lie, wasn't it?" asked the Earl of Fillington.

Cassie nodded.

She was walking along beside him with the skirt of her long white dress blowing about her legs. It felt strange to be dressed that way as herself, in the persona of Cassiopeia Suthorn. Cassie seldom wore dresses. Yet Uncle Chandy had suggested it, and Lady K had concurred.

"Why did you come back, then?" he demanded bitterly. "To rub my nose in my own folly?"

She stopped, turned to face him. "I don't know," she said honestly. "I suppose . . . to tell you I was sorry."

"Sorry?" he echoed, his tone become acid. " 'Sorry?' Your mercenary accomplices murder my people, and you think you can come here and tell me you're sorry? You abuse my confidence and my hospitality, you play shamelessly upon my sympathies, and all in the interests of that gross monster Chandrasekhar, and you think you can come here and say you're sorry?"

"No," she said. "I'm not apologizing for any of that. I did that for the Regiment. What I'm trying to say is, I'm sorry that I hurt you."

The Earl's handsome face went white above his lace collar. He raised a hand as if to hit her, but Cassie's eyes never left his. Only the color seem to shift slightly to the palest blue.

He caught himself, looked at his hand as if he'd just discovered it sprouting from the end of his arm, dropped it to his side.

"If I had tried to strike you," he said, "you'd have killed me, isn't that so?"

"Yes."

He took a deep breath. "Sometimes strong emotion tears aside a curtain within us, and we see things there we wish were not."

She said nothing. She turned and resumed walking, hugging herself against the cold.

After a moment he followed, catching up with long strides. "If it wasn't for the immunity Ninyu Kerai granted you, I'd see you and your friends prosecuted for killing my staff."

"We only killed one," she said, "and he was an ISF spy. He was trying to kill me, by the way."

"Yes." Percy stuck his hands in his pockets. "Ninyu admitted Gupta was one of his agents. Just a comment in passing when he found out the poor chap had bought it."

His brow furrowed. "But I suppose you didn't really kill that large black fellow?"

"Man Mountain's alive and charging ahead with his cooking lessons. He came through the battle unhurt." She looked up at him, and her eyes had paled again.

"Since you're being so pious about lives being taken," she said, "what about my friends?"

He nodded briskly. "Very well; it's my turn not to apologize. I could say that I was set up by our mutual friend Lord Kerai-Indrahar. But the fact is I welcomed a chance to take action against your employer. You've heard my reasons."

When Cassie didn't reply, he said, "I suppose you'll try to tell me, now, how mistaken I am about Chandrasekhar Kurita."

She shook her head. "All I came here to tell you was that I was sorry for hurting you," she said. "We have different perceptions of Uncle Chandy, though. I give you that much."

"You're an icy little bitch, aren't you?"

She looked up briskly at that, but her eyes were their normal gray. "If you were my friend," she said quietly, "would you see me the same way?"

He rubbed his cheek. "No," he said musingly. "No, I don't suppose I would. I rather think I'd feel the world was an altogether safer place if you were on my side."

They were on the crushed-shell path that led up past the stables to the big house. "I have to go," she said.

"Wait."

She stopped, turned.

"Is this your real appearance, Ms. Suthorn?"

She spread her arms and grinned. "As real as I get."

"I think you look lovelier this way than before."

She frowned, slightly, reflexively wondering what he wanted from her. Then she recalled long talks with Lady K in the gloomy aftermath of battle.

"Thank you," she said.

He held out his hand. She didn't move.

"Come on," he said, "give me your hand. My touch didn't poison you before, did it?"

"No," she said, and took his hand.

"I'm probably as big a fool as Ninyu Kerai and the late Marquis Hosoya and all the others took me for," he said, "but what I said earlier is perfectly true. I would feel safer if I could call you my friend. And I must confess, safety is not my only concern. You are by a respectable margin the most remarkable woman I've ever been privileged to meet. You possess—despite your deadly and deceitful ways—a substantial amount of charm. I think I should enjoy getting to know you better."

Cassie leaned toward him enough to raise his hand to her lips and brush the back of it very lightly with her lips. Then she let it go.

"Perhaps," she said, and walked away.

At the top of the path she turned back. "The people who think you're a fool think the same of Uncle Chandy," she said slowly. "But they're the real fools. Think about that, Percy Fillington."

And then she was gone.

Tai-sa Eleanor Shimazu leaned back in the leather-covered chair and put her boots on the broad desk before her, next to an insulated canister half a meter tall and only slightly less wide. *I could get used to this,* she decided, suddenly glad the penthouse office hadn't taken more battle damage.

She was a hero after all, as were her surviving Ghosts. So were the Caballeros. The media were still buzzing with it, how saboteurs from some unspecified power—read the Federated Commonwealth—had attempted to assassinate the Coordinator's beloved cousin in stolen BattleMechs. Only heroic joint action of the Combine's glorious Ninth Ghost Regiment and the foreign but almost equally glorious Seventeenth Recon had saved the day.

It was a remarkably thin story. A critical press and public would have torn it gleefully to shreds. But the Draconis Combine didn't *have* a critical press and public. The media swore the story was true; the public obediently believed.

The power of the press was something that might bear study, in light of her new responsibilities.

Sadly, Kazuo Sumiyama had been discovered to be party to the heinous plot against Uncle Chandy. Since he wasn't so obliging as to climb into an airplane and dash himself to pieces in the Trimurti foothills, it became the sad duty of the Ninth Ghosts to call him to account for his crimes.

Lainie had never seen sad soldiers grin so hugely as her Ghosts had when she led them against Sumiyama's skyscraper. They hadn't even seemed to feel the fatigue of the terrible battle the day before.

The telephone chimed, and the image of Miss Rajit, former receptionist to Sumiyama, appeared above the desktop.

"The *oyabu*n of Kuranosuke and Hawthorne just called, Colonel," she said. "They wish to know when to come to pay their respects."

That was expected. Most of the planet's other yakuza bosses had already checked in. The *oyabun* of Masamori was *oyabun* of Hachiman. That was one of Sumiyama's institution she intended to keep.

"They can come to the meeting on Thursday, like everybody else."

Miss Rajit moistened her lips. "I beg your pardon, Colonel, but they also wonder to whom they are to pay their respects. They are not . . . accustomed to bowing to a woman."

Lainie grinned. "Tell them that if they have any trouble with the idea of submitting to me," she said, "that they can take it up with the head on Thursday."

Miss Rajit frowned in discreet incomprehension. "I beg your pardon, Colonel?"

"Just tell them exactly what I told you. They'll figure it out."

The receptionist's image vanished. Lainie scratched her ribs, where the tape that held her bandages itched her. In the heat of battle she hadn't even noticed the splinter of ferrofibrous plate hitting her.

She had done a little research on the former *oyabun*'s receptionist, as part of her general stock-taking. Rather to her surprise, she'd discovered that Miss Rajit was more than just an ornament; she was sharp, tough, and quick. As soon as feasible, Lainie planned to shift her into a role in which *Sumiyama-kai*—she had to do something about that name!— could take full advantage of her abilities. That would also permit Lainie to get some blond muscular hunk with a good ass and a small brain to answer the phones for her.

She held up her left hand. The pink line around the base of her little finger where the neurosurgeons had grafted it back in place itched as abominably as the tape on her ribs. But she thought that a small price to pay for being whole again.

In more than just body.

It was a pity, she thought sardonically, that Kazuo Sumiyama would find it harder to get his missing body parts rejoined. For example, his head, which at the moment was packed in dry ice in the insulated canister sitting next to her boot.

She laughed. When she told Miss Rajit that the lesser *oyabun* could take up any problems they had with her succession with the *head* . . . that was exactly what she'd had in mind.

Cassie Suthorn stood amid the fleshy leaves and extravagant blooms of Uncle Chandy's greenhouse and said, "I want the truth."

He continued to putter with his orchids. "In the Draconis Combine inferiors do not make demands of superiors," he told her.

She stood and looked at him. After a time he began to laugh. "You should take up Zen, child; you have a knack for it."

He set aside his trowel and scrubbed fat fingers on his

apron. "Come, then. You have performed a great service to me. Enough to merit the greatest of rewards: the truth."

Their garb was unfamiliar, but something about the figures that seemed to sit on the holostage in Uncle Chandy's inner sanctum prickled the skin at the nape of Cassie's neck.

"Clanners," she said.

"Oh, yes. Jade Falcon, this lot."

"I don't recognize their caste marks."

"They're merchants. I see you're surprised; almost no one in the Inner Sphere has ever seen anyone from the Clan's merchant caste. Kerensky's children didn't come back to trade, after all."

She looked at the figures again. They were much as the nameless spacer had described them.

"Where are they?" she asked in a flat voice.

"Upstairs, in a pleasant corner apartment on the top floor. An appropriate place to keep Falcons, don't you think, in the penthouse? They had quite a view of your glorious battle with the Ghosts. They refused to go below to the shelters; they're almost as bellicose as the Warriors are."

Cassie looked at him. "So you're the—" She broke off, unable to voice the word.

"Traitor?" Chandy supplied.

She shuddered. It was not self-preservation that kept her from actually saying the word. It went much deeper than that.

He shook his head. "I'm not," he said. "A traitor, that is. But there was no convincing old Subhash and that chained-leopard heir of his of that, as you can well imagine. So it became necessary to frame the hapless Marquis Hosoya. Who, I might add, richly deserved it."

She spun away, squeezed her eyes tight shut, walked blindly forward a few paces, not caring if she blundered into a wall.

"Cassie." The vast man's voice was quiet, and more sober than she'd ever heard it. Even when the Compound was about to be besieged, it had held its note of avuncular banter.

"Don't tell me you didn't know, child."

She spun, glaring. He laughed, raised a hand. "Spare me the righteous indignation. You knew what was going on by the time you got back from your first jaunt to Stormhaven."

"How the hell can you say that?"

"Quite easily. You asked me to 'keep Percy out of it.' Or words to that effect."

She held her arms down stiffly by her sides and said a great deal of nothing.

"That was a most curious turn of phrase," Uncle Chandy continued, "if you truly believed what you had done was plant a bug in order to get evidence of Marquis Hosoya committing a crime. If you suspected, however, that what your little device was actually doing was gathering images of the Marquis and his surroundings, into which appropriately skilled computer technicians could splice images of our Sumiyama and our Clan visitors, your request becomes entirely comprehensible."

Cassie sat down among the plush cushions. "And when your bug produced such instant results," he said, "surely that must have settled any doubts you had that the whole affair was a set-up."

He lumbered to the holostage, smiled fondly down at the Clanners, as if they were well-loved dolls. "They're really marvelous technicians, by the way. Lyran nationalists, who seem to have found it prudent to relocate in the wake of the little tiff between the Archon Prince and his sister."

She looked up at him sharply. "Don't fret yourself, daughter; they're not dead. They're on their way to the Periphery with enough money to live like kings, or at least minor dukelings. I murder, child, but like you I try to do so judiciously."

Her nostrils flared. She didn't say anything for a moment. When she trusted herself enough to speak, she said, "What makes you think Ninyu will let you get away with this?"

He laughed, his usual uproarious laugh of cosmic Buddha mirth. "Dearest child, he has already let us get away with it! He and his adoptive father are now our most valuable accomplices."

She stared at him.

"I'm not mad, child," he said. "Or at least, I'm not delusional at this particular moment. Recall what we discussed before: the woeful state of forensic science in the Draconis Combine. Even the Smiling One would be hard pressed to prove that the evidence we concocted to hang Hosoya is false.

"Yet consider: having accepted it, old Subhash has no interest in proving it wrong. He has averted one possible scandal—that a Kurita might be treating with the greatest enemy the Combine has ever known—which might well have brought the whole elaborate structure of our empire crashing in ruins. And the ISF has officially anointed its villains in my place: Hosoya and Sumiyama. He wanted Percy, too, but I talked him out of it—as I directed my technicians to leave our good Earl out of our cooked imagery."

Uncle Chandy spread his hand. "We have an . . . accepting public, as the official explanations of the recent trifling disturbances show. But there's a limit to how much even Subhash's media wizard Katsuyama can make the people of the Combine accept. No one knows this better than the Smiling One. Should the official explanation be discredited, not only House Kurita but the ISF would be discredited as well. And Subhash Indrahar believes, rightly or wrongly, that the Dragon's Breath is the glue that holds the Combine together."

The explanation made sense—in a twisted way, but one that Cassie could grasp. But it left the biggest question of all.

"Why?"

"Your Japanese is immaculate. What does 'Hachiman Taro' mean?"

She blinked at him.

"Indulge an old man's folly," he said. "Answer me."

" 'The first-born son of the God of War,' " she translated in a dull voice.

"A name often associated with the ancient Japanese hero Yoshitsune, who was kind enough to bequeath his name to the largest of our moons. A name even our staunch traditionalists, like our late Marquis and *oyabun*, would have to approve for a Hachiman-based corporation. While never guessing its real significance."

He gazed down at the Clanners. The woman was reading, the man performing some kind of calisthenics. "The risk they run by being here is as great as mine in hosting them," he said softly. "The Jade Falcons are the most conservative of Clans. Most particularly they fear such contact as this. And most of all, they fear the cargo I shall send back with these fine specimens."

"What's that?"

"Holographic projectors," he said, turning from the display. "Video games. Washing machines. Toasters. Holophones.

Holophone answering machines. Consumer electronics. Labor-saving devices. Toys."

"They're afraid of *toys*?" she asked. She was beginning to wonder what kind of joke her employer was pulling on her. She refused to believe he was as crazy as he sounded.

"Absolutely. And do you know what? They're right."

He gestured at the Clanners again. "My fine merchant friends will go back with a hold crammed full of all the decadent comforts and conveniences that mad, bad old General Kerensky wanted to shield them from. They are not the first. Thanks to the efforts of you and your friends, they won't be the last."

He smiled like a happy moon. "We won't be strong enough to beat them when the truce expires. But if I can ship them enough goodies, by that time they may well have beaten themselves. The war god's first-born has found a way to gain by other means what the ways of war cannot, you see."

"But if that's true," she said, "why would they go along with you?"

"Because they have no idea what I am really doing. They don't understand the power of plenty. Who can blame them? Our own rulers have ignored it for centuries, despite the fact that they have never been able to crush the Steiners, who only in my lifetime have ever managed to field an army suitable for anything but playing the chorus in an ancient comic opera. The Lyran people have always fought like badgers to avoid coming under the benign protection of the Dragon. And why should they not? They had comfort and plenty. All we could offer them was hardship."

"But what about the risks involved?" Cassie asked. "You said yourself they were in danger."

"Oh, yes. The Warriors who dominate their Clan would kill them and anyone even remotely related if they so much as caught wind of this."

"They're risking that?"

"Oh yes, because what they do see is the enormous profit potential in the cargoes I'm selling them. And Clan merchants are every bit as obsessively goal-oriented as their MechWarriors and Elementals."

She sat and looked at her hands, which had gotten pretty banged up in the go-round with Ninyu's cohorts. Maybe she'd better get some cream on them before they turned into claws.

"They suspected me of conspiring against Theodore," the huge man said, as if to himself. "But I am his most devoted servant."

She wasn't listening. Not to him, at least. Cassie was listening to herself.

Well, he used you, and he used the Regiment, and he took you in six ways from Sunday, a voice said in her head. It was not the hateful voice that had pursued her all her life to tell her she was dirty and wicked and wrong; didn't sound a bit like that.

So what? You got paid. So did the Caballeros. And as for tricking you—that's the root of it, isn't it?

You're angry because he scammed you.

Cassie shook her head and sighed. Then she laughed.

Chandy's great head was sunk into his chins and reverie. He raised it as she stood.

"Child," he said, "I'm aware I've deceived you. But I've also done nothing to hurt you. And you have, in fact, come to mean something to me, with your impertinence and your keen rapacious mind. As you know, your Colonel is entertaining an offer to extend the Regiment's contract with me. I would like to ask, whether or not he accepts, that you stay with me."

And suddenly there was something awkward and vulnerable about him, and she realized that he was being honest with her. Not for the first time—she had to grant him that.

"I'll think about it," she said, and left.

"That's it? You told what might be the most powerful man in the whole Inner Sphere you'd *think* about it?" Kali MacDougall's voice throbbed with wonder as they walked across the Compound. The wind off the Yamato was honed like a DEST sword.

"Yes."

Lady K laughed and hugged her. "Good for you."

She had not asked for details of Cassie's meeting with the big man, and her friend hadn't volunteered them. They were a burden Cassie would bear alone, for the time.

"So what now?" Kali asked.

Cassie looked at her sidelong, almost shyly. "You think you might like to get away for a few days, just go camping or something before the snow really clamps down? Just go off and talk?"

"Is the bear a Catholic? Are they lighting candles and praying to poor batty Terry de Avila Chávez back in the Trinity? Sierra Foxtrot, Cassie, I was figuring if I had to stay cooped up in here with all the ghosts, the Virgin would start appearing to me. And I'm not even Catholic."

Cassie bit her lower lip. "What about, ah, Archie?" she said, marveling at her own hesitation. "Won't he object if you light out for a few days?"

"Hey," Kali said, "Archie's a lot of fun, no doubt about that. And if he's more than that, he won't object to my taking some time for myself. And if he does—" She shrugged. "Forget him."

She put her arm around the smaller woman and hugged her again. "Fun's fun, Cassie," she said, "but friends are what last."

Cassie nodded. "Yes," she said. "Only friends last."

CATAPULT

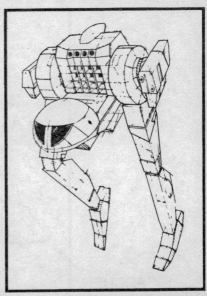

JENNER

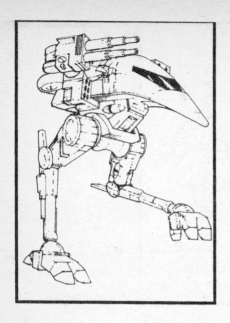

RAVEN

ARCHER

AWESOME

SHADOWHAWK

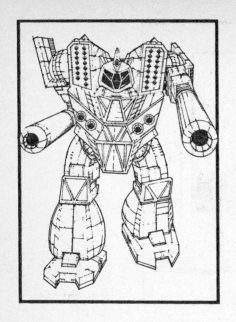

MAULER

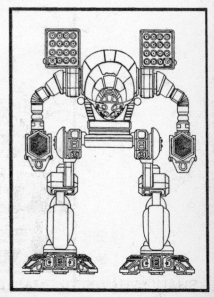

MADCAT

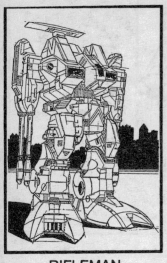

RIFLEMAN

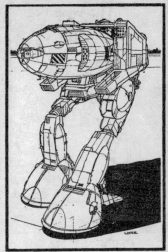

STALKER

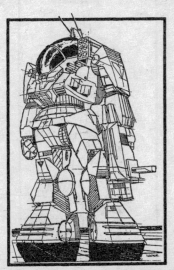

BATTLEMASTER

PHOENIX HAWK

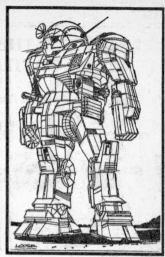

ATLAS

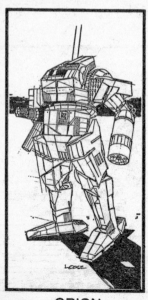

ORION